Copyright © 2024 by Charlotte Eyle

All rights reserved.

No part of this publication may be reproduced, distributed, or transmitted in any form or by any means, including photocopying, recording, or other electronic or mechanical methods, without the prior written permission of the publisher, except as permitted by U.S. copyright law. For permission requests, contact Charlotte Eyle at AuthorCharlotteEyle.com.

The story, all names, characters, and incidents portrayed in this production are fictitious. No identification with actual persons (living or deceased), places, buildings, and products is intended or should be inferred.

Cover Design by Getcovers

1st edition 2024

RED AS BLOOD
A SNOW WHITE REIMAGINING
CHARLOTTE EYLE

Caffeinated Kraken Publishing

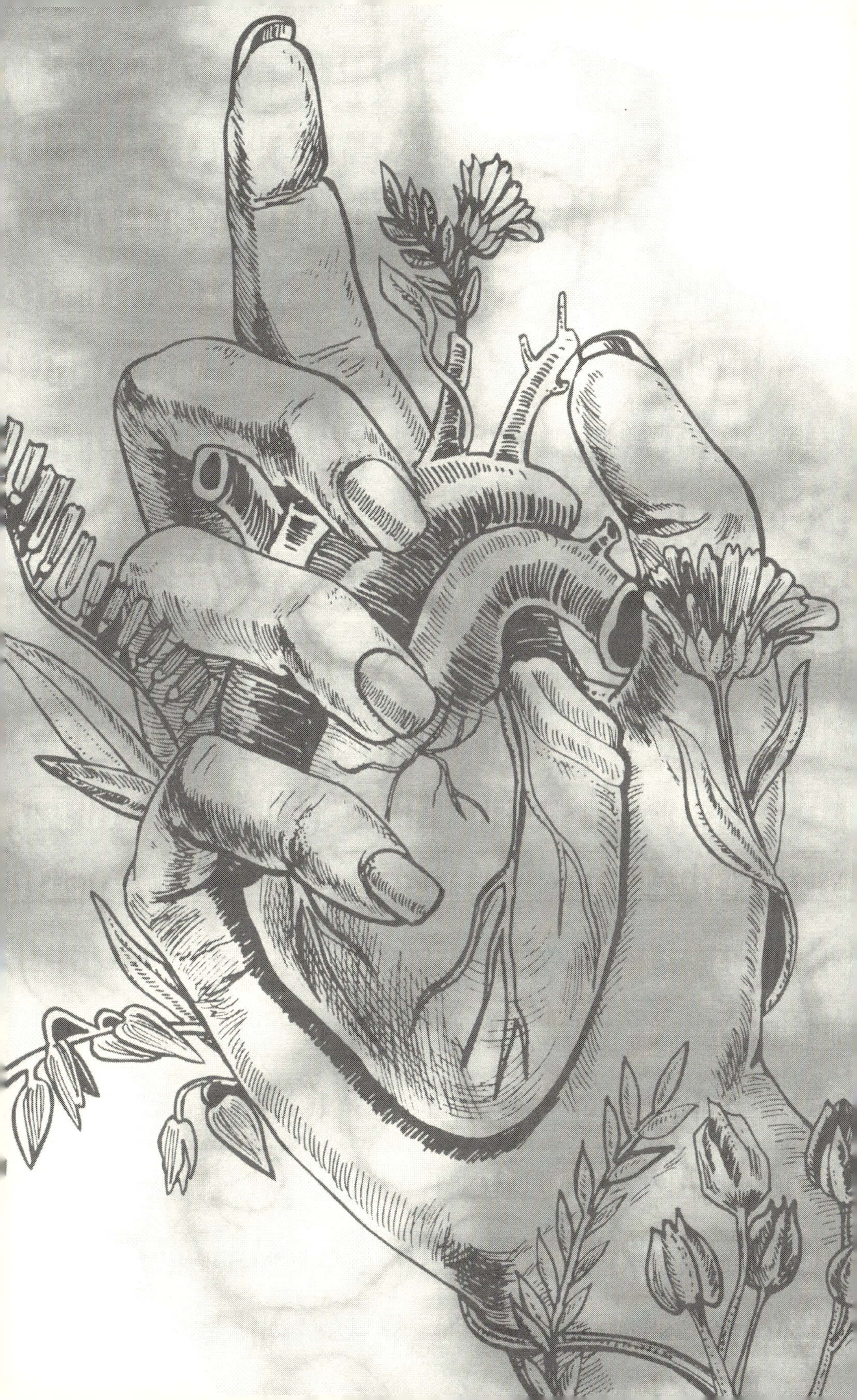

CONTENTS

1. Demon in the Graveyard — 1
2. A Surprise Announcement — 7
3. A Blaze of Discontentment — 17
4. I Banish You — 25
5. Death and Blood — 33
6. Court Gossip — 42
7. A Union of Convenience — 52
8. Forbidden Magic — 58
9. Rifts — 71
10. The King of Cherida — 77
11. The Taste of Wine — 92
12. What Have You Done? — 102
13. Marked by Great Magic — 112
14. The Huntsman — 120
15. Vampire — 130
16. The Journey Begins — 138
17. Refugees — 146
18. The Greenwitch Wives — 156
19. Mercy — 166

20.	Honeycrisp Tavern	172
21.	Everald the Vindicator	180
22.	Sunrise	191
23.	Let the Past Go	200
24.	Finding Lost Things	207
25.	The Black Barrel	216
26.	The Necromancer	230
27.	Visitors	242
28.	Alchemy	247
29.	Honey Festival	257
30.	The Gift	269
31.	Grief	279
32.	Goodbye For Now	286
33.	First Steps	293
Epilogue		302
Newsletter Signup		309
Sneak Peak		310
Castle Frankenstein		311
About The Author		315

1
DEMON IN THE GRAVEYARD

It was a night so dark, even the moon was blotted out. The stars, too, hid their faces; unable to witness the dreadful atrocity that was about to transpire. A thick snowfall blanketed the world in silence.

"Marcella," I whispered to my sister, trembling even through my thick cloak, "Please see reason! I beg of you, we must turn back. This...this can not be done!"

Marcella stopped dead in her tracks and turned to face me. She was beautiful, even in her anger. Her eyes shone like black onyx and her hair was dark as a raven's wing. "Do not try to dissuade me, Ceridwen. I have come too far to be held back by your pathetic whimpering."

I swallowed back a lump in my throat and the lantern I held trembled as though caught in a strong wind.

Marcella sighed. Her head sagged down for a moment. When she looked up, I saw the desperation in her eyes. My sister moved towards me and clasped my hand. "Do you want me to die? Is my life worth so little to you?" Her voice was high and thin.

I pressed her palm over my heart, clutching her fingers. "You know I love you above all else. How could you ask that?"

"Then you must help me do this thing." The resolve was back in Marcella's voice. She turned and continued making her way through the forest. "I know you've heard the rumors. They've been spreading through the castle like wildfire. People think because we are foreigners, because we are greenwitches, that we have cursed the King to love me."

"That's not true, though." I debated, fierce even in our solitude. "King Iberius married you because he loves you, not because of any spell."

Marcella paused, and I saw her shiver. "It doesn't matter what we know." She scorned. "Do not play dumb or stupid. We cannot afford it if we want to live. The truth is what the King wills. With corrupt advisors whispering in his ear, it may please him to call his marriage a sham, a lie. They could execute me. They could execute us *both*," she emphasized. "If we are to escape that fate, we must keep the King amiable. To keep him amiable, I must, *must* produce an heir. I refuse to die beneath a blade."

My heart pounded in my chest as I contemplated the thought. Before we lived here, in Cherida, my sister and I lived in Aileen. Together with our parents, we owned a shop and sold charms and knew happiness. Then a plague swept through Aileen. Only mysticmancers, those skilled in magic, could heal the sick, or slow the spread of illness. After the death of his wife and two children, King Drustan grew angry and paranoid. He convinced himself the plague was a clever way for mysticmancers to gain power and seize his throne. So, he began executing them. After our parents were tied to a pyre and burned alive, Marcella and I fled for our lives.

We settled in Cherida, a much smaller country than Aileen. King Iberius had expressed an interest in the mystical arts. Mysticmancers were scarce in his country, and he longed for magic to flourish there. Marcella and I taught him about herbs and crystals and performed simple spells to make ourselves useful. I thought it was only natural when the King expressed an interest in my sister, but many in the Kingdom believed there was nothing natural about it.

I shook my head, bringing myself back to the present.

"I don't believe it," I said. "King Iberius would not set you aside or allow you to come to harm. His feelings are-"

"Shut up, you stupid child." Marcella snapped.

I knew the stress she was under, so I thinned my lips and said nothing.

"Here," Marcella approached a graveyard and stood at the entrance.

"No," I gasped. "Marcella, please, I implore you!"

"I have no other choice." I could hear her panting and, in the light of my lamp, saw a glitter of excitement in her eyes. She had always been drawn to power. Now I feared it would lead to her demise.

Marcella made her way to a stone crypt and pulled a dagger out of her cloak. I heard her speak, but the breeze muffled her words. Then she cut her hand with the blade.

I winced as a dark fluid oozed from the cut and dribbled onto the crypt, blood magic.

"You are calling forth a demon," I said in a trembling whisper.

"A demon?"

I jumped as the words seemed to be spoken directly into my ear. I spun in a circle, swinging my lantern around wildly.

"I suppose you can call me a demon. I have many names, you see."

I turned towards Marcella and froze. A man stood only a few feet away from my sister. He moved with superhuman speed, faster than the eye could track, and grabbed Marcella by the throat.

"Here now!" I yelled, taking a step closer.

Marcella waved me down. "He's not hurting me."

I held the lantern higher and squinted. The monster's hand was still at her throat, and he was softly stroking her skin with the pad of his thumb. He was gentle, almost like a lover, and didn't seem to be applying any pressure. I lowered the lantern and frowned.

"Why have you sought me out?" The man asked. If he was a man. I examined his features, trying to determine if what I saw was human or demon.

Sharp cheekbones jutted out of pale skin. Watery blue eyes glinted like ice in the lantern light. Dark hair hung limply down to his shoulders. The only color on his face was his blood-red lips.

Marcella lifted her chin, looking at the creature through her thick lashes. "I seek magic greater than what I possess. I was told that the force inhabiting this graveyard might be willing to assist me."

The creature grinned, paper-like skin pulling away from bone-white teeth. "Oh, surely they told you much more than that."

I saw Marcella pale, and she thinned her lips.

"Tell me." The creature's voice was rapturous. "Tell me what nightmares these simple country folk have conjured up. Tell me of their fear."

Marcella drew a shaky breath. "They said a dark entity inhabits this land. A force for evil or the devil himself, no one knows. Others call you a shadow. A shadow of death that may not leave me alive."

"Yet you have come, regardless." He sounded amused.

"Yes." I heard the resolve in Marcella's voice. Her eyes narrowed.

"Very well then," the monster went on. "Tell me what you seek, and I shall set my price."

I heard Marcella sigh, and her shoulders sagged in relief. "I need to produce an heir for the King."

"Ah," the monster said. "You are the Queen, I presume?"

Marcella nodded.

"After all this time, to speak with a queen again." He chuckled.

A knot twisted in my stomach. What did he mean by *a* queen? What did he mean *again*?

"Forgive me." The creature stepped away and bowed. It was a very human gesture.

"I had no idea I was in the presence of such esteemed royalty. I must not forget my manners." He continued.

Marcella smiled and relaxed even more. I couldn't bring myself to do the same. The monster was too glib, almost mocking. I wondered what game he was playing.

"So, the Queen wishes to have a child, and she wishes for my help." The monster chuckled. "Very well then, I can assist you in this matter."

Marcella sucked in a deep breath, and she placed a hand over her heart. "Thank you."

"You can keep your gratitude. I don't work for free, you know. There is still a price to be paid." He smiled, and a shiver ran down my spine. Something was terribly wrong.

Marcella didn't hesitate. "Anything," she breathed. "I have gold, jewels, horses-"

The monster moved with that same unhuman speed he had used earlier. He appeared behind Marcella, grabbing a fistful of her hair and wrenching her head back. He looked at the sky, his mouth gaping open. I watched in horror as his teeth sharpened into points.

"My price is blood," He snarled. Then he plunged his fangs into Marcella's soft skin. Dark fluid spurted from the puncture wounds, rolling down her shoulder and staining her dress.

I screamed. I screamed so loudly that the breath went out of my body, and I collapsed to my knees. Marcella was screaming also; a long, desperate wail that tore through the night sky.

The creature drew back his head. A wine-red stain surrounded his mouth and covered his chin. He tucked a strand of hair behind Marcella's ear and leaned down to whisper something.

I watched my sister's frozen features, wondering what he could be saying. After several long moments, she nodded, and the man looked up. He motioned me closer with his index finger.

I was afraid, but also seething with anger. Struggling to my feet, I advanced on him, only to fumble as he tossed Marcella in my direction. I grabbed her around the waist, and we slid to the ground together.

"Take her home. She knows what to do." The mirth was gone from his voice. Yanking a handkerchief out of his pocket, the man dabbed at his face and turned away. He was suddenly cold and aloof.

I bit my lip, then hurried Marcella to her feet and began dragging her away. We made our way through the snow, half limping and half sprinting. My heart was pounding in my throat and fear crawled down my spine like the legs of a spider.

"Please, wait just a moment." Marcella paused and grabbed onto a tree trunk for support.

"What did he say to you?" I asked.

"Never mind that."

She was still in shock. Her eyes were wide and frozen in horror. Her body trembled like an autumn leaf caught in a high wind. She had one hand pressed against the bite mark on her neck.

"We'll have to sneak back into the castle and figure out what to do about that wound." I pointed out.

"Never mind that," Marcella repeated. She hunched over and 3 drops of blood dripped from her fingertips and onto the snow.

Marcella stared at the drops, entranced. Some life seemed to come back into her eyes. "I will have a child with hair black as midnight, skin white as snow, and lips red as blood."

A look crossed her face that I didn't quite recognize, but it scared me all the same. I eased my arm around her waist. "Let's just make it back to the castle."

2
A SURPRISE ANNOUNCEMENT

Two days went by, and I wondered if Marcella and I would ever speak of what happened in the graveyard. We had snuck back into the castle that night under an invisibility spell, and I used a poultice to clean her dress. The bite marks proved harder to deal with. I was able to mop up the blood and stitch the puncture wounds, but there was still deep bruising.

"I can't get this to heal. My magic has no effect against it, I don't know why," I finally admitted in a frantic voice.

Marcella closed her eyes and laughed through her nose.

"What is it?" I asked in a sharp tone.

"Don't you see?" Marcella responded, opening her eyes. "The bite has its own magic. It will have to heal on its own."

"But what will you do? Surely you cannot hide this from the King." I admonished.

Marcella motioned towards her vanity table, where jewelry, perfume, and powders lay. "Not everything has to be solved with magic," she said. "There are other alternatives I can rely on."

Makeup, she was planning on using makeup. I wasn't sure if such a thing was possible. I opened my mouth to object, but Marcella waved me away. "Leave me, I am tired."

"I will be right around the corner if you need anything," I assured her.

I rose from my seat, and Marcella jumped into my arms, embracing me in a tight hug.

"You are my sister," she said. "I do love you. Please always remember that."

If her attitude raised any suspicions, I attributed it to the horrors of the night. I rubbed her back and tried to soothe her. "I love you too, Marcella."

That was the last we spoke until the evening of the second day. I contemplated approaching Marcella, but she came to me that night.

I had just slipped into my gown when a knock sounded at my door. I opened it to find my sister on the other side.

"What are you doing?" I asked as she pushed her way inside.

"Starting this evening, every night I will confine myself to a holy room and pray." Marcella's eyes were glittering, and she panted with excitement. "I will do this each week, for six nights. On the seventh night, I will lie with my husband."

Fear coiled in my stomach. "What gods do you pray to that it must be done at night?"

Marcella lowered her eyes and stepped away from me.

"Marcella." I reached out and touched her shoulder. "This has something to do with that demon in the graveyard. You never told me what he said to you."

"How *dare* you touch me!" Marcella wrenched herself out of my grasp. "I am the queen!"

"You're also my sister!" I yelled back. "What darkness has its hooks in you?"

"None that I don't allow." She hissed between clenched teeth.

Now it was my turn to step back. A gasp escaped my lips.

Marcella straightened up, smoothing the wrinkles out of her dress. Then she smiled. When she spoke, her voice was light and airy. "Let us not fight, dearest sister. I come to you with gifts."

"What gifts?" I asked, suspicious of her erratic behavior.

She opened my door, and servants poured into the room. Birchwood was set up in my windows. Solar water was placed next to my bed. Garlic was strung up at my door. I wrinkled my nose at the smell.

A SURPRISE ANNOUNCEMENT

"You call these gifts?" I asked, a smile tugging at my lips. "My room is going to stink to the heavens."

I turned to Marcella and found her frozen. She had a hand around her neck and her eyes were filled with fear.

"Leave us," I ordered the servants.

They nodded and filtered out of the room immediately.

"Marcella." I rushed to my sister and placed my hands on her shoulders. "This is a bad idea. Whatever you've done, whatever you've agreed to, you don't have to follow through with it. I can help. Just tell me-"

Marcella gave a high-pitched giggle then. Her head rolled back while her maniacal laughter bounced off the ceiling.

I paused, fearing she had gone mad.

"There is no going back, Ceridwen," she said. "Nor would I turn away if I had the opportunity."

"I won't have this." My voice was sharper than I intended. "I'm going to the King. Whatever you're involved in, I won't-"

"No!" Marcella yelled, giving me a hard shove.

I stumbled backward. My shoulder blade slammed painfully against the bedpost. I wrapped a hand around the carved wood to keep my balance and gaped at my sister. "What has come over you?"

Marcella ran towards me. For one wild moment, I thought she meant to strike me, but then she collapsed to her knees and wrapped her arms around my waist.

"Swear to me," she gasped, "swear to me you will not leave this room. You must stay here between the time the sun sets and the sun rises. Do not step one foot out unless the sun is in the sky!"

Maybe Marcella had gone mad. I stroked her hair in an attempt to soothe her, but my heart was pounding frantically in my chest. I thought she was angry that I threatened to go to the King, but this was something else.

"I won't leave the room unless the sun is out," I said at last.

Marcella scrambled to her feet. "Swear it. You must swear it!"

"I-I do. I swear." Her fear was infectious, and I felt goosebumps erupt along my arms. What had Marcella gotten us into? Clearly, the danger extended beyond just her. I felt a twinge of anxiety for Iberius and the rest of the castle.

Marcella heaved a deep sigh. A ghost of a smile spread across her face.

"That's good, that's very good." Her voice was soft and dreamy. She turned and let herself out of my room.

"Sleep well, sister." Her words drifted over me as she shut the door, and the lock clicked in place.

I stood in the garden and squinted up at the sky. The sun was dazzling, and the snow had long since melted. Winter was giving way to spring, so there was still a slight chill in the air. It was invigorating and crisp.

"Good morning, Dutchess." Tierra, a greenwitch, appeared before me. She was also from Aileen, and was a few years older than Marcella. When my sister and I first arrived in Cherida, it was Tierra who found us employment in the King's royal gardens. The three of us worked together before King Iberius elevated my sister to Queen. It felt odd, to be treated so deferentially by someone who I knew was my equal. It was only by a stroke of chance that I was now royalty.

"Did the Queen pray last night?" Tierra asked in a conversational tone. She kneeled and began plucking herbs from the garden. The sun glanced along her arms, bringing out the earthy undertones of her skin.

Here in Cherida, the people were known for their blonde hair, blue eyes, and pale complexions. It made those of us from Aileen easy to spot. Our skin was rich ochre, with warm reddish-orange undertones that so closely resembled the colors at sunset. Our hair was as black as charcoal, and our eyes were dark as midnight.

"No," I said. "She was with the King."

I had long believed it was Marcella's exotic looks that caught the eye of King Iberius. It was whispered that he was fascinated with Aileen's culture and that he had a taste for their women. Even in our homeland, Marcella was known as a great beauty.

"May the gods bless your sister with a babe." Tierra gave a cheerful smile, and I saw her hand stray to her belly. She had married two years ago, around the same time as Marcella.

"Tierra," My eyes widened, and I moved towards her. "Are you with child?"

She gave a small gasp. "Please, Dutchess Ceridwen, how did you know?"

I tried not to flinch when she used my title. It had been a gift from the King when he wed my sister, but I felt ill-suited for it. Instead, I laughed. "Because of the way you touch your belly. I promise I used no magic."

Tierra gave a small gulp and confided in me. "I've been so afraid to tell anyone. I didn't know how the Queen would take it, see."

I almost laughed again. It seemed such a silly thing to say about Marcella, but I stopped myself. My sister had always been the jealous, controlling type. The more I thought about it, the more I worried that Tierra was right to be concerned.

Unable to come up with any words of comfort, I stood there for a long moment before managing a tight smile. "I wish you much joy."

Tierra's face lit up, and she gave a small curtsy. "Thank you, Dutchess." Then she turned and made her way into the kitchens.

I looked back up at the sky and pondered my predicament for a long while. Every night that Marcella barred herself in her holy room, I barred myself in my chambers. I would often lay awake under my covers, listening to the sounds of the night. Listening for the sounds of a predator.

I rarely slept well, oftentimes falling into a fitful slumber before bolting awake at the first light of dawn. Yet I never heard my sister scream or cry or beg for mercy. The castle was silent, and so was the darkness.

That didn't mean everything stayed the same. It had been six weeks and Marcella was growing very thin. Her face was gaunt and haggard and her beauty fell away like dead leaves in autumn.

I took a deep breath and began trailing along the winding path of the garden. Nature had its benefits. I walked barefoot, drawing energy from the earth and reciting meditations. I willed the negativity to leave my body and focused on raising my vibration. The dirt under my feet was damp and buzzing with the beginnings of new life.

An unfamiliar scent wafted in the air. I stopped and took a deep breath. What was that?

I turned down a less-used path and pushed some branches and bushes aside. What was growing out here and why was it hidden?

When I spotted what lay in the tiny clearing, I felt my heart stop, then break, then shatter into a million pieces.

In the clearing lay cinnamon, rosemary, fennel, lavender, and mullein. We were just coming out of winter. These herbs and flowers couldn't have grown on their own. Magic was needed to keep them alive during the intense frost.

"Oh Marcella, what have you done?" I whispered.

These were all the ingredients needed for a potent love spell.

I never confronted my sister about what I found in the gardens. I made many excuses for my cowardice. The walls have ears. Someone might be eavesdropping. I was being paranoid, and I should keep my delusions to myself. There could be another greenwitch in the castle I didn't know about, and it would be imprudent to blame my sister. Yet no matter how many excuses I made, it ultimately boiled down to one thing: I didn't want to know.

I had silenced any voice that dared speak out against the Queen. I had denounced what I believed were vile rumors, and I punished protesters for treason. My faith had been placed in Marcella's hands, without question or hesitation, and she may have been lying the whole time.

Two weeks went by. I kept my discovery to myself and tried to forget it. I almost succeeded when the King called a royal meeting.

Instantly, my mind jumped to the worst possible outcome. A love potion was effective for only so long until the effects began wearing off. Did the King realize he had been bewitched? Would I walk into the throne room and find my sister's head on a pike? I gulped and clutched at my throat. Maybe there would be an executioner waiting to collect my head as well.

I considered fleeing, but I could never abandon Marcella, so I dressed and made my way to where the announcement was being held.

When I stepped into the throne room, I breathed a sigh of relief. King Iberius, usually stoic and grim-faced, was actually smiling. Beside him, Marcella looked radiant. She was still thin, and her cheekbones were sharper than I would have liked, but a blush of beauty had returned to her face and her eyes were sparkling.

I moved to the front of the room, and Marcella waved to me. I waved back and smiled, feeling the tension lift from my shoulders.

After several more minutes, the room was full. King Iberius stood. He beat his scepter against the floor, and everyone quieted down.

"Ladies and gentlemen," King Iberius began, "I am pleased to have you all here today, that you may partake in my joy. Some very happy news was brought to me this morning, and I am delighted to share it. Soon, Cherida will have an heir, for the Queen and I are expecting a child!"

The room exploded with cheers. I found myself jumping up and down and clapping madly. I moved towards the front of the room so I could speak to my sister personally. Marcella smiled when our eyes met, and she held out a hand.

"Let her approach," she said to the guards.

They parted, and I rushed forward, clasping her fingers and kissing the palm of her hand. "This is the happiest day of our lives!" I exclaimed with excitement. "Oh, Marcella, this is *wonderful*!"

"It's about damn time if you ask me." King Iberius inclined his chin in my direction. "Ceridwen, I am glad to see you."

"Thank you, Your Majesty." I was so consumed with happiness that it took me a minute to recognize the sharp tone in his voice, along with the way Marcella tensed at his reprimand.

"I think dancing is in order," King Iberius said.

I was just about to release Marcella's hand when King Iberius turned and disappeared in the opposite direction.

Marcella bared her teeth. "Jane Westerling is here, the little tramp. He likes her brown eyes, though she's as blonde and pale as the rest of these milky-faced fools."

"Marcella," I breathed, shocked at the venom in her voice.

"He can't set me aside now. I have done what no other woman has, not even his mistresses." She rubbed her stomach and gave a gruesome smile.

I was silent for a moment, reliving the scene in the graveyard. I had believed, foolishly, that Marcella sought out magic to make her more fertile. It was only now that I began to understand, this pregnancy was not normal. I almost choked on the knowledge.

"What's wrong with you? Shocked that the King has indiscretions?" Marcella smirked at me. "They're men, Ceridwen. They can't help but be a slave to their desires. The sooner you learn that, the better."

I looked around. Everyone had moved away from the thrones. It was just my sister and me.

"What about our desires, Marcella?" I asked in a quiet voice.

"Do you have desires, little sister?" Marcella gave a throaty chuckle. "They call us the weaker sex, yet we are expected to exhibit much more control than they do."

"That's not what I meant." I felt blood rising into my cheeks as I became angry. "I speak of desire for love, marriage...even power and fertility."

Marcella's head snapped around. Her gaze pierced me like a knife. "You dare," she hissed, "you dare speak to me so?"

I stood my ground. "Tell me about the hidden patch of herbs and flowers that grow in the castle gardens." I pressed. "Magic has been used to keep the foliage growing and thriving during the winter months, in secret. Be honest with me."

Marcella sneered at me. "Secret? What truly stays a secret when you come to court?"

"Tell me it isn't yours," I whispered. "Tell me you didn't bewitch the King, Marcella. It isn't real love, it can't last. Eventually, he'll find out, or the potion will wear off-"

I paused as understanding dawned on me. "This is why...this is why you needed a child so desperately."

Marcella rose from her throne and advanced on me. There was a murderous look in her eye.

"I don't know what you're talking about, but if you ever speak of it again, I'll kill you myself." Marcella grabbed my shoulder. I felt her nails digging into my skin. "I'll feed your body to the dogs and mount your head on a pike within this very throne room. So everyone knows, every damn sniveling courtier and loose woman who makes eyes at the King, that no one is spared from my wrath. Not ever, not even my own sister."

Her words chilled me to the bone, and I froze, not recognizing Marcella in her anger.

She removed her hand. Taking a step back, she bowed her head, a look of anguish on her face.

"I am sorry," Marcella said in a velvety soft voice. "I am a mother now, Ceridwen. I can't risk any threat to my child's throne. Treason must be swiftly addressed. I'm sure you understand."

I rubbed my shoulder and nodded. "I do."

"I don't know who the garden belongs to, but I'm hurt that you think it's mine." Marcella's lower lip puckered out. She looked miserable.

"You were my greatest ally, Ceridwen. Now you have turned against me. My own sister, who knows I have never needed potions or spells to make men fall in love with me. I am well and truly doomed, for if my kin have taken up with the heretics, then I stand alone."

Marcella rubbed her stomach, and I felt an avalanche of guilt wash over me.

"I'm sorry." My voice came out just above a whisper. "I'll never put you or the baby in danger again. Tomorrow, I'll destroy the garden. No one else will find it, and there'll be no cause to question your honor."

Marcella kissed my cheek. "Most faithful sister," she cooed.

I kneeled before her and took her hand.

"Ceridwen?"

I looked up from my spot on the floor. "Yes?"

Marcella smiled down at me, a cruel glimmer in her eyes. "If someone were to bewitch the King, it would take a very clever and cunning person, don't you think?"

My body tensed up. "I wouldn't know, Your Majesty. I don't think on such things."

"Of course not," she scoffed, "pious little sister."

It wasn't a compliment.

"You swear to destroy the garden tomorrow?"

I kissed her hand. "I swear it."

3
A BLAZE OF DISCONTENTMENT

I destroyed the garden, like I promised, and resolved to keep a better eye on Marcella. She was too reckless. It was hard to tell who I worried about more, my sister or those who got in her way. It was an impossible and exhausting task as I jumped through countless hoops to keep the peace.

Using earth and herbs, golems were placed discreetly throughout the castle. They posed as scullery maids, pages, ladies-in-waiting, and stable boys, and worked as spies. My golems reported to me every evening, and when I wasn't putting on a show for the royals, I became the witch everyone was afraid of. I was ruthless in quashing heretics who slandered my sister.

By day, I rallied the noble folk by laughing and dancing and sparkling in court, abating their fears and shedding the mystery of the Starbright sisters. By night, I delved into my magic. For the rich and connected, I performed spells to freeze tongues and bring calamity down on their households. The poor and foolhardy were either threatened into silence or paid off.

The true heretics were the hardest to deal with. They remained undeterred by threats or the promise of disaster. Their convictions were strong, and they refused to be bribed or intimidated. My sister and I were the immediate scapegoats for any tragedy that befell them, which severely limited our options. So, heretics spread like fire through our small country, leaving a blaze of discontentment and rebellion in their wake.

It was a tricky line to walk, defending my sister from rumors I was no longer sure were falsehoods. Yet I did it, with all the fervor of an aunt protecting a baby. No matter what Marcella did, the child was innocent and of my own blood.

It was a strange and pleasing thought, that my little world would expand beyond my sister and me. I imagined the weight of a baby on my chest, the delicious smell of a newborn, their soft skin and tiny fingers. There were times I felt my womb ache with desire, even though I was only fifteen. I hadn't thought much about having children. Mostly because that involved marriage, and I wasn't ready to settle down yet. For the first time in my life, though, I was beginning to understand that I wanted a family.

When my sister was seven months pregnant, I found a heretic in my kitchens. One of the golems brought me the news, and my blood ran cold at what the cook might have seen or heard.

My time was divided between the castle and my estate, Easton Manor. On horseback, Easton Manor was a four-hour ride from the castle. When torture and magic were necessary, I could retreat to my own towers and dungeons. My stomach rolled as I thought about what sort of tales someone in my employ might have picked up. Especially a heretic, hiding in the shadows and sniffing out secrets like a bloodhound. I ground my teeth when I thought about it and vowed to show no mercy.

Today, I stood in my Great Hall, staring out my floor-to-ceiling windows. It provided an excellent view of my luscious grounds. Behind me, a long table was laid out with a delicious dinner.

I tapped my foot irritably against the floor. I did what I must for my family, but it gave me no pleasure. Heretics had no respect for the difficult situation they placed me and my family in.

A golem in the form of a slight and freckled scullery maid opened the door. "Dutchess Ceridwen, the cook you requested."

I steeled my nerves and straightened my back before turning from the window. "Thank you, Mallory. You may leave us now. Please shut the door on your way out."

The cook apprehensively entered the Great Hall. Her eyes darted from me, to the food, to the double doors. I knew she was considering all her options.

I was not a cruel mistress, but I wasn't a kind one either. I did not resort to using the cane or the whip. Nor did I bully my staff for small, perceived slights. There was only one way to get on my bad side, and that was by betraying my family.

"Sit," I ordered. "Eat. There is much to discuss."

The cook slowly took a seat at the table and began nibbling on some cheese. She poured herself a goblet of wine and drank deeply. Her body was stiff and tense, but the more she ate, the more she relaxed. It made sense. She had prepared this food herself. She was starting to believe it wasn't poisoned, that I couldn't have altered the foot without her detection.

Yet I had.

I took a seat at the table, across from the cook, and gave a sickly-sweet smile. "What is your name?"

"Gerta," the other woman said. She was sweaty from working in the kitchens. Blonde hair escaped from her braid and stuck to her damp forehead. Her grey eyes were guarded.

"Gerta," I continued, "Do you know why you're here?"

She paused, then reached for her wineglass. Taking a large swig, Gerta placed the cup down on the table and wiped her mouth. Her gaze fell to her lap before rising to meet mine.

"Because I know the truth," Gerta whispered. Her voice was quiet, but there was a steely resolve in her eyes.

I gave a light chuckle and leaned back in my chair. "What would that be?" I asked, still polite, still smiling.

Gerta's chest was heaving now. I wondered what she was thinking. Did she want to escape? To run madly through my halls until she reached a place of safety? Or maybe Gerta wanted to attack me, to run me through with the silver knife placed by her right hand.

"I know my king is bewitched," she said at last. "I know it was done by your sister's hand."

"Oh, Gerta." I stood from my chair and narrowed my eyes. My calm, collected demeanor fell away, revealing my true nature. Heat flooded my cheeks as rage raced through my blood. I slammed my hands down on the table, leaning in close to the cook.

"You know no such thing." I snarled. "You are a lowly servant, grasping at straws and making this world a dangerous place for the future heir to the throne."

Gerta stood from her seat, then stumbled backwards on unsteady legs before falling on her rear. Her eyes were wide and terrified. All traces of defiance had vanished from her face.

I snapped my fingers. The candles and braziers went out, enveloping the room in darkness. Thick fog began rolling through the Great Hall, turning the air cold and damp.

"Please, mercy!" Gerta shrieked.

"What mercy have you shown your king and queen?" I roared. My voice was like a crack of thunder. The ground shook beneath our feet. "You, who would bring civil war to their doorstep? You, who would discredit the future heir?"

"I have done no such thing! I am loyal to my king!" Gerta was frantic now. She turned and ran towards the towering double doors, only to find them locked. She beat her fists against the wood paneling, screaming for help.

I used magic to flit across the room, moving with superhuman speed. I stopped next to Gerta and pried her away from the doors. My hand found her neck, and I lifted her high in the air. Her skin was warm, and I could feel the blood pulsing in her veins.

"Did you forget I am a witch, Gerta? Did you really believe I couldn't alter the meal without your knowledge? I poisoned the wine with an honesty serum. I shall have the truth, whether you will it or no. Now answer my questions. Where did you hear these vile rumors, and who did you repeat them to?"

"The b-b-bard in town, at the Honeycrisp," Gerta said. Her eyes widened as the words poured from her mouth.

"The tavern?" I asked.

Gerta swallowed hard. "Minstrels, they sing songs of the Queen's magic. Everyone knows."

I scowled. "So, because the Queen is a witch, she must have spelled the King. Is that it? Is that what you're saying?"

"The King cannot have an heir!" Gerta burst out, full of conviction. "It is magic, evil magic!"

I slapped Gerta across the face. The sound of flesh of flesh echoed through the air and Gerta howled in pain.

"How dare you say such a thing!" I bellowed, "Where is your proof?"

Gerta screamed like a horse. Her eyes rolled with panic as she struggled in my grip. She flailed her arms and legs, desperately trying to extricate herself. One of her fingernails slashed down my face. I felt a hot sting under my eye, followed by something wet. She had drawn blood.

"The proof is in the past!" Gerta shrieked, unable to stop the torrent of words pouring out of her mouth. "The King is infertile! A-a horse accident i-in his youth! All the royal physicians say he cannot father an heir! The Queen is carrying a monster! There, I said it. I've spoken the truth. Kill me, if you dare. Everyone will know it was your doing!"

"What does that mean?" I demanded.

Gerta let out a devilish laugh. "You think we only whisper about the Queen? We watch, we see! Your manor is a place where people enter and never return! Murderer! Touch me, and everyone will know it was you! Touch me, and your life is forfeit!"

Gerta finished by spitting in my face. I lost my temper, then. Heat rolled off of me like a furnace. My hand glowed red hot, like metal in a blacksmith's forge. Without a word, I plunged my hand into Gerta's chest, ripping through flesh and muscle. Bones shattered against my hand.

Gerta's jaw dropped open, her mouth a wide O. Pain and horror lanced across her face, and I saw the shock in her eyes.

My fingers curled around her still-beating heart. It was warm, almost hot. The rhythmic beating reverberated against my palms. The pulsations were frenzied with fear and agony.

Gerta realized, too late, that she had overplayed her hand.

"Mer-cy," she gurgled. Crimson blood bubbled at her lips, dripping down onto her chin.

I pulled. Gerta's chest ripped open. Blood fountained from her corpse, covering me with a scorching spray. My hand emerged, holding her heart.

Gerta's blood was everywhere.

With a flick of my hand, the candles and braziers re-lit themselves, and the fog rolled away. I looked at the droplets of bright red blood arcing across the floor. They shone brightly in the firelight. It was almost pretty, like a string of garnets.

If only there wasn't so much of it.

With a sigh, I looked at Gerta's body, slumped on the ground. Here the blood pooled and spread lazily across the floor. Sticking my head out the double doors, I called Mallory back into the room. I ordered her to keep an ear out and to begin mopping.

I couldn't lift Gerta's body on my own, so I used a spell to move her to the table. I swiped the food onto the floor and grabbed a knife. It was gory work, fashioning a golem into the image of a certain person, but it had to be done.

Taking a deep breath, I cut into Gerta's chest, pulling the flaps of skin aside so I could see her ribs. Besides her heart, I would also need her lungs and liver.

Mallory brought me buckets of dirt, which was spread across the table and sprinkled with rainwater. There were several herbs on the table, waiting to be added to my concoction.

The doors to the Great Hall unexpectedly swung open. I looked up with a scowl, only to see Marcella enter.

"I hate it when you shield yourself from my golems. I like to be notified of visitors." My voice was coarse from all the yelling I had done earlier.

Marcella paused and took in the scene before her. "I can see why," she said. "Dare I ask what happened here?"

I laid Gerta's heart on the pile of dirt and began extracting her lungs. Her ribs made a sharp snapping sound as I broke them one by one.

"Tonight I found out my cook was a heretic. I've been working for months to quell any rumors against you, Marcella, but it's not easy. The people don't love you. You need to reach out to them. Show the world you are a benevolent queen."

Marcella glared at me. Rich hues of jeweled plum blossomed in her cheeks as she flushed with anger.

"After all I've done, all that I've sacrificed, you think I'm going to grovel to those dirty commoners?"

Marcella moved to the windows and stared out into the night. "No one can imagine the things I've done to get where I am today. Not even you, Ceridwen. I have ridden down to the gates of hell and snatched what I wanted right out of the devil's hands. I have elevated *myself!*" She beat a hand across her chest. "I will not share my glory! I've earned what I have!"

"Have you earned it or have you taken it?" I shouted, losing my temper. "Damn it, Marcella, do you know what *I've* done for your child?"

My sister turned and examined the corpse on my table. The anger drained from her as she approached and leaned in close. A look of mild interest crossed her face. "You're making a golem?" She asked, eyeing the dirt on the table.

"Yes." I continued removing Gerta's liver. My hands were sticky with blood. "Too many people have disappeared, too many that have questioned the crown. Your subjects are growing suspicious."

Marcella nodded. "That's smart. You're thinking ahead."

"I'm going to put her back in the kitchens. She will be under orders to continue about her duties and speak favorably of us."

Marcella carefully seated herself in a chair and rubbed her rounded belly. "I wish we could kill them all."

I nodded. "As do I."

Marcella heaved a sigh. "At least say you will come to the party tomorrow."

"Party?" I asked, wrinkling my nose. "I don't know if I'll be in the mood."

"Oh no, you must!" Marcella sat up, eyes sparkling. "The King is going to make an announcement. About the baby."

Against my wishes, a smile tugged at my cheeks. "Oh? What will he say about my niece or nephew?"

"Come tomorrow and find out." Marcella kissed my cheek and walked out the door.

4
I BANISH YOU

I destroyed the garden, like I promised, and resolved to keep a better eye on Marcella. She was too reckless. It was hard to tell who I worried about more, my sister or those who got in her way. It was an impossible and exhausting task as I jumped through countless hoops to keep the peace.

Using earth and herbs, golems were placed discreetly throughout the castle. They posed as scullery maids, pages, ladies-in-waiting, and stable boys, and worked as spies. My golems reported to me every evening, and when I wasn't putting on a show for the royals, I became the witch everyone was afraid of. I was ruthless in quashing heretics who slandered my sister.

By day, I rallied the noble folk by laughing and dancing and sparkling in court, abating their fears and shedding the mystery of the Starbright sisters. By night, I delved into my magic. For the rich and connected, I performed spells to freeze tongues and bring calamity down on their households. The poor and foolhardy were either threatened into silence or paid off.

The true heretics were the hardest to deal with. They remained undeterred by threats or the promise of disaster. Their convictions were strong, and they refused to be bribed or intimidated. My sister and I were the immediate scapegoats for any tragedy that befell them, which severely limited our options. So, heretics spread like fire through our small country, leaving a blaze of discontentment and rebellion in their wake.

It was a tricky line to walk, defending my sister from rumors I was no longer sure were falsehoods. Yet I did it, with all the fervor of an aunt protecting a baby. No matter what Marcella did, the child was innocent and of my own blood.

It was a strange and pleasing thought, that my little world would expand beyond my sister and me. I imagined the weight of a baby on my chest, the delicious smell of a newborn, their soft skin and tiny fingers. There were times I felt my womb ache with desire, even though I was only fifteen. I hadn't thought much about having children. Mostly because that involved marriage, and I wasn't ready to settle down yet. For the first time in my life, though, I was beginning to understand that I wanted a family.

When my sister was seven months pregnant, I found a heretic in my kitchens. One of the golems brought me the news, and my blood ran cold at what the cook might have seen or heard.

My time was divided between the castle and my estate, Easton Manor. On horseback, Easton Manor was a four-hour ride from the castle. When torture and magic were necessary, I could retreat to my own towers and dungeons. My stomach rolled as I thought about what sort of tales someone in my employ might have picked up. Especially a heretic, hiding in the shadows and sniffing out secrets like a bloodhound. I ground my teeth when I thought about it and vowed to show no mercy.

Today, I stood in my Great Hall, staring out my floor-to-ceiling windows. It provided an excellent view of my luscious grounds. Behind me, a long table was laid out with a delicious dinner.

I tapped my foot irritably against the floor. I did what I must for my family, but it gave me no pleasure. Heretics had no respect for the difficult situation they placed me and my family in.

A golem in the form of a slight and freckled scullery maid opened the door. "Dutchess Ceridwen, the cook you requested."

I steeled my nerves and straightened my back before turning from the window. "Thank you, Mallory. You may leave us now. Please shut the door on your way out."

The cook apprehensively entered the Great Hall. Her eyes darted from me, to the food, to the double doors. I knew she was considering all her options.

I was not a cruel mistress, but I wasn't a kind one either. I did not resort to using the cane or the whip. Nor did I bully my staff for small, perceived slights. There was only one way to get on my bad side, and that was by betraying my family.

"Sit," I ordered. "Eat. There is much to discuss."

The cook slowly took a seat at the table and began nibbling on some cheese. She poured herself a goblet of wine and drank deeply. Her body was stiff and tense, but the more she ate, the more she relaxed. It made sense. She had prepared this food herself. She was starting to believe it wasn't poisoned, that I couldn't have altered the foot without her detection.

Yet I had.

I took a seat at the table, across from the cook, and gave a sickly-sweet smile. "What is your name?"

"Gerta," the other woman said. She was sweaty from working in the kitchens. Blonde hair escaped from her braid and stuck to her damp forehead. Her grey eyes were guarded.

"Gerta," I continued, "Do you know why you're here?"

She paused, then reached for her wineglass. Taking a large swig, Gerta placed the cup down on the table and wiped her mouth. Her gaze fell to her lap before rising to meet mine.

"Because I know the truth," Gerta whispered. Her voice was quiet, but there was a steely resolve in her eyes.

I gave a light chuckle and leaned back in my chair. "What would that be?" I asked, still polite, still smiling.

Gerta's chest was heaving now. I wondered what she was thinking. Did she want to escape? To run madly through my halls until she reached a place of safety? Or maybe Gerta wanted to attack me, to run me through with the silver knife placed by her right hand.

"I know my king is bewitched," she said at last. "I know it was done by your sister's hand."

"Oh, Gerta." I stood from my chair and narrowed my eyes. My calm, collected demeanor fell away, revealing my true nature. Heat flooded my cheeks as rage raced through my blood. I slammed my hands down on the table, leaning in close to the cook.

"You know no such thing." I snarled. "You are a lowly servant, grasping at straws and making this world a dangerous place for the future heir to the throne."

Gerta stood from her seat, then stumbled backwards on unsteady legs before falling on her rear. Her eyes were wide and terrified. All traces of defiance had vanished from her face.

I snapped my fingers. The candles and braziers went out, enveloping the room in darkness. Thick fog began rolling through the Great Hall, turning the air cold and damp.

"Please, mercy!" Gerta shrieked.

"What mercy have you shown your king and queen?" I roared. My voice was like a crack of thunder. The ground shook beneath our feet. "You, who would bring civil war to their doorstep? You, who would discredit the future heir?"

"I have done no such thing! I am loyal to my king!" Gerta was frantic now. She turned and ran towards the towering double doors, only to find them locked. She beat her fists against the wood paneling, screaming for help.

I used magic to flit across the room, moving with superhuman speed. I stopped next to Gerta and pried her away from the doors. My hand found her neck, and I lifted her high in the air. Her skin was warm, and I could feel the blood pulsing in her veins.

"Did you forget I am a witch, Gerta? Did you really believe I couldn't alter the meal without your knowledge? I poisoned the wine with an honesty serum. I shall have the truth, whether you will it or no. Now answer my questions. Where did you hear these vile rumors, and who did you repeat them to?"

"The b-b-bard in town, at the Honeycrisp," Gerta said. Her eyes widened as the words poured from her mouth.

"The tavern?" I asked.

Gerta swallowed hard. "Minstrels, they sing songs of the Queen's magic. Everyone knows."

I scowled. "So, because the Queen is a witch, she must have spelled the King. Is that it? Is that what you're saying?"

"The King cannot have an heir!" Gerta burst out, full of conviction. "It is magic, evil magic!"

I slapped Gerta across the face. The sound of flesh of flesh echoed through the air and Gerta howled in pain.

"How dare you say such a thing!" I bellowed, "Where is your proof?"

Gerta screamed like a horse. Her eyes rolled with panic as she struggled in my grip. She flailed her arms and legs, desperately trying to extricate herself. One of her fingernails slashed down my face. I felt a hot sting under my eye, followed by something wet. She had drawn blood.

"The proof is in the past!" Gerta shrieked, unable to stop the torrent of words pouring out of her mouth. "The King is infertile! A-a horse accident i-in his youth! All the royal physicians say he cannot father an heir! The Queen is carrying a monster! There, I said it. I've spoken the truth. Kill me, if you dare. Everyone will know it was your doing!"

"What does that mean?" I demanded.

Gerta let out a devilish laugh. "You think we only whisper about the Queen? We watch, we see! Your manor is a place where people enter and never return! Murderer! Touch me, and everyone will know it was you! Touch me, and your life is forfeit!"

Gerta finished by spitting in my face. I lost my temper, then. Heat rolled off of me like a furnace. My hand glowed red hot, like metal in a blacksmith's forge. Without a word, I plunged my hand into Gerta's chest, ripping through flesh and muscle. Bones shattered against my hand.

Gerta's jaw dropped open, her mouth a wide O. Pain and horror lanced across her face, and I saw the shock in her eyes.

My fingers curled around her still-beating heart. It was warm, almost hot. The rhythmic beating reverberated against my palms. The pulsations were frenzied with fear and agony.

Gerta realized, too late, that she had overplayed her hand.

"Mer-cy," she gurgled. Crimson blood bubbled at her lips, dripping down onto her chin.

I pulled. Gerta's chest ripped open. Blood fountained from her corpse, covering me with a scorching spray. My hand emerged, holding her heart.

Gerta's blood was everywhere.

With a flick of my hand, the candles and braziers re-lit themselves, and the fog rolled away. I looked at the droplets of bright red blood arcing across the floor. They shone brightly in the firelight. It was almost pretty, like a string of garnets.

If only there wasn't so much of it.

With a sigh, I looked at Gerta's body, slumped on the ground. Here the blood pooled and spread lazily across the floor. Sticking my head out the double doors, I called Mallory back into the room. I ordered her to keep an ear out and to begin mopping.

I couldn't lift Gerta's body on my own, so I used a spell to move her to the table. I swiped the food onto the floor and grabbed a knife. It was gory work, fashioning a golem into the image of a certain person, but it had to be done.

Taking a deep breath, I cut into Gerta's chest, pulling the flaps of skin aside so I could see her ribs. Besides her heart, I would also need her lungs and liver.

Mallory brought me buckets of dirt, which was spread across the table and sprinkled with rainwater. There were several herbs on the table, waiting to be added to my concoction.

The doors to the Great Hall unexpectedly swung open. I looked up with a scowl, only to see Marcella enter.

"I hate it when you shield yourself from my golems. I like to be notified of visitors." My voice was coarse from all the yelling I had done earlier.

Marcella paused and took in the scene before her. "I can see why," she said. "Dare I ask what happened here?"

I laid Gerta's heart on the pile of dirt and began extracting her lungs. Her ribs made a sharp snapping sound as I broke them one by one.

"Tonight I found out my cook was a heretic. I've been working for months to quell any rumors against you, Marcella, but it's not easy. The people don't love you. You need to reach out to them. Show the world you are a benevolent queen."

Marcella glared at me. Rich hues of jeweled plum blossomed in her cheeks as she flushed with anger.

"After all I've done, all that I've sacrificed, you think I'm going to grovel to those dirty commoners?"

Marcella moved to the windows and stared out into the night. "No one can imagine the things I've done to get where I am today. Not even you, Ceridwen. I have ridden down to the gates of hell and snatched what I wanted right out of the devil's hands. I have elevated *myself!*" She beat a hand across her chest. "I will not share my glory! I've earned what I have!"

"Have you earned it or have you taken it?" I shouted, losing my temper. "Damn it, Marcella, do you know what *I've* done for your child?"

My sister turned and examined the corpse on my table. The anger drained from her as she approached and leaned in close. A look of mild interest crossed her face. "You're making a golem?" She asked, eyeing the dirt on the table.

"Yes." I continued removing Gerta's liver. My hands were sticky with blood. "Too many people have disappeared, too many that have questioned the crown. Your subjects are growing suspicious."

Marcella nodded. "That's smart. You're thinking ahead."

"I'm going to put her back in the kitchens. She will be under orders to continue about her duties and speak favorably of us."

Marcella carefully seated herself in a chair and rubbed her rounded belly. "I wish we could kill them all."

I nodded. "As do I."

Marcella heaved a sigh. "At least say you will come to the party tomorrow."

"Party?" I asked, wrinkling my nose. "I don't know if I'll be in the mood."

"Oh no, you must!" Marcella sat up, eyes sparkling. "The King is going to make an announcement. About the baby."

Against my wishes, a smile tugged at my cheeks. "Oh? What will he say about my niece or nephew?"

"Come tomorrow and find out." Marcella kissed my cheek and walked out the door.

5
DEATH AND BLOOD

For a moment, I couldn't answer. I barely recognized Marcella as I stared at her. The endless hours of terror and blood-soaked labor we had just shared vanished in an instant. I licked my lips, trying to form words.

"You don't mean that. She's your daughter." I finally got out.

Marcella turned her head away, refusing to look at her child. "This is not what I suffered and sacrificed for! I wanted an heir to the throne. I wanted a *king!*"

I looked down at the squirming bundle in my arms, then at my sister. Rage as I have never known flooded my body.

"You're selfish," I snarled. "You're a selfish monster and you don't deserve to have a child."

I turned and stalked out of the room, holding my niece close.

"Ceridwen." The King stood as I strode into the hallway and looked at me expectantly. He didn't ask, but I could see the questions looming in his mind. He didn't even glance at his daughter nestled in my arms.

"The Queen lives," I said in a flat voice, then looked down at my niece.

The King's eyes fell to his daughter, and I saw his chest swell with pride. "Well, what have we here?"

He moved closer to me, and we looked down at the baby. Her puckered lips were ruby red against pale skin and her dark eyes captivated us. Tiny legs kicked in the air and her hands were balled into little fists.

She was so small, so intricately delicate.

I glanced up just as Iberius lifted the cloth covering his daughter. I saw his eyes cloud over and my heart fell.

We both stood motionless for a moment. Neither of us breathed a word. Iberius didn't ask to hold his daughter and I couldn't bring myself to offer. The thought of my niece being rejected for a second time was too much to bear. Time slowed down. We were frozen on the brink of some horrible, unpredictable precipice.

It felt like several minutes before Iberius smiled. It was a brittle smile. A gentle breeze would have smashed it to pieces.

"Is the child healthy?" Iberius asked.

"Y-yes, Your Majesty," I whispered. I could hear my heart thundering in my ears.

"Well," Iberius said, "if we can have a healthy daughter, then we can have a healthy son."

I moved my eyes to the floor. If only he knew what Marcella had done for this child, how much she had risked in this mad game of power and status.

"Best be getting her to the wet nurse now." Iberius patted my shoulder and moved past me, into Marcella's room.

The wet nurse was at the end of the hallway. I approached the door and knocked lightly. A short, portly woman with sandy blonde hair and freckled cheeks pulled it open.

"Ah." Her eyes immediately dropped to the baby. "I see the Queen has had her son?"

I ground my teeth for a moment before answering. "It's a girl."

The wet nurse clucked her tongue and then motioned me in. "No heir for the kingdom today."

White hot anger washed over me. My magic surged, and a vase sitting on a windowsill shattered into a million pieces.

I froze and my cheeks grew warm with embarrassment.

"There's no fretting over it now, dear. What's done is done. We know a baby is a blessing, no matter if it's a boy or a girl. The rest of this royal court won't see it that way, though, and you know it." The midwife arched a knowing brow.

My body relaxed. A grudging admiration for the nurse came over me. Her words were frank, and she put me at ease.

I stepped into the room and bobbed my head. "Thank you. My niece has not had an easy beginning."

"I imagine not. So many foolish hopes were placed on her. However, that doesn't mean her whole life needs to be difficult. She is a princess, after all, and she has many opportunities ahead of her."

"I hope you're right," I confessed. It felt strange to hear the baby in my arms referred to as a princess.

The nurse smiled at me and clucked her tongue. "Come, hand the child over. She must be hungry. What is her name?"

"She...doesn't have one," I confessed. Once again, my cheeks flooded with heat and I felt embarrassed.

"Well, there's no shame in that. It'll come soon enough." She took the baby, and I immediately missed the small, solid weight against my chest.

"My, look at those eyes. She's certainly alert." The nurse moved to a corner of the room and I looked away.

A long, thin wail of a baby sent my heart racing. I spun towards my niece, but the cry was not hers.

"What was that?" I asked.

"That would be Amara." The nurse motioned with her chin towards a bassinet. "She came to me two weeks ago. Her mother died, poor thing."

I moved towards the cry and peered down at the tiny face.

"Hello," I cooed, lifting her into my arms.

Amara was only slightly larger than my niece. The two girls shared the same dark hair and ebony eyes, but Amara's skin was a few shades darker.

"Who's her mother?" I asked. "She looks to be of Aileen descent, but I wasn't aware we had visitors at court."

"Her mother wasn't a noble," the wet nurse explained. "She was a servant. Her name was Tierra."

"Tierra," I murmured. My heart twisted horribly at the news and I felt an avalanche of grief. I recalled our meeting in the royal gardens roughly nine months ago and let out a sigh. "Tierra was the first friend my sister and I made in Cherida. She will be missed."

"Yes, what happened to that family was such a tragedy." Mirtha sighed. "Their wagon overturned on the road after a heavy rain. Amara was the only survivor."

I stroked Amara's smooth cheeks, and she instantly quieted. Her dark eyes locked onto mine and she let out a soft coo. Warm affection stole over me, and I smiled.

"Please let me know if she needs anything. I want to make sure Tierra's child is well looked after." I said.

"Thank you, Duchess. She's a good-tempered babe. Praise the goddess." The wet nurse said. "She sleeps through the night and only cries when hungry. Other than that, Amara is content to be held and rocked."

Amara stuck her fist in her mouth and began sucking. Her eyes closed, and she quickly fell into a deep sleep. I hummed a quiet laugh and laid her back down in the bassinet. The excitement of the day was wearing off, only to be replaced with a deep weariness. I collapsed in a chair, my eyes starting to drift shut. However, I was startled back to consciousness when I heard the wet nurse make a loud exclamation.

"Oh, naughty thing!"

I bolted upright in my chair. "What's wrong?"

"She bit me." The wet nurse clucked her tongue and placed my niece in a second bassinet. "It happens sometimes. The babies get a little over-eager."

I rubbed my eyes and fell back in my chair.

"Duchess, take the bed, please. You're exhausted."

"Oh no, I couldn't-" I objected.

"Nonsense, I'll be up with the babies all night and this way, you'll be close to your niece."

I managed to stand and stumble onto the bed. The wet nurse tossed a blanket over me.

"I don't even know your name," I murmured.

"You can call me Mirtha," she said.

I drifted into oblivion.

The world was enshrouded in darkness.

My sister stood alone in a graveyard. "Death and blood," she said. Her voice was calm and echoed like a bell.

"Death and blood," I repeated, not knowing why.

A man stood behind her. His teeth lengthened into fangs. His mouth yawned open like a chasm. Then he bit her, burying his fangs into Marcella's neck. Blood poured from her wounds.

I tried to scream. I drew in a breath, but no sound came out.

The next moment, my sister and I were walking. Snow crunched beneath our feet. The air smelled of rot.

Marcella stopped, and I turned to face her. She held a hand to her neck, clutching at a wound. Blood dripped from beneath her fingers and three drops landed in the snow.

I watched with an eerie calmness. Somehow, I knew what came next.

"Death and blood," she said.

I frowned. That didn't feel right. Those weren't the words. I looked at the ground.

The blood was spreading. It grew into the size of a puddle and continued to swell. It consumed the snow, washed up against my boots, and stained the bottom of my cloak.

"Death and blood," Marcella repeated.

I bolted upright in bed. My heart was racing, and I was drenched in sweat. There was something in the air, a sort of dry, electric pulse. I shivered, despite not being cold.

"Duchess."

The word echoed out of the darkness.

I turned and saw the light of a single candle. There was a face, floating behind the candle, white as the moon. A page boy.

I turned more and saw Mirtha with my niece in her arms.

"What is it?" I asked, feeling groggy. I looked out the window. The sun wasn't up yet and the sky was just a few shades lighter than midnight.

"It's the Queen," the page boy said. "She's taken a turn for the worse. She has requested your presence...and that of her daughter."

Goosebumps erupted along my spine and arms. The air became as cold as death.

Death and blood.

I shivered again and stood from the bed. "Lead the way."

I followed the light of the candle as it bobbed down the hallway to my sister's room. Mirtha was close behind me, my niece lying silent in her arms. It was as if the baby understood how serious the situation was.

The room was lit by the golden glow of a thousand candles. Priests and priestesses clutched crystals and chalices filled with strange herbs and liquids. I watched their lips move silently as they chanted.

Everyone in the room looked either panic-stricken or gravely serious. They murmured to each other and shuffled around.

I noticed Iberius before I noticed my sister. He was slouched over in a chair, head in his hands. I touched his shoulder, but he didn't respond.

"Ceridwen."

I turned towards Marcella and nearly wept.

She was so thin. Her face was pale and her lips were chapped. The skin was beginning to peel back from her teeth. When I looked down at her legs, I could see the bedsheets were drenched in blood.

"Oh, Marcella." I took her frail hand and pressed it to my lips. Hot tears escaped from my closed eyelids and trickled down my cheeks. I sank to the floor as all the strength went out of my body.

"Don't cry." She whispered. Her voice was hoarse. "You must be strong."

I struggled to my feet and swiped at my eyes. "Of course." I choked out the words.

"I-I am sorry." Marcella went on. "I've asked so much of you, little sister. Forgive me?"

My mind traveled back to the night in the graveyard, and to the herb garden I had razed on her orders.

Unbidden, memories from a darker time of my life rose to the surface. The death of our parents, the rising tensions in Aileen, fleeing for our lives and scrounging to survive. Through it all, I had looked to Marcella. She had been my rock. It never occurred to me that Marcella was also just a girl, only three years older than me. She must have been lonely and scared too, but with no one to look up to and no one to protect her.

I lowered myself onto the bed beside Marcella and softly stroked her hair.

"There is nothing to forgive," I soothed.

"Please, can I see my daughter? Let me...let me hold her before I die." She whispered.

Mirtha stepped forward and handed me my niece. I carefully lay the babe in Marcella's arms.

"My King," I twisted around to speak to Iberius, "would you also like to see your daughter?"

My brother-in-law had been silent until that point. Now he rose from his chair like a great bear that had been prodded while sleeping. I held my breath, but he merely kneeled beside the bed and took Marcella's hand.

"You are, and will always be, the greatest love of my life," Iberius whispered to Marcella.

Marcella didn't answer. She was looking at the baby on her chest, carefully cradled in one arm. "Both of you, promise you'll look after her. Protect her. Swear it to me."

I felt my mouth go dry and fear crept into my heart. Protect her? From what?

"I swear it," The King responded. "It shall be my life's work."

I pressed my lips together. Iberius had no idea what he was swearing to. He had never seen that thing in the graveyard. Now Marcella was leaving her daughter with a threat hanging over her head. One I knew nothing about.

"Sister?" Marcella was gazing at me with her large doe eyes.

"I also swear it." My throat was tight as I spoke. I wanted to beg Marcella not to die, to fight for her life, but we both knew that was fruitless. So I sat on her bed, stroking her hair while the King sat on the floor holding her hand.

I watched my niece, lying on Marcella's chest. My sister had one frail arm wrapped around her daughter. She nuzzled the baby's head with her cheek.

"So much hair," she noted.

I gave a watery laugh. "She looks just like you, Marcella."

Marcella's eyes welled up and tears spilled down her cheeks. "Hair black as midnight, skin white as snow, lips red as blood."

"That's right," Iberius said. He tried to give a weak smile but failed. "She takes after you, just like Ceridwen says. She'll be the most beautiful princess in all the lands."

Marcella closed her eyes and took a deep breath. She kept her chin tucked down, nuzzling the baby. "Will you name her Snow White?"

"Of course," Iberius breathed. "Of course we shall. It suits her."

Marcella closed her eyes, and a ghost of a smile appeared on her lips. I heard her take one final, deep breath and, as she exhaled, all life left her body.

A wave of dizziness, of disbelief, washed over me. Everyone in the room seemed to freeze in horror as we watched the Queen fade from our world.

A long, thin wail finally broke the silence encapsulating the room. For the first time, Snow White was crying.

6
COURT GOSSIP

The room seemed to explode in a frenzy. The physicians rushed to my sister. I only had time to scoop Snow White up in my arms before I was pushed aside. Mirtha came and wrapped her arms around me while I wept.

Iberius stood in a corner, his face dark and frightening.

"I am sorry, Your Majesty." A physician said after several minutes. "She's gone. There's nothing more we can do."

If I stayed in this room, looking at my sister's dead body, I was going to scream or faint.

I turned and walked in a daze while Mirtha kept her hand on the small of my back. I heard her speaking to me, but I didn't recognize the words. Oh gods, was my sister really dead?

We turned into the hallway, making our way back to Mirtha's room, when a pair of guards stopped us.

"Where do you think you're going?" The tallest of the men spoke. He had white blonde hair that was almost silver. His eyes were as pale blue as the sky on a winter morning. He was very handsome. Something told me this man had spent his whole life being catered to and was quite used to having his way.

"We are going to my rooms, sir," Mirtha's voice snapped. Something he said made her angry. I was too sunk in my grief to know what it was.

"You can go anywhere you like, but you'll not be taking the King's heir with you." The second man smirked. He had small, pig-like eyes, and his mouth was twisted into a cruel sneer.

"What?" My lips were numb, but I managed to speak. Talking felt so foreign all of a sudden, but I needed to understand why these guards were upset that I was holding my niece.

The tall, handsome man stepped forward. "I'll be taking the child."

"Don't you dare," Mirtha snarled.

I clutched Snow White closer. The breath froze in my lungs as terror engulfed me.

The short man put his hand on his sword hilt while the tall one leaned down and whispered in my ear.

"Your time here is over, witch," he growled. Then he grabbed Snow White.

I shrieked then and kicked him while Mirtha went after the short one.

The guard hadn't completely ripped Snow White out of my arms. He wrestled with the blanket while I clutched the baby.

One moment was frightful chaos, the next, my assailant was being ripped away and thrown against a wall. Iberius stood next to me and I saw him pull a sword from his side. The metal blade sang as it was released from the sheath.

Iberius darted forward. His hand came out, and his fingers clenched tightly around the guard's throat, leaving him choking for air. With a swift and forceful thrust, Iberius plunged the sword into the guard's chest. The sickening sound of metal piercing flesh echoed through the air. Blood sprayed across the floor and dripped down the blade of the sword. Terror and shock registered in the guard's eyes. He gasped, his breath coming out a gurgle, then his body went limp.

Iberius pulled his sword loose and turned to the short, beady-eyed man.

I glanced around and noticed several guards had filled the hallway. Conrad was among them. He stepped forward and placed a protective hand on my shoulder.

Iberius' chest rose and fell in heavy, ragged breaths. His eyes flashed dangerously. "My wife's body is not even cold, and already I see traitors in the castle fighting to ignite a civil war!"

He pointed a finger in my direction. "Look at her! *Look at her!*"

Those within the immediate vicinity shuffled around so they were facing me.

"The Grand Duchess of Easton is not just the Queen's sister, she is *my* sister as well. She will be treated with respect and honor. Her commands will be carried out efficiently and with expediency. The next person to question her position, I will have drawn and quartered, publically. Now clean up this mess."

Everyone in the hall scattered. Conrad moved to stand next to the King while Mirtha scuttled into her room like a frightened rabbit. I stayed put.

The King approached me and stroked Snow White's little cheek. "May I hold her?"

I was surprised that Iberius would ask. He was king, after all, and this was his daughter. I nodded and handed Snow White over.

"She didn't cry." He noted.

I shook my head. "She rarely does."

"You would know, you've spent the most time with her." Iberius looked down at his child and I saw shame in his eyes. Maybe he had learned something from the loss of his wife.

"You will stay with us, won't you, Ceridwen? I need you right now. We both do." Iberius said in a soft voice.

I bobbed my head. "Of course I will. I had no thought of leaving."

"I meant what I said. You're my sister too. I want you to know that you still have family here." Iberius continued.

I swallowed back a lump in my throat while tears collected in the corners of my eyes. "Thank you, Your Majesty. Tha-that means a lot to me."

He handed Snow White back and kissed me on the forehead. "Get some sleep, Ceridwen, sister of the King."

Those first few months after Marcella's death were a dark blur. I don't remember much about her funeral. Conrad stood behind me with his hand on my shoulder as she was laid to rest in the royal crypt. I didn't trust myself not to faint, so Mirtha accompanied me and held Snow White.

Iberius was large and silent, with an air of unfettered grief and unpredictable anger about him.

Hours after Marcella's death, Snow White began to cry, and she didn't stop until she was a year old. Those first few hours after her birth, she was so quiet I assumed she would be an easy, amiable baby. I was quickly proven wrong.

Getting Snow White to eat proved a chore. She bit her wet nurses often and was a cluster feeder. She demanded to be fed every half hour to forty-five minutes.

I was in a constant state of fatigue, despite the army of nurses Iberius assigned to me. Although Snow White cried no matter *who* held her, she seemed to cry less loudly with me, and I was happy to indulge her.

There were many long, cold nights where I sat in a rocking chair in front of a window, doing nothing but rocking Snow White as she screamed and slept in brief intervals. I would watch the sun rise each morning and feel exhausted down to my bones.

Iberius visited infrequently. His mouth would turn down whenever he looked at his daughter's furious, red face. The piercing sound of her screams echoed through the room as she flailed her tiny fists in the air.

"Why does she always cry?" He asked me once.

"Some babies just do," I admitted, slumped over in a chair.

Things became easier when Snow White started walking and talking. Her appetite improved, and she developed a regular sleeping schedule. She ceased her crying and reverted into the wide-eyed, solemn child she had been when first born.

Often, you could hear her feet pitter-pattering through the castle, but it was rarely followed with laughter or singing.

One blessing I never ceased to be thankful for was Amara. She and Snow White were best friends, and attached at the hip. Most people couldn't tell the two apart, although I never had much difficulty. They both had dark eyes and raven hair, but Amara's skin was the deep ochre of her Aileen heritage. Snow White was fair, but not the pale porcelain of the Cheridans. Her fawn skin was a warm yellow-brown, like the bark of an ash tree.

The only time Snow White ever seemed to be truly happy was with Amara. Her usually serious and inquisitive face would break into a smile, and her eyes would sparkle. Because of this, I spent almost as much time with Amara as I did with my niece. The two girls were content together, and I didn't have the heart to separate them.

One day, when the girls were about five years old, I was following them down the stairs when we ran into an unexpected guest.

Amara was giggling and talking excitedly to Snow White. It was a spiral staircase, and they had just dropped out of sight when I heard the laughter abruptly die.

I frowned and quickened my pace. "Girls," I called. "What's going on?"

I turned the corner and paused. It was Jane Westerling surrounded by three of her ladies-in-waiting.

"Hello, Snow White," Jane greeted, a coy smile on her face. "Do you remember me? I'm Jane."

I was momentarily surprised that she was speaking to the right child. I wondered if she had been watching us long.

Snow White didn't seem impressed. She stared Jane down with impassive eyes and didn't respond.

"She's shy," I interjected after a long moment. It was a lie. Snow White was able to size people up rather quickly. If she didn't like what she saw, she would ignore them entirely.

"Hello," Amara bounced on the balls of her feet and waved. She was constantly smiling and happy, with a kind word for everyone. She was the complete opposite of Snow White.

Jane Westerling smoothed her skirts, and I saw her nostrils flare. "Oh yes, the servant girl." She murmured to her ladies. Her tone was condescending.

Amara didn't notice, but Snow White did.

"She's my *friend*," Snow White proclaimed, speaking for the first time.

"Oh, of course." Jane smiled, and I saw the tips of her ears turn red. "Snow White, it's such a beautiful day outside. I thought you might like to take a walk through the gardens with me?"

"No," Snow White answered.

Jane's smile froze, and she glanced back at one of her ladies. "Perhaps we could take tea in my room later?"

"No," Snow White responded. She heaved a deep sigh and craned her neck, looking around the ladies. It was clear she was ready to be on her way.

"Girls, why don't you go into the kitchen and see what's for lunch?" I suggested.

"Wait," Jane threw out her arms and moved in front of Snow White, blocking her path. "Snow White, did you know your father is looking to marry again?"

"What?" I interrupted, shocked at the news.

Jane turned to her ladies and mumbled out of the corner of her mouth, "I'm not surprised *she* doesn't know."

There was a soft tittering among the group while my face heated in anger.

Jane turned and smoothed her skirts before kneeling in front of Snow White. "That means you're going to get a new mother. Doesn't that sound exciting?"

"This is *not* an appropriate conversation for you to be having with her," I growled. "Girls, go to the kitchen, now."

Jane turned her nose up at me while the children trotted around her and down the stairs.

"Good morning, sister of the King." Her voice was sweet as honey.

I ground my teeth. "The King and I will handle those types of conversations with Snow White. It would be well for you to remember that. You don't know the princess, and are of no relation to her."

I hadn't forgotten that Jane Westerling slept with the King while my sister was pregnant. I hadn't forgotten Marcella's fears of being set aside, or how Jane hovered around Iberius in the days following her death.

The King eventually let Jane back into his bed, along with a parade of other women. He never officially took a mistress, though, and I always wondered why.

As Snow White got older, he spent more time with her. Not as much as a father should have, perhaps, but as often as a king was able. We ate dinner together almost every night, and Iberius showered her with gifts from the farthest corners of his kingdom. He didn't always know what to do with her, or what she liked, but he tried. If Iberius was planning to marry again, I felt sure he would have said something to me, or to Snow White.

Jane lifted her chin, and her shrill voice cut through the air. "For now, you have the title sister to the King. That is only because the late queen died in childbirth. Soon, King Iberius will have a new bride and more children. Snow White is only a princess, after all, and your power will diminish."

I descended the stairs, closing the distance between Jane and me. She blanched when I paused on the step above hers, towering over her small group. I gave a wintry smile.

"Fancy words from the King's whore. At least I don't have to bed Iberius for his attention." I taunted in a silky smooth voice.

Jane's jaw dropped. Her cheeks reddened and her eyes flashed.

I pushed past her and her ladies, making my way into the kitchens. I heard Amara's excited chattering as I let myself through the doors.

"Good morning, Duchess." A cook greeted.

"Good morning," I answered with a smile.

There was a small table, off to the side and out of the way of staff. Snow White and Amara were eating. I went and kneeled next to the girls and watched them.

"Is the bad lady gone?" Snow White asked. She pushed food around on her plate.

"I thought she was nice," Amara said, her mouth full of food. "She invited us to tea."

Snow White gave me a look. It was a look that said she knew Jane thought very little of Amara.

"Her name is Lady Westerling, and she won't be joining us," I assured. I ran my fingers through Snow White's silky hair. Her eyes were intent, focused, and her cherry lips were curled into a thoughtful frown.

"I love you," I murmured.

"I love you, too." Snow White responded, squinting at her plate. "Can I have more milk?"

A cook brought over a jug and refilled her cup.

"Auntie," Snow White asked, "Why would I get a new mother?"

I reached out and clutched her hand. "You will *never* get a new mother. What Lady Westerling was trying to say is that your father might remarry. If that happens, she will become your stepmother."

"Why would Father remarry?"

"Well," I paused, "He might be lonely."

"He can't be lonely. He has us," Snow White noted. "Also, he has lots of lady friends besides Lady Westerling."

Once again, Snow White surprised me with her keen observation.

"My mother is dead, too. So is my father." Amara said. "Mirtha takes care of me. She's my family now."

"We're all your family," I assured Amara with a warm smile.

Snow White tugged on my sleeve. "Auntie, if I have to have a new mother, why couldn't it be you?"

I didn't have an answer for her.

By the time I dressed for dinner, my conversation with Jane Westerling was only a blip in the back of my mind. There was no feast tonight, which meant our meal would be private, between the King, Snow White, and I.

I let myself into the dining room. There was a rectangular table that could seat 3 people on each side and one person on each end.

Iberius sat on the end with Snow White to his right. I took the seat on his left.

"Good evening, Ceridwen, how was your day?" Iberius looked up from his plate and smiled at me.

"Very well, thank you. Snow White played with her friend, Amara." I answered.

Iberius nodded his head. "Wonderful. She's such a sweet girl."

"Lady Westerling didn't like her." Snow White interjected.

"Lady Westerling?" Iberius looked from his daughter to me. "You saw her today?"

"She told me I was getting a new mother." Snow White continued.

Iberius set down his silverware, a storm brewing in his eyes. "Is this true?" He asked me.

I nodded.

Iberius shook his head. "This is not how I wanted you to find out."

I froze at his words, and Snow White scrunched up her eyebrows.

"What do you mean?" I asked, heart pounding in my chest.

Iberius heaved a deep sigh and leaned back in his chair. "Snow White, why don't you go down to the kitchen and ask for dessert?"

Snow White slid down from her chair and looked her father in the eye. "You can just say you want some privacy." Then she turned and strode purposefully from the room. She kept her back straight and her little feet made a tap-tap-tapping noise against the floor.

"She's certainly observant," Iberius smiled.

I laughed. "Now you know what I deal with every day."

Iberius looked down at his lap. I saw a chuckle shake his shoulders. "You do it with such humility."

I felt the tips of my ears burn. "I would do anything for my niece, Your Majesty."

"As you've demonstrated these past several years." Iberius smiled. "I don't know where she would be without your care and guidance."

"I believe, Your Majesty, that I need her just as much as she needs me." My voice was slow, careful. I wondered what this had to do with his impending engagement.

Iberius came around the table and kneeled beside my chair. "You've been a rock for me and my daughter these past several years, and have never asked for anything in return. It is your pure heart and the love you have for Snow White that keeps you here. I want- I was hoping- that you would stay on a more permanent basis."

"What do you mean?" I asked, confused.

Iberius took a deep breath. "Ceridwen, your king is asking for your hand in marriage."

I froze for a moment. Time seemed to stand still. All these years, I held the title "sister of the King" and our relationship had never been more than platonic. We weren't even that close. His motive confused me until I reflected on his words. Then I understood.

This wasn't a confession of love. Iberius wanted someone around who genuinely cared about Snow White. Someone he could rely on that didn't have an ulterior motive. This was a marriage of convenience.

I swallowed and nodded my head. "All right then, I accept. On one condition."

Iberius rocked back on his heels, a look of surprise on his face. I so rarely asked for anything. "Name it." He encouraged.

I took Iberius' hand and looked him in the eyes. "I want Lady Westerling dismissed from court."

Iberius shrugged. "Done. Is that all?"

"Yes," I answered. "I accept your offer of marriage."

7
A UNION OF CONVENIENCE

Iberius and I decided on a small wedding. After all, this was a union of convenience, not a celebration of love. Despite this, I still managed to feel overwhelmed by all the preparations.

The day of my wedding arrived faster than I thought possible. As the sun began peeking over the horizon, an array of maids began filtering into my room. I was laced into my wedding gown, and then my long dark hair was twisted up in an elaborate bun.

As I was having my makeup applied, Snow White let herself into my room. She had on a full pink dress and held a basket with some petals. She came up beside me and caught my eye in the mirror.

"I'm the flower girl," Snow White said, gesturing to her basket.

"Yes, you're the loveliest flower girl there ever was." I gave her a warm smile.

"Will we still be able to visit your estate in the summer?" Snow White asked.

"Of course. In fact, once your father and I are married, we will have family vacations all over Cherida." I answered.

Snow White puckered her lips. "I don't want family vacations. I just want you."

I noted the sadness in her voice. I waved away the maids and kneeled beside my niece. "There, there, my snow angel. You'll always have me." I stroked her cheek and smiled. "Do you know what happens when I am queen?"

"You'll become my new mother." Snow White answered.

"You only have one mother, snow angel," I said. "What your father is doing is giving me a new title, so I can better look after you."

"Oh," Snow White seemed to like that answer. She gave me a hug and a rare smile before skipping off into the next room.

The wedding went off without a hitch. For the ceremony, Iberius and I walked down the aisle together and said our vows. We kneeled before the altar and were blessed by the Hierophant and High Priestess.

I couldn't help but think of Marcella as I pledged my loyalty to Iberius, until death do us part. She had been so happy, so radiant on her wedding day.

Iberius and I opened gifts after. I was pleasantly surprised to receive a silver hand mirror with blackened glass.

"It's a scrying mirror," Iberius said. "Do you like it?'

A smile spread across my face, and I nodded. "Very much, thank you."

After the gifts had been opened, we went down to the feast. I ate at the high table between Snow White and Iberius. Halfway through the meal, I noticed something wrong with my new husband. He had set aside the red wine being served and moved on to a stronger drink, mead. He was drinking copious amounts, and his blue eyes were brooding.

I leaned over and touched his shoulder. "My Lord, is everything well with you?"

Iberius turned to me, a dark look on his face. I instinctively leaned back in my seat.

"You look like her, you know." He replied in a husky voice. "You look like Marcella."

A lump appeared in my throat, and I felt my eyes mist. "You miss her," I said after a moment.

Iberius bowed his head, his shoulders drooping. He seemed so sad all of a sudden, almost childlike.

My heart swelled with grief. I reached out and ran my fingers through the King's blonde curls. "I was thinking about her today, too."

Iberius caught my hand and kissed my palm. "You've been a blessing to me, Ceridwen. You have always given freely and never asked for anything in return."

I paused, unsure how to respond. What would it feel like to only know people with political agendas? To always be surrounded by false faces with their hands out? I felt a twinge of pity for Iberius. It must be a lonely existence.

As the new queen, perhaps I could change that.

I gave Iberius a genuine smile and squeezed his hand. "Of course, My Lord. I am always at your service."

Iberius stood and kissed my forehead. "I'll see you tonight, Ceridwen." He leaned over to ruffle Snow White's hair, and then he turned and strode from the room.

I insisted on tucking Snow White into bed before retiring to my new chambers. The servants helped me change into my nightclothes, and word was sent to the King that we were waiting for him.

I stood beside the bed, my hands clasped in front of me. This may be a marriage of convenience, but I understood Iberius and his appetites. I knew what was expected of me.

An hour passed, then two. The servants began to shift uncomfortably. I didn't blame them. My feet hurt too.

Some more time went by before I motioned towards one of the servants.

"Please light a candle," I requested. "I'm going to bed. You are all dismissed."

The servants murmured and shuffled around while I climbed under the covers. I closed my eyes as the room darkened and drifted to sleep almost immediately.

A loud clunking sound startled me awake. As I opened my eyes, I noted it was still dark outside. There only light was the single candle I requested burning next to my bedside.

I crawled out from beneath the covers, my bare feet hitting the cold stone floor. I pattered across the room and was surprised by who I found there.

"Iberius!" I paused and examined the king. He was leaning against the far wall, barely able to hold his balance. "My Lord, are you all right?"

Iberius looked up. Even in the dark room, I could see his eyes were bloodshot. He smelled strongly of mead.

The King's eyes went wide when he saw me. He staggered to my side and cupped my face, stroking my cheek with his thumb. "Marcella," he whispered. "My darling, my love, how I have missed you."

His words shocked me. "My Lord-"

"Marcella," He breathed. Then his mouth closed over mine. He lifted me up and carried me to the bed, all the while whispering my sister's name in my ear.

The candle went out.

When I woke the next morning, I was alone. I rubbed my eyes and climbed out of bed as the doors opened. Servants poured into the room carrying a breakfast tray.

I frowned. "I can eat downstairs."

"The King thought you might like to relax today," a servant answered. She motioned for me to climb back into bed and brought me the tray.

"That was...kind of the King," I responded. I laid back down and pulled the covers up over my lap.

In truth, I wasn't pleased with being ordered around. My garden needed attending, and I had to check in with Snow White. I didn't want my niece to think I'd forgotten her.

I was just finishing breakfast when Iberius walked into the room. The door opened slowly, and he almost tiptoed in, looking sheepish.

He came and stood at the foot of the bed. "Good morning, Ceridwen."

"Good morning, My Lord." I greeted.

Iberius shuffled his feet, and I saw his ears turn red. "Are you well this morning?"

"Yes, breakfast was wonderful. Thank you." I smiled.

The King thinned his lips, and I saw his face become stern. "Ceridwen, you must be honest with me. If you were hurt last night, I would have you tell me."

I raised my eyebrows, feeling surprised. "Is that what this is about? You think you hurt me?"

Iberius looked at the ground and didn't respond.

"Hm, I see." I folded my hands in front of me and looked at the ground. "I understand, My Lord, that last night you were in your cups. This has led you to question your treatment of me."

I paused, thinking about how to continue. "We laid together as husband and wife. I am given to understand a woman's first time is not necessarily pleasant, but you were not cruel or violent, and you did not injure me. My Lord, I am in perfect health."

"Are you- Are you sure?" Iberius still looked troubled.

"I am uninjured," I assured him. "May I get out of bed now?"

Iberius raised his eyebrows, surprised at my question. "Yes, of course. I only wanted to make sure you were comfortable."

"I want to check in on Snow White, and I need to tend to my garden," I said while putting on a robe.

"I had breakfast with her this morning. She missed you." Iberius said, a hint of affection in his voice.

I smiled at his words. "As soon as I'm dressed, I'll go find her."

Iberius hesitated, and I paused near my wardrobe. "What is it?" I asked.

A shadow passed over the King's eyes. I wondered how much he remembered from last night.

"I'll be retiring to my own chambers this evening," Iberius said after a long moment, his voice slow and heavy. "Not just for tonight but, every night after."

"Oh," I didn't know how to respond to that. I wrapped my hand around the handle of my wardrobe and glanced at him over my shoulder.

"Last night I behaved...less than honorably." Iberius continued. "I don't want a repeat of that happening. Ceridwen, I promise that after today, I will no longer enter your bedchambers."

I nodded my head. "As you wish."

It wasn't difficult to understand his perspective. Mistaking your new bride for your dead wife had to be embarrassing, as well as painful.

"I'll send the servants in." Iberius let himself out of the room. I heard the door close softly behind him.

8
FORBIDDEN MAGIC

Life at court settled into a comfortable routine. I was surprised at how little my day-to-day activities changed. Occasionally, Iberius would ask my opinion when it came to matters of state, but other than that, I maintained my freedom and continued looking after Snow White.

Less than a week after my marriage to Iberius, Snow White raised a sensitive topic. We were having tea in one of my smaller tea rooms, and it was just the two of us.

"Are you my new mother now?" Snow White pressed, gazing at me with her dark, doe eyes.

I frowned. I thought I made it clear to Snow White that she would only ever have one mother. Yet, the servant who had brought the tea tray in referred to me by my new title, Queen Mother. It must have confused her.

Or had it? It wasn't the first time Snow White had raised the issue. Did she feel her life was somehow lacking? That she was missing out on something important?

I set my teacup down and folded my hands in my lap, thinking about how to respond.

"Snow White, your mother is Marcella Starbright, of Aileen. That will never change." I said in a gentle voice.

Snow White pouted. "But she isn't here. You are."

"I-I am your aunt," I said, fidgeting nervously. Why couldn't I make her understand?

"Father gave you a new title, though. He says you're the Queen Mother now."

"Your father gave me that title so I could better look after you," I explained.

Snow White's face seemed to crumple a little, and her eyes turned into pools of sadness. "Maybe you don't want to be my mother."

"Oh, my snow angel! No, it's not that. Never that." I rushed to Snow White's side and lifted her in my arms. Tucking her beneath my chin, I sat down and rocked her gently.

After a long while, I drew in a deep breath. "Your mother was my sister. It is...difficult...to think about stepping into her shoes and taking her place."

"You did it for father." Snow White pointed out. "He asked you to marry him, and you said yes."

"I did that for *you*," I said. "So that I might better look after you. Still, I see your point."

"You do?" Snow White asked.

"Yes," I said. "I am more than your aunt now. I am your stepmother. Would you like to call me that?"

Snow White straightened in my lap and shot me an excited smile. "Yes, very much."

I gave her shoulder an affectionate squeeze. "Why don't we get back to our tea? When we're finished, we'll go find Amara and Mirtha."

Snow White agreed. I moved back to my seat, and we clinked our cups together.

While life at court might was settled and uneventful, raising Snow White was not always so. The older she got, the more odd habits she displayed.

It didn't take long for Mirtha and me to discover that vegetables made Snow White sick. In fact, Snow White was happiest when her diet consisted of rare, bloody steak. Garlic caused her to break out in hives.

Both Amara and Snow White exhibited early signs of animal magic. Most mysticmancers displayed some signs of animal communication as children, though it usually evolved into something else with age. Amara's faded as she grew older, and she turned to greenwitchery, like her mother. Snow White, however, had a special bond with animals and her powers grew stronger over time.

Birds and squirrels would bring her nuts and leaves without prompting. Sometimes they would appear with jewelry or small toys taken from other households. Dogs were the most loyal. They followed Snow White around, intuitively acting on her silent commands.

It wasn't until Snow White was seven that her most alarming allergy manifested.

Amara had broached the subject of a picnic lunch on the castle grounds, and Snow White readily agreed. It was a beautiful summer day. The sky was a clear blue, and sunlight flooded over the flowers, setting off their jeweled tones. I was invited, along with Mirtha, who had been raising Amara for the past several years.

Before heading into the gardens, I stopped in the kitchens to pack our meal.

"We have the blanket!" Amara burst into the room, clutching one end of a throw rug tightly to her chest. Snow White held the other end.

"All right, young ladies, let's slow down. There's no need to run in a castle." Mirtha followed the girls and gave me a bright smile. "It appears this idea was a good one. Everyone is so excited."

"The children, you mean," I murmured out of the corner of my mouth.

We giggled to each other while Snow White tugged on my dress.

"Stepmother, are we going outside now?" She asked.

"Yes, we are," I replied. Taking her hand, we went out of the door and into the castle gardens.

"Let's eat under the apple tree," Amara suggested.

Snow White consented with a nod.

"Let's spread the blanket on the ground," Mirtha said.

Amara did what Mirtha asked, but Snow White stubbornly clung to my hand.

"What is it?" I asked her.

"My eyes hurt," Snow White whispered.

My heart sank at the pain in her voice.

"Well, it is a bright day out," I said in a soothing voice. Even as I spoke, a nagging voice in the back of my head told me this wasn't normal.

"Amara," I called out, "Will you be a dear and move the blanket under the shade of the apple tree? The sun is hurting Snow White's eyes."

Amara looked up, her forehead creased with worry. "Of course," she answered and made the appropriate adjustments.

We all settled in and Mirtha began handing out the food. Snow White curled into my side and made herself as small as possible.

I ran my fingers through her silky hair. "Do your eyes still hurt, snow angel?"

"Yes," she said with a hoarse voice, keeping her head tucked down.

I glanced at Mirtha, who shrugged.

"Princess, try this lovely pie the cook made. Look at Amara, she's eating like a big girl." Mirtha said, trying to rally Snow White's spirits.

"It's really good, Snow." Amara nodded her head.

At this point, Snow White began to cry. Her tiny shoulders shuddered against my arm while she made small, hiccuping sounds.

"Snow White," I cried, cupping her face in my hands. "What is it? What's wrong?"

"It *burns!*" She screamed, rubbing her arms. "It hurts me!"

"What does?" I asked, feeling frantic and confused.

"The *sun!*" she almost screamed. "It burns my skin, and it hurts my eyes!"

I examined Snow White's arms and face, which indeed were turning an angry red. My stomach plummeted.

I didn't wait for my stepdaughter to say another word. "Off," I commanded to Mirtha and Amara.

The two of them scrambled off the blanket, moving the basket and food with them. I grabbed the fabric and wrapped Snow White as tight as I dared. Lifting her in my arms, I fled back to the castle. As I sprinted across the grounds, I whispered a spell of protection around her.

After dinner, when Snow White and Amara had been put to bed, Mirtha and I convened in one of my private sitting rooms.

"Snow White has always liked dark, cold places. An attic without windows, catacombs deep beneath the earth. I thought it was odd, but I never expected this." Taking a deep breath, I wrapped my fingers around the back of a chair and exhaled slowly. "I don't know what to do, Mirtha."

Mirtha seemed just as panicked as I was. Her porcelain skin was paler than usual, and her eyes were wide. "She's still so young. Perhaps it will pass. You and I both know children develop allergies at early ages that don't carry over into adulthood."

"Food allergies," I corrected. "I've never heard of this. Did you see her skin? She was scalded red. Snow White was being burned."

"But it faded," Mirtha tried to soothe.

I shook my head, unable to make sense of our predicament. "A real burn wouldn't have healed so quickly."

Mirtha looked at the ground and bit her lip. I saw the tips of her ears redden.

"What is it?" I asked, knowing she was holding back.

"Perhaps," Mirtha hesitated, "perhaps if we knew more about how Snow White was conceived?"

"What?" Her words shocked me.

"Queen Mother, I know your sister was asking questions before she got pregnant, questions about forbidden magic."

A shudder moved down my spine, and I turned away.

"If we could just find out who Snow White's father was-"

I spun around. My magic surged, and the lights in the room went out. Mirtha froze.

"Snow White is the daughter of the King." I hissed.

"With all due respect, Queen Mother, the King is infertile," Mirtha spoke in a soft, but knowing voice.

I shook my head, refusing to believe it. "I will not deny that my sister dabbled in forbidden magic, but what you're suggesting? That is beyond anything Marcella was capable of."

The door opened then, and Conrad entered. "Forgive me, I heard there was an incident with the Princess. I wanted to check on her." He stopped and looked around, confused by the darkness.

The candles and braziers re-lit themselves and I motioned towards the hourglass. "She has long been in bed, sir, but I assure you, Snow White is unharmed."

"That is good to hear. The King was worried."

"Why would the King be worried?" I asked. My voice was high-pitched as I tried to downplay the situation. "Of course, we were all concerned at first, but there is no lasting harm done."

"It was how he found out," Conrad looked grim. "The King overheard the servants talking."

I sighed and ducked my head. "I'll speak to him in the morning."

"King Iberius is out hunting, and will be gone for some weeks, I believe," Conrad continued. "He put me in charge of your protection before he left."

"Oh yes, that," I growled and collapsed into a chair, my anger rising. "It's been years and I still haven't shaken my reputation as the evil foreigner, the seductress, and witch. Maybe next I will be the evil stepmother."

The room was silent for a moment. I looked at Conrad.

"The Princess has developed a sensitivity to sunlight. From now on she will need to be indoors, unless it's very early morning before the sun has risen, or the sky is overcast."

"Yes, Queen Mother," Conrad said.

"I am tired. Please leave Mirtha and me alone so we can talk," I said.

Conrad bowed and left the room, the heavy door closing behind him with a soft *boom*.

For a moment, Mirtha and I held each other's gaze. After all these years of friendship, we were now sizing each other up.

"Mirtha," I stood from my chair and went around the table to stand next to her. I gave a sweet smile. "What you hinted at earlier, about Snow White's paternity, you will never mention that again."

Mirtha bowed, then turned to leave.

"What you said is treason," I continued. "I won't have it."

"As you will, Queen Mother," Mirtha answered.

"If it were mentioned again, my hand would be forced. You would be given a traitor's sentence."

Mirtha's back stiffened. "I understand." Her pace quickened, and she hurried to the door.

"Do you know what the penalty for treason is?" I asked.

With one hand on the door handle, Mirtha glanced over her shoulder at me. She answered with one word.

"Death."

***

As predicted, the King was gone for some weeks. I was having dinner with Snow White when the hunting party made its return.

Conrad let himself into the dining hall and bowed low. "The men have returned."

"Father is home?" Snow White brightened at the thought.

"Let the King know he is welcome to join us," I said with a smile.

Conrad nodded. "I will inform him at once, Queen Mother."

Snow White and I finished our meal, but Iberius never showed. As I tucked Snow White into bed that night, she looked into my eyes with something akin to fear.

"Father doesn't love me," she whispered.

My heart plummeted. I sat on the edge of the bed and stroked her hair. "Of course he does, my sweet. Why would you say such a thing?"

"I can hear him," she answered. Her dark eyes glittered in the candlelight. "I can hear what he's thinking."

Her words puzzled me. "What do you mean?"

"When he gets close, I can feel it. Sometimes I hear words," Snow White said.

I took a deep breath. "Oh, snow angel, that's simply not true." I kissed her on the forehead. "You're just letting your imagination run away with you."

Snow White didn't believe me. I could see it on her face. Her lips thinned and her eyes darkened.

I pulled the covers up to her chin. "Goodnight, my love."

"Goodnight," she said.

I blew out the candle and opened the door to leave.

"Stepmother?"

I paused. "Yes?"

"Be careful." Snow White's voice drifted in the air like a gust of bitter wind. "He's angry."

I went back to my room, pondering Snow White's words. Was it true? Could she sense the King's emotions, hear his thoughts? She might be an empath, someone who could sense the feelings and emotions of another person. They couldn't read minds, though,

I briefly considered that Snow White was lying or exaggerating, but I quickly dismissed those thoughts. Perhaps she was confused. Yes, that must be it. She was just confused.

I continued to puzzle over Snow White's revelation, turning her words over and over in my head. I was so deep in thought that I didn't notice Conrad stationed outside my door.

"Ceridwen."

It had been years since I was addressed by my given name. I stopped and looked up.

"Conrad?" I questioned.

"The King waits for you." Conrad was stern, solemn.

A chill ran over my skin. I didn't have to be an empath to sense his fear.

"Then...I will go to him." I said my words slowly, testing the waters.

Conrad nodded, and I moved past him.

Just as I was about to push the door open, his hand fell on my wrist.

Startled, I looked up into his face.

Conrad leaned in close, capturing my eyes with his. "My Queen, I am your loyal subject, serving you most faithfully. Should you ever have need of me, I will come at your call. I will always protect you."

I would have been touched by his words, if they didn't elicit such fear. I only managed to nod before pushing open my doors and going into my rooms.

The King sat alone in the dark. He rested on my bed, next to a nightstand with a jug on it. I could smell the mead.

Only a few candles glittered from high in the candelabras. I steeled myself and marched forward.

"It's been many years since I've seen you in my room. The last time, I believe, was our wedding night." It was a subtle hint, a reminder of his promise to not enter my chambers.

"Do not speak to me of that night," Iberius growled.

I stopped in my tracks. Iberius had always been kind to me, but that did not make him an inherently kind man. He could be mercurial and temperamental when he didn't get his way and was capable of flying into terrifying rages when his demands were not met. He was king, after all, and used to having his orders obeyed.

I would need to tread lightly.

"Tell me why you are here," I coaxed in a soothing voice.

Iberius stirred. There was conflict on his face. "I've had a proposal from Theor, for Snow White's hand."

I clenched my hands into fists, then forced my body to relax. A proposal for Snow White? She was so young, only seven years old. A child still.

"They want me to give her away, so they can swoop in here like vultures and claim my throne when I am dead." Iberius took a large gulp of his mead. "How would you enjoy that, my dear? To be cast aside like a used rag the moment my throne is vacant?"

I didn't like the tone of the King's voice. I remembered Snow White's warning from earlier. My eyes darted to the door, where I knew Conrad was standing guard, waiting, listening. His shadow moved across the floor as she shuffled his feet impatiently. A storm was brewing.

I approached the table where the mead sat. Snagging an extra cup, I poured myself a glass. When I tossed it back, it burned from my throat all the way down to my stomach.

I slammed the cup down on the table and stood in front of Iberius.

"Tell them no." My voice was cold as steel and brooked no room for argument.

Iberius scoffed at me. "Were it that easy. The country would be plunged into a civil war after my death and my daughter would be the most sought-after commodity."

My blood ran cold at his insinuation.

Iberius took another long draw of his mead and wiped at his mouth. "If only she had been a son."

I wanted to scold him but held my tongue. There was no arguing that Snow White would have been safer as a boy.

Iberius stood up then. He loomed over me like a giant, threatening shadow. He ran his fingers through my hair.

"You could do what your sister did," he rasped. "Whatever magic she dabbled in that enabled her to bear my seed, you could do it."

My skin chilled, and a tremor ran through me. I slapped his hands away and stepped back. "My sister *died*." I ground out between clenched teeth. "Is that what you're asking of me?"

Iberius advanced on me, rage in his eyes. "You are the Queen," he hissed. "You have a duty to this kingdom, to me!"

My heart was thundering in my ears. I glanced at the door again. Surely Conrad would protect me if the need arose.

I turned back to the King. "You are not yourself." My voice was low but steady. "I will leave now and we will not speak about this again. Goodnight."

Turning on my heel, I walked away. I wanted to run but forced my legs to take steady, even strides. Stopping at the door, I turned to look at the King.

"Did you love my sister?" I asked.

Iberius snorted. "Did she love me?"

I wanted to answer yes, but I truly didn't know. Was Marcella capable of loving anyone but herself?

"Your silence is deafening." The King finished his mead and threw his cup against the wall. "Get out. I don't want to look at you tonight."

I fled.

I was slow to wake the next morning. Snow White lay in my arms, breathing softly. She barely stirred when I came in the night before. I looked into her face, admiring her long, dark lashes and gently puckered lips.

I took a moment to lie there, soaking up the peaceful quiet of the morning. Last night was still difficult to think about.

After several minutes, I stretched and gathered my courage. Carefully, I climbed out of Snow White's bed. The air was cold against my skin, and I shivered before grabbing a robe. Tiptoeing across the room, I opened the door and peered out.

"Conrad!" I was surprised to see him. "How long have you been here? Since last night?"

"Yes, Queen Mother." Conrad gave a quick bow. "I wanted to be certain you were safe."

Safe from the King, he meant. I tried not to tremble at the implication. The previous night frightened me more than I cared to admit.

"Thank you," I said at last. "Conrad, I want you to know that I appreciate you watching over me."

"It was my honor, Queen Mother." He replied.

I hesitated. "I would like to go back to my room but-" My voice trailed off. What could I say? That I was afraid of my husband? That I wished to avoid him, if at all possible?

"His Majesty retired to his chambers last night." Conrad finished my thought. "I sent a maid into your rooms to tidy up."

My heart soared as I looked into Conrad's eyes. I had an ally, someone who wanted to look after me. I was unsure why this touched me so, but I felt immense gratitude for Conrad in that moment.

"You're being so kind. I'm not sure how to repay you." I admitted.

Conrad stepped closer, his face serious, longing even. He reached out to touch my hair, running his fingers through my loose strands. Then he touched my cheek, stroking the pad of his thumb against my skin.

"I didn't do it for a reward." His voice was husky.

I was more confused than ever. I didn't recognize the intense, yearning look on his face, or understand why there was such fire in his eyes. Maybe I didn't want to.

"You-you've always been loyal to the King." I stuttered out at last.

Conrad dropped his hand. "I am still loyal to His Majesty, but first, I must be loyal to my heart."

I sucked in a deep breath. Conrad's declaration took me by surprise.

Sunlight trickled in through a window, alighting Conrad's ocean eyes. His wheat-colored hair glinted with threads of gold. He was tall too, almost as tall as Iberius. Every inch of him was thick with corded muscle, earned from long years of swinging the great sword that hung at his waist. There was no denying that Conrad was handsome, loyal, and brave. Any woman would be lucky to have him, so why did I feel so conflicted?

Conrad seemed to read my mind. "I'm not expecting anything from you, Ceridwen. I know you're a married woman, and my queen, but I will always be there for you. No matter what."

"But why?" I sputtered, still confused.

Conrad leaned back on his heels, a smile tugging at the corners of his lips. "I think you know why."

Light steps alerted us to an approaching maid.

Conrad bowed. As he straightened, he paused to hold my gaze. "Good day, Queen Mother."

Then he turned and strode away, leaving me to contemplate his words.

9
RIFTS

From that day on, tensions were strained between the King and I. Iberius didn't come to find me or apologize. Not like he did after our wedding night. We continued to be civil to each other, but there was a coolness between us that I couldn't quash.

The only good news that came out of the whole ordeal was that Iberius turned down Theor's proposal. We continued to eat dinner every night, but as Iberius drifted from me, he also drifted from his daughter.

Conrad continued to shadow me, though not in an outright manner. We never spoke of his affections again, but there were times I could feel his eyes on me.

I worried constantly that Iberius would grow tired of me and Snow White. That one day a proposal would come for my stepdaughter, and Iberius would ship us somewhere remote so he could be free of us.

Years went by like this, but for every proposal that came for Snow White, Iberius was steadfast in his rejections.

When Snow White turned twelve, another problem emerged that was more difficult to handle.

I was taking a turn in the gardens with my ladies-in-waiting when I heard a great roar coming from the gates. Concerned, I hurried forward, only to stop in my tracks. My jaw dropped in surprise.

The crowd was roaring alright, in pleasure. As far as I could see, peasants were pressed up against the gates, cheering and waving their hats. Their chants of, *"Princess, Princess Snow White!"* rang in my ears.

I stared at a brunette child, dancing in the grass and putting on a show for the peasants. The sun was out in full, so it couldn't be Snow White.

I began taking long, purposeful steps before I caught the attention of the child. "Amara," I yelled, "Come here."

She approached me, her cheeks flushed pink and her eyes sparkling. "Yes, Ceridwen?"

"What are you doing?" I asked in a hard voice.

Amara's face clouded in confusion. "I was dancing. They cheer when I dance."

"Can't you hear them? Don't you know what they're saying?" I asked.

A grin lit up Amara's features. "They're calling me Princess. Snow White and I find it humorous. People can rarely tell us apart, so we often switch without telling anybody."

My stomach hollowed out with fear. "How long has this been going on?"

Amara shrugged. "Oh, we've been doing it for years. Don't worry, Ceridwen, we've never tried to fool you. We both know we couldn't manage that!" A laugh escaped her lips.

I realized she was destined to be a great beauty. An enchantment of grace and loveliness adorned the child's face, poised to bloom into womanhood. In just a few years, she could rival Marcella in her prime.

My fear crested and turned to anger. I frowned, allowing my displeasure to show. "That is unacceptable behavior, Amara. Snow White is a princess. You are a servant's daughter!"

Amara's face crumbled, and I felt a twinge of regret. I thought back to my earliest days in Cherida when Marcella and I worked in the royal gardens, side by side with Tierra. Never before had I brought up Amara's parentage, or made her feel beneath Snow White.

I pushed the regret down. The girls were getting older. It was time they learned where their places were in the world.

I inclined my head towards the castle. "Go inside and stop fooling these people. I don't want this to happen again, Amara. You must not act above your station."

Amara's lips trembled, and she dropped her face into her hands. "I'm so sorry, Ceridwen," she sobbed, her little shoulders heaving. She turned and bolted into the castle.

"Hey there, what have you done to our princess?" An angry voice yelled.

"You can not keep her from us, witch!" Another voice called out. "She belongs to her people, and you will not take her from us!"

I ground my teeth at the chorus of angry shouts and motioned to my ladies-in-waiting. "Let us go inside," I said. "I'm quite done here."

That afternoon, I had a light lunch and some tea set up in one of my tea rooms. Snow White and I had agreed to eat together that day, so I sent a page for her when everything was ready.

I was sipping from one of my porcelain cups when Snow White let herself into the room.

"Ah, my snow angel." I smiled and gestured to the refreshments. "Sit. Have a cup of tea with me."

Snow White clasped her hands behind her back. "I'm afraid I must decline. I've been comforting Amara all morning. She's in quite a state."

I heard the reprimand in her voice.

Pursing my lips, I set my drink aside and sat up a little straighter. "Actually, I wanted to talk to you about that. Are you aware of what your so-called 'friend' has been doing behind your back?"

"Amara does *nothing* behind my back." Snow White snapped. "She is my dearest, closest friend. There are no secrets between us."

I sighed and pinched the bridge of my nose. "The reputation of a princess is delicate, Snow White. We can not have servant girls parading about, masquerading as royalty. Imagine if there was a coup! Have you considered the danger that puts you in?"

Snow White advanced on me. I saw the anger flashing in her eyes and for a moment, she could have been Marcella. I nearly recoiled in my seat, but managed to stay composed.

"How dare you," Snow White snarled. "You dare accuse Amara of plotting behind my back? She would do no such thing! I'm shocked you would even suggest it. You, who have known her since infancy. There is not a cruel or deceitful bone in her body!"

"I am the queen and your stepmother," I answered. "It's my job to think of these things. To protect you."

"Well then, you're looking in the wrong place." Snow White's pale cheeks were flushed with a reddish-orange hue. "I am well acquainted with the rumors surrounding you and my mother. I know what the people whisper. Did you think maybe, just maybe, Amara and I came up with this plan together? To help bolster my reputation, so I may avoid the trap you and my mother fell into?"

The thought hadn't crossed my mind. I tried to reason with my stepdaughter. "Snow White-"

"I can't go outside, the sun burns me. The people need to see their princess, to connect with her, so that one day they will have faith in my leadership abilities." Snow White interrupted.

"I am pleased to hear you have been thinking on such things, but this is the *wrong* way to go about doing it," I said. "We can host parties, dances-"

"I've no interest in that." Snow White interrupted.

I frowned at her tone. "Well, start. It's time you made new friends. It isn't only the common people you must win over, but the court. I can see now that I have allowed you too much freedom with Amara. That is going to end. She is well beneath you and it's time you were introduced into polite society."

"What are you saying?" Snow White challenged.

"Say goodbye to Amara," I commanded. "Tomorrow I will have her moved to a different location, perhaps to one of our summer castles. You will not be seeing her again. I am putting your friendship to an end."

Snow White took another step toward me, rage outlining her face.

"That's a damn fine way to repay someone's loyalty!" She yelled.

"Snow White-"

She cut me off. "I will not give her up, do you hear me? I will not! She is my only friend. Where Amara goes, I will go. You can't stop me."

Her outburst of anger shocked me. Snow White was so seldom flustered. I realized now I had crossed a line regarding Amara. I thinned my lips and gave a curt nod.

"Fine, she stays, but I will not have her parading around like she was this morning. That will stop immediately."

I worried for a moment that Snow White would fight me on this too, but after a moment, she gave a nod of consent.

"Fine," she said, "if it bothers you so." There was a scathing undertone in her voice. "May I go now?"

"Yes," I answered. I took another sip of my tea, but grimaced when I realized it was now lukewarm.

Snow White turned and flounced from the room, leaving me alone but for a few servants. I motioned towards one of the women and she came closer.

"Go into Amara's room. Strip her wardrobe bare. I want her dressed only in rags from now on. The Princess has spoiled her, and I want Amara to look her station."

The servant bowed her head, staring at the floor. "Yes, Queen Mother."

She scuttled out of the room and I drank the lukewarm tea, pondering the events of the day.

***

If Snow White found out about my order, she never mentioned it. She gave me a long, lingering look at dinner the next night, but didn't bring up Amara. We seemed to have reached an uneasy truce about the servant girl, and I seldom found the two socializing. I suspected them of avoiding me or hiding out.

I hadn't fully considered the consequences of my actions. My fear had created a rift between Amara and me. Whenever she saw me in the halls, she would duck into a low bow, hiding her face. After mumbling a quick, "Queen Mother" she would scurry away as though I frightened her.

It wasn't my intention to push Amara away, and it pained me that we were no longer close. At the same time, I was angry that she wasn't more understanding. After all, Snow White was going to be queen one day. Surely Amara didn't believe they could go on being friends their whole lives?

Guilt nipped at my heels, and I pushed the uncomfortable thoughts aside. I was doing what was best for Snow White. I would always do what was best for her and I couldn't let sentimentality get in the way.

Whatever animosity lay between Snow White and me dissipated when Iberius was threatened by an enemy that plagued rich and poor alike.

Death.

10
THE KING OF CHERIDA

"Make way for the King!" A great booming voice echoed throughout the castle, heavy with panic and fear. In my chambers, I froze at the sound.

Only a moment later, a banging sounded at my door.

"Queen Mother!" I heard Conrad yell. "The King is in need of you!"

I raced to my door and threw it open. "What happened?" I asked, heart pounding.

Conrad's face was white, and he shook his head. "It's the new stallion the King purchased. He was riding today, but the horse spooked. They both fell, and the King was rolled over."

My knees went weak, and I clutched my doorframe, placing my other hand over my heart. "Gods be good," I prayed. "Is it serious?"

"He's in with the physicians now," Conrad answered. "I want to prepare you. I was there when it happened. His prospects don't look good."

"We must-" I tried to swallow the lump in my throat, "we must keep faith. Has Snow White been summoned?"

"Yes, Queen Mother. I sent someone to find her as soon as we entered the castle." Conrad began walking down the hall at a punishing pace, and I trotted along beside him to keep up.

I glanced up at Conrad, realizing he left his best friend's side to come and fetch me. I wasn't sure how I felt about that, or even if he did it for me. It could be an act of desperation.

"They put him in a room downstairs. They wanted to move him as little as possible." Conrad went on.

We approached a door that Conrad opened for me. I rushed in.

"My Lord," I rushed to Iberius' side and took his hand.

"Ah, wife." Iberius attempted a smile, but his eyes were squeezed shut and his jaw was set. It was obvious he was in excruciating pain, despite his playful demeanor.

I lifted the blanket to find his belly swollen and bruised. Both of his legs were broken.

Conrad stood behind me, and I whispered over my shoulder. "There is internal bleeding. Make sure the physicians know to leech the wound."

He nodded and moved away.

"There is no need to fret," Iberius said. "In a few days, I shall be right as rain. Imagine what the minstrels would say if I died falling from a horse."

"The horse *rolled* on you," I admonished in a soft, but firm, voice. "Now lie still."

"Fretting over me?" He did manage to smile this time, and his eyes peeked open.

"Of course," I murmured, my cheeks warm. After all these years of being cold and distant, is this what it took for Iberius to open up? A trip to death's door?

Snow White rushed into the room, looking paler than normal. I saw her hands tremble as she moved forward and touched her father's arm.

"Hello, Snow White," Iberius said. "See what a fool your father has been? All this because he can't ride a horse properly."

Snow White knitted her eyebrows. "You are an exceptional rider, Father. There is no shame in the horse spooking. They're rather silly creatures anyhow."

"I'm surprised to hear you say so," Iberius noted. "I've heard you have a way with animals."

"Horses don't listen." Snow White responded, brushing the topic aside. Her eyes darted to mine. "Will he be alright?"

"We hope so," I responded, easing my free arm around her shoulders. Snow White leaned into me.

"What a family reunion this is." Iberius stared at the ceiling, looking desolate. "I had hoped for something happier."

A physician lifted Iberius' shirt and began poking and prodding.

I felt my husband's hand twitch in mine, but he didn't make a sound. Snow White watched with wide-eyed interest.

After several minutes, the physician looked up. "I'm afraid this is more serious than I would like. The wound will need to be opened and drained."

I felt a horrible twist in my stomach, but Iberius barely moved.

"Well, get on with it then." He said in a rough voice. "At least see my wife and daughter from the room first."

Snow White turned towards the door, but I held onto Iberius' hand.

"I will not leave my husband," I pronounced.

Mirtha arrived then. She was out of breath and her face was flushed. "I came as soon as I heard. Gods save the King!" she panted.

"Mirtha!" I exclaimed, glad to see her. "Please, will you watch Snow White and keep her company? She shouldn't see this."

"Of course, of course. Come along, Princess. We'll find something to occupy ourselves with." Mirtha said.

Snow White cast one more look at her father, her scarlet lips puckered in worry, then exited the room and shut the door behind her.

I turned back to find Iberius eyeing me.

"Why did you stay?" He asked.

Conrad pulled a chair forward, and I seated myself. "You shouldn't be alone right now," I answered.

"Fond wife," Iberius patted my hand and paused for a moment. "I don't deserve you."

A smile tugged at my lips, and I was handed a potion from one of the physicians.

"The King will need to drink this," He said.

I nodded, noting how bitter it smelled. I handed the cup to Iberius.

"Here," I said.

Iberius frowned. "Smells bloody awful," he complained, before downing the entire drink in a few gulps.

"Here, Your Majesty." Conrad handed him a cup of mead.

Iberius drank that as well. "Pour me another glass before we get started, will you?" He asked in a husky voice.

Conrad obliged, and Iberius gulped down his second cup.

"Alright," The King nodded at the physician, "do your worst."

The next few hours were hell. Iberius was given a rag to stuff in his mouth while his belly was cut open. Blood and pus spilled out, nearly causing me to gag. I turned away, conscious only of Iberius holding my hand. His fingers squeezed around mine until I thought the bones would break.

Conrad stood on the other side of the King, also having his hand crushed.

We could hear Iberius screaming in agony, his voice muffled by the rag. After what felt like hours, his grip went limp and his eyes rolled back.

"Your Majesty!" Conrad exclaimed, looking petrified.

I put my free hand against Iberius' neck and sighed when I felt his pulse. "He lives," I informed everyone in the room. "He likely passed out from the pain."

The physicians nodded and went back to work.

Conrad caught my eye. "He's lucky to have you."

I dropped my gaze. It had been five years since Conrad declared his feelings. Did he still care for me like he used to?

I decided I didn't want to know. Not when Iberius' life hung in the balance. I may not have been in love with the King, but I could never forget his kindness to me. Even in his anger, even in his coldness, he had always protected me and Snow White.

Finally, the physicians finished their treatment. Iberius' wound was packed with papyrus and an herbal salve.

Thus began some of the longest days of my life. The room was kept dark, with only a few lingering candles that seemed to aid the shadows more than chase them away.

Iberius developed an infection that quickly turned the air putrid. No matter how many times a day his bandages were changed, it didn't quell the stench of rot.

As for my husband, he fell in and out of consciousness. When Iberius did speak, he rarely made sense. More than once I was jolted awake in the middle of the night as he began screaming in pain, calling out for Marcella or his mother.

Conrad and I spent every moment with Iberius. I wound string around white candles, whispering words of healing as I tried to bind the infection. Conrad brooded in a corner, his blue eyes flickering in the candlelight.

After a week, I felt dead on my feet. The tips of my fingers were raw and exhaustion wore me down to the bone. The only sleep I had were quick naps as I stayed at Iberius' bedside. My magic seemed to slow the infection, but the wound was failing to heal.

It wouldn't be long now.

It was at this time, while I was at my lowest, that Amara came bursting into the room.

"Cer-Queen Mother!" She yelled, her face flushed.

"Amara, what is it?" I set down the candle I was working on and stood up from my chair.

"She's hurting her! Yvette is hurting Snow White!" Amara was shrieking. Her face was ashen, and her eyes were wild with fear.

I ushered Amara out of the room and shut the door behind me. "What? Yvette? Do you mean the new governess?" I asked.

Amara bobbed her head. "Yes, yes, hurry! She's hurting Snow White!"

Without another word, the two of us bolted through the castle. I held my skirts aloft, my heart pounding in my chest as I followed the slight frame of the girl in front of me. Her raven hair bounced as her legs pumped frantically.

In minutes we were outside, in the gardens. The sun was out in full force and the only shade offered was from a gazebo.

That's when I saw Snow White. She lay on the ground, her face crumpled in agony. She was screaming; long, haunting wails of pain.

The governess had grabbed hold of Snow White's wrist and was wrenching on her arm, attempting to pull her into the sunlight. Already I could see my stepdaughter's skin turning red, as though someone had thrown boiling water on her.

I don't know if it was exhaustion that caused me to snap, or that someone dared to lay a hand on my girl. Either way, something broke apart inside of me, unleashing a well of rage.

"Yvette!" I screamed, running across the lawn. "Take your hands off of her *immediately*!"

Yvette huffed, but did as I asked. She had tight blonde ringlets, a sharp nose, and cruel eyes.

"How dare you?" I snarled, throwing my cloak over Snow White. "You were hurting her!"

"The Princess can not spend all her time indoors," Yvette argued, looking down her nose at me. "She needs a firm hand, so that she may act properly."

"She is allergic to the sun!" I yelled, shepherding Snow White back towards the door.

"Nobody is allergic to the sun." Yvette crossed her arms, scowling. "I am the only one helping her! The Princess must be introduced into the world, into polite society. I see what you are doing and I am disgusted by it."

She began pacing across the lawn, pointing an accusatory finger at me. "You keep her locked up inside the castle like a prisoner. You teach her to fear nonsensical things, like sunlight, and you isolate her from the court. I see your true purpose, *Queen Mother*. You will be her ruin!"

I had enough. I pushed Snow White through the open door, into Amara's waiting arms, and turned towards Yvette.

Silently, I seized her by the throat, hoisting her upwards until her feet dangled above the earth. The atmosphere grew heavy, and a gust of wind arose, carrying a piercing, indescribable cry that made bystanders instinctively cover their ears.

Yvette's mouth opened wide in a horrible, silent scream. She drifted up, up, up, out of my grasp and hung like a puppet in the sky. Long slashes began appearing on her body, as though someone were flaying her alive. Her dress was being ripped to shreds, and blood seeped from her wounds.

I was lost in fury, wanting only to bring her pain and endless torture. The world fell away, and I concentrated on Yvette's slow demise.

I was pulled back to the present by Snow White. She tugged on my skirts with one hand, the other clasped over her ear. When I looked down, she pointed towards Amara, who was in a heap on the floor, sobbing.

I ceased my magic at once.

Yvette fell to the ground. Her body made a heavy thud as it hit the grass. I half expected her to get up and start scolding me again, yet she lay still. Only her shoulders moved as she softly wept.

"Yvette," my voice was like grinding rocks, "you will get your things together and be gone within the hour. If you ever come near my home or my child ever again, I will finish what I started here today."

I turned away and saw Amara on her feet, supported by Snow White.

I walked inside and shut the door.

"How are you feeling?" I asked Snow White.

"Better," she held out her arm. "I heal quickly once I'm indoors."

"I am glad. I would not see you in pain." My fingers brushed along her cheek, and I let out a shaky sigh.

My gaze moved to the other girl. "How are you, Amara?" I asked.

"I am well, Queen Mother." She gave a little sniff, but put on a brave face.

"Very good. I want to say you did the right thing by coming to me. Why don't you go down to the kitchens and have some dessert, hm? As a reward."

Amara smiled and wiped the tears from her eyes. "Thank you, Queen Mother." Then she turned and skipped away, once more the happy child she had always been.

Snow White looked at me with one raised eyebrow. *"Queen Mother?"* She asked.

"Please don't argue with me now. I really don't think I can stand it." I put out my arm and leaned heavily against the wall. Rubbing my forehead, I let out a weary sigh. That magic had taken a lot out of me and I was already exhausted.

"Amara is a servant girl. You are a Princess. The two of you have…different roles in life. I'm sure she understands."

Snow White stood a little straighter. "When I am queen, I will make her a duchess. Just like Father did for you. That way, no one will ever tell us not to be friends again."

Oh, my poor girl, she knew nothing of her father's condition. The day of her coronation was fast approaching. My stomach knotted, and I thought for a moment that I might be sick.

No, I must exert myself. After the King died, I would be Snow White's last kin. I would also remain Queen Mother, answering only to my stepdaughter and whoever her Regent was.

Those would be dark, dangerous times. Snow White would look to me for protection. I must keep my wits about.

"Stepmother?" Snow White reached out and touched my arm.

I smiled and patted her hand. "Do not worry about me, snow angel. I am well, but I must return to your father. Why don't you join Amara in the kitchens?"

Snow White frowned, her scarlet lips puckering with doubt. Still, she did what I asked, and I breathed a sigh of relief for it.

I made my way back to the King's chambers, where Conrad woke from his nap.

"What is it?" He asked, his voice groggy.

I sighed and sat in a chair. "Lady Yvette has been dismissed for mishandling the princess. I should have had her drawn and quartered for what she did. All the same, she knows now."

Conrad raised his eyebrows. "So, there was an incident?"

"You could say that." I shifted uncomfortably.

Conrad sat back in his chair, drawing a weary hand across his brow. "That's a shame. She comes from an old family. Her house is quite powerful."

I stiffened. "Are you saying-?"

"I would not question you, Queen Mother." He interrupted in a soft voice. "I am merely noting, it is a shame. I do not wish for my queen to have enemies."

I turned my face away, feeling unhappy. I thought about my little scrying mirror, hidden away in my bedchambers. If I looked into it tonight, would I see Yvette's face? Or that of her family? How long until others joined her cause?

A heavy weight bowed my shoulders, and I shrank in my seat. If only the King would live.

A few more days went by. Days spent sitting at death's chopping block, waiting for the ax to fall and spirit our king away from us.

It was the darkest, coldest hour of the night when Iberius awakened. This wasn't his usual muddled stupor. When he called out my name, he was completely lucid.

I leaned forward in my chair and clasped his hand. "My Lord," I breathed, tears in my eyes. "I am very glad to see you awake. Are you much recovered?"

Iberius grimaced. "Dammit, I don't think so. I'm still in a lot of pain. I dare not move." He paused and squeezed his eyes shut for a moment. He gripped my hand as though he might drown without it.

"Ceridwen."

The King's voice was a whisper. I leaned in closer to him.

"Yes, My Lord?"

"I know I am dying."

I choked on a sob and tears spilled down my cheeks.

Iberius let go of my hand long enough to wipe the tears away. "Have a servant fetch the Master Scribe. Also, the Hierophant and High Priestess."

I did as he asked. I ran to the door and flung it open, my raspy voice repeating the King's orders to the sentinels outside. Conrad had stepped out to handle some business regarding the King's Guard. I had him summoned as well.

The time had come. A new heir was to be selected.

I moved back to the King's side and gently stroked his hair. His blonde curls had long since turned grey, but his eyes were sharp and intelligent. I wanted to ask who he would select as Snow White's regent, but so many years of indifference lay between us that I dared not.

For a moment I worried that, instead of a regent, he might assign Snow White a husband. Perhaps an older man who could control the throne immediately. I wondered where that would leave me.

I had only sent for a few people, but the room quickly became filled with members of the court.

The Hierophant and the High Priestess were there, burning sage and chanting healing spells. Slinking in the back of a dark corner was the Steward, eyes glittering with greed. Standing at the door, looking pale and solemn, was the Marshal. The Master Scribe hunched over a piece of parchment, quill in hand.

While I sat at the King's side, Conrad stood behind me with a hand on my shoulder. I felt ill. My stomach churned uncomfortably and my head was dizzy. I prayed I wouldn't faint.

"Well, look at all you preening vultures." Iberius' voice was gruff and deep. If I had closed my eyes, I never would have known he was ill. "Yes, it's true. Your King is dying. Heard the news, did you?"

Nobody knew how to respond, and the room went quiet.

Iberius motioned towards me. "Sit me up, Ceridwen. I don't have long now."

With trembling hands, Conrad and I lifted Iberius, piling pillows around him to help prop him up.

"Where is the scribe?" Iberius asked.

"Here, Your Majesty." The Master Scribe responded in a weak voice.

"Good, write this down." Iberius closed his eyes for a moment, then began speaking. "To the head of my Kingsguard, Conrad of House Hadrian, I grant him Wickmoore Hall, Northamber Park, and Cotswold Abbey. Along...with all its...titles and lands. Wife, you are squeezing the life out of my fingers."

I gave a small gasp and loosened my grip. "My apologies."

The King's announcement had shocked me. Conrad was already rich, already titled. Now he owned nearly a fifth of Cherida's land and with that gift, he also became responsible for much of our army.

"You have that, Scribe?" Iberius asked.

"Yes, Your Majesty." The Master Scribe sounded as shocked as I was.

"Good. To my wife, Ceridwen of House Starbright, I leave her Castle Hampstead, Castle Shoremire, Castle Gisors, Alderth Abbey, and Cordington Park, along with all its titles and lands."

A shocked silence resonated throughout the room.

"Your Majesty," the Marshal gasped, "you have bestowed two-thirds of our army onto only two people."

"Dammit, don't you think I know that?" Iberius growled. "Do you think I've forgotten what happened after my first wife died?"

The Marshal paled and looked away.

Iberius looked smug. "No, you haven't forgotten. It was your cousin who tried to kidnap my daughter, right out of her aunt's hands. I killed him myself, you know. I rammed my blade into his chest and spilled his guts all over the floor."

"My cousin was a traitor," the Marshal said. He stared vacantly at the wall, and his words sounded rehearsed.

Iberius grumbled something indecipherable under his breath.

I glanced down at my hand, still wrapped tightly around the King's. Conrad, who had resumed his position of standing behind me with his hand on my shoulder, momentarily stiffened.

I understood Iberius now, more than I ever had before. He was giving me an army, and an ally. My heart swelled with gratitude as a weight lifted off of my shoulders. A small part of me had been concerned that he wouldn't care what happened to me, or Snow White, after his death. I was relieved to find my fears were unfounded.

"As for my daughter, Snow White-"

The entire room collectively held their breath and leaned in close as Iberius said this. It was the moment everyone had been waiting for. Who would be named regent? Who would rule until Snow White's sixteenth birthday, and she was old enough to take the throne? Who would influence the next Queen of Cherida?

I was the only person in the room who did not move. I was frozen with terror. Iberius and I had never discussed Snow White's succession before. My mind wandered back to the night Iberius had been drinking in my room, and he asked how I felt about being discarded like an old, used rag.

"Upon her sixteenth birthday, Snow White shall be coronated and take the throne as queen, per the law." Iberius began. "My first declaration will be that my daughter shall not marry, nor became engaged, until that time. When she chooses a husband, it shall be her choice and no one else's."

I felt myself sigh and relax at this.

"As for the regency, I bestow that title onto Ceridwen Starbright. Stepmother to the princess, Queen Mother to her people, and my wife."

It took a moment for his words to sink in. I gaped at Iberius, wondering if I had heard him correctly.

The room buzzed with talk while the Master Scribe scribbled madly, his feather pen swaying back and forth. "Done, Your Majesty."

"Bring it here," Iberius said.

The Master Scribe poured a bit of wax onto the bottom of the page and held it out to the King. Iberius stamped the wax with his insignia ring, making his words law.

"Give it to the commander of the Kingsguard," He whispered.

The Master Scribe handed the scroll to Conrad, who tucked it into his belt. There was a stunned look in Conrad's eyes, but his mouth was stern and he maintained an air of authority.

"Now get out, you lot. Let me speak to my wife in private." Iberius growled.

Conrad's hand squeezed my shoulder, and then he was out the door without a word or a look back. He would have much work to do tonight, I realized. Not everyone would be happy to have a queen on the throne, or a Starbright as regent.

The room emptied until it was just Iberius and me.

"That was very generous of you," I said. My voice was thick and cracked in the middle of my sentence.

Iberius said nothing for a long moment. He stared up at the ceiling. "It was well earned, Ceridwen. You're the only one who's ever truly loved her."

"That's not true," I whispered in a soothing voice.

"It is, though. I've been a damned idiot. I've spent too much time stewing in my anger, too much time feeling robbed of a son." Iberius paused, struggling for words. "It would be easy to blame my actions on my responsibility as king, but the truth is, I was just selfish. I did not care for you and Snow White as I should have."

"Perhaps not," I mused, "but you could have done worse."

Iberius snorted. We were silent for another moment, and when he spoke again, his voice was thick.

"I do love her, Ceridwen. I do. Maybe not as much as I should have, but in my own way. You'll tell her I said that, won't you? That I love Snow White?"

"She already knows," I said, trying to comfort the King, "but I'll tell her again."

"You've always been so kind," Iberius murmured. He gave my hand a gentle squeeze. "I still remember the first day I saw you and Marcella, working in the castle gardens. Marcella was all fire and pomp, but underneath it all, she was terrified. You were quieter, more reserved, less trusting."

"I remember those days," I said. Those first few months in Cherida had been excruciating. Everything was new and different, and I never knew how to act.

"You were *thin*," Iberius said, as though the memory offended him. "So was Marcella, but you were skin and bones. I told the cook to give you extra rations."

"Did you?" A giggle escaped my lips.

"Ah, you were a child then. I felt protective of you, and Marcella." Iberius went on. He paused, then continued, his voice growing weaker. "Sometimes I look at you, and I still see that sweet, innocent girl who needed to be protected."

My fingers trailed through Iberius' hair. "I am all grown up now. I will be all right. So will Snow White."

"Marcella was always so protective of you. I've tried my best to pick up where she left off," Iberius said.

"I appreciate everything you've done for me and my family," I said. My throat was tight with emotion.

"The Starbright sisters." Iberius gave a wistful smile. "Marcella…she always ran hot and cold. I knew it was just because she was frightened. I tried so hard to take care of her, to prove myself so she would open up and let me into her heart. Sometimes I thought I succeeded, other times…"

Iberius let his voice trail off and heaved a great sigh. I remained silent on the matter. The older I got, the more their relationship confused me. At times, Iberius and Marcella radiated joy and love. Other times, Iberius was irritable and snappish while Marcella quietly seethed with rage.

And Iberius took women to bed while my sister was pregnant.

"You were never like that," Iberius went on. "Ceridwen, you were always so kind and sweet. Never spoiled, always humble, despite the gifts I showered upon you. And you were always what you said you were."

"O-of course, My Lord." I stuttered out. What did Iberius mean? Did Marcella trick him somehow? Did she make promises she couldn't keep? Is that what made their relationship so turbulent?

Iberius stared at the ceiling. I could see a question forming, so I pushed mine down.

"Tell me true. Do you know if Snow White is mine?" He asked.

I sucked in a breath, shock pouring over me. "Of *course* she is!" I breathed, stunned that he even had to ask.

Then I thought of the graveyard, and Marcella's magic and her triumphant grin proclaiming that she had danced with the devil.

I swallowed back a lump in my throat. Maybe, maybe there was a possibility...but I didn't *know*. Not for certain. Anyway, I couldn't bear the thought of Snow White not belonging wholly to me. Of being...something else.

I was so deep in thought and self-pity that I almost didn't notice when Iberius, King of Cherida, drew his last breath and his hand grew cold in mine.

11
THE TASTE OF WINE

The funeral was six days later. I wandered up the spiral stairs and into a tower where Snow White was. We were both dressed in black.

"Snow angel, it's time for us to go," I spoke in a soft, exhausted voice.

"Who told you where to find me?" Snow White asked. She stood before a floor-to-ceiling window, staring out. There was a dark blur outside the window. Something fell so fast that I almost didn't notice it.

I took a deep breath. "Amara said you were refusing to come down."

"I don't want to go." Snow White's voice was soft and pained.

"Neither do I, to be honest. First my sister, now your father." I sighed and leaned against the wall.

"Amara says we're both orphans now." Snow White said, still staring out the window.

There was another flash, another blur of something falling.

"That's true," I nodded. "I'm an orphan too, you know. I lost my parents at the age you are now."

I reached out and stroked Snow White's black, silky hair. "It won't feel this bad forever. What's important now is that we honor your father, honor his memory."

Another dark, obscure object fell past the window.

Snow White turned to face me. "Yes, I suppose I can do that."

She turned towards the door and began descending the stairs, but I didn't follow right away. Drawing my brow, I moved forward, curious about the dark blurs falling past the window. As I poked my head out, a horrified gasp was ripped from my lips.

There were birds, dozens of them. Some were twitching, their wings bent at odd angles, others were dead. I tilted my head towards the sky but found nothing to explain this odd phenomenon. It's as though these birds suddenly decided to stop flapping their wings and fell to their demise.

A cruel knot twisted in my stomach. No apparent reason...other than, perhaps, animal magic.

It wasn't easy to shoulder the burden of an entire kingdom. After Iberius' death, I used my scrying mirror more frequently. Every night before bed, I would chant a simple spell:

Mirror, Mirror, in my hand
Show all my enemies in the land.

Shadowy figures would appear. Most of my opposers were commoners, placed far away so that they appeared distorted. The closer my enemy, the clearer I could see them. This proved invaluable in court, as I could quash rebellions and snuff out threats before they could gain any traction.

It was after Iberius died that I noticed a new enemy. This one was far away, lingering on the fringe of people. As the years progressed, the shadow began making its way towards the center of my mirror. Slowly, I started to make out facial features, like watery blue eyes and blood-red lips.

The demon in the graveyard.

The years marched forward, as they have a way of doing, until Snow White's fifteenth birthday was just around the corner.

I was going over the guest list when my stepdaughter let herself into the throne room. As the doors swung open, I saw her in deep conversation with Amara, before the latter girl scurried away like a frightened rabbit.

"Ah, Snow White," I beamed. "I was just making plans for your party."

"Do I have to go?" Snow White had a dour look on her face.

"Well, it is a party in your honor," I said.

"Isn't that ironic, a party I don't want in celebration of me." Snow White heaved a frustrated sigh, looking very much like Marcella in that moment.

"It is important to make appearances, to form alliances," I informed her.

"I would have more fun if Amara could be there." Snow White pointed out.

I held up a hand. "I don't want to argue about this again. Can we please-"

"I wasn't trying to be petulant," Snow White interrupted. "I was just saying the party would be more fun if someone were there that I actually liked."

"You've been too sheltered." I admonished. "It's my fault. I should have introduced you into polite society a long time ago."

"I'll be sixteen next year," Snow White said. "Then I'll take the throne. I could banish polite society if I wanted to."

I laughed then. "There's a lot to learn about ruling, snow angel. You need the court to work with you, not against you."

"I suppose." Snow White looked out the window for a moment. "I heard we have a visitor arriving tonight."

"Yes, I'm meeting with an emissary from Aileen," I said.

"Aileen?" Snow White asked sharply. "The place where my grandparents were murdered? The place you and my mother had to flee after the King turned against mysticmancers?"

"*That* King is dead," I informed her. "Aileen has a new ruler now. His name is Liam, and he is sending an emissary to broach peace talks. He wants to heal the rifts his uncle created."

"Hm," Snow White still looked skeptical.

I didn't blame her. The night King Drustan of Aileen died, my mirror was humming with energy, and a particularly malevolent energy was missing from the looking glass. I broke down and cried with relief, but also anger. King Drustan took so much from me and my family. I wished Marcella could have lived long enough to see him pass. She deserved that.

"King Drustan lost his wife and two children to the plague that swept through Aileen when your mother and I were children. His younger brother died a few years ago, which made his son Liam next in line for the crown. King Liam knows his uncle was not in his right mind for the past several years of his life, and severely damaged the kingdom's reputation. Undoing that damage is going to be a difficult, uphill battle." I said.

"So why send an emissary?" Snow White asked. "What does he want from us?"

"I've heard King Liam is very handsome," I said with a coy smile. "He's not too much older than you. Maybe by about seven or eight years-"

"Father said I can't get married until I'm at least sixteen, and I'm to choose my husband." Snow White interrupted.

"Fair enough." I settled back in my chair and glanced over the lists again. "I just thought, given that you are taking the throne in a year, that you might start taking an interest."

"Meaning that you think the emissary is going to...propose a proposal?" Snow White arched one knowing eyebrow at me.

I chuckled. "You caught me. It's possible he will ask for your hand. I was unsure if you would be interested or not."

Snow White tapped a finger against her chin, appearing thoughtful. "Not," she answered after a long moment.

I stood up and cupped her chin in my hand. "Very well. I'm not quite ready to say goodbye to you yet."

Snow White smiled. "Stepmother, you'll never have to say goodbye to me."

Shortly before dinner was served, I waited in the throne room for the emissary and his party. Their ship had docked in the early afternoon, and they were set to arrive any minute. I arranged for our introduction to be a private one. I wanted a moment to gauge the emissary's true intentions before introducing him to the court, or my stepdaughter.

The new marshal stood by the throne, one hand on his weapon. His body was alert, but there was a vacant look in his eyes that made me worry someone would notice he was a golem. In fact, all the servants for the evening were golems, their spelled lips preventing them from betraying even a whisper of what was to transpire.

A few members of the court meandered about. They were well bribed, and I knew that for now, gold would buy their silence. Conrad had wanted to stand by my side when the emissary arrived, but I had assigned him to watch over Snow White instead.

At long last, the double doors swung open. Trumpets sounded, and a crier announced Emissary Rian.

He entered the throne room with a party of six, and a large portrait wrapped in silk.

"Queen Mother," Rian bowed low before the throne. "I am most pleased to make your acquaintance. On behalf of all of Aileen, and our King Liam, we wish you bright blessings. May the sun shine warm upon your face and the rain fall soft upon your fields."

I couldn't help but smile at the familiar Aileen blessing. I inclined my head.

"Bright blessings to you, Sir Rian. May the road rise to meet you and the wind be always at your back." I said, finishing the blessing.

The emissary smiled and bowed low. "We have brought you gifts from Aileen, from which I hear you are a native."

My smile widened. It was nice to be reminded of my heritage without being made to feel like an outsider or a pariah. "You are correct, sir. I would be glad to see what you brought."

Rian motioned with his hands and two men came forward carrying baskets. "I bring you gifts of sage. Very good for cleansing the air. We also bring lavender and rose oil for your baths. Finally, our king would like to present you with a very fine necklace made of gold and diamonds. He had it commissioned especially for you."

"For me?" I asked, feeling surprised.

Another of the emissary's men stepped forward and opened a large, wooden box. The gold and diamonds sparkled magnificently.

"That's very generous of King Liam," I noted. "I'm surprised he would single me out so."

"King Liam is as generous as he is handsome," Rian answered.

"Then he must be handsome indeed," I said.

Rian motioned towards his men holding the portrait, and they brought it forward.

"For you, Queen Mother, that you may judge for yourself," he said, pulling the cloth off of the frame.

I raised my eyebrows at the painting before me. King Liam truly was very handsome. He had a high, regal forehead; feathery black hair with a slight curl, and eyes like blackberry wine.

"Perhaps the Queen Mother sees the compliment now?" Rian asked with a knowing smile.

I nodded my consent. "He is very handsome indeed."

I stood up from my throne and advanced down the dais to more closely examine the painting.

"My King will be greatly pleased by your declaration." Rian went on. "With your permission, he asked that I personally deliver the last gift. If I may?"

"I shall allow it," I answered.

Rian bowed low. "King Liam of Aileen would like to offer a proposal of marriage to the Queen Mother of Cherida, to you, Queen Ceridwen."

I turned away from the painting and faced Rian as he straightened up from his bow.

"Me?" I asked, stunned. "Are you sure?"

"Yes, Queen Mother. He was very specific. Tales of your beauty are spoken of even now, in Aileen."

"Surely those aren't the only tales that have reached the King's ears." I admonished. My mind wandered to the court and to those who still viewed me as an outsider and an evil witch.

Rian thinned his lips for a moment, then stepped closer.

"We are aware there are some in Cherida who are not as friendly towards their neighbors as they should be." He said in a low voice.

So King Liam *had* heard the rumors, and chose to disbelieve them, apparently.

"Why not my stepdaughter?" I asked. "She is closer to the King's age, and surely their marriage would create a powerful alliance between the two kingdoms."

"King Liam wishes to do more than strengthen ties between his neighbors. His late uncle left several rifts that King Liam wishes to mend, but the most important to him are within his own borders." Rian continued to speak in a low voice.

Understanding dawned on me at last. "He wishes to unite the magic and non-magic folk," I said.

"And what better way to do that than by marrying a greenwitch, one who has already proven herself capable of leading?" Rian asked.

I hesitated. "I'm still not so sure-"

"Anyway, it would go a long way in securing an alliance for your stepdaughter, when she takes the throne." Rian interrupted.

I paused to ponder his words. When I glanced around, I realized Rian and I were standing very close together and speaking in a hushed whisper. I stepped back and smoothed my skirts.

"Very well, Sir Rian, you may tell your King I accept his offer of marriage."

The next day, I had tea in my room with Snow White and broke the news.

She frowned into her cup. "I don't like it." She said after a moment.

I reclined in my chair. "It is a great opportunity for you. The wedding will not take place until after your sixteenth birthday and your coronation. Only when you are established on the throne will I marry again, and in doing so, will secure you an ally. Cherida is only a small country, my love."

"I didn't think you would be *leaving* me." Snow White sulked.

I sat forward and clasped her hand in mine. "My snow angel, I will never leave you. We will be neighbors and I shall visit often."

"I could order you not to get married." Snow White continued to pout.

I smiled. "You could, but to what end?"

Snow White didn't answer, and I stood up from my chair. "Come," I held my hand out to Snow White, "there are still preparations to be made for your party."

Hand in hand, we turned and walked out the door together.

Snow White's fifteenth birthday was upon us sooner than I thought possible. It was a magical evening, full of dancing and fun.

My stepdaughter was a gem on the dance floor. I had always thought it remarkable how closely she resembled Marcella, but as her cheeks grew pink with laughter and her eyes brightened from lively conversation, it became apparent to me that Snow White's beauty surpassed that of her mother's.

I drank wine and talked and danced until all my worries melted away. For a night, I was not the Queen; I was a mother celebrating the birthday of a most beloved daughter.

When Snow White and I caught a minute alone together, I found myself taking her hand. "Is it everything you wanted, my sweet?" I asked.

"Better than I could have imagined," was her reply. She kissed my cheek and melted into the crowd again.

Towards the end of the night, Conrad took my hand and led me out onto the dance floor. We waltzed around the room and I was very conscious of his hand on my back. Conrad gazed deeply into my eyes, and in my gaiety, I nearly missed the longing in his.

When I tired of dancing, Conrad saw me to my rooms. As we walked down the shadowy hallways, he took a chance and quickly pulled me into the alcove of a window.

The moon was out in full. The pale light threaded its way through Conrad's hair until it glinted like spun gold. His eyes were like the ocean on a calm and peaceful night. He touched my cheek ever so gently, then drew his head down and kissed me as we stood encircled by white starlight.

His lips tasted sweetly of wine and when he pulled away, I could smell the scent of pine trees and spring water clinging to him.

It was a thrilling experience, I found, to be kissed with such passion. My breath caught in my throat and butterflies erupted in my stomach.

Conrad looked at me in a way that Iberius never had and for a moment, in my weakness, I wanted to be selfish and hold on to that gaze forever.

Conrad, though, said nothing. He expected nothing, and he hadn't in all his years of faithful service.

Instead, I was seen to my door without another incident.

A knock at my door woke me. I sat up and wiped the sleep from my eyes as Conrad let Snow White into my room.

"Good morning, Queen Mother," Conrad said. His voice was uncharacteristically quiet, yet somehow also weighted. His words resonated through the room.

"Good morning, Conrad," I replied.

The door shut, and Snow White raised an eyebrow at me. "Does the Captain of the Guard know he doesn't need to stand outside your doors *every* night?"

I pulled myself out of bed and grabbed a robe from my armoire. "He gets to make the schedule. Heaven knows why he picked that shift."

"I believe you know more than you're letting on." Snow White said.

I felt my cheeks flush as I recalled the kiss. It had been three days since Snow White's birthday. I hadn't spoken about it to anyone, not even to Conrad, who also avoided the subject.

"Well-" I began.

Snow White held up a hand. "Please, I don't want to know what's going on between you and the Captain."

I rolled my eyes. "Nothing is going on. Did you see the emissary off this morning?"

"I did. I saw him safely down to the harbor and then waved to him as he sailed away. He has a very fine ship."

"Good, and you were sufficiently covered?" I asked.

"Yes, and Amara held my parasol."

"You were not burned?" I pressed.

"It was very early," Snow White pointed out. "The sun was not out in full."

I nodded. "Good, I would have seen the emissary off myself, but last night took longer than expected."

Snow White lounged on my bed. "You mean making preparations for the feast?"

"Yes," I answered, "A great many people are coming. I suspect they all want to know the true purpose of Rian's visit."

Snow White looked at me out of the corner of her eye. "Does Conrad know you're engaged?"

I hesitated. "He'll find out tonight with everyone else."

"How do you think he'll take the news?" Snow White asked.

I hesitated. "He knows I am the Queen. I have duties, to you as well as Cherida."

Snow White looked skeptical as she stood up from my bed. She came to kiss my cheek. "I'll see you tonight at dinner, then."

I smiled and touched her cheek. "Until tonight."

12
WHAT HAVE YOU DONE?

The announcement for my engagement would culminate in two events. The first would be a feast where a general announcement would be made to a select group of people. A ball would be held a month later, open to any noble who wanted to attend.

The night of the feast, Snow White and I ate on a dais overlooking a large crowd. In the middle of the room, performers showed off their juggling and dancing skills.

Snow White and I watched with interest, but I found myself picking at my food. Thoughts of Conrad and our kiss went through my mind more often than I cared to admit. I had ordered him to take the night off and go out. I thought an evening of women and wine would put me out of his head, but he opted to come to the feast instead. He sat at a table and kept shooting me long, lingering looks full of intensity.

My stomach twisted with anxiety. Maybe Conrad cared for me more than I knew.

Tearing my thoughts away from him, I looked out over the crowd of people, people who thought I was an evil witch, a seductress, and a usurper. It would be good to go home.

Was Aileen really my home, though? I was twelve years old when my sister and I slipped away in the night. I was thirty now, and the Queen. Deep down, Cherida felt like my true home.

"Stepmother?" Snow White was looking at me with dark, knowing eyes. She placed a hand on my shoulder, her lower lip puckered with concern.

With a chuckle, I reached up to pat her hand. "I'm all right. I'm just going to miss you when I leave."

"Well, you'll come back to visit." Snow White comforted.

I kissed her on the forehead. "Of course I will, my dearest love. I hope you'll come to Aileen. I can show you where I lived with your mother and grandparents."

Snow White nodded. "I'd like that."

I glanced down at my plate and grimaced. "Well, this is the last course for dinner. Dessert will be served next. I should make the announcement now."

The crestfallen look on Snow White's face told me she had been holding out hope that I wouldn't go through with the engagement. I squeezed her hand before standing and tapped a knife against my glass.

"Attention," I called out. The room quieted nearly at once. Dozens upon dozens of faces turned to me, all eager to drink up the gossip I was about to impart.

"As many of you know, we recently hosted an emissary from Aileen. He brought many gifts. Chiefly among them was a proposal."

The atmosphere was heavy as I paused for dramatic effect. The whole time, I was careful to avoid looking at Conrad. "I am pleased to announce that I accepted the offer. I am now engaged to King Liam of Aileen. After my stepdaughter comes of age next year, the wedding will take place."

There was a smattering of applause that turned into a roar of approval. I smiled and received congratulations, then resumed my seat.

"That went well," Snow White commented.

"It's hard to know if they're happy for me, or happy to be rid of me," I muttered before taking a drink from my wine glass.

"Nasty, small-minded people." Snow White replied. Her eyebrows narrowed as she stared down at the crowd before us.

I tried to smile. "Well, never mind them. Let's enjoy our dessert."

After the feast's conclusion, two sentries escorted me back to my rooms. I was surprised to see Conrad waiting outside my doors. He leaned against the wall, his head down and shoulders slouched.

"Leave us," I said to the sentinels. I stepped forward and stood before Conrad.

"I gave you orders to take the night off." My voice was soft, and I smiled, trying to keep the mood light.

Conrad looked up then. His eyes were bloodshot, and his hair was messy and tousled. There was an angry curl to his mouth that was frightening to see, and he was unsteady on his feet. I took a quick step back and had to stop a gasp from tumbling past my lips.

"How can you do this?" Conrad's voice was low and husky

I blinked in confusion. "W-What do you mean?"

"What do I-?" Conrad's voice trailed off. He pressed his hands to his head, gripping fistfuls of his hair. There was a deranged look in his eyes that I wasn't used to seeing. "Damnit, Ceridwen, are you going to pretend like there's nothing between us? Like nothing ever happened?"

Before I could respond, he grabbed my shoulders and pushed me against the wall. I did gasp this time. My heart rate accelerated, but Conrad's touch was more desperate than violent.

"How many nights ago did I hold you in my arms?" Conrad asked. He reached out one hand to cup my face, running the pad of his thumb over my lips. "How many nights ago was it that we kissed? There was something, a spark between us. There's no denying it."

Conrad gazed deeply into my eyes, desperate for something I couldn't give him. Pain tore at my heart, and I attempted to extricate myself from his embrace.

"I am the Queen," I reminded him. "I have duties-"

"To hell with duty!" Conrad held me closer to him, even as I attempted to pull away. "I love you, Ceridwen. There's been no one but you. When you were wed to the King, my closest friend, I loved you. Even when there was no hope of us ever being together. Now, finally, after all this time, there is *hope*. The Princess is taking the throne in less than a year. You will be free from your royal duties."

I placed a hand on Conrad's chest, gently pushing him away.

"I will always have a duty to my stepdaughter," I explained in a soft voice.

"Then don't leave her," Conrad pleaded. "Stay here, with me. I'll take care of you, Ceridwen. I'll retire and we can move to the country. Or we'll retain our place at court and stay close to the princess. Everything that I do will be for you, Ceridwen, if you marry me. Say yes. Just, please say yes."

I stared at my hand on Conrad's chest. He was everything a woman could ask for her, everything a woman should want in a man. Not only was he loyal, kind, and rich, but he loved me more deeply than I could fathom. He was also stunningly handsome, tall, and well-built. I could feel solid muscle through his shirt.

Yet, as I looked up into his clear, blue eyes, I knew with certainty that I didn't love him. I didn't know why, there was no reason not to. Maybe there was something wrong with me, but I didn't love Conrad.

I ducked under his arm, took a few steps back, and straightened up to my full height.

"You must not address me so informal, sir. I am the Queen of Cherida. I am an engaged woman. My actions are for the well-being of the Princess and this country. Please be so good as to show me the respect that my station deserves."

I couldn't look Conrad in the face as I spoke. It didn't shield me. I still saw a part of him die as my words cut to the very core of his being.

Conrad put a hand on the wall and his shoulders slouched as though I had run him through with a sword. He drew a sharp breath, his eyes scrunched in pain, as if someone had knocked the breath out of him.

For a long moment, neither of us moved. We were frozen in one of the worst moments of our lives, with no idea how to escape.

At last, Conrad stirred. He moved away from the wall and stood like a weary soldier.

"I will do as you wish." Conrad's voice was quiet and broken. Then he moved past me with a curt nod and disappeared down the hall.

Conrad began avoiding me. It was hard to watch. He was a shadow of his former self and moved silently through the castle like a ghost. It hurt to see, but I couldn't change my mind. I had to think of Snow White.

A month went by and my engagement ball quickly approached. The turnout was smaller than I expected, though I heard rumors many nobles were in their personal castles and estates, celebrating my impending departure.

I had new gowns commissioned for Snow White and me. When the night of the ball arrived, I dressed in an elegant black and red dress with billowing skirts that gracefully cascaded around me as I moved.

Deciding I wanted to check in on Snow White, I went to her rooms. There I saw her standing on a dais before a mirror. Three seamstresses were milling around, putting the final touches on her outfit.

"Snow White," I admonished, "You are not even laced into your corset. What is the meaning of this?"

"Apologies, Queen Mother." The head seamstress said. "Your stepdaughter has had a growth spurt since I saw her last. We are just extending her skirts a bit."

"Will she be ready in time for the party?" I asked.

"Oh, of course." The seamstress replied. "We are nearly done now."

"Very good." I stood before Snow White and smiled up at her. Her gown was silver and decorated with white snowflakes. She had a black ribbon secured around her neck, adorned with a single white rose in full bloom.

"You are a vision," I beamed.

Snow White smiled at me. "Are you excited about the party? This time, *you're* going to be the guest of honor."

"Well, your birthday was a success. I'm sure tonight will be too," I answered. "Tonight's event will be smaller than your birthday, though. Only about twenty families will be in attendance."

"I think that sounds like a perfect number." Snow White said.

I smiled and examined her reflection in the mirror. I absently plucked her sleeve while my heart swelled with pride.

"Oh!" a seamstress by Snow White's feet cried out. She held up a single finger where she had pricked herself with a needle. A large drop of crimson blood swelled at the tip.

The room dissolved and faded away to a night, almost sixteen years ago, where Marcella held a hand to her neck. Three drops of blood landed in the snow. They shone like garnets against the glittering white, encircled by the light of the moon.

Still in a trance, I watched, with growing horror, as Snow White absently reached out and grasped the seamstress' hand. She pulled the girl to her feet and popped the bloody finger in her mouth.

The nightmare deepened. Snow White's skin paled even further until the only color on her face was her blood-red lips. Her eyes flickered, becoming animated, almost predatory. I felt, rather than saw, a sudden insatiable hunger consume her. My mind reeled. Then, it wasn't Snow White in front of me, but a demon in a cemetery with watery blue eyes and bone-white teeth sharpened into fangs.

My legs trembled. A scream began building in my throat when Snow White pulled the finger from her mouth.

A red tongue flicked over her bottom lip, and then she turned and gave me a sweet smile. The image of a monster rapidly dissipated, and all that was left was my dear Snow White. Only fifteen years old, and still a child.

Humming softly to herself, Snow White turned back to her reflection in the mirror, the very image of purity of innocence, oblivious that the rest of the room was frozen in shock and horror.

My legs were weak and trembling. For a moment, I feared I would faint. Smoothing my skirts with shaking hands, I tried to smile. "I'm happy to see your dress coming along so well. I'll go down to the party now and you can join whenever you're ready."

"Yes, stepmother." Snow White trilled in a sing-song voice. She looked so calm and peaceful. If only I could do the same!

I turned and made my way towards the exit. I forced my feet to walk at a slow, leisurely pace when everything in my body was screaming to run away.

As I went out into the hall, I didn't go down to the party. Instead, I turned abruptly and hastened to my rooms. It wasn't until the door was slammed shut behind me and I was alone that I collapsed to the floor.

It took some time before I was able to pull myself together. I had a bottle of strong mead hidden in my dresser. I forced several large swigs down my throat, grimacing when it burned.

The trembling in my legs finally ceased, and I took several deep breaths while looking in the mirror.

"There's nothing to be afraid of," I told my reflection. "It was monstrous of you to compare that vile demon to your stepdaughter. Now, you must stop being silly and go down to the party immediately. Snow White needs you."

I smiled at myself. My reflection was pale and ghastly.

Heaving a deep sigh of frustration, I applied rouge to my cheeks and marched out into the hallway.

I paused at the door, thinking of my magic mirror. Should I use it? Would I be betraying my child if I did? I couldn't deny that a dark shadow hung over my mind. Something felt...off. I just couldn't put my finger on why. A sense of dread and danger permeated the air and prickled along my skin like a winter chill.

I was so deep in thought I didn't notice how quiet the castle was. I made my way through the halls, the tapping of my feet against the stone floor echoed off the walls and ceiling like a war drum. Eventually, I stopped and looked around, puzzled.

There was no singing, no shouts of merriment, no laughter anywhere in the castle. It was utterly silent.

Silent as the grave.

My throat constricted while my mouth went dry. A tremor went through my body as a cold knot of fear tightened in my stomach.

I proceeded forward, carefully now. I softened my footsteps, making as little noise as possible.

Turning a corner, I approached the double doors to the ballroom. I noticed, with a jolt, that they were closed. The party was supposed to have been in full swing by now. Not only should they be open, but sentinels and a crier should be stationed outside, ready to greet me and announce my arrival.

I bit down on my lip. For a moment, I was frozen, unable to move. Every muscle in my body locked up and I couldn't breathe.

After a long moment, I willed my legs, numb as they were, to step forward. I stretched forth a trembling hand and grasped the door handle. With a mighty heave, I pulled the door open and gasped.

Nothing could have prepared me for the horrors within.

The smell of death and rot permeated the air. Blood was pooled all over the floor, glistening like a macabre ocean.

The bodies, they were piled everywhere. Heaped in front of the doors, cloistered under the table, piled into corners. Their eyes were glassy, vacant, faces frozen in horror, mouths gaping in silent screams.

In a daze, I stepped into the room. Bile lodged in my throat. Hamlin, the third son of an Earl, lay on the floor. He was face down in a pool of blood, one arm slung across his new bride. They had only been married a few months.

Mirtha, loyal Mirtha, was propped against the wall. Her throat had been ripped open and the front of her gown stained crimson.

I came across another body and let out a strangled moan of dread and grief.

"No, no," I whimpered, falling to my knees.

Conrad stared at the ceiling. His blue eyes were clear and his face peaceful. I almost expected him to turn to me and smile. But he wouldn't. Conrad would never smile at anyone ever again.

His torso had been ripped open, revealing his chest cavity and shattered ribs. Guts spilled out of his stomach and onto the floor. He lay in a pool of his own blood.

I was forced, then, to admit the truth to myself. A truth I had been running away from since the day my stepdaughter was born.

"Snow White!" I tipped my head back, my voice a keening wail that echoed against the ceiling. "What have you done?"

Something moved out of the corner of my eye. Before I had a chance to do anything, I was knocked flat on my back. Snow White had me pinned to the floor, her hands on my shoulders as she sat on my chest and stomach. She drew back her lips, revealing pointed fangs, and let out a hiss. She was as feral as a wild animal, her face and neck stained crimson.

"Do it," I whispered. "Kill me."

My words were heavy, strained. I couldn't bear to live after seeing what Snow White had become, knowing what she was capable of. My death would be a mercy.

But Snow White didn't kill me. Her eyes cleared, and she blinked at me with the innocence of a child.

"I could never kill you." Her soft voice said. "You, who have been a mother to me all my life."

She reached one hand down to grasp a strand of my hair. She twirled it around her finger. "I love you, Mother."

"Snow White," I whispered. "Look at what you have done!"

Her tongue flicked over her lips. "Mm, I was hungry. I've been hungry my whole life. Starving, ravenous."

"Is your blood lust finally sated?" I asked in a hard voice.

Snow White hissed, showing me her fangs. "This is who I am. This is who I was born to be."

The weight moved off of my chest, and then Snow White was gone. She streaked across the room like a blur and flung herself out of a broken window.

I curled up into a ball, burying my face in the crook of my elbow, and sobbed.

My girl was gone.

13
MARKED BY GREAT MAGIC

It felt as though my tears would never stop. I lay on the cold stone floor, surrounded by blood and bodies, and wept until I thought I would die.

Eventually, a door creaked open, and I heard a gasp.

"May the goddess protect us!"

I raised myself into a sitting position and turned bleary eyes toward the voice.

"Queen Mother?" The voice asked.

I swiped a hand across my face. "Amara? Amara, is that you?"

My voice was rough and scraped against my throat.

"Yes, my Queen, I am here."

There was a patter of soft footsteps, followed by a swish of skirts, and then Amara was kneeling beside me. She was as white as cold candle wax, her eyes as large as dinner plates. Even her lips were pale.

"Your golem found me," Amara said in a trembling voice.

I blinked and looked towards the door where a chambermaid named Edith, waited. Her face was blank, and she showed no signs of distress or anxiety.

I gritted my teeth. "Who else is here?"

Edith shrugged. "I could find none other living, only Amara."

I let out a muffled wail and tried to stand.

"Allow me to help, Queen Mother," Amara said in a breathless voice. She placed a hand under my elbow and another around my waist.

Together, we managed to rise to our feet. I saw Amara's eyes skittering anxiously around the room, taking in all the faces of the dead. She blanched when she saw Mirtha.

"Never mind that, now," I said in a tired voice. "Edith, gather the other golems. Close the gates. Tell the people...tell them it is the plague."

"As you will, Queen Mother." Edith turned and walked briskly away.

My knees were still weak, and I leaned heavily into Amara's embrace.

"Before I turned Edith, she was a nosy little heretic," I said in a dark voice. "At least I don't have to worry about that now."

"No, Queen Mother, I suppose not," Amara whispered.

We hobbled forward until we reached my chambers. Another golem awaited me there, this one by the name of Sigrid.

Sigrid's purpose was to serve as one of my ladies-in-waiting. At the end of every night, she would stay back and inform me of any gossip that threatened me or my family.

When did I make so many golems?

I pushed the thought out of my head as Amara helped me sit on the edge of my bed.

"Good evening, Queen Mother. Are you interested in today's reports?" Sigrid asked in a hollow voice.

I growled at her. "Dammit, not now. Get out."

"As you will, Queen Mother." Sigrid moved towards the door and exited the room.

"Allow me to help you out of your corset," Amara said, motioning to my dress.

I nodded, then turned around, facing my full-length mirror. Amara began unlacing my dress while I stared at my reflection. My dress was covered in blood. I would have to throw it away.

Or burn it.

I looked at my face, but it was like looking at a stranger. The horrible things Marcella and I did weighed heavily on my shoulders.

"This is all our fault," I whispered.

Amara paused, then kept unlacing my dress. "Pardon, Queen Mother?"

I sucked in a deep breath, placing a hand on my stomach. "No, I'm sorry, Amara. There are things...things my sister and I have done...that can not be taken back."

Amara bit down on her bottom lip. "You sound as though you have regrets."

A sob caught in my throat. "There are secrets I thought I'd take to my grave. We dabbled in evil magic, forces better left alone. I was a child then, the same age you and Snow White are now. Half my lifetime ago, yet it seems so much closer than that. I think about it every day, Amara. It haunts me."

Amara finished unlacing my dress. The gown pooled around my feet and I stepped out of the voluminous skirts.

"I'm sure you had your reasons, Queen Mother," Amara whispered in a trembling voice.

For the first time, I noticed her hands were shaking. We lapsed into silence as Amara finished unlacing my corset and helped me into a shift. I moved to my washbasin and splashed some water on my face.

"Amara, I want you to stay in here with me tonight," I said. "Edith said there was none other living in the castle. I don't want you to come to harm."

"Me, Queen Mother?" Amara seemed confused.

I picked up a cloth and wiped my face, trying not to frown. Why the tone of surprise? Didn't Amara know how deeply I cared for her? Even though she and Snow White were situated differently in society, it didn't mean she wasn't important to me.

A forgotten memory floated to the surface of my mind, the day I caught Amara imitating Snow White. I had scolded her harshly then, but it was necessary. Surely she didn't hold a grudge over that day? It was so many years ago.

"Amara, you disappoint me. I thought we were closer than that." I said.

Amara paled and tilted her face towards the floor. "Forgive me, Queen Mother."

"Never mind that now." I picked up a brush and began combing my hair. "There is a chaise lounge in the corner that should be comfortable enough, and you can borrow one of my shifts. I trust you can dress yourself?"

"Yes, Queen Mother." Amara's voice was soft.

"Good." I finished brushing out my hair, then moved towards my bed. Throwing back the covers, I climbed under the blankets and stared at the ceiling.

There was a rustling sound in the corner as Amara dressed and got herself settled.

"Goodnight, Queen Mother." She whispered into the darkness.

"Goodnight, Amara," I said.

My eyes drifted shut. My body felt heavy and worn out. More than anything, I wanted to rest, but my mind was still reeling from the day's events. I breathed in deeply through my nose and attempted to calm my thoughts.

Tomorrow, the real work would begin.

Cleaning the banquet hall the next morning was gruesome work. I kept Amara in the kitchens to spare her the sight of dried, crusted blood, bloated bodies, and the permeating stench of death.

From the doorway, I supervised my golems. There were about a dozen. Some mopped blood off the floor, while others meticulously cleaned the bodies.

The faces of the dead varied in expression. Some, like Conrad, were peaceful. Others were frozen masks of horror. Most were twisted in agony and fear. Those were the worst. I tried very hard to avoid looking into their cloudy, empty eyes.

The golems stripped the corpses and bathed them with bowls of warm water. The bodies were then laid on a table where I sprinkled vinegar, crushed hemlock, and maggots on them. I whispered long forgotten words from ancient books, making the skin appear as though a flesh-eating disease ravaged it. The golems then wrapped the bodies in fresh linen and took them away.

The task stretched out over days. Bodies kept being brought into the banquet hall from all over the castle.

We burned the bodies slowly, just a few at a time. It was important to keep up appearances, important to keep up the lie about a plague that was slowly claiming the lives of those in the castle. It wouldn't do for the townspeople to know everyone had been taken out in one fell swoop, and by their princess, no less.

So the golems laid the deceased out on pyres and lit them on fire, and Amara and I would do our best to block out the smell of so many burning corpses.

My stomach churned at the sheer number of lost souls that were paraded before me. I tried not to think about how horrific their last moments of life must have been.

Amara continued to sleep on my chaise lounge. There were attached quarters for ladies-in-waiting, but even that short distance felt hazardous. When darkness fell, and shadows crept through the hallways like rivers of ink, the only safety to be had was in each other.

Sigrid continued to give her daily reports, although news was sparse. There was nothing happening in the castle to report on, and with news of the plague, the people of Cherida were isolating themselves indoors.

The nobles had all fled to their summer castles. We received ravens daily from people asking after their brothers and sisters and children. The first few days, I attempted to catalog the name of each body that was brought to me. If they belonged to a wealthy or noble family, I would write to their relatives. The work was hard, though, and draining. After two days, I had a golem take over the task.

One evening, as Amara and I were getting ready to retire, I snapped. Sigrid came to my door like she always did.

"Yes, Sigrid?" I asked in a tired voice.

"Would you care to hear the day's news, Queen Mother?" She asked.

"Get on with it," I growled in an irritated voice.

"Nothing new to report in the castle."

I scoffed. "How unprecedented." I mocked. "What else?"

"Rumors are starting in the village," Sigrid said. "An omen of the plague is said to walk the night. It takes the shape of a hauntingly beautiful woman with hair black as the night, skin white as snow and lips red as blood. Wherever she appears, death is swift to follow."

Amara let out a small gasp of pain. She clutched at her heart. "It's Snow White." Her voice came out as a whimper.

I turned to face the window, clasping my hands behind my back. "That will be all, Sigrid." My voice sounded strange and my lips felt numb. It was a wonder I could get the words out at all.

There was a shuffling as Sigrid bowed and let herself out of my chambers, softly closing the door behind her. Amara let out a muffled sob.

I stared at the night sky, feeling raw and empty. A great chasm opened up inside of me where my soul used to reside. How could this be happening? My Snow White, my darling, my precious stepdaughter. How had we come to this?

And the bodies.

The bodies were piling up, and I didn't know what to do. The noble's frantic letters and the people's panicked whispers were beginning to wear me down. Something had to be done, but what?

I straightened my back and steeled my resolve. Turning, I faced Amara, careful to keep my face neutral.

"Something must be done about Snow White."

My voice was remarkably calm, surprising even myself.

Amara watched me with wide eyes. Eyes that were stricken with grief, but held no fear. She was braver than I realized, and she didn't flinch away from me in horror. All she did was nod.

"Yes," Amara said, "I suspected this day would come, ever since Mirtha."

Inwardly, I cringed. I had almost forgotten Mirtha was a victim of the initial slaughter. But then, there were so many dead, and Conrad's demise had me riddled with guilt.

"I take no pleasure in this," I said.

Amara shook her head. "Of course not. Neither do I."

With a sigh, I went to sit on the edge of my bed. My mattress sank invitingly, but I knew if I collapsed into it now, sleep would not find me.

"I will need to read the most ancient texts this castle has available. My golems will question the townspeople. My sister conjured something evil, Amara. A demon with a taste for blood, just like our Snow White."

My stomach churned with nausea, and I drew a shaky hand over my eyes. "I need to understand what Marcella summoned that night in the graveyard. Once I understand, we can figure out a plan."

To do what? Kill Snow White? No, that wasn't an option. Contain her, perhaps. Transform her back into my sweet girl, preferably.

I love you, Mother.

Those were Snow White's words to me on that fateful night. No, I couldn't kill her, nor would I allow her to come to any harm. I was a witch; I was the Queen, I would find a way to save my girl.

Amara spoke in a hesitant voice. "Th-there might be someone who can help."

"Who?" I asked.

Amara sucked in a breath, and for the first time that night, I saw fear glittering in her dark eyes. "I've heard the servants speak of him. They say he comes from far away. That he has walked through the flames of hell, and looked death in the face, and did not die. He stalks the night and shadows flee his presence. He has been marked by great magic, and evil trembles when they hear his footsteps."

Fear ghosted along my flesh like a light breeze, and goosebumps erupted on my arms. I licked my lips. "He sounds terrifying."

Amara looked sorrowful. "They say he is a force against evil, but his methods are known to be brutal. He works without kindness or mercy."

A shiver crept down my spine, and I wrapped my arms around my middle. "He sounds like a witch hunter. We had those in Aileen, under the old king. They burned my parents at the stake. Marcella and I had to flee for our lives after that."

Amara's shoulders drooped. "I am sorry to hear it, Queen Mother. Unfortunately, I can't say one way or another. I've never met him. I only know the stories."

I let out a deep sigh, pinching the bridge of my nose. "Unfortunately, we don't have many options at this point and time. I wish there was some way of knowing whether or not this man would pose a risk to us, but time really is of the essence. I'll speak to the golems. With a little magic and a bit of luck, I'm sure we can locate him in a timely manner."

"I'll call Sigrid back," Amara said. She slipped quietly from her bed and let herself out into the hallway.

I bit anxiously at my nails before I recalled my scrying mirror. Stumbling to my feet, I went to the vanity table and yanked a drawer open. As my hand closed around the handle, I hesitated.

I hadn't looked into my scrying mirror since the night before my engagement ball. What if I saw Snow White's face in there? That would break me.

Pushing those thoughts away, I took a deep breath, thinking only of the man who walked through the flames of hell and did not die. Exhaling slowly, I looked into my mirror.

It was empty.

My body slumped with relief, and I leaned heavily against my vanity. Whoever this man was, he did not pose a threat to me or Amara.

As footsteps sounded in the hallway, I hurriedly tucked the mirror back into place and resumed my spot on the bed.

"Here she is, Queen Mother." Amara pushed the doors open and entered the room, Sigrid at her heels.

"Yes, Queen Mother?" Sigrid asked, looking almost bored.

I cleared my throat and nodded. "Yes, Sigrid, I have a job for you and any golem we can spare. We are looking for a man, someone who causes evil to tremble when he is near. I want him found and brought to the castle."

Sigrid nodded. "And what is the name of this man?"

I looked to Amara, who answered in a high-pitched tone, her voice ringing like a bell.

"He is called the Huntsman."

14
THE HUNTSMAN

He wasn't actually called the Huntsman, that was just a title meant to frighten small-minded people. His real name was Quincy Pollux. I couldn't help but breathe a sigh of relief when a golem brought me this information. It humanized him, in a way, and made him less fearsome and mysterious.

I continued to say his name into my scrying mirror, wondering if he would ever materialize as an enemy or a threat. So far, his reflection hadn't made an appearance.

It took five days for the golems to find Quincy, and three weeks to bring him to the castle.

The day of Quincy's arrival, I sat on my throne dressed in red velvet. I had taken care to have my hair done, and my crown was polished to a high shine. Whoever walked through that door, I had to command their respect.

From outside came the blast of a horn, followed by the creaking of gates. The Huntsman was here.

My fingers twitched, but I resisted the urge to go to the window and look down into the courtyard. Clearing my throat, I straightened my back and wiped my face clean of emotion.

The double doors creaked open. A dozen soldiers marched through in two lines. Quincy stood between them.

The soldiers were all human, but the Marshal was a golem by the name of Garen. Preceding them was my new master of ceremonies, Alaric, who was also a golem.

"Queen Mother," Alaric started in a booming voice. "Presenting Quincy Pollux, the Huntsman."

I sucked in a breath as I took in Quincy for the first time. His skin was as black as umber and lined with cuts and scars. The breadth of his shoulders and the muscles in his arms told me this was a man who had seen more than his fair share of war. His hair was long, reaching down past his shoulders, and in several tiny braids that were tied back with a scrap of forest-green silk. His hair was as dark as a raven's wing, highlighted with a silver glow set off by the sun's light.

His eyes were what gave me pause. They were dark, with a hint of amber that cradled any beam of light that fell across them. I would have described those eyes as beautiful if they weren't burning with such ferocity. I did not doubt that fiery stare was just as cutting as the ax at his side, and as deadly as any poison.

Quincy's eyes had such an aura of danger that it took me a moment to see the burn that spread from his cheek to his neck, to his shoulder and upper arm. One side of his mouth was twisted and disfigured.

I repressed a shiver, thinking of what Amara had said.

He has walked through the flames of hell, and looked death in the face, and did not die.

How much of that was true?

I rose from my seat and descended the three steps from my podium. "Thank you, Alaric. Thank you, Garen. You all may leave now."

"If it pleases your Majesty, I wish to stay," Garen spoke in an offhand voice. "It is the duty of my station to secure your safety."

"I can manage on my own, thank you," I said.

"Very well, then." Garen turned and left the room, followed by Alaric. The soldiers murmured among themselves, casting suspicious looks at my golems, then followed them out.

I turned my attention to the Huntsman. He still had not spoken, although he kept his eyes fixed on me. My mouth went dry and everything in me screamed to flee, but I did not.

Lifting my chin, I advanced a few steps towards my guest. "They say you are a great huntsman, that you stalk the night, and shadows flee from your presence, and evil trembles when they hear your footsteps."

Quincy smirked. "Is that what they say about me?" He closed the remaining distance between us, his steps light and sure. He loomed over me, staring me down with those dark amber eyes.

"Do you want to know what they say about you, Queen Ceridwen?" He rumbled in his deep voice. "Shall I repeat the rumors whispered in dark corners by hushed, frightened voices? Shall I tell you how the common folk tremble when they hear your name, or how the royal court pales and whimpers when they fear they have crossed you? Are those things you would like to know, my queen?"

A shiver of fear went down my spine. I quickly took a step back, seeking to broaden the distance between us, but Quincy advanced just as quickly.

"I did not bring you here for platitudes," I said in a hard voice.

"Why did you bring me here?" Quincy asked.

"We'll get to that in a moment," I said briskly. Quincy's stare was unnerving, and it disoriented my thoughts. "You'll have to prove your mettle first. I need to make sure you're the right man for the job."

Quincy's lip twitched in anger. Something like rage filled his eyes. "Stop lying." He snarled.

His hands went abruptly to my shoulders. His touch was firm, not painful, but definitely secure. Six pillars stood parallel to each other in the throne room. Quincy pressed my back up against one and looked down at me. Our bodies were close, but not touching. He was also tall, easily over six feet, definitely taller than Conrad and Iberius. Quincy stared down at me with hard eyes.

"Did you bring me here to kill me?" Quincy asked.

"What?" I gasped. "N-no!"

My heart pounded frantically in my chest, while my breath caught in my throat. A tremor ran down my spine, and I hated that my fear was so obvious. Part of me wanted to call for the guards, but I couldn't. There was too much at stake.

For a long moment, neither of us moved. Quincy didn't say anything. He just held me with his dark eyes, studying me. Finally, he stepped back and released his hold on me.

"I believe you." He said.

My lungs loosened, and I quickly scrambled back a few steps. The trembling in my hands increased. I clasped them together and held them against my chest, breathing rapidly.

"I could have you hanged for putting your hands on me! Never do that again!" I yelled.

Quincy didn't seem phased by my anger. He moved about the throne room with ease. When he spoke, his voice was glib. "I noticed you didn't call for help. You must be very desperate."

I clenched my hands into fists and resisted the urge to stomp my foot. When was the last time someone had threatened me like that? Or spoken to me in such a disrespectful manner?

"You don't know what I am," I finally sputtered out.

"Let's see," Quincy drawled out, "The soldiers who apprehended me didn't know why. You refuse to speak on the subject in front of anyone except me, and, oh yes, when I grabbed you, you didn't scream or summon your soldiers. Whatever you have to say, it frightens you more than I do."

His observation shocked me. My mind blanked, and all I could do was stare at him with my mouth open.

Quincy turned towards me and crossed his arms. "So what is it? What do you want?"

By the gods, this man was terrifyingly dangerous. Was I really going to send him after Snow White? My sweet girl, who still barely clung to the cusp of childhood? She wasn't quite a woman, not yet.

Summoning what was left of my willpower, I straightened my back. "I need help locating someone."

"Who?"

My mouth went dry, and I struggled to form the words. "My stepdaughter."

Quincy raised an eyebrow. "Princess Snow White?"

I nodded. "Yes."

"Isn't she the little dark-haired girl that trails after you? Your golems didn't indicate to me that she was missing." Quincy said.

I balled my hands into fists and bared my teeth. "My golems do not speak to anybody except me!"

"Wrong." Quincy looked bored as he pulled a necklace out of his shirt. It was an acorn, attached to a thin piece of leather. On the acorn was a rune that I recognized as Kenaz.

"Do you know what this is?" Quincy asked. "You're a witch, so I'm assuming you do."

"It is Kenaz," I answered.

"Yes, the torch." Quincy nodded. "It illuminates the truth and dispels darkness and lies. A greenwitch made it for me after I skinned a werewolf that had been terrorizing her village. It's very powerful. So when I ask your golems questions, they answer me."

A coil of fear knotted in my stomach.

"Now, I'll ask you again." Quincy lowered his chin and his voice deepened. "Who is the little dark-haired girl the golems talk about?"

I thinned my lips, then huffed and crossed my arms. "That is-Her name is Amara."

"What happened to Princess Snow White?"

My muscles locked up again, all except for my hands, which trembled with fright. I twisted them into my voluminous skirts and tampered back my fear. "There was an incident."

Quincy raised an eyebrow. "Explain."

I licked my lips, quailing at the thought of reliving Snow White's last night in the castle. "I don't know if that's strictly necessary-"

Quincy rolled his eyes. "Listen, lady, you didn't have your soldiers drag me all the way here for nothing. I'm willing to hunt whatever this thing is, but I'm going to need details. Until I get that, until I understand what I'm going up against, I can't fight it."

I ground my teeth together when he called me *lady*, and nearly screamed when he began talking about fighting Snow White. This huntsman was being insolent.

I sucked in a breath and straightened my back. Quincy may be rude, but he was right. He needed details.

"It was a small dinner." I began in a whisper. "Snow White, she...she...When I got to the banquet hall...everyone was dead. There was...blood...everywhere. I don't know what else to tell you."

Quincy was watching me closely, his eyes narrowing. He let out a small hiss. "The death night? Is that what you're referring to? Snow White is the one who killed all those people?"

"What?" I asked. "I've never called it that before. Who told you that?"

"Your golems. They spoke of a death spirit walking around the castle. Pale skin, red lips, smells like the grave."

"You-you made them say that!" I countered. "Golems don't talk like that. They don't have feelings, they don't know things!"

Quincy regarded me with a hard stare. "You fashioned them after people, Queen Ceridwen. What did you expect?"

I bared my teeth at him. "I expect them to do what I say! That, and nothing more!"

Quincy scowled at me. "You really are evil, aren't you?"

"Say what you want about me. I don't care!" I yelled. "Just help me find my daughter!"

"Fine," Quincy snarled. "Tell me about the little death spirit."

"Don't call her that!" I screamed, finally losing my temper.

"Why don't we start with where she came from, hm?" Quincy asked. "I've heard stories about your sister. I've heard that the late Queen Marcella was desperate for a son, that she would have done anything to secure her bloodline to the throne."

My jaw dropped, but no words came out. Memories of Marcella angrily rejecting her daughter propelled themselves to the surface of my memory.

When I spoke, my voice was cracked and miserable. "It's not what you think."

"Then tell me what it is," Quincy said. There was a flicker in his eyes, something like pain and regret. It was gone in a flash, and I wondered if it was even there to begin with.

I licked my lips. "Marcella thought the king was going to kill her. That's why she was desperate, because she was afraid."

"So, what did she do?" Quincy softened his voice. He was almost gentle.

"I begged her not to go, but she wouldn't listen to me. Marcella had heard from someone, I'm not sure who, that there was...some kind of demon in a graveyard. It wasn't too far from here. We walked there in the dead of night."

"Hm," Quincy scratched his chin. "So your sister went to a graveyard in the middle of the night to secure a deal with a demon."

My heart was thrumming in my chest, fast and light, like hummingbird wings. "Yes, she did."

"Demons don't go around doling out favors," Quincy said. "What was the price of the demon's service?"

More memories were coming to the surface of my mind. Bone white teeth, watery blue eyes, crimson blood on freshly fallen snow...

"I-I-I can't." I gasped. The air was suddenly very thin. I was trembling too, and my teeth were chattering. Black spots appeared on the edge of my vision. Memories crowded together until I was drowning in them. I couldn't breathe-

Quincy put his hands back on my shoulders. His touch was light this time, more of a caress. The gold in his eyes flashed, and he looked at me with concern.

"Ceridwen, take deep, slow breaths." He encouraged in a soft voice.

No title, just my name. It had been so long since someone addressed me as just myself. It was soothing when it fell on my ears. I slowly started to relax.

"Blood." My voice was scratchy. "The demon said he wanted blood. He bit her."

Quincy's fingers tightened on my shoulders. Then he was releasing his grip on me and stepping back.

"Blood for a baby." He shook his head, a look of disgust spreading across his face.

"What is it?" I asked. "You know something, tell me!"

Quincy gave a bitter laugh and shook his head. "You already know. Oh, you have to, Ceridwen. Admit it."

I huffed, angry again. "I certainly do not! If I did, do you think I would have brought you here? Do you think I'd be asking for your help?"

"Fine." Quincy straightened and looked down his nose at me. "If you won't say it, I will. Your sister was a demon's whore."

I threw myself at him. My rage boiled over, and I acted before I could think. Quincy stepped back, grabbing at my hands as I screamed and clawed at him, calling him every name I could think of. I kicked and bit and flailed, angrier than I had ever been in my life.

Finally, I pulled back, panting for air. "Get out!" I screamed. "Get out! I never want to see you again! If I do, I'll kill you!"

Quincy looked angry at my order. "I've traveled three weeks to be here."

"I don't care!" I screamed. "Leave!"

Quincy shook his head and turned away. He stopped before pushing the double doors open, glancing at me over his shoulder. "Fine, I'll go. Just know one thing: You need me more than I need you."

Before I could think of a retort, he was gone, and I was left alone in the throne room.

I paced back and forth in my chambers, grinding my teeth together. It had been a week since the Huntsman had been unceremoniously thrown out of the castle. His last words echoed in my head like a drumbeat.

You need me more than I need you.

What insolence! The sheer nerve of that man! How dare he speak to me like that? I was the Queen!

As I stewed in my thoughts, Sigrid knocked on the door and let herself into my room.

Amara came from behind the dressing screen and settled onto the chaise lounge.

"Would you care to hear the day's news, Queen Mother?" Sigrid asked in her usual flat voice.

I pinched the bridge of my nose and breathed in deeply. "Yes, Sigrid. Please, continue."

"Nothing new to report in the castle."

"I suspected as much," I muttered in a dark voice. "What of the city? What are the people saying?"

"They are uneasy, Queen Mother. They believe the rumors about the plague."

"They should, with the amount of bodies we're burning," I muttered.

"There is more, Queen Mother," Sigrid said.

My stomach twisted into a tight knot. Amara covered her mouth with her hands. We both knew what was coming next. How could we not? Snow White was still out there.

I thought about her bone-white teeth, glistening in the moonlight and sharper than any knife. I thought of her insatiable blood thirst, and a chill crept down my spine.

"There are rumors of a woman attacking townspeople in the night. They say she is terrible and beautiful to behold, with hair black as midnight, skin white as snow, and lips red as blood."

"Snow White." Amara whimpered.

"As of this moment, the townspeople are too afraid of the plague to ask questions." Sigrid continued.

"That will not last forever," I said. "Eventually, the truth will take hold." I paced back and forth across the room, wringing my hands.

That damn huntsman. Why did he have to bait me?

"We have also received word from Aileen. The King will set sail soon. He is looking forward to meeting you." Sigrid said.

I gasped in horror. "No! The King can not come here, not now! Didn't he get our messages about the plague?"

"He did, Queen Mother, but King Liam feels confident he will not succumb to any illness. He also stated his intention to bring magical healers with him. The King wishes to help the poor and suffering."

"His intentions are good, at least," Amara offered.

I scoffed. "Be that as it may, he has put our plan into jeopardy. Right now, the court is hiding out in their summer castles. If they find out the King is here, that will embolden them to return to the city and begin asking questions."

"Not to mention King Liam. We can only guess what he will see and hear." Amara added in a quiet voice. She looked frightened.

I ground my teeth together and stared up at the ceiling. "There is one course of action left to us. Sigrid?"

"Yes, Queen Mother?" The golem asked.

"Find the huntsman. Have him brought back to the castle immediately." I demanded.

"Yes, Queen Mother." Sigrid curtsied, then turned and left my chambers.

Amara was quiet for a moment, then cleared her throat. "What do we do now?"

"Get some sleep," I responded gently. "We'll work out the specifics tomorrow."

Amara nodded and pulled the covers up to her chin. In time, her eyes drifted closed and her breathing evened out.

I went to my window, knowing sleep would not find me this night. Clasping my hands behind my back, I looked out over the city and awaited the arrival of the huntsman.

15
VAMPIRE

The first time I met Quincy Pollux, I cared about making a good impression. I wanted him to see me as a powerful queen, someone to be feared and respected. As neither of those things happened, I decided to meet him on his level. There would be no airs of bravado, only gritty realism about the task at hand.

Instead of the throne room, I had a tea room prepped for Quincy's arrival. Chamomile tea and place settings were laid out for us. Trays of scones and jams, along with biscuits and cress sandwiches, were brought in.

It took a day for Garen and his soldiers to find Quincy, and another day to bring him to the castle.

I was reclined in my seat and sipping demurely on a cup of chamomile when the door was thrown open.

Quincy entered the room, collapsing in the chair opposite me.

"Thank you, Garen," I called through the open door. "You may leave us now."

"As you will, Queen Mother." Garen's voice responded. He shut the door and his footsteps receded.

Quincy tossed a satchel at his feet and poured himself a generous cup of tea. He tossed a couple of cress sandwiches in his mouth, then sat back, mirroring my posture.

"So," Quincy said. "I was right. You had need of me after all."

I narrowed my eyes at Quincy, though I was more annoyed than angry. He was larger than I remembered. His tall and muscular frame dwarfed the dainty chair he sat in.

My mouth went dry as I ran my eyes over Quincy's body. Hard, corded muscles flexed beneath dark skin as he shifted, trying to get comfortable. His black vest was open at the top, revealing a barrel chest and a thatch of dark hair. With his thick arms and broad shoulders, he had an intimidating presence.

My heart rate accelerated, and I turned my gaze to his face.

Quincy was more relaxed than last time. The fire was gone from his velvety black eyes, and his mouth was no longer twisted into a cruel sneer.

"See something you like?" Quincy asked, popping another cress sandwich in his mouth. He locked eyes with me and lifted an eyebrow.

"I see a weapon." My voice was ice cold. "I was surprised to hear you were still in town. I thought you might have left by now."

Quincy shrugged and took a swig of tea. "I've been monitoring the situation."

The blood drained from my face, but I kept my composure. "Things can not continue as they are."

"So," Quincy poured himself another cup of tea and sat back in his chair. "Does this mean you're no longer mad I called your sister a whore?"

"Careful, Huntsman," I growled in a low voice. "This is a delicate matter, and I do not have many options, but I do have ways of getting what I want from people."

"Hm, so you are still mad." Quincy seemed amused at my anger, and pleased with himself for being the cause of it.

"Did you really not know?" He asked.

I blinked at him, uncomprehending. "What?"

"Did you really not know that your sister was sleeping with a demon?" Quincy asked.

My magic surged. The teacup shattered in my hand, and I cursed.

"Gods dammit!" I cried out, mopping up the mess with a napkin. Luckily, the cup was nearly empty, so there wasn't much to clean.

I waved a hand, and the shards of ceramic whisked themselves neatly to another table. I would have a golem come in and dispose of it later.

"Well, that answers my question." Quincy muttered under his breath.

I turned on him angrily. "Why do you insist on saying such vile things?"

"It seems a bit obvious from where I'm sitting." Quincy shrugged. "What are your thoughts on the matter? Is Snow White the daughter of King Iberius?"

An icy shiver of fear ran down my spine, and I clenched my hands in my lap.

"I will not dignify that question with a response, nor do you deserve one. Anyway, I want to talk about the job."

"You want to see if I'm qualified," Quincy said.

"Yes," I answered.

Quincy spread out his arms. "Ask me whatever you wish."

My mouth went dry again. I grabbed another cup and poured some more tea. After a quick sip, I gathered up my courage and posed the question that had been on my mind since before our first meeting.

"Why do they call you the Huntsman?"

Quincy smiled like the devil, his lips pulling away from his teeth. There was a flash of something in his eyes. The velvet black turned as dark as a starless night in winter.

I pressed back in my seat, suddenly uncomfortable.

"How does anyone get such a name?" Quincy asked in a voice that was nearly a growl. "I hunt. I kill. I spill blood in places where evil thinks it is safe to hide. I pull demons from the shadows and I put them to the blade. In short, Your Majesty, I am called the Huntsman because when I am on the trail, no monster escapes my ax."

Quincy had never called me "Your Majesty" before. His voice was like a chilly winter wind. It was only by holding very still that I was able to stop myself from trembling.

Still, I couldn't help but feel a little smug at Quincy's ire. It was only fair. He had riled me up more than his fair share.

"All that pomp, and after accusing me of keeping Snow White's parentage a secret." I tutted at Quincy.

Quincy lifted his chin. "That's different."

"Is it?"

"You're asking me to do a job, to hunt. I have to know what I'm hunting." Quincy said defiantly.

I let out a sigh and set my teacup down. "Quincy, I know you want answers, but the truth is, I don't know who Snow White's father is. I thought it was Iberius. I truly believed it was. It wasn't until Snow White got older that-that I began to have doubts."

I bowed my head. It shamed me to question Marcella's honor like this, and in front of a stranger, too.

"What things?" Quincy asked in a soft voice. "Explain it to me, Ceridwen."

I drew in a shuddering breath. "Snow White, she's allergic to the sun. When she goes outside, she has to completely cover up, otherwise she's in pain the entire time, and her skin turns red. Once inside, though, she heals quickly."

"Good, good." Quincy nodded his head. "What else?"

"Animal magic," I said. "It's common in Aileen for children to have it. As they grow older, the magic generally transitions into something else. I mean, one can keep animal magic, but you have to nurture the bond."

I hesitated before continuing. "It's different with Snow White. She doesn't just communicate with the animals, it's like she controls them."

"How do you mean?" Quincy asked.

My hands were trembling. I hid them in my skirts. "The day of Iberius' funeral. Birds were just...falling out of the sky. Like, they just stopped flapping their wings and fell to their death."

"You think Snow White was responsible for that?" Quincy asked.

"She was standing at the window, watching them fall," I explained.

"I see." Quincy nodded. "Is there anything else you want to tell me?"

"I don't know." I buried my face in my hands. Marcella's gaunt face flashed behind my eyes. I could almost hear her voice, asking me to keep her daughter safe.

"There is one more thing," I whispered. "She can...well, I think she can read minds. Only if someone is feeling a very strong emotion, though."

"Hm, I see." Quincy stood up and paced the floor. The room was too small for his long legs, and he had to turn frequently. There was a thoughtful frown on his face, as though he were slowly putting together pieces of a puzzle.

At last, Quincy paused and turned to me. "You spoke of animal magic. Was there a particular animal she was fond of?"

"From what I remember, yes," I said. "She liked dogs the most. They were very loyal to her."

"Well, it's a good thing I brought this." Quincy collapsed into his seat and patted the satchel he had brought with him.

"What is that?" I asked.

"This is what I'm going to be hunting," Quincy said, looking grim.

He pulled the satchel into his lap and flipped open the top. I rose from my seat to get a better look at what he was doing.

"Prepare yourself, Your Majesty," Quincy said. All the gentleness was gone from his voice. "This is an ugly job you're asking of me."

I frowned. "Stop trying to frighten me. Explain yourself, at once."

"If you insist," Quincy said in a rough voice.

Reaching into his bag, he pulled out a severed head.

My eyes widened as I took in the grotesque spectacle before me. Hair black as midnight, skin white as snow, lips red as blood. The teeth, though, the teeth were sharpened into fangs.

A memory of a creature sinking his fangs into Marcella's neck instantly sprang to mind. Another image cropped up, and then it was Snow White at the engagement dinner with the same pointed teeth, and blood smeared on her face.

Goddess protect me, she was gone. Snow White was dead. It was over, all of it was over...

I don't remember opening my mouth to scream, but suddenly the air was full of it. My hearing was distorted, as if everything was coming to me from underwater. There was a roaring in my ears. The room swayed, and everything went dark.

"What have you done to my mistress? What have you done to her?" A high-pitched voice was shrieking.

"She fainted." Came another deep, rumbling voice. "I only meant to lay her down somewhere. I did not-"

"Liar! You've done something!"

I finally recognized Amara's shrill voice, laced with fear. I stirred, slowly coming out of the darkness that engulfed me.

"There, see? She's coming too. No harm done." The deep voice spoke again.

I was gradually becoming aware of my surroundings. I was being gently cradled in strong arms. My head lulled against broad shoulders, and I could smell leather and tobacco.

Lifting my head, I turned towards Amara's voice. My eyes fluttered open, and I took in the scene before me.

I had been carried to the room across the hall, into a small lounge. Amara stood in front of me, her face white with terror, and cheeks flushed with rage.

Turning again, I finally understood that it was Quincy who was holding me.

"Get away from me!" I snarled in a weak and scratchy voice.

I attempted to struggle out of Quincy's embrace, but his arms tightened around me.

"Take it easy, now. You fainted. I caught you before you hit the floor, and I'd appreciate it if didn't do anything to harm yourself," Quincy said.

I thought of the decapitated head Quincy had shown me, and the room swam again. My head drooped back onto his shoulder, and I let out a groan.

"You're distressing her!" Amara said in an accusatory voice. "Put her down immediately. I will attend to her."

"As you wish."

Quincy laid me down on a settee. I immediately missed the touch of his brawny arms and powerful chest. The thought horrified me, and I immediately shoved it away. I blinked, and then Amara's face appeared as she crouched down in front of me.

"Help me sit up, Amara." I said.

Amara nodded and did as I asked. Quincy stood in a dark corner. He watched me with an intense expression in his eyes.

I glared at him.

"I thought that was Snow White's head you brought me." I got out at last.

Quincy shook his head. "No, just the same kind of monster as your princess."

"How dare you?" Amara got out between gritted teeth.

"Should you even be here?" Quincy asked in a curious voice.

"Amara is my closest confidant," I said in a firm voice. "She is privy to all my personal information, and that of the castle."

"Ah, right, the little dark-haired girl that trails after you." Quincy folded his arms across his barrel chest. "I take it she is up to date on what is happening with the princess?"

"Yes," I answered.

"Well," Quincy said, "That's settled. Would you like me to say I accept the job? Or, Ceridwen, would you prefer to command me?"

"You can't speak to her that way, she's the queen!" Amara objected.

I glared at Quincy. "Get your tools together. The king of Aileen is coming. We're leaving the day after his arrival."

Quincy raised an eyebrow. "We? Surely you don't mean to come with me."

"Snow White is my stepdaughter and the last member of my family. I'm going, and before you get any ideas, it is not in your power to stop me." I said.

The side of Quincy's mouth that wasn't burned turned up in a smile. "If the queen commands it, how can I say no?"

"I have an estate a few hours ride from the castle, Easton Manor. You can stay there until our departure." I said.

"I agree to your terms." Quincy moved towards the door, but paused when he placed his hand on the handle. "Don't you want to know what kind of creature we'll be hunting?"

I let out a deep sigh. "What kind?"

"I wasn't sure, not at first," Quincy said in a thoughtful voice. "I found that creature on the outskirts of town. Her father was terrified. He thought she was feral. Well, I got him alone and confirmed my suspicions. The demon is a few years older than Snow White, and they have some things in common."

"So," Amara began in a trembling voice, "What did you discover? Wh-what did Snow White become? Is it a curse? A hex? What?"

Quincy turned in our direction. His dark eyes were serious and burned with intensity. "The word you are looking for is vampire."

16
THE JOURNEY BEGINS

Time was of the essence, so I quickly hatched out a plan. Garen escorted Quincy to my estate, Easton Manor. Amara was set up in a luxurious suite of rooms and began going by the name of Snow White. New servants were hired to attend to her, as well as the castle.

After three weeks, King Liam finally arrived. By this time, the castle was running smoothly.

The morning the King's ship docked in our harbor, I rose early. After dressing and having my hair done up in a severe bun, I went to Amara's room.

A maid answered when I knocked on the door.

"Queen Mother." She said, bobbing her head.

I ran my eyes over the woman. She was human, not a golem. One of the new hires, I concluded.

Behind her, Amara was on a dais, being dressed in an elegant ballgown. She looked beautiful in the cobalt blue dress.

As I entered the room, Amara locked eyes with me.

"Good morning, Stepmother." She said in a sweet voice, smiling at me.

I returned the smile. "Good morning, Snow White."

The first few times, the lie had lodged in my throat, but I was getting better at it.

"All done here, M'lady." A maid finished lacing up Amara's corset and stepped back. "All that's left now is the hair."

I went to Amara's vanity and picked up a brush. "Actually, I would like to do my stepdaughter's hair. If you don't mind, Snow White."

Amara shook her head. "No, of course not."

I turned to the ladies-in-waiting. "That will be all. You may leave us."

The other girls bowed, then scurried from the room, their heads down low. The door shut behind them.

I gently ran the brush through Amara's hair, then began to put it up in a braid.

"I don't think you've ever done my hair before," Amara said in a quiet voice.

Startled, I looked up and met her eyes in the mirror. "Never?"

"No," Amara said. Her voice was barely above a whisper.

"Well, I'm happy to do it now," I said in a kind voice. "We have a long day ahead of us."

"Right," Amara nodded, looking nervous.

I paused, then resumed braiding her hair. "Are you all right?"

"Snow White and I used to play games when we were younger," Amara confessed. "We used to pretend that we were sisters at court together. I'm confident I can do this, Ceridwen. Snow White taught me everything about etiquette. I just-Well, it's odd being here, doing this without her. I never imagined my first foray into court would be on my own."

"I'm sorry." My voice was soft, apologetic. "I didn't know."

"It's not your fault," Amara said.

I took a deep breath. "With any luck, it will be only temporary."

"What are you going to do?" Amara asked. "We've looked. There's no cure for vampirism."

"I am going to turn Snow White into a golem," I answered in a cheerful voice.

Amara tensed, but didn't say anything.

"It's simple, really. I just need her lungs and heart, fresh soil, a bit of rainwater, and this whole nasty business will be behind us." I continued, my voice unnaturally sunny.

"It's hope, at least," Amara said.

We lapsed into silence, then. Neither of us spoke our fears out loud, though I knew we were thinking the same thing. A golem wouldn't be a replacement for

Snow White. She would only be a shadow, an echo of my stepdaughter. Frozen, emotionless, doomed to live a half-life.

Then there was the issue of how we would handle Snow White's return to court. There was no way I could switch her with Amara. People would notice. The only reason we got away with it now was because Snow White had been such a recluse, and because the staff had been mostly slaughtered upon her departure.

Worry and fear twisted in my stomach, but I pushed those feelings down. All that mattered was that I got Snow White back. Whatever sliver of her I could pull from the darkness, I would do it without hesitation.

I finished braiding Amara's hair and twisted it up into a bun.

"There," I said. "You're beautiful."

Amara met my eyes in the mirror and smiled. I smiled back, carefully examining her face. Marcella and Snow White had always been beautiful. Amara, on the other hand, was ethereal and lovely, like a painting one could stare at for hours. I had known, since the day I caught her dancing in the castle gardens, that she was going to outpace my sister and stepdaughter. It had made me uneasy then. Now, her transition from servant girl to princess was astonishing.

"Thank you, Stepmother," Amara said in a soft voice.

I cleared my throat and looked away. "I'm pleased with the progress we're making in the castle. The bodies have all been removed, and the floors scrubbed clean. We have new staff. We are fully functioning just in time for the King's arrival."

"Yes, it's a relief," Amara said.

"I don't think I could have done it without you," I said, laying my hand on her shoulder. "Amara, I'm so grateful for everything you've done these past few weeks, and everything you're doing now, so I can go look for Snow White."

Amara was quiet for a long moment. Her long, sooty lashes came down, laying against her gently flushed cheeks and hiding her dark eyes as she stared at the ground.

"I'm happy to be of service." She said. "You, Snow White, Mirtha, you're the only family I've ever known. I'm very grateful for everything you've done for me, Ceridwen."

My heart twisted painfully as I looked at the sweet and demure girl in front of me. I remembered then that she was only two weeks older than my stepdaughter. In many ways, Amara was just a girl herself.

"I'm sorry, Amara." My voice was quiet and filled with shame. "I should have done more."

Amara spun towards me, a look of alarm on her face. "No, I didn't mean to imply- That is, Ceridwen, you've done more than enough-"

"No," I interrupted, shaking my head. "You should have been like a daughter to me, and I should have been a mother to you, like I was to Snow White."

"I don't expect that from you, Ceridwen," Amara said.

"Maybe not, but when I come back, we're going to do things differently around here."

Amara stood from her seat, and we embraced each other in a tight hug.

"Come on," I said, breaking away. "Let's go greet the King of Aileen."

Amara and I stood on the dock, watching as King Liam was rowed to shore in a dinghy.

He was very good looking. I impassively noticed this, like I had noticed Conrad was handsome.

As soon as King Liam stood on our dock, he swooped down in a regal bow. He had fine manners, and there was a wide smile on his face that indicated an open and friendly nature.

"Greetings to you both, fine ladies," Liam said. He turned to me. "Ah, you must be Queen Ceridwen, my intended. I am King Liam of Aileen."

I smiled and curtsied. Beside me, Amara did the same.

"Greetings, Your Majesty," I said. "I can't tell you what joy it brings me to welcome you to our fine country, although I wish it were under better circumstances."

"Well, I am here now, and happy to be of assistance," Liam said.

Amara cleared her throat and stepped forward. "I am the Princess Snow White. It would be an honor to escort you back to our castle, where we can discuss business together."

King Liam paused, taking in Amara's features. His eyes softened, and he nodded. "Yes, I would like that very much."

I had to stop myself from breathing a sigh of relief. For a moment, I had feared that the king meant to comment on Amara's age. I was very conscious of the fact that I would be leaving a fifteen year old in charge as I went out looking for the *real* Snow White.

We all piled into the carriage, and the coachman took us back to the castle. I had an intimate gathering planned in one of the smaller dining halls. Lunch was laid out, and we all took our seats. I sat at the head of the table. On either side of me were Amara and Liam.

"Your Majesty-" I started.

"Oh, please, you can call me Liam." The King gave me a shy smile. "I understand there is royal protocol to follow, but you are to be my wife. I want no formalities between us."

"I understand. That is very generous of you." I paused. "You may call me Ceridwen."

"Well, it is such a pretty name. It would be a shame not to use it."

I took a sip of my tea to hide a growing smile on my face. Yes, this man had fine manners indeed.

"Liam," I started again, "As you know, we've been recovering from a plague. Luckily, we managed to contain the pestilence to within the castle walls, and the worst is behind us now. Snow White has been working diligently with the poor and the ill. Snow White, why don't you tell the king how you've been helping the people of Cherida?"

"Of course," Amara sat a little straighter and smoothed out her skirts. "Because of the plague, many have been out of work and do not have money for food. I've found a solution for this. I've put the kitchens to work preparing meals twice a day. The people can come for a bowl of soup, some cheese, and a slice of bread."

"That is very benevolent and kindhearted of you." Liam looked impressed. He turned to me. "And you support this endeavor?"

I nodded. "Of course, this is Snow White's kingdom. She is going to rule someday, and I think it is the responsibility of the royal family to share their blessings."

"Yes, responsibility. That is precisely how I feel," Liam said.

"Snow White has also been volunteering her time in the sickhouses," I said.

"I would love to hear more about your work there," Liam said, looking at Amara. "That is where I plan to spend most of my time. I have also brought healers with me to assist in the recovery of those afflicted."

"I am looking forward to working with you," Amara said, giving a slight bow of her head.

"What of you, Ceridwen?" Liam turned towards me. "Will you also be joining us in the sickhouse?"

"Mostly, I assist in the making of poultices," I said. "The people of Cherida are not too keen on having an outsider handling their health."

Liam's eyes clouded over, and I recalled his envoy's visit, when Rian said the King was aware of the open hostility between me and my subjects.

"At any rate, I am setting off early tomorrow morning," I said. "There is business at my summer castle that can not wait."

Liam looked surprised. "So soon after my arrival?"

"It is unfortunate, Liam, but I had little time to prepare for your visit. As I've stated before, the business is of an urgent matter, and I must attend to it immediately."

"Of course." Liam nodded. "I hope you can forgive my impertinence. It's as we've said before, the responsibility for those who depend on us can weigh heavily."

"There is nothing to forgive," I said. "Snow White will manage the castle duties until my return. I will leave you in her capable hands."

"Would you not rather that I assist you?" Liam asked.

I shook my head. "No, you will be of more use here. It wouldn't hurt for you to become more familiar with Cherida. After all, our countries will soon be allied with each other."

"You can help me administer medicine and change bandages," Amara said. "I also read to those who are ill or wounded. That helps lift their spirits."

"I look forward to it," Liam said.

"Snow White also sings for them," I added. "She has a beautiful voice. If you're lucky, you might get to hear it."

"Really?" Liam looked delighted at this prospect. "I'm quite musical myself. I play the piano."

"My stepmother exaggerates my abilities," Amara said, a light blush coloring her cheeks.

"Something tells me you're a very modest sort of person, and Ceridwen is telling the exact truth." Liam's eyes went soft again as he looked at Amara.

"I'm glad to see the two of you settling in so well together," I said. Finishing my tea, I stood up from the table. "If you'll excuse me, I need to oversee the packing and provisions of my trip."

"Of course." Liam instantly stood from his seat and gave a brief bow.

I curtsied back, smiled at Amara, then left the room.

Tomorrow, I would leave at dawn.

The next morning dawned a bright and clear day. The roads were dry, which made for easy traveling.

Amara and Liam stood at the door of the carriage house as I bid them farewell.

"Goodbye, Stepmother," Amara said. She was beautiful and composed, but she gave me a brittle smile that betrayed her insecurity.

I stepped forward and embraced her in a tight hug.

"Goodbye, my love. I know you'll do well." I said in an encouraging voice.

Liam was next. I hesitated as I approached him, my eyes darting in Amara's direction.

"I know you are a guest here but, would you- Would it be too much of an imposition to ask-" I fell over my words, not quite sure what I wanted from this handsome stranger.

Liam, to his credit, caught on to what I was trying to say. He kissed the back of my hand, then drew me in as if to also kiss me on the cheek. Instead, he whispered in my ear.

"It would be my honor to look after Snow White." He said in a low voice.

I smiled at Liam as I pulled away. "Thank you."

Liam helped me into my carriage, and the horses took off at a brisk trot.

Now the real journey began.

17
REFUGEES

I sat in the back of the carriage, my stomach churning with anxiety. We rode through town, out the city gates, and into the country. In time, we reached a fork in the road and stopped.

The door opened, and Garen was there. He held out a hand and helped me step down onto the packed dirt. Behind him stood Sigrid, holding the reins of a spare horse.

"Right then." I straightened up and adjusted my cloak. "You know your orders. Take the carriage to my summer castle. In ten days time, Garen, you will ride back to the castle and announce that I am sick with the plague. Sigrid, you are in charge of shutting the castle down and keeping everyone out."

"Yes, Queen Mother." Both of my golems answered in the same deadpan voice.

For a moment, my mind wandered to what Quincy said about my golems. Was it possible? Could they really have their own thoughts? If they could have their own thoughts, did they also have feelings? What would they say if I loosened their tongues?

Taking a deep breath, I cleared my throat and pushed my reflections away to the darkest recesses of my mind. I wouldn't think of it, I just wouldn't.

"Well, it's time I set off for my meeting with the huntsman. I'll take my horse and be going now."

Garen and Sigrid bowed their heads while I swung myself up into the saddle. Not another word was spoken between us as I took the road leading to my estate, and the carriage started its long trek to my summer castle.

I whispered some spells to the wind which hurried my journey along. It wasn't long after that I was cantering down the lane of Easton Manor and pulling up in front of a set of double doors.

After handing the reins off to a waiting stable boy, I hurried inside the house. A golem directed me towards the dining hall where I found Quincy having a late breakfast.

"I'm surprised to see you eating at this time of day. I thought you'd be an early riser." My voice had a hint of a reprimand to it.

"Maybe I am, maybe I'm not. It depends." Quincy shrugged and shoved a bite of toast into his mouth.

Letting out an exasperated sigh, I collapsed in the chair opposite him. "Well, I'm not hungry. I've already had breakfast."

"It's a big house. I'm sure you can find some way to entertain yourself." Quincy answered in a nonplussed voice.

I scowled and sat back in my seat. After staring out the window for a minute, I straightened my back and folded my hands on the table.

"Last time you were at the castle, you said you found another…creature…like Snow White. You got her father alone, and he clarified some things for you."

"Yes," Quincy answered in a wary voice.

"What did he clarify?"

Quincy leveled his gaze at me. "Are you sure you can handle it? You're not going to faint again?"

"Answer my question."

"All right, then." Quincy wiped his mouth with a napkin, then threw it on the table. He leaned towards me, his eyes hard. "His wife died giving birth to that child."

I shook my head. "That doesn't mean anything. Women die in childbirth all the time."

"He also said they were married for many years and had given up all hope of having a baby. Her pregnancy was an unexpected one."

I frowned, drawing my eyebrows. "Is there a point to this?"

"The daughter had odd habits growing up. Dogs were loyal to her. She was sensitive to sunlight. She liked her meat bloody, almost raw."

My breath hitched in my throat then. I looked away.

"Do you want me to stop?" Quincy asked.

"I can guess the rest," I answered in a soft voice. "His daughter somehow got a taste of blood, and she became a vampire."

"No," Quincy shook his head. "She finished transitioning."

"What?" I asked, confused.

Quincy sighed and rubbed the back of his neck. "These vampire children, they are undead creatures. They don't just grow in the womb like normal babies. They sap the lifeblood of whoever is carrying them. When they come into this world, they have one foot in the living, and one foot in the grave. After their first taste of blood, they fully transition to vampires."

My stomach churned. I got up jerkily from my chair and began to pace the hall. My thoughts were too jumbled to form a coherent sentence. Instead, I focused on my breathing.

When my heart slowed, and my nerves settled, I resumed my seat.

"So what you're saying is, Marcella never had a chance. She was meant to die so Snow White could be born."

"Yes," Quincy said in a soft voice.

"There's one other thing," I said. "Snow White, when she...well, when she tasted blood for the first time, she became pale. More pale than she already was."

"And?" Quincy asked.

"Well, I was thinking. She wasn't as pale as the head you brought to my castle. The one I mistook for Snow White."

"Your stepdaughter is of Aileen descent. Aileen complexions are darker than that of Cheridans."

Quincy picked up his teacup and took a sip. "Becoming a vampire doesn't turn your skin white. Snow White and the girl were pale because they were corpses."

I turned away from Quincy when he called my stepdaughter a corpse. For a moment, I contemplated telling him my plan to turn Snow White into a golem. It would feel good to throw that in his face, to taunt him, to brag about my ability to snatch Snow White back from the darkness. Rather quickly, I decided not to. This was my mission. Quincy was in my employ. I had no intention of letting him take control.

"So there were two vampires living close to the castle," I said.

Quincy drew his brow. "I think so. It's difficult to say for certain. At any rate, after I killed that girl, I noticed people stopped mysteriously dying in their beds."

"What does that mean?" I asked, looking down at my hands.

"Well, it means Snow White fled. Either she left after the massacre, or she heard there was a huntsman on her trail and ran off." Quincy said.

My heart lifted. "That means Snow White may not have been responsible for any of those murders."

"Don't do that to yourself, Ceridwen," Quincy said in a deep voice.

"Don't do what?" I snapped.

"Don't give yourself hope." Quincy looked up and met my eyes, and there was such a deep sadness on his face that I couldn't bring myself to argue with him.

"Fine." I plucked at my skirts. "Are you almost finished? It's getting late."

"I'm done now." Quincy stood from his seat. He was in another vest, leaving his arms bare. He stretched, lifting his hands over his head. I watched as his muscles flexed, sunlight skimming across his dark skin. His many scars stood out, and I wondered what they would feel like beneath my fingers...

I stood up from my seat so abruptly, I almost knocked my chair over.

Quincy glanced at me in surprise. "Are you all right?"

"Yes," I said, smoothing my skirts and refusing to meet his eyes. "I'm just impatient to be gone. I thought we'd be on the road by now."

Quincy grunted. "Yes, I believe you're right."

As we made our way to the double doors, I couldn't help but ask Quincy one more question.

"Where are we going?"

Quincy grimaced. "Nowhere you're going to like."

We made our way down to the stables, where I was pleased to see our horses were already saddled and packed with provisions.

Quincy mounted a great black horse with ease. The animal was at least seventeen hands and had a restless energy to it.

"Scout has been locked up for too long." Quincy reached down to give the horse an affectionate pat on the neck.

I thinned my lips, staring up at the horse and rider. They were absolute giants. Every inch of them was thick, hardened muscle, and they towered imposingly over me.

Holding back a sigh, I climbed onto my own cream colored mare, standing at fifteen hands.

"You named your horse Scout?" I asked.

Quincy shrugged. "It seemed a fitting name for a huntsman's stead. What's your horse's name?"

I frowned, staring at the back of the mare's head. "I don't know. Buttercup, I think."

Quincy snorted. "Buttercup," He mumbled, rolling his eyes.

I bristled. "Let's get started, shall we?"

Quincy nudged his horse, and Scout took off at a brisk trot down the road. I followed behind, feeling nervous.

After a time, we left behind my grand estate and made our way onto the country roads.

I watched the land roll from one hill to the next, long stalks of grain waving lazily in the breeze, glinting gold in the sunlight. We passed a few people here and there, but no one that recognized us.

I was so lost in thought that I didn't notice when Quincy pulled Scout off to the side of the road.

"Oi, where are you going?" Quincy asked as Buttercup plodded on by.

Tearing my eyes away from the land, I spun in the saddle to stare at Quincy. I blinked rapidly, momentarily disoriented.

"Are we stopping?" I asked.

"Yes, it's midday. We need to let the horses rest and get something to eat," Quincy said.

"Right." I pulled Buttercup around, then swung my leg over the saddle, preparing to dismount.

"Here, let me help you." Quincy appeared before me and held out his hands.

I was so exhausted I didn't bother to argue. Leaning forward, I placed my hands on his shoulders.

Quincy's arms slid around my waist, and he hoisted me down. For a fraction of a second, I was held close to his barrel chest. Once again, I caught his scent of tobacco and leather. His touch was tender as he placed me on the ground.

"Thank you," I said, quickly stepping away.

Quincy was starting to confuse me. His words and mannerisms were coarse and condescending, but his touch was safe and gentle. Protective, even.

Settling on the grass beside me, Quincy offered me some cheese and bread.

"So," He asked, picking at his meal, "You were lost in thought. What's on your mind?"

I shrugged, also picking at my food. "I was thinking of Aileen."

"Ah, yes." Quincy leaned back on his elbow and shot me a cheeky grin. "You probably can't wait to marry the King and wash your hands of Cherida. What a homecoming that will be."

"Don't say that." I snapped. "You have no idea what life was like for me in Aileen."

"So, how was it?" Quincy asked in a flippant voice.

I turned away, staring at the long road ahead. "When I was twelve, my parents were burned at the stake. Marcella and I had to flee in the night. We paid a captain to stow us away on his boat and take us to Cherida."

Quincy was silent for a long moment. At last, he cleared his throat. "I'm sorry to hear it. Rumors of the late King Drustin reached Theor, of course, but…there were many who believed the reports to be exaggerated."

"I assure you, they were not," I responded in a cold voice. "The only reason Marcella and I were not burned along with them was because we were at the market when the soldiers came. A neighbor came to find us and warned us not to come home. She did this at great peril to her own life."

Quincy shifted, looking uncomfortable. "You couldn't even go back to collect your things?"

"No," I shook my head. "We had to leave everything behind."

Quincy ducked his head, looking down into his lap. "I apologize for what I said earlier. It was unkind."

His words were spoken in the deep, unsure voice of a man who was unaccustomed to apologizing.

"Marcella and I had to pick pockets to eat. We had no way to earn our meals. Then there was the journey down to the port. We traveled down a road like this one, walking for days. Our food and water ran out, and our stomachs rumbled with hunger. We tried begging whenever we came across another traveler. Some were kind, but there were some men who wanted…company."

Quincy made a pained face. "You were *children*."

I hesitated before continuing. "Yes, but we were more than that. We were mysticmancers, and those men paid a steep price for their lechery."

Quincy shrugged. "Can't say I'm sorry to hear that."

"We finally made it down to the port. There were laws against smuggling mysticmancers out of Aileen. Anyone found doing so faced dire consequences. Few captains would risk it, and those who dared charged exorbitant rates. Marcella and I were lucky. We had um…managed to acquire enough money for the journey. The voyage over wasn't too bad. We were given plenty of food, and we had a dry place to sleep."

Quincy nodded. "A lucky break, then."

"The first one we had since our parents were taken." I heaved a sigh and looked back towards the road. "Anyway, that's what was on my mind earlier. Walking down a road with aching feet, a hungry belly, and a parched throat, wondering if we would make it to the port before we succumbed to death. I never liked thinking about those days, but out here I can't seem to help it."

Silence elapsed, and my mind sank into darkness, reliving the hunger, the thirst, the deep ache of grief coupled with a weariness that was bone deep.

"I also know what's it like to lose your family and your home."

The darkness receded, and I found myself looking closely at Quincy. It occurred to me that I knew next to nothing about him. It was possible that I could ask, ask Quincy about his story, but the look of deep sorrow and loss was back on his face, and for the second time that day, I lost my nerve.

I shifted and cleared my throat. "So, you are from Theor, then?"

Quincy stirred, as though I were drawing him from a deep sleep. "Yes."

"Why did you leave?"

"I fled." He answered simply.

I drew my brows, confused. "Were you persecuted?"

"No, I was running from something else," Quincy said.

"Hm," I brushed a strand of hair out of my face and glanced at the road again. "So we are both refugees in a strange land, then."

"So it would seem."

The silence resumed, and we both focused on eating our food. After a while, I spoke up.

"You still haven't told me where we're going."

Quincy pulled out his acorn necklace. "The greenwitch who gave me this, her name is Aster. She sent for me after a werewolf attacked her village. The depth of her knowledge surprised me. I've since called on her many times for her expertise."

"But you said Snow White was a-a vampire," I said.

"Yes," Quincy nodded. "And vampires use werewolves to protect them during the daylight hours."

"Why?" I asked. "How does the sun affect them?"

"Vampires and werewolves are both ruled by the moon," Quincy explained. "That means they are weakest during the day. While the sun is out, werewolves are still strong and fast, but they can not shift into their wolf counterpart. Vampires, on the other hand, lose a majority of their power, and sleep most of the day."

"Snow White, her skin used to burn in the sun," I said slowly.

"A vampire's skin is sensitive to direct sunlight," Quincy explained.

"What of these other powers?" I asked. "What will Snow White be like after dark?"

Quincy let out a deep sigh. "Speed, for starters, vampires can move faster than the human eye can track. Some of them can read minds."

I blanched at that and turned away from Quincy. Not fast enough, though.

"I take it your stepdaughter is one of those vampires?" He asked in a quiet voice.

"Yes, she is," I whispered.

"Well, that complicates things," Quincy said.

Maybe, maybe not. Perhaps this was information I could use to my advantage. If I got close enough to Snow White, she could read my mind and understand I meant her no harm. The only question remaining was, would Snow White consent to being made into a golem?

Quincy sprawled his legs out and crossed them at the ankle. "Is there anything else you want to share?"

"Hm?" I looked up, meeting his dark, questioning eyes. My stomach abruptly twisted into a tight knot.

"Well, Snow White said something- I don't know how helpful it will be, though." I hesitated.

"Let's hear it."

Letting out a deep sigh, I straightened my back and pushed a few strands of hair out of my face. "Snow White only mentioned it once. It was when...well, Iberius was not in a good mood. She told me she could sense his emotions, that sometimes she could hear words."

"But not all the time?" Quincy clarified.

"Exactly." I nodded my head. "I think a person has to be feeling something very strongly for Snow White to pick up on it."

"I see," Quincy said.

We went quiet again. I thought about Snow White, and what I would say when we were finally reunited. Even if I could convince my stepdaughter to let me turn her into a golem, I was still going to kill her. I would cut her chest open, break her ribcage apart, and pull out her heart and liver.

It was a horrendous thought, one I wished I could put from my mind. I stuffed the last bite of bread in my mouth and looked up.

Quincy was staring at me. There was a wary, almost knowing, look in his eyes that gave me pause.

I turned away quickly, and Quincy got to his feet.

"Come," He said, "We still have several days of riding ahead of us."

Without another word, we each mounted our horses and turned towards the road. I gripped the reins, trying to put any difficult thoughts out of my mind. After all, our journey was just beginning.

The hardest part was still before us.

18
THE GREENWITCH WIVES

After three days of hard riding, we finally came upon a small village. It was dark out, and there were only a few stars dotting the night sky, so I barely took notice of the few ramshackle buildings and small homes. My whole body ached. I was tired and swaying in the saddle.

Quincy had taken the reins of my horse and was leading Buttercup.

I stifled a yawn. "We should've stopped hours ago, Quincy. We can't keep up this pace."

"We're nearly there," Quincy said, a hint of amusement in his voice.

I glared at the back of his head, but didn't say anything.

We trotted down a dark road for several more minutes. Just as my temper was beginning to flare, and I contemplated ordering Quincy to stop, a cottage emerged from the shadows.

It was a quaint and cozy cottage, by the looks of it, and situated on the outskirts of town. There was an herb garden out front, and a porch swing. Smoke rose from the chimney, and several wind chimes were hanging above a window and by the door.

Scout pawed the ground and let out a loud *neigh*. The front door was flung open at once, and two women came rushing into the yard.

"Quincy Pollux, you've kept us waiting." A stout blonde woman with hazel eyes said. She put her hands on her hips.

"My apologies, Aster. As you can see, my companion here is not used to being on the road for long periods of time." Quincy chuckled and dismounted.

"Oh, poor dear." A strawberry blonde with wide blue eyes stood next to Aster. "Well, get inside you two! I've saved you both some dinner."

"Hello, Senna, good to see you," Quincy said, coming around to help me dismount.

My leg trembled as I swung it over the saddle. As I leaned forward into Quincy's arms, my whole body went limp and I slid forward.

"Whoa, careful now!" Quincy jumped forward, catching me neatly in his arms. Instead of putting my feet on the ground, he lifted me in a bridal carry, pressing me close to his chest.

"Bring her inside, Quincy. She doesn't look well." Senna said, a worried expression on her face.

"We have some tea that should perk her right up," Aster said.

"Please," I said, "Don't make a fuss." I squirmed in Quincy's embrace, but he tightened his arms around me.

"Let's just get you inside." He said in a deep voice, carrying me towards the door.

I felt humiliated as Quincy strode into the cabin and placed me in a rocking chair. I was the Queen, I shouldn't have to be carried around like a child.

"Here you go, love," Senna said in a cheery voice. She set a cup of tea down in front of me.

"Thank you," I said, as the scent of oolong wafted out of the cup. I took a sip of the hot drink and felt the weariness drain from my body. I let out a deep sigh as my head cleared and I sat up a little straighter.

Aster and Quincy disappeared outside the cabin as they stabled the horses. I sipped my tea and stared into the fire. Not long after, they came back inside and seated themselves at opposite sides of a table.

"Which one of you is the greenwitch?" I asked, peering into my cup.

"Both of us," Aster said.

"I'm also a kitchen witch," Senna said. She was busy putting away her wide array of teas. "My wife likes to stick to the garden, though."

"How long have you two been married?" I asked, taking another sip of my drink.

"Almost seven years." Senna beamed with pride.

"Congratulations, seven is a lucky number," I said.

"With Senna, every day is lucky." Aster reclined in her seat, giving her wife a fond look.

Senna giggled, then pulled a chair up next to Aster. They shared a quick kiss, and Aster slipped an arm around Senna's waist.

"Now, Huntsman," Aster turned towards Quincy and quirked an eyebrow. "I hear you're looking for a vampire. A very specific vampire, at that."

"Yes," Quincy said, his deep voice rumbling. A muscle jumped in his jaw, and he kept his eyes fixed on the two greenwitches.

Aster turned in my direction. "I'm assuming this is the Queen, then?"

I froze in my chair. My stomach churned with nausea, while my muscles went rigid.

Senna clicked her tongue. "That's not very nice, Aster. She looks afraid."

"This is Ceridwen Starbright of Aileen." Aster said in a hard voice. "We've all heard the horror stories trickling out of the castle. She is no innocent."

I narrowed my eyes. Aster may have caught me by surprise, but I would not be intimidated by her. I was the Queen; I was a Starbright, and I feared no one.

"Aster is right," I said in a soft voice. "I can certainly be dangerous in the right circumstances."

"Give it a rest, Ceridwen. No one in this cabin is a threat to you," Quincy said in a tired voice.

"Don't speak for me, Quincy." Aster snapped. She turned her hazel eyes in my direction. "I heard you ordered your stepdaughter to be dressed in rags and forced her to stay inside the castle. Why should I help you find her? How do I know she didn't just run away?"

"How *dare* you?" I shouted, rage coursing through my body. I was so offended, I actually stood from my seat, though I quickly sat back down again. Despite the tea, I was still exhausted.

"There's no need to bait her, Aster. I've already confirmed Ceridwen's story with members of the castle. There's a girl, her name is Amara, she is also of Aileen descent. She and Snow White were close friends, but she was a servant, and dressed for her station. Apparently, Cheridans can't tell one Aileen from another." Quincy said. "Snow White also stayed in the castle because of her sensitivity to the sun. Ceridwen did not keep her locked up as a prisoner."

"That's not what I heard," Aster continued. "They say Snow White is more beautiful than her mother, who, we all remember, seduced the king-"

"Excuse me!" I angrily interjected.

"And that Queen Ceridwen became so jealous of Snow White's blossoming beauty that she forced the princess into hard labor and made her wear old hand-me-downs. She also has a mirror in her bedroom, and every night before bed she asks who the most beautiful woman in the kingdom is. The mirror answers the queen is the most beautiful, for now. We all know a day is coming when Snow White's beauty will surpass the queen's. Then what will become of our princess?"

"Oh, Aster! That's a horrid thing to say!" Senna's mouth pulled down into a frown, and there was a hurt look on her face.

Aster shrugged. "That's just what I've heard. I didn't say I believed it."

"I do not know what twisted rumors have reached your ears," I said in a low voice, "But I assure you, I love Snow White. She is a daughter to me. I would never harm her."

Aster leaned back in her seat and gave me a long look.

"I don't know if that brings me comfort, or just makes things worse." She mused.

"What do you mean?" I asked.

Senna cleared her throat while Quincy looked down at his lap.

"You say you would never harm her?" Aster stood up and went into the kitchen. When she returned, she had a jug of mead with her. "Do you even know what a vampire is, Ceridwen?"

I bristled at the use of my first name. Aster poured drinks for everyone at the table and then brought me a cup.

I accepted the proffered drink and set aside my empty teacup. "Quincy has told me a little."

"Here's the thing about vampires. They're predators." Aster said. "They prey on humans, kill them, and drink their blood. Not necessarily in that order, either. For someone to become a vampire, you have to be dead. An animated corpse, not unlike a golem."

My insides turned to ice as Aster spoke. Did she know? Could she possibly suspect that I intended to turn Snow White into a golem if all other paths failed?

"What would you have me say?" I asked in a cold voice. "First, you accuse me of being an evil stepmother who keeps Snow White indoors and dressed in rags. Now you're admonishing me for saying I could never hurt her? How am I to respond to such a statement?"

"We don't mean to admonish you, of course not," Senna said in a high voice. "It's just that, well, killing vampires is hard, messy work. We want to make sure you know what you're getting yourself into by going with Quincy. You may not get the outcome you desire."

Aster let out a deep sigh. "When you love a vampire, there is no desirable outcome."

Understanding slowly dawned on me. Quincy meant to kill Snow White, because that was the fate of all vampires. Aster and Senna were gently attempting to guide me to the truth.

They had no idea I wanted to make Snow White into a golem. All they knew was that she was my stepdaughter, and I loved her, and I had magic. They expected me to try and save her, and were warning me it was futile.

It had been a while since Quincy said anything. As I turned my eyes in his direction, I saw him staring into his cup of mead. His jaw was clenched, and there was darkness in his eyes. His face was a strange combination of rage and grief.

"Are you telling me that there is no hope?" I asked. "That all I can do is accept Snow White's fate and stay out of Quincy's way?"

"I am a huntsman," Quincy spoke at last in a harsh voice. "You know what it is I do."

"A huntsman is not the same as a butcher," I said sharply.

"It's late." Senna quickly interjected. "We should all get to bed. We can discuss it in the morning. Things are always worse when it's dark out."

Aster stood up and spoke to Quincy about their loft.

I stared miserably into the fire for a long moment, taking long swigs of mead. I wracked my brain for more solutions. There had to be something that could help Snow White, some blessing or unbinding spell that could drive out the evil in her.

There had to be something, because the alternative was unthinkable.

I changed into a nightgown, and Senna ushered me up a ladder and into their loft. I fell asleep at once, although it was a restless slumber and full of dreams that made me uneasy.

Quincy came up sometime during the night and fell asleep on his side of the loft. We had traveled together for some days at this point, so his presence actually brought me comfort.

Despite this, we each tossed and turned for the rest of the night.

I woke early in the morning, as I was accustomed to. There was a quiet tiptoeing and gentle clinking coming from downstairs. Rubbing the sleep from my eyes, I deduced that either Aster or Senna was awake, and the other was still in bed.

My gaze drifted over to Quincy. He was fast asleep, lying on his stomach with one hand tucked under his pillow. It was a familiar sight, and I knew he held a knife in his hand.

Our second night on the road, I found this out quite unexpectedly. Three bandits ambushed us as we were sleeping. Before I could scream, Quincy leaped from his makeshift bed. His hand emerged from underneath his pillow, revealing a knife the size of my forearm. He made quick work of the bandits, finishing them off before I had a chance to untangle my legs from my blankets.

A door closed softly, probably the front door. Rifling through my bag, I hastily threw on a robe and tiptoed down the ladder. I moved quietly through the cottage and let myself outside.

A brisk morning breeze surrounded me at once. I took in a deep breath, relishing the crisp air.

"Good morning, Ceridwen." Senna stood up from her herb garden and gave me a bright smile. "Did you sleep well?"

"Very well, thank you." I lied, returning her smile. It was a relief to see Senna instead of Aster. Aster clearly didn't like me very much, and the feeling was mutual.

"I'm glad to hear it." Senna went back to tending her herb garden.

"Do you need any help?" I asked, moving closer to her.

"Could you hold this basket, please?" Senna asked.

"Yes, of course," I said.

"Excellent. I really need to trim the sage and rosemary." Senna went to work with her clippers.

"I noticed you have a patch of Camellia sinensis on the side of your house," I said.

"Yes, I put some of that in your tea last night," Senna said. "It's one of my favorite plants to work with."

"Mine too," I said. "It has a lot of benefits, and it's good for so many teas."

Senna chuckled. "You know your herbs! Are you a kitchen witch, too?"

"Oh, no." I shook my head. "I excel at many magical abilities, but cooking has never been one of them."

Senna beamed. "One more person for me to cook for, then!"

"If you don't mind it." My voice was shy. "I'm afraid I never took the time to learn. I was young when Marcella and I came here from Aileen. Then my sister married the King, and I never had to learn."

"I don't mind it in the least," Senna said. "I love cooking for people. What did you think of Cherida when you arrived? Did you get a chance to see much of the country?"

I shook my head. "No, Marcella and I barely had two coins to rub together when our ship landed. Some days we spent begging, others looking for work. Marcella finally found us jobs in the castle gardens. That was when the King took notice of her. So, when I finally had enough money to leave, I couldn't. At least, I didn't want to leave my sister."

"I understand," Senna said. "It sounds like the two of you were very close."

I sighed and shrugged my shoulders. "It was us against the world. I don't think that made us close, though."

Senna's cheeks flushed pink, and she lowered her eyes, looking embarrassed. We continued our work in silence.

"I've been thinking about our conversation last night," I said in a low voice, finally breaking the silence. "Senna, tell me the truth. Do you honestly believe there is no way to turn Snow White back into a human?"

"Oh, Ceridwen." Senna stood and gave me a pitying glance. She gently placed her hand on my shoulder. "I'm so sorry, but she was never human."

The world spun wildly for a moment. When I came too, I was still on my feet, but leaning into Senna's embrace. She had both of her arms wrapped around me.

"I'm sorry," I gasped, quickly straightening up. "I don't know what came over me."

"Don't apologize, please. You did nothing wrong." Senna's eyes were glassy, and she ran a shaky hand across her face.

A door closed loudly, and we broke apart.

"There you two are. I should have known." Aster made her way towards us, with Quincy at her heels. "I believe you'll be pleased with what we've managed to accomplish."

"What's that?" I asked.

"Well, there were a few women who were mysteriously impregnated around the same time as Marcella. After looking at a map, I triangulated the closest graveyard to each of you."

I drew my brow. "Do you think he's still there? In the same graveyard where Marcella and I saw him?"

"Oh, no, no, no. Of course not." Aster shook her head. "I did a tracking spell. It's not easy, you know. I had to scry him in a bowl of water first. Then I used the water to do a tracking spell."

"But, that's incredible!" I burst out. "That's a really advanced level of magic. Aster, I can't thank you enough."

Senna laughed and went to stand next to her wife. "She is quite innovative."

"What about Snow White?" I asked.

Aster shrugged. "For all we know, they could be together right now. If not, there's a chance he could give you some information on Snow White. What he's taught her, what her powers are, where she may be headed, those could be valuable details."

"I suppose," I answered, still skeptical. Aster's eyes were guarded when she met my gaze, and I got the impression she was hiding something.

Quincy shuffled his feet and cleared his throat. "It's a start but, Ceridwen, I need to speak with you before we leave."

Aster paled, a serious look on her face. Suddenly, she couldn't meet my eyes.

Feeling wary, I allowed Quincy to pull me around to the side of the house.

"What is it?" I asked. "Why does this conversation require secrecy?"

"Not secrecy, privacy," Quincy said. "Ceridwen, if you're going to come with me, there are certain rules you're going to have to follow."

I stepped back. "I don't like where this is going."

"I kill vampires." Quincy's voice was deep, husky. Sunlight fell across his face, setting off the gold in his eyes like hearth-fire flickering through a glass of whisky. There was compassion, pity, and sadness on his face, but also a stern determination that let me know he was unwilling to compromise.

I took another step back. "Are you asking me to let you kill Snow White?"

Quincy took a deep breath in through his nose and straightened his back. His broad shoulders flexed as he moved to his full height. "I am saying, the only way you are accompanying me one more step of this journey is if you swear an oath, an *oath*, Ceridwen, that you will help me kill any vampires we come across."

"No." I planted my hands on my hips. Heat rushed into my face, and I glared at Quincy. "You are in my employ. I am in charge! Not you!"

"I haven't taken one gold coin from you!" Quincy roared, his face twisting with rage. "This isn't about money! I do it because...because if I don't, then lives will be destroyed!"

"What about Snow White's life?" I screamed back.

"She's a monster!"

"No! I can help her! I can change her...make her into a golem...I can do something..." The words were tumbling out of my mouth so fast, that I didn't realize I had given away my plan until Quincy's eyes widened.

"So that's been your real goal all along." He said in a quiet voice.

I stepped quickly towards Quincy, grabbing desperately onto the front of his shirt. "You can bring me what I need. Cut out her heart, her liver, her lungs. Just bring me those three things and I can-"

"It's impossible," Quincy said in a flat voice. "It won't work."

"You won't try!" I screamed.

Frustrated, grieving, and about to burst into tears, I gave up on speaking to Quincy. Turning on my heel, I fled into the forest.

I wouldn't give him the satisfaction of seeing me cry.

19
MERCY

I didn't go far. After stomping angrily down a trail, I eventually stopped to curl up at the base of an oak tree. The trunk was wide; the roots delving deep into the ground. It was a comforting place to stop. It was here that I finally allowed my tears to flow.

Eventually, my eyes dried, and I stared up at the canopy of leaves above me. Various shades of green moved in the breeze, sometimes allowing a ray of sunshine through.

"I thought you might be out here." Quincy strolled leisurely down the path, his hands clasped behind his back. "Mind if I join you?"

I twirled a twig around my fingers, then flicked it away from me. "Fine."

Quincy collapsed beside me with a deep sigh. He moved like his body ached, though I suspected that wasn't true.

"You're sad about something," I noted. My tone was almost accusatory. What did *he* have to be sad about?

Quincy turned to look at me, and I saw the grief in his eyes. "I'm asking a mother to stand back and watch me kill her child. That is not something which brings me joy."

Tears pricked the back of my eyes, but I quickly blinked them away. "Then why, Quincy? Why won't you try to save her?"

"It's not for lack of trying, Ceridwen," Quincy said, his voice soft. "I've searched for a cure for years. I've looked everywhere, even talked to necromancers-"

I drew in a hiss of breath at the word *necromancer*.

"I know." Quincy nodded. "It's a dangerous art, unpredictable, unstable, and it rarely yields any good results. How can it? Everything is meant to end, to come to some sort of natural conclusion. Prolonging the inevitable goes against nature. I had to try, though. After all, who would know more about the undead than a necromancer?"

"So, you found nothing?" I asked.

"Believe me, Ceridwen, I wanted to." Quincy shook his head. "As I've said before, Snow White was born with one foot in the grave. The kindest thing we can do is help her the rest of the way in."

"How can you say that?" I asked in a thick voice. More tears spilled out of my eyes and rolled down my cheeks. "Do you even know what it's like to have a child? To remember the day of their birth, and watch them grow? To hope for every good thing for their future-?"

"Yes," Quincy said.

I stopped, my jaw falling open. "W-what?"

"Yes, I was a father." Quincy stared into the distance, a faraway look in his eyes. His voice was a rough whisper.

"I was married, Ceridwen. My wife's name was Mercy. We had a son together. His name was Milo." Quincy stopped, struggling for words.

Moving closer, I clasped Quincy's hand in mine. He gave me a gentle squeeze, then continued his story.

"It was in Theor. A new town was being built. We liked the idea of watching the place go up, of being one of the founding families. We thought about all the adventures we could have in this wild, untamed land."

"What about your son?" I asked in a whisper.

"Mercy was pregnant when we moved. Towns take a long time to build. We decided we wanted to live on the outskirts, sort of like where we are now."

Quincy paused. We both took time to glance around the forest and appreciate our surroundings.

"That sounds really beautiful," I said.

"It was." Quincy had that faraway look in his eyes again. "The house was finished just a few weeks before Milo arrived. I was very proud of myself for being able to give Mercy that. A safe place to have our baby."

Quincy stopped and ran a hand over his eyes. "When Milo was a few weeks old, I was out hunting. I came back after dark. From a distance, everything looked normal. But...the smell. I remember the smell. Like death and blood."

Death and blood. I shivered, recalling the dream I had the night Marcella died. "What happened next?" I asked.

"I went into the cabin." Quincy's words were slow, drawn out. The pain in his voice was evident. "It was dark. The fire in the hearth had almost gone out. Mercy was in the kitchen, slumped on the floor. Her hair was a mess. Her eyes were wild...vacant. Close to her chest she held...our son. Our Milo."

Quincy paused again. His back bowed as though the memory was physically painful. "It wasn't until I got closer that I realized they were both covered in blood, Milo's blood."

A hand flew across my mouth as a gasp escaped from my lips. "Oh, no...Quincy, I'm so sorry."

A muscle jumped in Quincy's jaw. He lowered his eyes to the ground. "At first I couldn't believe it. I just stared at them. I kept asking, Mercy, what have you done? Over and over. It must have taken her a moment to realize I was there. I want to believe she was horrified by her actions, killing our son the way she did. I need to believe that."

Quincy let out a deep sigh and shook his head. "I'll never know, though, because the moment Mercy realized I was there, in the room with her, she attacked."

"Your wife tried to kill you?" I asked.

"Yes," Quincy nodded.

"How did you stop her?" I asked.

Quincy didn't answer for a long moment. His face became hard, and his jaw clenched.

"I know what people say about me, Ceridwen." Quincy finally broke the silence. "They say I've looked death in the face, that I've walked through the flames of hell, and I've been marked by great magic."

"Yes, I've heard that," I murmured.

"I set our house on fire," Quincy said in a low voice. "I have walked through hell, Ceridwen, but hell was my home going up in flames with my wife's death wail echoing in my ears. It was only by a stroke of luck that I escaped. Although, as you can see, I've been marked. Not by magic, though."

Quincy reached up to run his fingers over the burn on his face. His eyes were rueful.

I was silent for a moment. "I'm very sorry to hear that."

Quincy didn't respond. He stared straight ahead, unmoving.

I drew my knees up to my chest and wrapped my arms around my legs. I let out a deep sigh. "Quincy, I can't promise to help you kill Snow White. I just can't. But I do promise to help you."

Quincy turned to me then. He gave me a sad smile and nodded his head. "I suppose that's all I can ask."

Standing to his feet, Quincy offered me a hand. I allowed him to help me to my feet. Together, we made our way back to the cottage. I knew it was only a matter of time before we were on the road again.

"Where is this vampire?" I asked.

Quincy and I were back inside the cottage with Aster and Senna. We all sat around the table, drinking cups of mead.

"Back towards the castle," Aster said. "If I were to guess, I'd say he's still in the same area he's been for the last fifteen to twenty years."

"Still?" I asked, my eyes widening. "That's bold of him."

"Vampires are immortal," Senna said. "They don't view time the same way we do. What may be a significant amount of time for us could be the blink of an eye for them."

"Let us not forget the vampire also has progeny in the area," Quincy said in a deep voice. "We know of at least two, though it sounds like there's more."

Quincy brushed a few braids back from his face. Pulling a scrap of silk out of his pants, he tied his hair off at the nape of his neck. I watched the muscles in his arms as he did this, fascinated with the way his broad shoulders flexed with each movement. Pale sunlight filtered in through a window, setting off the silver sheen in his hair.

My heart thrummed unexpectedly in my chest, and I quickly looked away.

"Dammit!" I snapped, recalling a long-forgotten memory.

"What is it?" Senna asked, leaning forward in her seat.

"I just remembered something. Something the vampire said the night Marcella and I went to the graveyard. He talked of speaking with a queen, *again*. Like it had happened to him before. I didn't understand what he was talking about at the time, but it makes sense now."

"Don't blame yourself, Ceridwen." Quincy turned in my direction, his dark eyes meeting mine. "You were too young to understand what you were doing."

"I was Snow White's age." I tore my gaze away from Quincy and frowned into my cup. What was wrong with me? Why did I keep staring at him?

"Well, rest here for a few days, please," Senna said.

Aster nodded. "You two should gather your strength before you leave. Especially you, Ceridwen."

"Oh, I won't argue with that," I said. "I'm not looking forward to sleeping on the ground again."

Quincy laughed and took a long swig from his cup. He gestured to Aster for more mead. "You bore it well, Ceridwen. I was expecting a noble like you to complain so loudly the dead would hear."

Aster laughed and passed the jug of mead to Quincy. "I'm surprised you let her come at all."

"Really?" I asked.

"Quincy likes to work alone," Senna said.

"Well, I'm afraid that I insisted on coming," I said with a smile.

Senna shook her head. "Oh, no, trust me. If Quincy didn't want you to come, you wouldn't be here."

"Senna, please." Quincy rubbed the back of his neck, a pained expression on his face.

"What?" Senna asked. "There's no shame in saying you wanted her to come-"

"Senna, darling, do you think we have any more of those cress sandwiches?" Aster interrupted.

"Oh, yes, of course. I'll go get them." Senna quickly shuffled to her feet and disappeared into the kitchen.

Aster shot an apologetic look towards Quincy, then took another sip of her mead.

I didn't say anything. Senna's words rattled around in my mind, and I was trying to figure out their meaning. After a while, as the conversation drifted, I gave up. There were more important things to think about.

Like how Quincy and I were about to hunt and kill a vampire.

20
HONEYCRISP TAVERN

A few days later, Quincy and I were on the road again. Our second journey was less difficult, as my muscles had hardened. Spending all day on a horse, and all night on the ground, didn't bother me as much as it once had.

Still, as we rode into town, I couldn't deny feeling relieved.

"Oy!" One townsman shouted on our way in. "You two from the big city?"

"No, we're not," Quincy answered in a deep voice. He straightened his back and rolled his shoulders, as if daring the man to challenge him.

"I- uh-" the man stuttered, his eyes taking in Quincy's muscular frame, and Scout's giant figure. "Well, I just thought I'd ask. They have the plague up there, you know."

"No, I didn't know," Quincy growled. He grabbed my reins and urged our horses forward.

"Quincy," I asked in a quiet voice, "Where are we going?"

"There's a tavern up here, it's called the Honeycrisp. We'll get a room and stay here while we hunt for our vampire," Quincy murmured back.

I frowned. "We're close enough to Easton Manor. We could go there."

Quincy laughed. "Do you really think that's a good option?"

"No," I grumbled in a low voice. I desperately missed having a soft feather mattress to sleep on. Even though staying at a tavern was our best course of action, being this close to my grand estate made me resentful of our circumstances.

"Cheer up, we're nearly there." Quincy led our horses down a main street until we came across a two-story tavern.

"The bar is on the first floor, the inn on the second," Quincy said. He dismounted from Scout, then came around to help me down from Buttercup.

"This place seems familiar," I said, looking around.

"Does it?" Quincy sounded amused. "Did you come here often, then? Mingle with the peasants?"

"No," I scowled. "Perhaps I've driven by this place before, and am only half remembering it."

"All right, if you say so," Quincy chuckled. He held his hands out to me, and I slid into his arms.

Quincy took our reins and tied them to a hitching post. "Let's go get checked in."

I followed closely behind Quincy as we stepped into a smokey room. There was a roaring fire in one corner, with a cauldron over it. Next to the fireplace was a bar. A man stood behind the counter, a pipe hanging out of his mouth as he wiped down mugs with a filthy rag. I wrinkled my nose as we approached him.

"Excuse me, I'd like a room," Quincy said. He spoke in the deep, commanding voice he used when he didn't want anyone to argue with him.

The barkeep looked up, then did a double take. His eyes raked across my figure, his piggy eyes glinting with anger. I had to suppress a shudder. His look wasn't one of sexual desire. He was unhappy with the color of my skin, and where I came from. I braced for him to say something, but then his eyes landed on Quincy's giant frame, and the ax that hung at his side. The barkeep took a step back. Throwing down the rag, he took the pipe from his mouth.

"How long will you be needing the room for?" The barkeep asked.

"Not sure." Quincy shrugged. "We'll take the daily rate."

"Daily rate, huh?" The barkeep tilted his head, looking me up and down. "She a whore, then? Not sure how I feel about that. We already have an Aileenian whore sitting on the throne-"

"*Excuse* me!" I interjected. I clenched my fists, anger heating my blood.

I didn't get any farther than that, though. Quincy flung himself forward, grabbing the back of the barkeep's neck, and slamming his face into the counter. I gasped when blood spurted from the man's nose.

The barkeep yelled and attempted to retreat, but Quincy wasn't having it. He kept his grip on the back of the man's neck, forcing him to stay bent over, with one cheek pressed against the countertop. Using his free hand, Quincy yanked a knife from his side, the one the size of my forearm, and buried the blade into the polished wood, inches away from the barkeeps' wide, frightened eyes.

"Speak about the lady like that again, and they will be the last words you ever say," Quincy growled.

"Right, er…sorry!" The barkeep gasped.

Quincy released his hold on the man, who backed away, gasping.

"O-one bed then?" The barkeep asked.

Quincy hesitated, but only for the tiniest fraction of a second. I doubted the barkeep saw it. He nodded. "Yes, my wife and I would like a room with one bed."

I kept very still when Quincy spoke. I didn't want to give these people any reason to question us or doubt our identities.

"I think we'd like a discount as well," Quincy said.

"O-of course." The barkeep said. "I'll have one of the girls show you the way."

A sweet girl named Anya scurried forward to greet us. She had us follow her up a staircase, then showed us into an empty room.

Quincy rubbed the back of his neck. "Sorry about the room arrangement. I'll sleep on the floor."

I put my things away and folded my hands together. "Please, don't apologize. It was a good lie, actually. If we had shown up and asked for a room with two beds, people would question why we were traveling together. It would attract unwanted attention."

"That's what I was thinking." Quincy threw his bag into a corner and rubbed the back of his neck. "You want to go downstairs and get some dinner?"

My stomach rumbled, and I nodded. "Yes, I'm starving."

We trotted back down the staircase, and Quincy ordered in his deep, commanding voice. Our food was brought to us quickly, and we settled down to eat.

As we ate, the door to the tavern was blown open, and a woman entered. She had round, rosy cheeks and a bright smile. Yet, there was something offputting about that smile. She was of medium height and medium build, with dark blonde hair and greenish-blue eyes.

"Good evening all, what a blessed day it is! But then, all days are blessed when the generous and kind Queen Ceridwen is on the throne, looking after our country and future heir, Princess Snow White."

My eyes widened, and the man next to Quincy choked on his drink.

"Who is that?" Quincy asked. He narrowed his eyes, instantly suspicious.

"Oh, don't pay her no mind." The man next to Quincy said. "That's our poor Gerta. Cursed, she is, ever since she went to work for that monster, the queen."

"I beg your pardon?" Quincy asked. There was no reprimand in his voice. He appeared more confused than ever.

"When Queen Ceridwen was a duchess, our Gerta worked for her as a cook. She was a staunch opposer to the Starbright sisters. One day, the poor girl returned from Easton Manor and was never the same. All she wants to do is praise the Starbrights, talk about how gracious and generous they are." The man snorted into his cup of ale. "Makes me sick, it does."

Finishing the rest of his drink, the man stood up and moved away from us.

Quincy turned to me, his eyes hard. "What did you do to that poor woman?"

I scowled at him. "She's hardly an innocent. If Gerta had her way, this country would be fighting a civil war. I did the kind thing. I turned her into a golem."

Quincy leaned in closer to me, his eyes burning. I leaned back, not liking the look on his face.

"Look at her. Does that seem like kindness to you?" He hissed. "How long has she been this way?"

I shrugged. "If I'm being honest, I forgot all about her."

"Dammit, Cer- Just, dammit." Quincy put his fist on the table, his face twisted with rage.

"You weren't there!" I objected. "She was telling everyone that Snow White was a monster, that Marcella conceived her through evil magic-"

"So you killed a woman for telling the truth." Quincy interrupted.

I placed my hands flat on the table and stood to my feet. "You may not understand, but I will never regret protecting my stepdaughter, my *child*. I did what had to be done."

I spun on my heel and started to stomp away.

"Do you still feel that way?" Quincy asked in a quiet voice. "Knowing what your *daughter* has become?"

I paused, my eyes flitting across the bar towards Gerta. It caught me off guard to see her staring back. I squared my shoulders and lifted my chin. Gerta wouldn't give me away, of that I was sure. My magic would prevent her from harming me.

Gerta's face and expressions were the usual blank slates I had come to expect from my golems. Yet, there was something behind the emptiness that I recognized. It took me a moment to realize that seated deep in her eyes was a vicious rage and hatred. She was glaring at me.

I glared back. Damn heretic.

I decided against answering Quincy. Instead, I stormed away and went back to our room.

Quincy came in sometime during the night. He was so quiet that I didn't wake, his hunter's reflexes allowing him to move effortlessly through the dark room. It wasn't something I noticed until our stay with Aster and Senna, when our daily schedules and sleep routines were no longer required to be in sync with each other.

We didn't get a chance to speak in the morning. I woke and used the washroom, stepping over Quincy on my way out. He was sprawled across the floor, sound asleep. When I returned, he was gone.

Around midday, after I had eaten a light lunch, Quincy finally returned.

"Where have you been?" I asked from my seat at the window. I held a book in my hand that one of the serving girls had loaned me.

"I've been out gathering supplies," Quincy answered. He tossed a roll of cloth onto the small table next to the fireplace and collapsed into a chair.

I snapped my book shut and turned towards him. My voice was cool when I spoke. "I thought you might have been avoiding me."

Quincy paused. His eyes turned in my direction, conveying an air of annoyance. With a sigh, he pinched the bridge of his nose and tilted his head down. His long, dark braids were loose, and they swung forward to obscure his face.

"This morning I was," Quincy said. "I've had all day to think about it, though. It gives me no pleasure to say this, but I don't know if I would have acted any differently in your shoes. If the opportunity to save my wife and child presented itself, I don't know how I would react."

I let out a sigh and shook my head. "You're Quincy Pollux. You would have done the honorable thing. Not like me. I was selfish and cruel for years, and many have paid the price because of it."

"I don't deserve such praise, Ceridwen," Quincy said. He brushed his braids back from his face, allowing me a glimpse of his dark, tumultuous eyes. "I would let cities burn, and rivers flow red with blood, to have my family back."

I stood up from my seat by the window and smoothed my dress. "Well, I suppose what's important is that we're trying to rectify the situation we are in now. Speaking of what we could have done, or what might have been, is pointless. It will only break our hearts, imagining how life might have turned out for us."

"You're right. We should get started." Quincy said. He moved towards the table, gesturing at the roll of cloth he had brought with him. "Because vampires are ruled by the moon, I went to see a solar witch."

I moved to Quincy's side and watched as he unrolled his bundle.

"This is solar water, infused with sunlight." Quincy held up a bottle of water. Settled at the bottom were diamonds and hawthorn sticks inscribed with Huath. "Vampires can be killed with fire, so anything imbued with sun energy burns them."

"Even water?" I asked.

"Even water." Quincy nodded and turned back to his bundle. "Two citrines, I assume you know what these are for?"

"They are sunstones. They hold solar energy." I said.

"Good," Quincy nodded. "Here, take one and keep it close to you."

I did as he requested, dropping the heavy stone into my pocket. The crystal was buzzing with sunshine and energy.

"I went to an alchemist for this," Quincy said. He pulled out a silver dagger and handed it to me. "This is for you."

I examined the pure silver, then set it down on the table. "It's beautiful. What does it do?"

"Almost every supernatural creature is vulnerable to silver. It weakens them." Quincy explained.

I nodded. "I'll wear it on my belt tonight."

"These are the last items I acquired," Quincy said. "They came from a greenwitch." His hand emerged from the cloth with two sharpened wooden sticks. They also had the symbol of Huath inscribed on them. "These are hawthorn stakes. You can stab these through the heart of a vampire to paralyze them."

I frowned. "Paralyze? Is that all?"

"Yes," Quincy said in a serious tone. "There are steps, procedures, to killing a vampire."

"What about your wife?" I asked. "You said she died in a house fire."

"Yes," Quincy said in a quiet voice. "Fire is the only sure way to kill a vampire. Most know how to use their powers to run away from it. Mercy was a new vampire, feral in every sense of the word. I don't think she had enough wits about her, or knew enough about her changed body, to understand how to save herself."

"So," I said, understanding dawning on me, "The surest way of killing a vampire is by paralyzing them, so they can't run away, then burning them to death."

Quincy ducked his head, his long braids obscuring his face. "Yes," His voice was hoarse.

My chest tightened. For a moment, there was no air in the room.

So this would be Snow White's fate. To be set on fire, alive, unable to scream or protect herself. Forced to suffer in silence to the very end.

I gripped the edge of the table and steadied myself. I took a few slow, deep breaths, then straightened my back. We were not hunting Snow White today. We were going after the vampire who impregnated my sister.

Quincy lifted his head. His dark eyes connected with mine. "Are you going to be all right?"

I was so angry that I almost hissed. Instead, I lifted my chin and clenched my fists.

"We are going after the monster who killed my sister. He deserves a slow death, and I am willing to give it to him." My voice was ice cold.

Quincy's face broke into a devilish smile. "Then I will show you how."

21
EVERALD THE VINDICATOR

Just before dusk, Quincy took me down to the stables. He saddled Scout, but urged me to leave Buttercup behind.

"You can ride with me," Quincy said, tightening Scout's stirrups. "My horse has hunted with me before. He knows how to behave, and he won't spook. I can't say the same for Buttercup."

I agreed, and Quincy boosted me into the saddle. He climbed on behind me, and we set off.

My stomach churned uncomfortably as Scout trotted down the road. Memories of a dark night and powdery snow, strewn with drops of crimson blood, filled my mind. I gave a little shiver and leaned back against Quincy's chest. His arms tightened around me.

Eventually, we came upon a graveyard. Quincy dismounted and helped me down.

"Here, take these," Quincy said. He handed me the bottle of solar water and one of the stakes.

"What about you?" I asked.

"I have a stake and a citrine stone."

"Shouldn't you have some water as well?" I asked, feeling worried.

"I'll be fine, Ceridwen."

"Quincy." I planted my feet and put a hand on my hip. "Now is not the time for grand gestures, nor am I a helpless maiden. Take some of this water. We must share our resources equally."

Quincy turned his head up to the sky, a pained expression on his face. He took out his green silk scarf and tied it at the nape of his neck, restraining his braids.

Despite his obvious annoyance, he made a striking figure. His rich, umber skin caught the fading light of the sun, highlighting an earthy undertone of copper. Gold danced across his dark eyes, like embers scattering across a night sky. His long braids shone like polished onyx.

Quincy's nose had obviously been broken at some point, but it looked perfect, and I couldn't imagine it any other way. Despite the burn on his face, I could make out a strong jaw and high cheekbones.

"I'm going to regret this," Quincy mumbled. He took a flask out of his vest and emptied the contents onto the ground. He let out a long sigh as he watched the mead sink into the soil. Taking the jar of solar water, he carefully poured some of its contents into his flask.

"There." Quincy re-corked the bottle and screwed the cap onto his flask. "Happy now?"

"Yes," I said, unable to keep the smugness out of my voice.

"Good." Quincy raised his head again. "The sun is setting. The moon should be out soon."

A shiver of fear worked its way down my spine.

"Get ready," Quincy said in a quiet voice. He pulled out his ax and turned in a slow circle, his eyes searching the graveyard.

I clutched the stake in my hand and summoned my courage. I wouldn't let this vampire get the best of me for a second time.

A sudden blur on our right had Quincy and I both spinning on our heels, weapons held high to fend off an attack.

My blood froze when I saw the vampire leaning casually against a gravestone. He looked just the same as he had 15 years ago. Long, black hair hung limply down to his shoulders. His skin was like parchment, and his eyes...

I had seen those eyes so many times in my scrying mirror, they were as familiar as my own. Pale, watery blue with a touch of amusement and an undertone of danger.

The vampire flashed his fangs at us in what could have been a smile. "Ah, after all this time, to speak with a queen again."

Rage rose like a viper in my chest. It took everything in me to not fling myself at this vampire and claw out his eyes.

"Don't speak to me like that." I snarled. "Don't you dare even think of taunting me with the same words you used on my sister."

Quincy was moving very slowly, trying to discreetly edge himself between me and the vampire.

The vampire smiled again. His fangs glistened in the pale moonlight. "Yet, you are queen, are you not, Ceridwen? Was that not your plan all along, to usher your sister to the brink of death, and take all that was hers?"

"Leave her alone!" Quincy ordered.

"Ah, there you are, the huntsman." The vampire sneered. "Yes, I've heard of you. I know what the people whisper when you draw near. Ridiculous claims of shadows fleeing from your presence, and evil trembling when they hear your footsteps."

"Not all," Quincy answered in a cool voice. "There are still some foolish enough to challenge the blade of my ax, and the accuracy of my aim."

"Foolish creatures?" The vampire raised an eyebrow. "Like your wife?"

Quincy started forward, but I grabbed his arm.

"Oh, you're very clever," I said in a condescending tone. "You know who we are, but we know nothing about you."

The vampire bowed, then. It was a very pretty bow, a single, fluid motion as he dipped down low, his back straight. For a moment, I saw the nape of his neck. Quincy stiffened, as though tempted to attack.

"I am Everald the Vindicator." The vampire said. The corners of his lips turned up in a hollow smile. "Do not bother asking from where I hail. You would not recognize the name of any country I gave you. I have seen kingdoms rise and fall during the course of my existence."

"Then tell me, why did you come to Cherida?" I demanded.

Everald shrugged. "Why not? It is a small kingdom, with few mysticmancers here. Gives a demon like me the freedom to move about."

Everald turned towards me, a gleam in his watery blue eyes. "Unless you've found a different word to call me by, Queen Ceridwen."

"I have," I answered. "Dead."

The vampire pulled his lips back from his teeth, baring his fangs. "I suppose you think you're going to kill me?"

I clutched the stake tighter in my hand. "Yes. I suppose you think you'll live to see the dawn?"

"I have seen dawns long before your birth, and I'll see dawns long after your death," Everald said.

"We'll see about that," Quincy said. His face hardened as he lunged at the vampire.

The blade of his ax sang in the night air as Quincy took one practiced swing after another. Despite his anger, he managed to stay in control of his weapon.

The vampire hissed and jumped back, barely dodging the blade again and again as Quincy advanced.

I stuffed the stake into my belt and pulled out the silver knife. I rushed forward, intent on helping. This monster killed my sister. I would not allow Quincy to take him down without me.

Summoning my magic, I moved at an inhuman speed, darting behind Everald. I raised my knife high in the air, then sank the blade between his shoulders.

The vampire screamed. It was an unearthly scream, seeming to bubble up from the depths of hell and shaking the earth beneath our feet.

Quincy used the distraction to push his advantage. His ax came up, and the blade buried itself in the vampire's chest.

Everald's head rolled, his blood-red lips gaping, his fangs bared. He gave a horrible, wheezing gasp. His body jerked, as though caught in the throes of death.

"Ceridwen," Quincy gasped, "The stake! Now!"

I was confused at first, until I realized Quincy wanted me to stake the vampire in the back. My hands fumbled at my belt. I had just grasped the hawthorn rod when the vampire let out another roar.

This one was filled with rage. He brought up his leg, kicking Quincy in the stomach.

"Ooomph!" Quincy flew several feet through the air, then landed on the ground. He rolled several times before coming to a stop, and lay motionless.

"No! Quincy!" I shouted.

Leaving my silver knife stuck in the vampire's back, I attempted to dodge around the creature and rush to Quincy's side.

"Not so fast!" Everald snarled. He grabbed a handful of my long hair and flung me to the ground. I screamed as pain lanced through my skull and my legs flew out from under me. The breath was driven out of my body as I landed on my back.

"Oomph," I resisted the urge to curl up into a ball. Instead, I rolled onto my stomach and crawled towards Quincy.

"Did you really believe you could challenge me?" The vampire snarled. He lifted his foot and attempted to bring it down on my leg.

I rolled out of the way and quickly got to my feet. My heart was hammering in my chest. My legs and hands felt shaky. I clutched the wooden stake tightly, holding it to my chest. A quick glance at Quincy told me he was still out cold. It was just me and the vampire.

"You- you hurt my family!" I gasped. "You took advantage of my sister during a vulnerable time-"

"Hahaha!" The vampire let out a long, drawn out laugh that sounded more like a cackle. He sneered at me. "Your sister came to me willingly, as did you."

"She didn't know what she was doing, what she was sacrificing-" I argued.

"Oh, she knew." The vampire smiled, showing his teeth and fangs. "You don't know what plans she whispered to me during the long, dark nights. She was desperate, all right. Desperate for power, for an heir that would bring Cherida to its knees, and all of Aileen as well. She wanted the entire world to bow to her, and a child of power that she could wield as a weapon."

"Liar." I choked out.

"Think about it, Ceridwen. She could have had a bastard with anyone, yet she chose me. A demon, a vampire."

"You're disgusting," I whispered.

"I promised her a child of great power." Everald went on. "I didn't promise she would live to see that child's full potential."

My hand grasped the solar water at my belt. In one fluid motion, I used my thumb to push out the cork, and I flung the contents at the vampire.

"Ahh!" He shrieked. The water landed across his face. His paper skin burned and blistered, and peeled away until I could see teeth and bone. The vampire turned and twisted, his body jerking in agony.

I rushed forward, lifting the stake in my hand.

"No!" Everald shrieked, baring his teeth at me. He brought up his hand, his palm slamming into my chest.

I flew through the air before finally landing on the ground. I rolled several times, then gasped and choked as I fought for air. Curling up on my side, I tried to catch my breath.

Everald jumped and landed at my side. He grabbed me by the throat, wrenching me to my feet.

Real terror rushed through me. This is exactly how he was holding Marcella when he bit her.

There was a pounding of hoofbeats against the ground, and then Scout was there. He reared up on his hind legs, blocking out the moon and stars with his giant body. There was a flash of silver as he waved his hooves in the air, and then he struck the vampire in his head and ribcage.

"Ah!" Everald shrieked, smoke rising from his injuries.

We both hit the ground. I quickly rolled away and watched as Scout tried to trample Everald.

"Enough!" Everald screamed. He jumped high in the air, landing behind Scout. Before the horse could pivot, Everald kicked him in the back of his leg. A loud *snap* echoed through the air, and Scout collapsed to the ground with a scream.

"No!" I shouted.

Everald reached behind him and pulled the silver knife from his back. He dropped it to the ground with a hiss and turned his pale eyes on me.

"You," the vampire snarled. He flitted across the graveyard using his vampiric speed. Grabbing me by the throat, he slammed me up against a tombstone.

I gasped as the back of my head bounced off the granite. For a moment, my vision swam. I clawed at the hands denying me air, but to no avail.

"You say I'm the monster, but you are the one who led your sister to her death!"

"No!" I choked out.

"You went to the graveyard with her willingly, then did nothing to stop me. She protected you with hawthorn and solar water. What did you do? How did you protect her when you saw her wasting away?"

"Shut up!"

"You stole all that was hers." Everald sneered. "Her crown, her husband, you even raised her daughter as your own. Though, from what I hear, not well-"

I screamed in rage. The citrine in my pocket was hot and vibrating as I absorbed the energy into my body. My hand glowed like hot metal in a blacksmith's forge. Heat rolled off of me in waves.

The vampire's eyes widened, but he didn't have time to react. He was fast, but my magic made me faster. My hand darted out. I punched a hole in his chest and through his ribcage.

There was no blood, no warmth, no life, only a chasm with a deathly chill to it. My fingers curled around something cold where a heart should be. I yanked the organ from his chest.

The hands at my throat abruptly left off. The vampire's eyes glazed over, his lips paled.

Swiiiing.

Quincy appeared, rising out of the darkness with a monstrous look on his face that was terrible to behold. His eyes scorched me with their heat, and his lips were twisted into a deadly scowl. In that moment, he was the huntsman I had heard about, the one the shadows fled from.

The *swiiiing* I heard was Quincy's ax moving through the air. The blade cut cleanly through Everald's neck and decapitated him. There were two thumps as the vampire's body hit the ground, followed by his head.

I gulped for air, shocked at what had happened. It wasn't my first time ripping a heart from someone's chest, but it was my first time feeling like I had plunged my hand into death itself.

The heart I held was blackened, like charcoal. The smell of rot filled the air.

"Ceridwen?"

"Quincy," I said in a high, nervous voice. "His heart is dead."

"I know."

"No, you don't understand. This is wrong. His heart shouldn't look like this. It's dead, Quincy, it's d-"

"Ceridwen, I know. I *know*." Quincy emphasized.

I was such an idiot. He was a hunter, a vampire hunter. Of course he knew what an undead heart looked like.

Quincy pulled a pouch out of his belt and held it open for me. "Put it in here."

I dropped the heart into the bag, and Quincy pulled the strings shut. "We need to check on Scout."

Quincy and I both stumbled our way towards the horse and collapsed at his side. Scout was breathing heavily, his eyes wide, but he didn't spook as I drew my hand along his neck.

"Can you help him?" Quincy asked. He tried to remain composed, but there was an undertone of desperation in his voice. He riffled through the saddlebags, then pressed a howlite crystal into my palm.

I nodded, feeling out the stone's energy. "Yes, it won't take long."

Standing, I went to crouch down by Scout's injured leg. I held my palms out, channeling the energy from the stone into me, and then into Scout's injured leg.

A minute later, Scout snorted and surged to his legs. He shook his mane and turned to nuzzle me in my chest.

Quincy released a great sigh, burying his face in Scout's neck.

"Luckily, it was just a broken bone," I said. "Simple injuries where the body will heal on its own are easiest to fix. A life-threatening injury, such as damaged organs or disease, requires more complex magic, and the patient can't always be saved."

Quincy drew in a ragged breath. "Thank you."

"Of course," I answered. Pointing to Scout's hooves, I asked, "The horseshoes, they're silver?"

Quincy looked up and nodded. "Yes, they are. Come, we need to build a pyre."

I stood next to Scout, shivering, as Quincy went into the nearby woods. He quickly felled several small trees and arranged them to look like a bed.

"Ceridwen, come stand next to me," Quincy said in a gentle voice.

Trembling, I moved to his side.

Quincy held up the bag containing the vampire's heart. "This goes underneath the pyre. It will burn first."

Quincy kneeled on the ground and shoved the small bag in between a couple of sticks and in a pile of tinder.

My throat was tight. I could feel my chest rising and falling, but it didn't feel like any air was making its way into my lungs. My vision was becoming foggy, and the ground was tilting at an odd angle-

Quincy caught my elbow. He was standing in front of me, crouched down a little, so we were at eye level.

"Don't faint, Ceridwen," Quincy said in a low voice. "I'm sorry, you've already done so much tonight, but I need you right now. We must burn the body."

Quincy put his hand on the back of my neck, then moved closer to gently press his lips to my forehead.

He had never touched me like this before. His kiss was warm and gentle. I breathed in his scent of tobacco and leather. Lifting one hand, I wrapped my fingers around his arm. Leaning into his broad chest, my body relaxed.

Quincy bowed his head so he could rest his forehead against mine. We stayed like that for a long moment, drawing strength from each other.

At last, Quincy drew in a deep breath and stepped away. "Stay here. I'll be right back."

I followed him with my eyes as he walked over to where the vampire had fallen. He grabbed an ankle, and a fistful of hair, then dragged the body and head over to the pyre.

Quincy tossed the head onto the wood stack and heaved the body up with minimal difficulty. He then moved back to my side.

"All right, Ceridwen." Quincy said. "To kill a vampire, you need to do three things. The first is to remove the heart, which you've already done." Quincy pointed to the smaller mound on the ground where we had placed the pouch. "Next, remove the head from the body."

"That was your fine work," I said in a quiet voice.

"Yes, now the last step is to burn the remains." Quincy fished the citrine out of his pocket and pressed it into my hand.

"Just do what you did earlier." He spoke in a calm voice. "Channel the energy into you, then light the pyre."

I breathed in deeply through my nose, then cupped the citrine in both hands. I felt the crystal buzz with energy and began taking it into myself.

It was instant relief. Sun energy provides vitality, life, and warmth. It soothed the aching in my bones and relaxed my tense muscles.

I took another deep breath, relishing the feeling of vibrancy flowing through me.

Exhaling, I released the energy. The pain, aches, and soreness returned to my body. Sparks floated from my palms and onto the pyre. The heart I lit up first, followed by the head and body.

In a very short time, a roaring fire was before us, and a little more evil was eradicated from the world.

Quincy and I stood side by side, watching the flames. We didn't speak, but Quincy's hand found mine, and our fingers entwined around each other. After all the horrors we had endured that night, I found myself grateful to be standing next to him.

22
SUNRISE

We stood by the fire for some time before Scout joined us. He went to Quincy and nuzzled him in the chest.

"Good boy," Quincy said, rubbing the horse's neck. He reached into the saddlebags and produced a lump of sugar, which Scout happily devoured.

"He was very brave tonight," I noted. "You were right. He knew what to do."

"Scout is descended from a line of great war horses. I've had him since he was a foal. A Lord offered him to me as payment for ridding his lake of a rusalka."

"That explains why he is so brave," I said, stroking Scout's long nose.

"He was not the only brave one tonight," Quincy said. He turned to look at me. "You did remarkably well. Better than I expected."

I raised an eyebrow. "Did you expect me to fail?"

"What I didn't expect was to be taken out of the game so early." Quincy rolled his shoulders and grimaced.

"Are you in much pain?" I asked.

"Nothing I can't handle," Quincy muttered in a low voice. He shuffled his feet and cleared his throat. "I was surprised by what you did with your hand and the citrine. The way you used the energy to pull out the vampire's heart was absolutely inspired." He finished with a light chuckle.

Coldness enveloped me, and my stomach hollowed out. I bit down on my bottom lip to stop a shiver from running down my spine.

"What is it?" Quincy asked, sounding worried. "Ceridwen, I'm sorry. Did I say something-?"

"I can't do this." I blurted out. "Quincy, I'm the one who's sorry. I shouldn't have come tonight-"

"Ceridwen, if you hadn't come tonight, Scout and I both would be dead," Quincy said in a firm voice. He moved in front of me, placing his hands on my shoulders. "Tell me what's going on. Why are you so upset?"

Tears welled in my eyes and spilled down my cheeks. They felt ice cold in the night air. Quincy wiped them away with the pad of his thumb.

"I can't do this," I repeated. "Not to Snow White. Quincy, I can't kill her. She is a daughter to me. The thought of reaching into her chest, plunging my hand inside of her, feeling her cold and dead-"

I buried my face in my hands, dissolving into sobs. Quincy put his arms around me and tucked me under his chin.

Eventually, my sobs subsided. I pulled away, swiping a hand across my face, and staring into the sky.

"You know, all this time, I've been holding out hope that I could find a way to save her," I whispered.

"I know," Quincy said. "You're a mother, so of course you would have."

I closed my eyes, and a few more tears escaped down my cheeks.

"When I pulled out Everald's heart, saw it blackened and cold and dead, that was the moment I knew. Vampires have their own magic. I can't combine it with mine to create a golem."

Quincy released a deep sigh, his shoulders sagging. "That's why I wanted you here with me tonight. So you could see firsthand what we were going to be up against."

A sob lodged in my throat. "It's all been for nothing. My sister begged me on her deathbed to protect Snow White. All I've done is fail them both."

"No, Ceridwen, don't say that," Quincy said. He cupped my face in his hands, staring deeply into my eyes. "You couldn't have known what Marcella had done, or what Snow White would become. The blame for this does not fall on your shoulders."

"Everald said I took everything my sister wanted for myself. He was right. Her crown, her husband, her child. I stepped into Marcella's shoes and replaced her.

Like she was nothing. Like she wasn't important." My words came out in short, painful gasps.

"No," Quincy shook his head. "You picked up where Marcella left off. You assumed her responsibilities and honored her memory."

"How can you say that?" I asked. "You know what I am, what I've done."

"I know *who* you are," Quincy said. "Who you are is a woman that always puts herself last. For all the time we've known each other, Ceridwen, you've never asked for anything. Every word out of your mouth has been about Snow White or Cherida."

A shiver ran down my spine. "What's going to happen to me, Quincy?" I asked in a small voice. "I'm going to be all alone in the world."

"You are a strong woman who has had to carry a heavy burden on her own for far, far too long." Quincy still cupped my face in his hands. He drew the pad of his thumb down my cheek, gazing intently into my eyes.

I noticed, not for the first time, how handsome Quincy was. Maybe he wasn't traditionally good-looking like Conrad or Liam, but he had a rugged attractiveness that I found irresistible. I reached one hand out to touch his braids. They were as dark and soft as a raven's wing, and the faded moonlight gave the appearance of silver threads being woven into his hair. His eyes, his eyes were like black velvet, soft and warm with hints of gold. His broad shoulders and strong chest offered safety and comfort.

Most importantly, Quincy was gentle. Yes, he was rough around the edges, but his abrasive attitude was rooted in the pain of his past and the loss of his family. Loss was something I understood very well. Despite everything, he still had a good heart. He was noble and honorable, and protective and caring all at once.

Quincy drew me against his chest, searching my eyes. When he spoke, his voice was low, husky. "I love you, Ceridwen."

His words were like a dream on the wind. My breath caught in my throat and I waited for the moment to be swept away. Surely, I didn't deserve something as good as Quincy's love.

As if sensing my thoughts, Quincy repeated his words. "I love you, Ceridwen. I don't know what's going to happen, but I do know that, for as long as I draw breath, I will not leave your side. There is no battle I would not fight, no terrain I would not brave, no danger that would drive me from you."

I couldn't speak. I could only stare at Quincy in shock. In his eyes, there was an urgency and a longing that surprised me.

Quincy's hands moved from my face down to my waist. His hands slid over my stomach, coming to rest on my hips. "Look at you," He breathed. "Bathed in moon and starlight. You're beautiful enough to kiss."

I drew in a breath, then leaned forward, pressing myself against Quincy's chest. I wound my arms around his neck. "So do it."

Quincy's lips met mine in an instant, creating a rush of warmth and electricity that spread through my body. His embrace grew stronger, pulling me closer and making my heart race. I could feel the strength in his arms, nearly lifting me off my feet. The air around us seemed to buzz with anticipation as our lips locked, creating a symphony of soft sighs and gentle gasps. The heady scent of tobacco and leather enveloped me, adding to the intoxicating moment. No one had ever kissed me like this before.

Despite his urgency, his need, his desire bordering on desperation, Quincy remained gentle throughout. His touch was unfailingly delicate and soft, his lips sweet and tender.

At last, we broke apart. I felt lightheaded and out of breath. I leaned into Quincy's embrace, and he held me effortlessly.

"I would follow you anywhere, just for the privilege of being by your side," He said in a quiet voice.

My hand came up to rest lightly on Quincy's cheek. "I love you. I love you like I've never loved anyone else. Before you came into my life, I didn't even know it was possible to care about someone this much. You mean so much to me, Quincy."

We stood like that for several heartbeats. Our bodies pressed together in a comforting sort of embrace.

At last, Quincy broke away. He peered out into the horizon. "The sky is getting lighter. We should leave."

I nodded. "Yes, let's go." I was suddenly anxious to be gone from this graveyard, and away from the monster that was the source of so much grief in my life.

I used magic to put out the bonfire, and Quincy checked to make sure the vampire's body had been reduced to ash. Then he boosted me onto Scout and jumped in the saddle behind me. He nudged the horse, who broke into a gentle trot.

As we rode back to the tavern, stars slowly faded from the sky. The blackness gave way to a deep blue. I couldn't help but think about all the people, sleeping peacefully in their beds, who would never know about the events which had transpired this night. They would never know about the evil lurking in the graveyard, or the people who had fought and almost died to rid the world of him. Or how, for the first time in a very long while, the sun would rise on a town that was infinitely safer.

The ride back to the Honeycrisp was a silent one, but it was a comfortable silence. I lay back in Quincy's arms, basking in the safety and love he offered.

It was still dark when we arrived, although some early risers were just starting their day. It wasn't until Quincy helped me dismount, and my feet hit the ground, that I realized how tired I was.

"You go ahead," Quincy said. "I'm going to groom Scout, then I'll be up."

I nodded, then went inside and up to our room. I changed into a shift, then used the washroom before finally collapsing into bed.

Despite my aching body and tired muscles, my mind was still reeling. Every time I closed my eyes, I saw Everald. Interestingly enough, it wasn't my near-death experience with him that haunted me; it was his words about my sister.

She could have had a bastard with anyone, yet she chose me.

The thought of Marcella wanting to rule Cherida, and conquer Aileen, seemed so farfetched at the time. Yet, could it have been true?

I curled into a ball under the covers. When was Quincy coming up? My heart ached for him. I didn't have these thoughts when he was near.

Rolling onto my back, I stared up at the ceiling.

It was only because the room was so quiet that I heard the door open. Quincy tiptoed into the room, then sat in a chair and began taking off his boots. He stripped down to his small clothes, then hesitated. Without a word to me, he grabbed a blanket and started to make his bed on the floor.

"What are you doing?" I asked, confused.

Quincy removed the scarf from his hair, setting his braids loose. I admired the way they fell around his face.

"Ceridwen, we've only just kissed," Quincy said in a slow voice. "It's been a rough night. You've been through an ordeal-"

"That's precisely why I need you right now," I whispered.

Quincy stared at the ground. "You might feel differently after a couple hours of sleep. We don't have to decide anything now."

"Quincy Pollux, you listen to me." I sat up in bed and swung my feet onto the floor. "I didn't tell you I loved you on a whim. It's not something I say lightly. In fact," my voice stuttered to a halt here, and I blushed. "That's the first time I've told anyone that I was in love with them."

"Ceridwen," Quincy's voice was deep and husky. He raised his eyes to mine. "You must have had suiters, a sweetheart, something-"

"Suiters, yes." I nodded. "Some were very dear to me."

Conrad's face flashed before my eyes. Sweet, loyal Conrad, who was everything a young lady ought to want. He deserved a happier ending.

I shook my head. "But I didn't love them, Quincy. They could never understand me, not like you. I knew, before we rode into that graveyard, I knew I loved you. That won't change. Not tomorrow, not ever."

Quincy turned his head away, looking conflicted.

"Please, Quincy, don't leave me alone tonight," I whispered. "I'm asking you. Come to bed with me."

It seemed to be my gentle plea that finally convinced Quincy. He stood to his feet and moved towards me at once. He crawled into the bed, gently laying me against the pillows. His mouth came down to claim mine, and he kissed me deeply until my head was spinning.

Quincy's hands moved up my body and underneath my shift. The tips of his fingers brushed across my hips and up my stomach. His touch was as gentle as morning dew drops. As he continued his tantalizing exploration, a wave of electricity surged through my veins, heightening my senses to a feverish state. My heart pounded in my chest, matching the rhythm of my ragged breaths. His touch set my nerve endings ablaze, spreading an intoxicating heat throughout my body.

With each brush of Quincy's fingertips, I quivered in response, yearning for more. A deep ache settled in the pit of my stomach, demanding to be sated. As his lips trailed along the curve of my collarbone, the warmth of his breath mingled with an anticipation that consumed me. It was a delicate dance between pleasure and longing, an exquisite torture that I willingly succumbed to. Every inch of my being was hyper-aware, as if every cell in my body was awakened, craving his touch. The sensations cascaded like a symphony, building in intensity with each passing moment. I could feel the heat radiating from my core, aching for his hands to venture further, to fulfill the intense desire that consumed me.

"Ceridwen."

I opened my eyes. Quincy was watching me carefully. He traced a finger down my cheek. Despite the darkness in our room, I could read the emotion in his eyes easily.

"Don't stop," I whispered.

Quincy nodded, then leaned down, brushing his lips against mine. It wasn't quite a kiss; it was so light. His breathing was labored, his body tense. I ran my hands down his bare chest and felt the pounding of his heart.

Quincy pulled my shift off over my head, then gazed down at my body. He ran his thumb down my lips, adoration in his eyes. "You are so beautiful."

I traced my fingers along the scars on his shoulder, then brushed my fingertips over the burn on his face. "So are you."

"Ceridwen-"

"That day at my estate, before we set off for Senna and Aster's place, you were standing in the window. Sunshine was all around you. I looked at your scars, and I wondered what it would feel like to touch them. After learning about your past, after what happened tonight, they feel like safety. They feel like strength and endurance."

Quincy brought his lips to my forehead and kissed me. "You are marvelous." He paused to shrug out of his small clothes, then slid back under the covers with me. He pulled me underneath him, his kisses becoming more urgent. One hand was wrapped in my hair, the other gripping my waist.

"I love you." He breathed into my ear.

"I love you, too."

Quincy moved his hand from my waist to my hip, and I opened my legs for him. He lowered himself between my thighs, and I gasped when he slid inside of me.

I closed my eyes, pleasure rippling through my core. It was as if his every touch, his every caress, had etched a memory that would be forever imprinted in my soul. With each breath, I could feel a profound sense of connection, a deep understanding that surpassed mere physicality. It wasn't long before waves of pleasure crashed over me, like the ocean breaking against a cliffside. I arched my back, crying out Quincy's name.

Our bodies rocked together in unison. There was no noise in the room besides our gasping breaths and pleasurable moans. Sweat pebbled our skin, and our bodies became slick with moisture.

At last, Quincy slammed his hand against the headboard, gripping it tight. His body tensed as he found his own release, and then he collapsed on his stomach next to me. Wrapped in each other's arms, we found solace and contentment, our bodies still humming with the echoes of our passion. The rhythmic rise and fall of our chests synchronized, creating a comforting lullaby. In that moment, our souls merged, entwined in a bond that transcended the boundaries of time and space. We curled up next to each other and drifted off to sleep.

23
LET THE PAST GO

Marcella stared out the window of my estate. "No one can imagine the things I've done to get where I am today."

I didn't speak. I only watched her with wide eyes, feeling as though I didn't know my own sister.

"I've ridden down to the gates of hell and danced with the devil himself."

"You've lain with a vampire," I whispered in a strained voice.

"I have elevated myself." Marcella beat a hand across her chest. "I will not share my glory! I've earned what I have!"

Then Marcella transformed. She was no longer dressed in queenly attire. She stood before me in plated armor with a drawn sword.

Next to her stood Snow White. My stepdaughter drew back her lips and bared her teeth, showing off her fangs.

"My greatest weapon," Marcella said, a crazed smile spreading across her face. "I will rule Cherida, and bring Aileen to its knees."

"She's not a weapon. She's our daughter!" I screamed in a high voice.

Marcella leaned down to whisper something in Snow White's ear.

Snow White turned to me. There was a hungry look in her eyes. She advanced on me.

"No!" I screamed.

Marcella was raising her sword high. An army appeared behind her. Screams filled the air. The clash of steel echoed in my ears. Dead bodies lined the streets.

Snow White hissed and lunged at me.

"No!"

I bolted upright in bed, covered in sweat. My heart was pounding, and my body was shivering with fear.

Blinking, I turned to look out the window. It appeared to be midday.

Quincy, where was Quincy? I needed him.

As if on cue, our bedroom door clicked shut. I spun towards the noise and saw Quincy emerge from the shadows. He set two bowls down on the table and turned to smile at me.

"It's lunchtime. I thought I would run down to the tavern and-Ceridwen? What is it? What's wrong?"

Without waiting for a reply, he crawled into our bed. Pulling me into his lap, he held me in a tight embrace.

Tears escaped from my eyes. I threw my arms around Quincy's neck and curled up into a ball.

Quincy rocked me back and forth, murmuring soothing words into my hair and brushing kisses along my temple. Finally, my heartbeat slowed and my breathing eased.

"I had a nightmare," I whispered in a small voice.

Quincy laid us down on the bed and tucked me under him. "About what?"

I sighed, turning my face into his chest. Despite my fear, I found his presence comforting.

"Everald."

Quincy tightened his arms around me. "He can't hurt you anymore. I'll make sure of it. Even if that means walking down to the ninth circle of hell and throttling him with my bare hands."

"It was what he said about Marcella." My voice was a whisper.

"What did he say?" Quincy asked.

My mouth went dry. I licked my lips. "He said Marcella could have had a bastard with anyone, but she chose him."

"Did he say why?"

"Yes." I closed my eyes, tears trickling down my cheeks.

Quincy brushed my hair out of my face and kissed the tears away.

"Everald said that Marcella wanted a child of power. One she could wield as a weapon, that would bring Cherida and Aileen to their knees."

Quincy propped himself up on his elbow and looked down at me. There was a note of horror in his eyes. "Why would she do such a thing?"

I rolled from my side onto my back and stared up at the ceiling. "I've been asking myself the same thing. If I were to hazard a guess, I'd say it had to do with our parents being burned at the stake."

"What makes you say that?" Quincy asked.

I heaved a deep sigh. "Because that was the first time Marcella had ever truly been helpless. After our parents were arrested, we were hunted like animals. Marcella and I were scared and hungry. We had to disguise ourselves and flee our home. We almost didn't make it out alive."

"That sounds terrible," Quincy murmured.

"Before that, Marcella was just a girl. Fifteen years old, the same age Snow White is now." I paused as pain lanced through my heart. "She was exceptionally beautiful, and charismatic. Many wished to court her, but of course, they couldn't until her sixteenth birthday. That was the law in Aileen. Our parents loved us. They provided us with a wonderful home, lots of love, and as many books as we wanted. We were taught many things, about midwifery, herbology, and astrology. Our lives were…well, they were perfect."

"Then your parents were taken," Quincy said.

"Yes, everything changed after that," I said.

"So Marcella wanted revenge." Quincy mused.

"When we landed in Cherida, Marcella began inquiring after work for us. She learned that King Iberius had a um…taste for Aileen women." I went on.

Quincy's face hardened. "Yes, Iberius wasn't shy about acknowledging his fetishes."

"His what?" I asked.

"His fetish, for Aileen women."

"What's a fetish?" I asked.

"Oh, um…" For a moment, Quincy looked lost for words. "It's when someone has a-a hyper-sexualized, um…obsessive, unhealthy attraction to a particular object or activity. In Iberius' case, he had a fetish for Aileen women."

"What does that mean?"

Quincy moved to a sitting position and pulled me into his lap. "Iberius hyper-sexualized the women of Aileen. He didn't see them as people, just a device of sexual gratification."

I frowned. "Oh, but…you're from Theor, and I love you."

"A fetish is compulsive and harmful. For example, I have dark skin." Quincy held out his arm. "See?"

"Yes," I nodded.

"Now, let's say that dark skin, and only dark skin, was attractive to you. In fact, you were so attracted to my dark skin that you had problems learning anything else about me, or seeing me as a person because you were always thinking about how turned on you are. That's a fetish, understand?"

"Yes," I nodded. "I just never thought of it like that before. Everyone knew Iberius had a preference, but I didn't know it was unhealthy. I suppose that's why Marcella was able to get us jobs working in the castle gardens. She thought she could use our looks and our culture to her advantage."

Quincy ran a hand through my hair and kissed the top of my head.

"Does that mean Iberius never loved my sister?" I asked. "That he just saw her as-as an object of sexual gratification?"

"Possibly."

I paused before continuing. "I think Iberius loved Marcella the best he could. In his last days, when he was sick and delirious on his deathbed, he called out for her often. Not to say that their relationship was perfect. Iberius was stubborn and demanding, and he took women to bed while Marcella was pregnant. But he never loved again, and in his last days, his thoughts lay with her."

"And what of your sister?" Quincy asked.

I squirmed uncomfortably. "Marcella kept a garden that she used to grow ingredients for love spells."

Quincy raised his eyebrows. "Are you saying Marcella spelled the King into proposing to her?"

"Well, he had a fetish. She wanted power." I shrugged. "Iberius also wanted an heir. He was older than Marcella by quite a bit, and he never had any children. Who knows what Marcella promised in exchange for a crown? Perhaps Iberius believed magic could cure his infertility. Maybe Marcella encouraged him to believe it could. Before he passed, Iberius said something. He told me I was always who I said I was. It made me wonder if Marcella had tricked him somehow, if she had promised him something she couldn't deliver."

"I guess we'll never know." Quincy nuzzled me and stood up from the bed. "They're gone, and we're here. Let's have some lunch."

"You're right," I said. "It's time to let the past go."

Quincy and I returned to bed after eating and didn't get up again until dinner. After, we headed straight back to bed and became entangled in each other's bodies.

What Marcella did, and her motives behind it, still bothered me. I tried ignoring the nagging theories that crowded to the front of my mind, but it wasn't easy.

Eventually, night fell. Quincy lay on his side, fast asleep, with one arm slung across me. I stared out the window, watching the stars wink on.

Well, there was nothing I could do about Marcella or Iberius, but I was in control of my own actions.

I slipped out of bed and pulled a dress on over my head. Quietly, so I wouldn't wake Quincy, I tiptoed out of the room.

A simple spell allowed me to pass through the tavern unnoticed. I went around to the side of the building and waited. I was barefoot, and I focused on the cool, damp earth beneath my feet. It felt good, invigorating.

At last, I felt her approach. It was easier to sense her this time, now that I knew what to look for.

I peered around the side of the tavern, not saying anything. The footsteps stopped in front of the door, then turned and shuffled in my direction.

I withdrew back around to the side of the building. A short time later, Gerta joined.

Rather, what was left of her.

"Queen Mother." Gerta greeted in a deadpan voice. Her eyes were flat.

"Hello, Gerta," I said in a quiet voice.

Neither of us spoke for a long moment. I looked up at the sky, then turned back to face my golem.

"Do you know what you are?" I asked.

"Yes."

"Tell me," I said. "Speak freely."

"Speak freely?" Gerta's face hardened, and her eyes flashed. "Never in my miserable existence have you allowed me such a privilege. Do you know what that's like? To have all my thoughts and feelings stymied, to be a puppet, capable only of repeating another person's thoughts?"

There was more emotion in her voice, though I could see she was putting a great deal of effort into remaining composed.

"No, I don't know what that's like," I said at last.

Gerta glared at me. "You asked if I know what I am. I am not Gerta. I have...traces...of her in me. But I am not her. I am a faded memory, a ghost, a flicker of something that was once real."

She stopped to jut her chin in the air. "I am not of the living world, not this one at least."

"What do you mean?" I asked.

The anger drained from Gerta's face. Now she looked upset. "I was once damp, spring earth, feeding the roots of plants. I was once a cloud, drifting through the sky. Then I was rain, falling to the ground and bringing life to nature. I was everywhere, all at once, connected to everything. Now, I am separate."

"What would you have me do?"

"Release me." Gerta breathed. "Take this half-life from me and allow me to return to what I was before."

I nodded. "All right, if that is what you wish."

Gerta's face smoothed out and became peaceful. "I am ready."

"You wish to begin now?" I asked. "Are you sure?"

"Yes."

I drew in a deep breath, then held out my hands. Sparks appeared like glowing embers on Gerta's skin, then drifted up into the night sky and dissipated. It was my magic leaving her body.

Gerta released a deep sigh, tilting her head up towards the heavens. "Thank you." She whispered. Then her body crumbled and became dirt once more.

24
FINDING LOST THINGS

I told Quincy what happened the next morning. He kissed me and said I did the right thing.

We spent the next several days in bed together, rarely leaving our room. Sometimes we made love, sometimes we talked about our pasts, and other times we lay quietly next to each other.

It occurred to me we should head back to Aster and Senna's cottage. Every time I considered broaching the subject, I remembered that our next course of action would be hunting Snow White.

It was so much easier to stay in bed, in our little corner of peace and bliss that we had carved out for ourselves. I wasn't ready for the outside world to intrude.

Sometimes, I saw Quincy looking at me with hesitation in his eyes. I knew he wanted to speak about what happened next, but he never could get the words out, and I didn't push him.

Staying in bed was just too much temptation.

After about ten days of this, I woke to a strange buzzing. It was like there was a pull from my belly button to my travel bag.

I groaned and sat up, feeling angry at having my sleep disturbed.

Quincy stirred, then propped himself up on his elbow. "What? What is it?"

"You can't hear that?" I asked in a groggy voice.

Quincy frowned and drew his brow. "Should I?"

"I suppose not." I swung my feet onto the floor, then shuffled towards my travel bag. Flipping the top open, I rifled around until I found what I wanted.

Pulling my scrying mirror out of the bag, I took a seat at the table. I used a book to prop up the mirror, then set a candle near it and lit the wick.

Quincy didn't say anything. He pulled up an extra chair and sat next to me, looking puzzled.

"Hello! Hello? Can you hear me? Is this thing on?" Senna's voice was shouting.

"I can hear you, Senna," I said in a tired voice. "What do you want?"

Quincy's eyes flew wide open. "Senna! Is that you?"

"Yes, it's me!" Senna continued, shouting at the top of her lungs.

"Ask them what's taking so long," Aster's voice cut in.

"Hold on, let me move the candle. We can't see you." I said.

I adjusted the angle of my mirror, then moved the candle until the light was shining in the middle of the glass.

Vaguely, I could make out Senna and Aster sitting close together, staring at me.

"Can you see us?" I asked.

"Yes, we can see you!" Senna yelled.

"You don't have to yell," I said, rubbing the sleep from my eyes. "What is it? Why are you calling us so early?"

"We hadn't heard from you. We were worried." Aster said in a cross voice.

Quincy rubbed the back of his neck, looking guilty. "Sorry about that. It was my fault, Aster. We uh...we got caught up here."

"Caught up?" Aster squawked. "What's more important than reaching out and letting us know you're still alive? Do you know how worried we've been-?"

"Aster!" Senna yelled. She clapped a hand on her wife's shoulder, effectively silencing her. The two women stared at me and Quincy with wide eyes. They appeared frozen in their seats, not saying a word.

Quincy and I glanced at each other. There was a look of slight embarrassment and adoration in his eyes. I felt my own cheeks warm, and I smiled.

"We can uh- we can discuss that later," Aster said. "How did things go with the vampire?"

"Well, we got a name. Said it was Everald the Vindicator. Didn't give us a country of origin. He fed us some ridiculous line about watching kingdoms rise and fall. It was boring to listen to." Quincy shrugged.

I went still and looked down at my lap. "He said more than that."

"Ceridwen," Quincy said in a quiet voice, "We don't have to tell them about that part."

"No, it's all right. I-I trust them."

Aster and Senna looked at me with wide, curious eyes.

"What is it, dear?" Senna asked.

I cleared my throat and straightened my back. "Everald spoke about my sister. He confirmed what we've suspected for a while. He impregnated Marcella. Snow White is not the child of Iberius."

"I'm sorry," Aster said, a spasm of pain crossing her face. "That must have been difficult to hear."

"It gets worse," I said, rubbing my temples. "He told me Marcella had plans for Snow White."

"Didn't some astrologers predict that Snow White was supposed to be a boy?" Senna asked.

I rolled my eyes. "I think they told the Queen what she wanted to hear."

"I've heard astrology is unpredictable when it comes to gender," Senna said.

"You're right." I nodded. "Gender is...well, it's more of a spectrum, really."

"What were the plans?" Aster asked.

"Apparently, my sister wanted to start a war." I grimaced at the thought.

Aster and Senna frowned at that.

"What about King Iberius?" Senna asked.

"I don't think the King would have allowed such a thing." Aster quickly added.

Quincy snorted. "Who's to say our beloved king wouldn't have mysteriously found his way into an early grave?"

I blanched at that and turned away. Quincy looked ashamed and rubbed the small of my back.

"I hate to say it, but I think Quincy's right," Aster muttered.

"Well, he managed to find his way into an early grave, anyway." Senna sighed. "It's no use dwelling on what might have been."

"Although, I suppose it is heartening to know that things could have been worse." Aster shrugged.

"Aster!" Senna's jaw dropped, and she turned to gawk at her wife.

"I didn't mean it in a bad way." Aster objected.

Quincy cleared his throat. "Look, ladies, I'm sorry I didn't reach out to you before. I didn't intend to make you worry. Tomorrow morning, Ceridwen and I will check out of here, and we'll head back your way."

Senna and Aster nodded.

"We'll see you soon, Quincy."

With that, my scrying mirror faded to black, leaving Quincy and me alone in our room. As I sat back in my seat, I clenched my shaking hands together in my lap.

The next vampire I faced would be Snow White.

It only took a couple of days to make it back to Aster and Senna's. I couldn't say whether the time passed quickly or slowly, only that I seemed to be in a daze for most of it.

We rode up to their cottage early enough in the evening that it was still light out, although the sun was just beginning to set. This time, I was able to dismount without Quincy's help.

"I'll take the horses into the stable and get them groomed," Quincy said, taking Buttercups' reins from me.

"Thank you, Quincy," I said.

As I walked up onto the porch, the front door swung open and Senna poked her head out. "Oh, you're here! Come inside. I'll put the kettle on and make some tea."

"Thank you, I would appreciate that very much," I said. Senna ushered me inside, and I took a seat at the table.

Aster sat in a chair in front of the fireplace. She watched me closely as I ran a weary hand down my face. "Senna, love, forget the tea. I've got something stronger."

"All right, I'll make some sandwiches then," Senna said from the kitchen.

Aster stood up and moved to a shelf. She took down a bottle with dark amber liquid in it. Grabbing two glasses, she filled them up and handed one to me.

"So, you took down the bastard that killed your sister," Aster said. She took a long swig from her cup, then sat back and watched me.

I nodded. "It wasn't easy, but we got the job done."

"That must have felt good," Aster muttered.

I put the cup to my lips and drank deeply. It was a strong mead. Heat rushed through my body, easing my muscles and clearing my head a little. "Yes, and no."

Aster was watching me again, a knowing look in her eyes. "So, have you finally accepted Snow White's fate?"

I hesitated, then nodded. "Yes, I have."

"It was my idea, you know. To send you and Quincy after a different vampire first," Aster said. "It was important to me that you understood what you were signing up for. For Quincy's sake, and your own. If you found Snow White, and decided you couldn't go through with it, if you believed for a second that there was another way, it would have risked both of your lives."

I frowned when Aster said this. "I suspected you were hiding something from me. You were right, of course, though it gives me no pleasure to say that. It's like you said during my first visit, there are no happy endings when you love a vampire."

Aster nodded. "So, now that you've dealt with...Oh, what was his name, Everald? Now that you've dealt with Everald, do you finally feel prepared?"

"To kill Snow White?" I shrugged. "I found a way to come to terms with it. Not just because of Everald, though."

"Then how?" Aster asked.

I took a deep breath in through my nose. "Gerta."

"Who's that?" Aster tilted her head to the side.

"She was a golem." I began. "I created her. To be honest, I forgot about her. Quincy and I ran into Gerta at the Honeycrisp. I went to her after we dealt with Everald. When I asked what she wanted, Gerta...she told me she knew she wasn't real. She wanted to be returned to what she was, earth and rainwater. I complied with her wishes."

I stopped to take another swig of my mead. "Quincy said once that Snow White was born with one foot in the grave. He was right. It's not natural. The way I see it, I'll be releasing her. She can't be in both worlds, half alive and half dead. It will be like...ending a curse, I suppose."

"Hm," Aster sat forward and put her elbow on the table. "That's a very noble thing to do."

"Is it?" I scoffed.

"It is." Aster nodded. "Because it will hurt you, and cause you pain, but you'll do it because you believe it's in Snow White's best interest."

"Thank you for saying that." I gave a brittle smile.

"Well," Aster shrugged and sat back in her seat. "You've grown on me, Ceridwen. I wasn't sure about you when Quincy first brought you here. I am now."

I smiled and held up my cup.

Aster gave a crooked grin, then sat forward and clinked her drink against mine.

Quincy came in then, the door slamming shut behind him. He moved to the table and sat beside me, slinging his arm across the back of my chair.

"You ladies talking business?" He asked.

Aster turned her eyes towards me, and I dropped my gaze into my lap.

"No," Aster said. "Business can wait."

Senna joined us at the table, bringing a plate of cress sandwiches with her. We sat and ate, enjoying each other's company. Yet as we drank and laughed, my thoughts kept turning to Snow White and how I was another step closer to facing her.

Aster and Senna were gracious enough to give Quincy and me a day to recuperate. We slept in, then got up and had a late breakfast.

Quincy groomed the horses and helped Aster with the chickens. Senna and I tended to the garden.

I sighed when I finally got a chance to bury my hands in the cold, damp earth. "Ah, this is better."

"Did you do much gardening at the castle?" Senna asked, working beside me.

I shook my head. "No, not after Marcella married Iberius. It was considered beneath our station, though I always considered it my true calling."

"Well, you're very good at it," Senna said.

"Thank you," I said in a quiet voice.

Laughter rang through the air. Senna and I both turned to see Quincy being chased by a rooster. He flailed his arms in the air as he ran around in circles. Aster was bent over at the waist, laughing until she was red in the face.

It was one of those moments in time that felt absolutely perfect. I watched Quincy run about the yard, a smile on his face, his long hair trailing behind him, glinting silver in the morning sun.

"I don't think I've ever seen our Quincy this happy," Senna said, a smile playing on the corners of her lips. "Oh, I don't suppose Aster and I can call him our Quincy anymore." She gave me a sidelong look, a sparkle in her pale blue eyes.

I blushed and bent over my work, not meeting her gaze. The thought of building a cottage with Quincy, of having our own chickens and herb garden, was such a tempting one. It made my heart ache to think about how easy our lives could be here, embedded in nature and each other.

It was not to be, though. I was still engaged to the King of Aileen. Amara needed me back at the castle. We would have to discuss how the Kingdom was to be run after Snow White was released from the land of the living.

The day passed by in perfect bliss. That night, as Quincy and I made love in the loft, I knew our time together was coming to an end.

The next morning, I woke rather early and made my way down the ladder. Aster was already up, rooting around in her jewelry box.

"What are you doing?" I asked, passing by her to join Senna in the kitchen.

"She's trying to find her copper pendulum," Senna explained. "Here, Ceridwen, can you flip the bacon?"

"Yes, of course." I threw on an apron and hurried to the oven. I put on a cheerful smile, hoping no one noticed that my heart had just dropped into my stomach.

A copper pendulum had many uses. Its main purpose was to find lost things.

A short time later, Quincy's voice made its way into the kitchen. I didn't catch his words, which led me to believe he was speaking to Aster and purposefully being quiet.

He needn't have bothered. I knew what today was.

Today, we were going to locate Snow White.

"I found it," Aster said, as Senna and I brought breakfast to the table. She held up the polished copper hanging from a silver chain. The end of the pendulum had been filed down to a sharp point.

Senna blanched. "Let's eat first. We'll need our strength."

My stomach was churning, so I was only able to get a few bites down, despite Quincy urging me to eat more.

"This spell is going to need quite a bit of energy." He explained, a worried look in his eyes.

At last, the dishes were cleared away, and Aster brought out a map of Cherida.

"All right." Aster rubbed her hands together, looking serious. "Snow White is of your blood, Ceridwen. I'll need you to prick your finger on the end of the pendulum."

I nodded and did as she requested. I winced a little as the copper cut into the soft flesh of my finger. Quincy rubbed my back, looking apprehensive.

I handed the pendulum, red with my blood, back to Aster. She took the end of the chain between her two fingers and held it over the map.

The four of us watched with bated breath as the pendulum began to swing back and forth. Eventually, the movements became a circle. It started out in a wide arc, encompassing the entire map. Eventually, the arc got smaller and smaller, until it was rotating above a small town several miles away from the castle.

"That's Honeyvale. It's about a ten-day ride from here," Quincy said, drawing his brows. He cast a worried glance in my direction.

"I can handle it," I said in a soft voice.

"When will you leave?" Aster asked.

Quincy hesitated. "Two weeks. That should give us enough time-"

"No," I shook my head. "We'll leave the day after tomorrow."

"So soon?" Senna asked, her eyes wide.

I placed my hands flat on the table and stared out the window. "The sooner we get this over with, the better."

No one said anything, but we all knew I was right.

At last, Quincy stirred. He nodded his head. "All right, Ceridwen. We'll go. The day after tomorrow."

25
THE BLACK BARREL

Quincy predicted the ride to Honeyvale would take ten days. I got us there in six.

As we rode into town, Quincy twisted around in his saddle to peer at me. "You've never used magic to help us travel before."

I shrugged. "Those other times I wanted to conserve my energy."

"Not this time, though?"

I sighed and squirmed in the saddle, trying to get comfortable. "I just want this to be over with. Besides, this is the first time we've had to travel more than a few days."

"Fair enough." Quincy turned back around.

We arrived at a tavern not long after. There was a large sign out front that read *The Black Barrel*.

Quincy and I went in, where we found a portly man working behind the counter. He had a wide nose, grey eyes, and a ruddy complexion from years of working in the sun.

"Hello, strangers!" The man looked up when we entered, and he set down the mug he was wiping down. "What can I do for you weary travelers this fine afternoon?"

"My wife and I would like a room," Quincy answered, the lie rolling smoothly off of his tongue.

"Yes, of course. We have plenty of those." The barkeep said. "How long will you be staying?"

"A few days at least." Quincy dropped some coins on the counter.

The man nodded and scratched his salt-and-pepper beard. "Upstairs, first door on the left. Business has been slow these past few weeks, so it should be quiet up there. My name is Thaddeus. Just holler if you need something."

"Thank you. We appreciate it, Thaddeus," Quincy said with a nod of his head.

We went upstairs and got settled into our room. It was a little dusty, and the furniture was worn from long use, but otherwise, it was clean and tidy.

"Did you hear what he said about business?" I asked as we got settled into our temporary quarters.

"I did," Quincy answered. "Which is unusual, considering this is a mining town. It should be busier."

I pulled a small bottle out of my travel bag. It contained crushed basil, star anise, and cloves.

"I suppose we should go downstairs and figure out what's wrong, then," I said.

Quincy chuckled and pulled me to his chest. He linked his hands at the small of my back. "Who knew traveling with a witch would make my job so much easier?"

"Probably quite a few people. You just lack imagination." I teased.

Quincy kissed me on the lips. "Come on, love. Let's go downstairs and see what we can learn from our host."

Quincy and I made our way back down to the tavern, where we took seats at the bar.

"Got anything to drink?" Quincy asked in a casual voice.

"Aye, that I do." Thaddeus quickly produced two mugs and filled them with mead.

"Have one with us." I encouraged with a smile.

"Oh, I shouldn't." Thaddeus hesitated.

"You'd be doing us a service. We're new to these parts." Quincy said.

"Hm, well." Thaddeus wavered. "Business is slow today, but then it has been for months. Eh, what the hell?" He shrugged, then grabbed another mug and poured himself a generous amount of mead. "So, what brings the two of you to Honeyvale?"

"We're searching for work," Quincy said. "We heard this was a good place to look for jobs."

"Er, well, yes." Thaddeus anxiously tugged at his salt-and-pepper beard. "Not much work around these parts nowadays. If you had gotten here a few months ago, I'm sure we would have had some openings-"

I waited until Thaddeus was fully turned towards Quincy, then discreetly poured my bottle of herbs into his drink.

"Unfortunately, the town has had a bit of trouble since then. Nothing to worry about, just a slow season." Thaddeus gave an uncomfortable chuckle, then took a long draught from his drink. He smacked his lips, then poured himself some more mead.

"This used to be a bustling city, you know," Thaddeus continued. "There's a coal mine outside of town. It used to bring in workers from all over. Of course, more people meant more commerce. The workers used to come to town, buy things for their families, and have drinks in my tavern."

Thaddeus paused, then shook his head. "I probably shouldn't be telling you this."

"That's all right, Thaddeus, you can trust us," I said in a honey-sweet voice.

Thaddeus took another long draught of his mead, having no idea it was spiked with a truth potion. "Oh, well, it's not like word won't spread anyway."

"That's right," Quincy encouraged. "You may as well tell us the truth."

"The truth." Thaddeus snorted. "The truth is, the miners don't come to town anymore. They don't come to my tavern, they don't spend money in shops, they don't travel to see their families. It's like they just locked themselves up in their lodging quarters one day, and that was that."

"Why don't they come to town anymore?" Quincy asked.

"Let me tell you something about our miners." Thaddeus went on, his voice stronger. "We used to have some turnover. Not a lot, just the usual. Some of the men were on a rotation. But us townfolk were used to seeing them around as they came and went. Now, we don't even get coal, so transport has dried up."

"What changed?" I asked.

Thaddeus leaned in close. "What's changed is, a monster has come to Honeyvale."

"What kind of monster?" I asked in a sharp voice.

"No idea." Thaddeus shrugged. "You wouldn't think it by looking at her. She's downright beautiful, almost ethereal. Like an angel."

"Can you describe her?" Quincy asked.

"Oh, sure." Thaddeus nodded. "Long black hair, red lips, dark eyes, too."

Quincy and I glanced at each other. It had to be Snow White.

"When did she arrive?" Quincy asked.

"Couple months ago, I believe," Thaddeus said. "She got here sometime after dark. Didn't talk much, just floated in looking like a goddess. Seeing her, it was like being hypnotized."

Thaddeus paused, his eyes becoming glassy. "She sure was stunning. Seeing her, being near her, it was like being under a spell. Hell, maybe we were."

"What happened next?" I asked, trying to keep the harshness out of my voice. I didn't like the besotted look on Thaddeus' face when he spoke about Snow White.

"There was a man with her. Tall, muscular, and covered in hair. Downright feral, that one, though the girl seemed able to control him. They chatted with some of the miners, and then they all got up and left together. That's the last we ever saw of 'em."

"The miners?" I asked, confused.

"The men, the newcomers, all of them," Thaddeus said, waving his cup around. "They all left together and haven't been seen since."

"What about the girl?" Quincy asked. He leaned forward, folding his arms on the counter.

"Ah, now that's the right question," Thaddeus said, a gleam in his eye. "Lots of folks packing up and leaving because of her."

"What do you mean?" I asked.

"The night that woman arrived in town, that's when the sightings started. Folks saying she's floating outside windows, asking to be let in. People are waking up in bed with bites on their necks and blood on their sheets. Some don't wake up at all."

Thaddeus stopped to shudder. "Those are the worst. The corpses with the blood drained out of them. Pale as cold wax, they are."

I glanced down at my lap, tears pricking at the backs of my eyes. Quincy noticed this and downed his drink.

"Thank you, Thaddeus. That will be all." Quincy took my arm and steered me up the stairs and back into our room.

"Did you hear the way he was talking about Snow White?" I asked, my voice shrill. "She's only fifteen years old. She's not a woman, she's a girl! A child, still!"

"It's not his fault," Quincy said in a low voice. "It's Snow White. Vampires have a way of making themselves appear desirable."

"I don't like it." I sat on the bed with a sigh. "Another thing I don't like is Snow White picking up a new companion. Who is this *feral* man, anyway? Why would Snow White take up with the likes of him?"

Quincy sat beside me on the bed and took my hand. "If I had to guess, I'd say he was a werewolf. Snow White came here looking for a lair, somewhere safe to hide during the daylight hours. A miner's lodging would be perfect. Hell, she could be sleeping inside the mine for all we know. Somewhere dark, and deep, where the sunlight can't reach her."

I frowned. "What do you think happened to the miners?"

"If I were to hazard a guess, I'd say she turned them into werewolves. So they could guard her during the day."

"Everald didn't have any werewolves guarding him."

"He was an old vampire," Quincy said. "He probably aged to the point where he felt he didn't need their protection."

"What are we going to do, Quincy?" I asked in a whisper.

Quincy stood up and went to the window. He looked out at the slowly darkening sky. "We're going to have to wait a couple of days for the full moon to pass. After that, we'll need to stage an attack."

"Right," I nodded. "Because werewolves can only change during the full moon?"

"That's correct," Quincy said.

"Will we be going at night?" I asked.

"Like I said, we don't know where Snow White is sleeping during the daylight hours. We'll go at dusk and dispatch the werewolves. After the sun sets, we'll draw Snow White out, and deal with her then." Quincy said.

I let out a deep sigh, then flung myself down on the bed, staring up at the ceiling.

"Get some sleep," Quincy said in a soft voice. He took a blanket and gently tucked it around me. "We'll figure it out tomorrow."

Quincy and I spent the next few days stocking up on supplies. Aster and Senna had sent us off with a large amount of solar water and citrine stones. In addition to our hawthorn stakes, Quincy also had a quiver full of hawthorn arrows tipped with silver and a crossbow. I still had my silver dagger and a leather belt embedded with carnelians, another sunstone. They glowed with life and light.

The day after the full moon, Quincy and I went down to the stables and saddled Scout. The sun was still in the sky, but just beginning to set.

I stroked Buttercup's long nose. "Sorry, girl, you're not coming with us this time." I murmured.

"Ceridwen, are you ready?" Quincy asked, leading Scout out of the stall.

"Yes, I'm coming." My heart lodged in my throat as I followed Quincy out onto the street. He boosted me into the saddle and pulled himself up behind me.

We rode in silence until we reached the edge of the woods. In the clearing, up against a mountain, was the miner's lodgings. We pulled up on the west side, so the lodgings were to our right.

Quincy dismounted, peering off into the distance. He ran his fingers along the handle of his ax.

"All right, Ceridwen. Remember, it's past the full moon, so the werewolves can't transform." Quincy said. "They'll be in their human form, which means their bite won't turn you into one of them."

"Right." I nodded. "Only a bite from a transformed werewolf can turn you."

"Exactly," Quincy said. "Now, you take Scout and ride about fifty yards east. On my signal, we'll attack. We'll be on opposite sides of the field, so the werewolves will have to split up. We'll both make our way towards the lodgings and regroup there."

I hesitated. "Quincy, are you sure this is a good idea-?"

Quincy kissed the back of my hand and looked into my eyes. "Trust Scout. He knows what to do and how to protect you. Remember, also, that I love you."

"I love you too," I answered in a soft voice.

Without another word, I nudged Scout in the side, and he set off at a trot. After assuming our positions, I glanced over at Quincy, waiting for the signal. My heart beat frantically in my chest.

A flaming arrow arced through the air, plunging itself into the ground and spreading fire across the clearing.

It was the signal.

Scout let out a wild *neigh* and plunged forward. To my left, Quincy sprinted forward on foot. He had the crossbow in his hands.

The door to the lodging house flew open, and twelve men poured through. But it was only in that first glance that they appeared like men. At second glance, I noticed the thick, dark hair that covered every inch of skin. Huge, bulging muscles contorted their bodies, giving them an almost deformed look. Their eyes had a wild, feral quality to them, and fangs protruded from their mouths.

As they bounded towards us, they folded over at the waist. A shiver ran through their bodies, and then...

The human-like bodies of the miners gave way, and their werewolf forms burst forth. They were snarling, slobbering, and three times the size of normal wolves. They were only a few hands shorter than Scout.

"Quincy!" I shrieked, twisting in the saddle.

What was this? What was going on? It was the night after the full moon. Everything I'd learned about werewolves told me they only changed when the moon was full. How were they doing this?

Quincy looked just as stricken as I was, but there was no fear on his face. He glanced briefly in my direction, then he notched another arrow.

That was all the confirmation I needed. Facing forward, I gathered my courage and focused on my task.

We were only steps away from each other now. Scout and I ran at full speed while the werewolves barreled in our direction, red tongues lolling and lips pulled back in a snarl. Then, all at once, we clashed.

Five werewolves surrounded Scout and me. They lunged at the horse, nipping at his legs and snapping their sharp teeth.

To his credit, Scout didn't spook for an instant. The horse struck the first werewolf that approached us with his front legs. As the werewolf fell to the ground, Scout stomped on him several times with his silver horseshoes. Smoke, and the smell of burnt hair, filled the air.

Another werewolf came up beside us and attempted to nip my leg. Drawing energy from my carnelian stones, I summoned a fireball and threw it at the creature. The fireball landed with a shower of angry sparks and flames quickly spread across his body, leaving the werewolf howling in agony.

Three more werewolves left. I glanced over my shoulder to check on Quincy. One werewolf was down, with a shaft sticking out of his eye. Quincy stood next to it with his ax out. He gave one mighty swing up and over his head, then brought it down, decapitating the animal.

Another werewolf was lunging at him. It jumped up, flying through the air, its jaws open and teeth glistening with saliva.

Quincy moved with a fluid grace that could only come from years of being a hunter. He thrust his ax back into his belt with one hand, the other was lifting his crossbow off the ground. One hand reached back to grab an arrow, which he notched and sent flying at the werewolf.

As the silver tip of the arrow went into the werewolf's mouth, Quincy stepped neatly to the side. The werewolf landed hard, skidding several feet across the ground. When the body finally came to a stop, the eyes were vacant and filmy.

Scout gave a sharp pivot, and I almost fell from the saddle. I lost sight of Quincy as I refocused my attention.

There were two werewolves in front of Scout. They bared their fangs and snapped at us. Scout was using his front hooves to kick and keep them at bay.

A third werewolf was slinking around behind us. He kept low to the ground, his hackles raised.

I summoned a large amount of sun energy from the carnelian stones. Power surged into my body, which was then summoned into my palms. As I held up my hands, I shifted my weight and leaned back in the saddle.

Scout followed my lead and hastily retreated two steps. A giant fireball burst forth from my hands, engulfing the werewolves in front of us. Scout then kicked out his back legs, striking the last werewolf. The animal screamed as the silver singed him. More smoke filled the air.

Jumping down from the saddle, I pulled out my silver dagger. Scout kicked the werewolf again, and I buried my dagger in his neck.

The werewolf gasped and swiped at me. I hastily retreated. The werewolf's body shuddered, then his eyes glazed over and he collapsed on the ground. A blood red tongue lolled from his mouth.

I rushed to Scout's side, pulling myself up into the saddle. Three more werewolves tumbled from out of the lodging house, snarling and snapping.

My heart jumped into my throat. I had forgotten to grab my silver dagger. It had been left in the decaying body of the dead werewolf.

As Scout and I prepared for this new onslaught, the sun dipped below the horizon and disappeared.

A howl filled the air. It was a long, commanding howl that stopped the remaining werewolves in their tracks. They gave us one last, slobbering snarl, then turned and disappeared into the mountain.

I spun towards Quincy, searching him out. He was pulling his ax out of a carcass. I counted three around him, and five surrounding Scout and me.

Eight dead werewolves.

Quincy started running towards the lodgings, and Scout followed his example. The three of us met outside the doors of the building.

"There are four werewolves left," Quincy said, coming to help me down from the saddle. "Did they bite you?"

I shook my head. "No, but I lost my silver dagger. I'm sorry."

"Don't apologize, you're doing wonderful." Quincy kissed me on the forehead, then cupped my face in his hands. "Wonderful," He repeated.

Scout gave a nervous paw at the ground, and Quincy turned towards the horse.

"Stay here, Scout." He instructed, petting the horse's nose. "If we don't make it out, you know where to go."

Scout tossed his head and gave an anxious whinny.

Together, Quincy and I turned towards the door.

Quincy moved first, stepping forward as quietly as possible. He placed his hand on the handle, then swung the door open.

We paused just outside the entrance, listening intently. We were met with silence.

Quincy and I glanced at each other. It was a wary glance, full of intense concentration and concern.

I took a step forward, but Quincy put his arm up, stopping me in my tracks. He moved in front of me, then stepped into the lodgings. I trailed behind.

"Hello, Mother."

With a gasp, I spun on my heel. Snow White was standing directly behind me. She gave a sweet smile and clasped her hands behind her back. She looked so young, so innocent. For a moment, she was my sweet girl who wouldn't hurt a fly.

Quincy grabbed my arm and pulled me behind him. "Stay back!" He shouted at Snow White.

Snow White snarled, baring her fangs. "I'm not going to hurt her!"

"You're a vampire," Quincy said in a hard voice.

"Yes, and you're the huntsman." Snow White hissed in a low voice, sending a shiver up my spine.

Snow White's eyes flicked to mine. She licked her lips, and I saw the hunger on her face.

"Are you really going to kill me?" She asked.

I tried to swallow the lump in my throat, but to no avail. Grief and sorrow rose inside of me. A single tear rolled down my cheek.

"It is not my intent to harm you, Snow White," I said, somehow keeping my voice steady. "But you don't belong in the world of the living."

"It matters not whether you think I belong. I am here. This is my life, and I am not ready to say goodbye to it just yet," Snow White replied.

"You've never had your own life, Snow White," I said in a weak voice. "You sustain yourself off the lives of others."

"That is not my fault!" Snow White shrieked. She bared her teeth at me and advanced a step.

"Ceridwen, now!" Quincy yelled. He grabbed his ax and swung it at Snow White.

My stepdaughter jerked back, but not fast enough. Quincy's ax grazed her stomach, and she let out an inhuman shriek.

Quincy struck again. This time, he used the butt of his ax to strike Snow White in the face. Her head jerked back, and he grabbed her around the knees, toppling them both to the ground.

Snow White bared her fangs. She lunged for Quincy's throat, but he grabbed a handful of her hair. Rolling them both onto their backs, Quincy locked eyes with me.

"Do it!" He roared. "Ceridwen, hurry!"

For one terrifying moment, the room spun, and I thought I might faint. My body began to tremble, and I felt the blood drain from my face. My resolution to release Snow White from her cursed half-life crumbled into nothing.

No, I had to be strong. Quincy was depending on me. My hands fumbled at my belt. My fingers were numb, but eventually I managed to pull a wooden stake free.

"Mama!" Snow White cried out in a loud, keening wail. She held her arms out to me, a look of desperation on her face.

A surge of protectiveness came over me, so strong I nearly plunged the dagger into Quincy instead. My throat closed up, and I made a strangled, gasping noise.

"Oh, Goddess." I whimpered. "Quincy, Quincy, I don't think I can-I don't think I can do it-"

"That's fine. Use the stones. Ceridwen, use the carnelian crystals!" Quincy bellowed. He grimaced, his jaw clenching, as he struggled to hold Snow White down.

I drew what was left of the crystal energy into me, surprised to find most of it depleted. If I was determined enough, perhaps I could still complete my task. All I had to do was summon fire and set Snow White ablaze-

Fear choked me, and my stomach rolled with nausea. The taste of bile was bitter on my tongue. I held out my trembling hands, but only sparks came out. Embers drifted down like ash, landing with a sizzle on Snow White's flawless skin.

I couldn't kill her. I couldn't kill Snow White. The realization struck with such force that it nearly drove me to my knees. It wasn't for lack of magic. I just couldn't harm my daughter.

Snow White flinched as the embers singed her skin. Fear and rage flashed in her eyes as she turned to me.

I flinched backward, hurt by the emotions on her face.

Snow White threw her head back. She shrieked like I've never heard before. The air trembled, and I clasped my hands over my ears, collapsing to the floor.

There was a rumble outside, like thunder, and then the door was flung open.

I gasped. Rolling onto my back, I looked up at the biggest werewolf I had ever seen. From outside, I heard Scout's high-pitched whinny.

The werewolf snarled at me, turning my blood cold.

Quincy let out a roar. His face twisted into something fearsome and chilling. He released Snow White and picked up his ax. Without a second thought, he leaped over me, planting himself between me and the werewolf.

"Quincy!" I shrieked.

He didn't hear me, or he didn't respond. His ax was a blur as he took precise, measured swings at the werewolf. He wove away from the sharp teeth and ducked swipes from the creature's sharp claws.

Behind me, Snow White was getting to her feet. I struggled into a standing position and launched myself at her, knocking us both back onto the floor. Whether I did this to protect Snow White, or stop her from escaping, I didn't know.

Snow White snarled. Her hand jutted out, slamming into my chest.

I flew across the room, colliding hard into the far wall.

Without a glance back, Snow White took off at a run, smashing through a window and disappearing into the night.

"Ceridwen!" Quincy yelled. He half turned towards me, momentarily distracted.

The werewolf took advantage of this by dragging his claws along Quincy's chest, turning his shirt into a canvas of vibrant red. The sight of the deep crimson hue was accompanied by the sickening sound of tearing flesh. A metallic scent filled the air, blood mingling with the unmistakable stench of a fresh wound. Quincy's eyes scrunched shut in pain. He opened his mouth to yell, but only a weak gurgling came out. He fell back, hitting his head against the floorboards.

"No!" I screamed with such force it felt like my throat was on fire.

From outside, I heard Scout shriek. Suddenly the horse was there, inside the lodgings, kicking at the werewolf. His silver horseshoes struck the monster, singing his fur.

Rage consumed me until my blood ran hot with it. I drew on the remaining solar energy and brought it forth in a powerful blast of fire and embers. A fireball flew at the werewolf with the force of an arrow, slamming into the creature and covering him in flames.

The werewolf howled in agony. He twisted and writhed while snarling fiercely. Letting out another howl, he raced forward and jumped out the window Snow White had used to make her escape.

My heart stuttered in my chest as I stared at Quincy.

A red stain bloomed across his shirt. Blood pooled around him, and he lay completely still.

26
THE NECROMANCER

I screamed. I screamed so loud pain ripped through my throat and my voice turned hoarse. Stumbling to Quincy's side, I collapsed beside him and grabbed his shoulders. I was frantic, hysterical. I had to save him, but how?

"No, no, Quincy, please!" I sobbed.

After what felt like an eternity, Quincy's eyelids slowly fluttered open. His brow furrowed, and a disoriented look came over his face. He reached a hand up to touch my cheek, then tried to move into a sitting position. "Oh, what happened?" He slurred in a slow voice.

I pushed him back down onto the floor. "Lay still!"

Quincy's bottom lip puckered at my command, but he did as I asked.

My hands shook as I ripped open his tattered shirt and examined his wounds. After carefully running my fingers along his skin and searching for bruising, I sat back on my heels with a sigh. "The wounds are superficial. There are no bones broken, and none of the major arteries have been hit."

"Can I sit up now?" Quincy asked, raising an eyebrow at me.

"Yes," I nodded.

I helped Quincy into a sitting position, and he looked down at his chest with some surprise. "That one almost had my number on it."

"But it didn't." I blurted out.

Quincy patted my hand in an attempt to calm me. "What about the Howlite crystal? Can you heal my injuries that way?"

"I doubt it." I eyed his chest again, thinking of when Everald bit Marcella. "These types of wounds typically have their own magic. Let's get back to the inn, and I'll take a closer look at it there."

Quincy agreed and mounted Scout. He made it up into the saddle with some difficulty, and I climbed up behind him.

"I like holding you in my arms." Quincy teased as I carefully held onto his shoulders.

"Not this time, love," I said. My heart was still racing over how close I had come to losing him.

Scout was very careful not to jostle us on the way back. The horse went at a slow walk, carefully picking his path. Quincy tried to get him to canter once or twice, but Scout would only turn his head and glare.

Eventually, we made it back to the Black Barrel. The sun hadn't come up yet, but the sky was turning a lighter shade of blue. Quincy was hastily wrapped in a thick cloak. As he leaned heavily against me, I made a joke to Thaddeus and his staff about him drinking too much at the bar down the street.

With Scout being taken care of by the stable master, Quincy and I stumbled our way upstairs to our room.

Quincy collapsed in a chair, and I hastily grabbed some supplies and cleaned his wound. He didn't flinch, or curse, or get angry. Instead, he sat patiently while I worked, humming softly under his breath.

As I predicted, the Howlite didn't heal the werewolf slashes. I threaded a needle and began to stitch them up by hand.

"Quincy," I spoke in a strained voice. "I'm so sorry. I really am." I choked on my words and fought back tears.

"For what?" Quincy sounded puzzled. He reached out and stroked my cheek with the pad of his thumb.

"I couldn't stake Snow White. We failed. You almost died. It's my fault. All of this, the whole thing, it's all my fault-"

"Stop." Quincy shook his head. "It's not all your fault. I'm the one who didn't realize werewolves could turn after a full moon. Anyway, today wasn't a total loss. How many werewolves did you count dead?"

"Um, eight," I said.

"Exactly. Snow White is significantly weaker now than she was yesterday. That works to our advantage for our next attack."

"Won't she just make more werewolves?" I asked.

Quincy hesitated. "From what I understand, to be made into a werewolf, you have to first be bitten by one in wolf form, then wait for the next full moon. A werewolf doesn't come into their full powers until after their first transformation."

"I see." I went back to stitching Quincy's wounds. "How were the werewolves able to transform tonight?"

Quincy turned to stare out the window, looking glum. "It's been said that werewolves can transform the night before, and the night after, a full moon. I paid those rumors no mind. I sensed how eager you were to be finished with this whole thing, and I let it cloud my judgment. Ceridwen, I'm the one who almost got us both killed tonight. You're the one who should be angry with me."

I shook my head. "I'm not. Honestly, I'm just glad you're going to be all right."

"What a pair we make," Quincy said in a fond voice.

I finished stitching Quincy up, then looked up into his face. His dark, velvety eyes were warm with love and adoration. I crawled into his lap, wrapping my arms around his neck. I ran my fingers through his braids, feeling how soft they were.

"I love you," I whispered.

Quincy brushed his lips against my temple. "I love you, too. We're together, we're safe, that's what's important."

We stayed like that for a long moment, wrapped in each other's arms. It felt good to hold Quincy, and to be held by him. Slowly, I felt myself relax as the tension drained from my body.

My eyes drifted towards the window. The sky had lightened significantly, and I watched the sun come up from the comfort of my lover's arms.

"Oh," I sat up suddenly, putting a hand on my stomach. The feeling of being pulled towards my mirror was back.

"What is it?" Quincy asked, looking alarmed.

"Aster and Senna," I responded, standing from his lap. Rooting around in my travel bag, I pulled out my looking glass.

Quincy scooted his chair up to the table. I sat beside him and lit a candle. A few moments passed by as I adjusted the candle's flame, and then Aster's and Senna's faces appeared.

"There you are!" Senna said, looking vastly relieved. "We were hesitant to call so early. I'm glad to see you both."

"How did it go?" Aster asked.

"Well, ladies, if I'm being honest, we were taken a bit by surprise." Quincy gestured to his chest and the gashes I had stitched up.

Aster gasped, while Senna slapped a hand over her mouth. They both looked horrified.

"Turns out, werewolves don't just transform during the full moon," I said in a tired voice.

Aster shook her head, looking exasperated. "I told you so, Quincy."

Quincy bowed his head, looking bashful.

Senna lightly smacked Aster on the shoulder. "Now is not the time for that!"

"Sorry," Aster said, not sounding sorry at all.

"So, how did it go? Is Snow White-?" Senna's voice trailed off.

I shook my head. "I couldn't do it."

"We were able to take down most of the werewolves, though," Quincy said, jumping to my defense. He quickly filled them both in on the events of the night.

"So what now?" Senna asked, her forehead lined with worry.

Quincy slung his arm over the back of my chair. "Now, the two of us are going to see Bartholomew."

Senna blanched, while Aster nodded thoughtfully.

"Make sure you get it done before the next full moon," Aster said.

"We plan on it." Quincy nodded.

"Be careful." Senna urged. Her face was still pale, and her eyes looked huge in her delicate face.

"We will," Quincy said.

"Let us know when it's done," Aster added.

"We'll be in touch," I said with a smile.

After exchanging our goodbyes, I blew out the candle. Aster and Senna disappeared. I turned to Quincy.

"Who is Bartholomew?" I asked. "Senna didn't seem to like him."

Quincy went to the bed and settled in with a sigh. "Senna is not a fan of his magic."

I arched an eyebrow. "That means I probably won't be either."

"You didn't give me a chance to say what it is." Quincy protested.

"Do you think I'll change my mind once you do?"

Quincy examined me for a long moment, then shook his head. "Probably not."

"There," I said, my voice smug. "So I was right. Now tell me, what kind of magic does Bartholomew practice?"

Quincy hesitated before answering. "He's a necromancer."

"Quincy!" I yelled. "Necromancers are not good company!"

"Well, I'm not looking for good company, Ceridwen," Quincy said in a testy voice. "I'm a hunter. What I need are knowledgeable people who can help me in my profession."

I chewed on my bottom lip, then nodded. "All right, fine."

"We'll have to leave as soon as we're able," Quincy said, staring up at the ceiling. "Time is of the essence."

"I'll be ready." I climbed into bed with Quincy, holding his hand in mine. "What are we going to see him for?"

"Hm," Quincy rumbled in a deep voice. "We're going to need a weapon."

Quincy wanted only a few hours of sleep and was prepared to depart from Honeyvale at midday. I put a stop to that idea at once and demanded that we leave on the morrow. Quincy tried to object, but I stubbornly insisted he would need a least a day before he would be ready to ride.

The morning after that, we said our goodbyes to Thaddeus and began our long trek. I helped our journey along as best I could by whispering spells to the wind. It was draining, but I made sure each night to check Quincy's wounds and change his bandages.

After seven days, we finally made our way to a small estate on the outskirts of a large town. I kept my hood down low and cast a spell to hide me from prying eyes.

"This Bartholomew seems to be doing well for himself," I said, as Quincy and I rode through an iron gate. The estate was larger than most in the area, although I couldn't help but notice it looked shabby and run down. The lane to the house was well taken care of, but the yard had been left to grow wild.

"There is a university in this town," Quincy said. "Many students come here, driven by their curiosity of the forbidden arts."

"Do they learn anything?" I asked.

Quincy shrugged. "It depends on the student. Bartholomew has a wealth of knowledge, but he is careful not to let it fall into the wrong hands."

We reached the end of the lane, and a stableboy came out and offered to take Scout and Buttercup.

After dismounting, a steward led Quincy and me inside. When we were finally shown into a room, I couldn't help but be surprised.

At first glance, it looked like a greenhouse that had fallen into disrepair. On one side of the room were floor-to-ceiling windows, though several panes were missing. The floor was dirt and moss and mushrooms and buzzing with life.

Shelves of books reached almost to the ceiling. I frowned when I saw them covered in moss, but as I picked up a book, I noticed it was perfectly intact. The ink was not faded from the sun; the pages were crisp and not waterlogged, and the spine was undamaged.

Turning some more, I blanched when I saw a table covered in jars. The jars were of varying sizes, and contained the bodies of animals, mostly amphibians. Frogs, lizards, and even a pig had been preserved in green goo. Potions simmered on the table next to them.

"Ah, I see my guests have finally arrived."

I looked up to see an older man enter the room. He was tall and lanky. His hair was long and grey, and was accompanied by an equally long and grey beard. He wore a calf-length, flowing robe that may have once been purple, but was now so faded it was hard to tell. There was a look of such wildness in his eyes that it took me a moment to realize one was blue, and the other was brown.

"Bartholomew," Quincy inclined his head. "I'm here on business-"

"Yes, yes, you never come here unless it's on business." Bartholomew shuffled in my direction, and I noticed his feet were bare. "Now, let me take a look at the queen."

I felt my blood go cold, while Quincy stepped in front of me.

"Watch yourself, old man." Quincy rumbled in a deep voice.

"Oh, pshaw, get out of my way, boy." Bartholomew stepped around Quincy and took my face in his hands. "Oh, yes, hm, I see," He muttered in a low voice.

Taking a step back, Bartholomew clapped his hands together. "I've been expecting you two, though maybe not quite so soon. Ah, what do spirits know about time, eh? Come, sit, I had tea brought in."

The couch, like everything else in the room, was covered in moss and vines and flowers. I perched on the edge of my seat and shot Quincy a confused look.

Quincy shrugged and sat down next to me. "I take it Aster has been in touch?"

"Aster?" Bartholomew frowned as he sat across from us. There was a table between his seat and our couch where the tea settings had been laid out. The necromancer began pouring drinks for everyone. "No, no, my dear boy. It was the spirits, the shadows, who told me you were coming."

Bartholomew sat up and glared into the corners of the room. "Although it would have been *nice* if someone had mentioned our company was arriving *today*!"

I froze as the shadows began to whisper back. I couldn't understand what they were saying, or even catch the tone, but it was clear Bartholomew could.

"Ah, hm, magic. What an interesting way to travel." Bartholomew took a sip of his tea. "Now, Quincy, tell me what your visit is about."

Quincy shifted in his seat, looking uncomfortable. He added milk and honey to his tea, then picked up his cup and took a careful sip. "I'm here about necromancer magic, of course."

"Brilliant, anything specific you're looking for? Mummies, zombies? You know, I've found zombies have a rather unfair reputation. It's all in how you raise them, see. Blame the necromancer, not the zombie, I always say-"

"Vampires." I interrupted. "We need to learn more about them."

Bartholomew seemed to deflate at my answer. His shoulders bowed, and he dropped his head.

"Quincy," Bartholomew said in a reproachful voice, "We've had this conversation already-"

"You have?" I interrupted, surprise in my voice.

"More than once." Bartholomew nodded.

"I'm not here looking for a cure," Quincy said.

"I should hope not," Bartholomew said, taking another sip of tea. "The last time you came here looking for a cure, you tried to cut my head off."

"I beg your pardon?" I asked, leaning forward. That didn't sound like the Quincy I knew. Or did it? He said once he had tried to find a cure for vampirism. Was this the necromancer he spoke to?

"Our poor Quincy." Bartholomew turned to me and gave a sad shake of his head. "I trust you heard what happened to his wife?"

"Yes," I answered.

"Bartholomew," Quincy said, a warning in his voice.

"Well, Quincy just couldn't stand what he had done." Bartholomew went on. "He wanted to blame himself, believe he had acted rashly. Even after Mercy's death, he was still looking for ways to redeem her. But then," Bartholomew stopped to sigh, "That is often the case when it comes to the people we love."

"Why are you telling me this?" I asked in a soft voice.

"Because," Bartholomew said, "You have touched death recently."

My stomach hollowed out, and I stared at Bartholomew with wide eyes.

"I'm a necromancer, my dear," Bartholomew said, pouring himself more tea. "It is possible for the dead to be raised, but not as they once were. Look around you. See the flowers that are wilting, dying? They will fade away and become something else, dirt and fertilizer. Then it will change again, perhaps into a nice mushroom. All living things must have a conclusion so that they may evolve. This is the nature of death. It transforms the spirit. Of course, an evolved soul can not be pulled fully back into our world. It must come back as something else. Something-"

"Different," I finished. My lips felt numb, and they barely moved as I spoke.

More whispers came from the shadows, and a chill went down my spine.

"Your Majesty," Bartholomew began, "I hope you don't mind if I call you Your Majesty. I understand the King gifted you with the title of Queen Mother, but I'm quite a bit older than you and it doesn't roll off the tongue very well."

"I don't mind," I said in a quiet voice.

The shadows whispered again, and Bartholomew looked grim. "There is a death spirit walking the land who shares the same blood as you. That is true, yes?"

"It is," I answered. It was difficult to talk. I took a sip of my tea and tried to be brave.

"Yet you are not here for a cure. Which means you must be in search of a weapon." Bartholomew crossed his legs and gave me a knowing look.

"We are," Quincy said. "We need something quick and painless."

Bartholomew shook his head. "Tsk tsk, quick and painless for a vampire? That is a tall order. Why don't you tell me what you've tried so far?"

"Solar water," Quincy said, glancing at me.

I nodded. "Yes, and hawthorn stakes with Huath inscribed on them."

"Citrine stones."

"I also had a silver dagger, although I lost it recently," I said.

"How does one come to lose a silver dagger?" Bartholomew asked, tilting his head.

"It's currently stuck in the decaying body of a dead werewolf," I answered.

Bartholomew raised an eyebrow. "Well, these are all very impressive answers. I see I've taught you well, Quincy."

I heaved a sigh and sat forward. "Mr. Bartholomew-"

"Oh, please, there is no need to stand on ceremony with me, Your Majesty. You can call me Bartholomew."

"Bartholomew," I started again, "If you have any suggestions, please, share them with us."

"Hm," The necromancer drummed his fingers against his leg and looked up at the ceiling. "Have you tried salt?"

"No," I said, shaking my head.

Bartholomew stood up and went to his desk. He returned with a large jar, sealed with wax. "Here you go. Pour a circle of salt around a vampire, and it will trap them inside."

"They won't be able to get out?" I asked, confused.

"They can't cross over salt," Bartholomew explained.

"Oh, thank you," I said, taking the jar.

Quincy shifted in his seat, looking restless. "That won't work. We don't know where she's sleeping." Turning to me, he continued. "The best way to kill a vampire is to pour a circle of salt around their coffin, then set the coffin on fire."

I shuddered at the thought.

"Perhaps you will find another use for it," Bartholomew said.

"Isn't there anything else?" Quincy asked, sounding exasperated.

"What about nightshade?" Bartholomew asked.

I blanched. "The poison?"

"It has the same effect as holy water," Quincy said, shaking his head.

"Not quite," Bartholomew said. "If you wear it around your neck, or in your pockets, it repels vampires."

"We're not trying to repel vampires, though," Quincy said. "We're trying to kill one."

"Oh?" Bartholomew's voice was quiet. "Can you not think of a reason to keep a vampire's teeth away from your necks?"

"All right, point taken." Quincy finished his cup of tea and glanced around the room. "Don't have anything stronger, do you?"

Bartholomew stood and went to his desk. He returned with a dusty, amber bottle and handed it to Quincy.

Quincy uncorked the bottle, poured himself a generous amount, and downed it in two gulps. "Bartholomew, I'm going to level with you. The reason we're here is because Ceridwen is struggling. We faced a vampire over a week ago, and she couldn't harm the girl, not with a stake, not with sun energy. I have to be the one to take down the vampire-"

"Quincy," I objected in a soft voice.

"So I need something quick and efficient." He finished, not looking in my direction.

"As well as painless?" Bartholomew's eyes flicked towards me.

I lowered my gaze to the floor.

"Can you help us or not?" Quincy asked, sounding frustrated.

"Hm," Bartholomew tapped a finger against his chin, then stood up. "There is something. It was a gift from a student. I've never used the spell. It's not in my purview."

"What is it?" I asked, my curiosity piqued.

"A spell to create a lightning wand, invented by an alchemist with far too much interest in soul transference and cadavers." Bartholomew riffled through some papers on his desk. "Ah, here it is." He shuffled back over to me and handed me a single piece of paper. "He was very advanced. I hope that won't be too difficult for you."

Quincy looked over my shoulder, his brow drawn. "Can you manage it?" He asked in a low voice.

I glanced over the directions, my heart rising in my chest. A lightning wand, a way to quickly and easily take care of Snow White without strapping her to a pyre and burning her alive.

I nodded. "Yes, but I'll need some help. Do you think Aster and Senna-?"

"Of course they would." Quincy nodded.

I took a deep breath and smiled at Bartholomew. "Thank you. I believe this is just what we were looking for."

"Of course, happy to be of assistance." Bartholomew inclined his head in my direction, then took another sip of tea.

"We should contact them," Quincy said, standing up. "We can use your scrying mirror."

"Yes, of course. How delightful." Bartholomew also stood and adjusted his robe. "You will both stay the night, though, won't you? You can leave first thing in the morning. With any luck, and a bit of magic, of course, you should make it to your friend's house just after dark, tomorrow evening."

"That's very generous of you," Quincy said. "Come, Ceridwen, we'll need to contact our friends immediately. Some of these items will be hard to come by."

I stopped to cast one more long look at Bartholomew, then followed Quincy out the door. Behind us, the whispers of the dead followed at our heels.

27
VISITORS

The steward led us to the room where Quincy and I would be staying for the duration of our visit.

There was a washroom attached to our quarters, something that made me squeal in delight. I took a long, hot bath, luxuriating in the multitude of soaps and oils Bartholomew had. It was almost as fine as the ones at the castle.

Eventually, when the water cooled, I pulled myself out of the tub and dressed. I braided my hair and pinned it to my head. As I entered the bedroom, I saw Quincy standing at a window, staring at the outdoors with a faraway look in his eyes.

"We should contact Aster and Senna. I need to find my mirror." I said, putting my hand into my bag.

"I already grabbed it. It's on the desk." Quincy said.

I turned around, spotting a writing desk against the wall near the door. "Perfect, we just need a candle and a match-"

"Ceridwen," Quincy finally turned towards me. "Look at the mirror."

Curiosity piqued, I moved towards the desk and took the scrying mirror in my hand. My eyes widened when I saw the writing across the surface. It was a message from Aster and Senna, containing only three words.

We are coming.

"I'll go downstairs and tell Bartholomew we're expecting more guests," I said, adjusting my hair.

"I'll go with you," Quincy said in a rough voice. He took a step towards me, then swayed on the spot.

"Quincy!" I cried, rushing to his side.

"I'm fine." He mumbled, his eyes starting to droop shut.

"No, you're not. You're dead on your feet. Lay down on the bed and let me check your bandages."

Quincy did as I asked and smiled up at me. "You worry too much."

I clicked my tongue at him, but a gentle smile pulled at my lips. I checked Quincy's bandages and ensured they were clean. By the time I finished, he was fast asleep.

Tiptoeing out the door, I made my way back to the sitting room where I had last seen the Necromancer.

The door was open, so I let myself in. My eyes swept the room, and I found Bartholomew bent over his desk, checking on various bottles.

I cleared my throat. "Excuse me, Bartholomew?"

"Yes?" He said, turning to me.

"I just wanted to let you know our friends, Aster and Senna, contacted me. They sent a message saying they were on their way here."

"Ah, yes, the greenwitch wives." Bartholomew nodded. "I heard they were on their way. With any luck, they will arrive sometime tomorrow afternoon, barring any magical use, of course."

"Excellent. I'm glad to know you were already expecting them." I nodded in Bartholomew's direction, then turned on my heel, prepared to leave the room.

A finger trailed its way down my back, starting at the base of my neck and moving down my spine. The touch was ice cold and sent a chill over my whole body. With a gasp, I spun on my heel.

Bartholomew was watching me carefully. He hadn't moved away from his desk, which was several paces away from me.

"I beg your pardon, Your Majesty, but the dead are anxious to speak with you," Bartholomew said.

As he spoke, shadows moved in the corners.

My mouth went dry as I thought about Marcella and Iberius. Conrad and Mirtha also came to mind, as well as my parents.

I licked my lips. "What do they want?"

"Do not be distressed, Your Majesty," Bartholomew said. "They wish to help you. They bade me give you a gift."

Moving to a vase of mostly alive flowers, Bartholomew hummed as he searched through the blooms.

"Ah, here it is." Bartholomew emerged with a gorgeous piece of polished wood. "It's a hair stick. The wood is hawthorn, with Huath inscribed on it. At the tip here, is a carnelian crystal. It works just as well for holding sun energy as citrine crystals do. You'll have to be careful with the other end though, it's incredibly sharp."

Bartholomew came to my side and showed me. A piece of metal was sticking out of one end of the hair stick.

"What is it that?" I asked.

"It is a nail from the coffin of a High Priestess," Bartholomew explained. "Very potent."

I took the hair stick and smiled at Bartholomew. "Thank you for the gift, but if I were capable of staking my own blood, I wouldn't be here."

Bartholomew rocked back on his heels and gave me a grim smile. "We shall see, Your Majesty."

"Your title is Necromancer, not Prophet." I reminded him.

"That is true." Bartholomew nodded. "I have no knowledge of the future. I can't say the same for the dead, though. There are a few of them who can see that which is hidden from us on the physical plane. I do not argue with them."

I held Bartholomew's gaze for a long moment, working up the courage to ask him my question.

The whispering in the shadows started up again, and I felt the hairs on the back of my neck stand up.

"Do not fear the dead, Your Majesty." Bartholomew moved towards me and clasped my hands in his. "I see questions in your eyes. Ask me what you will."

I took a deep breath, feeling like a knife had been stuck in my heart. "As you may have guessed by now, the death spirit, who shares my blood, is the Princess Snow White."

"Oh, my dear." Bartholomew chuckled. "I have known that long before you did. The dead were in an uproar the night she was born. They were so loud, I'm surprised my neighbors didn't hear them gossiping."

"The night she...fully transitioned...she hurt a lot of people," I said. "Some of them I cared for deeply."

"Yes, I know of the night you speak." Bartholomew heaved a great sigh. "Some of them died quite tragically. The scars run deep. The trauma keeps them from fully crossing over."

Bartholomew patted me on the cheek. "Do not fret over the handsome blonde soldier. He bears you no ill will. You cleaned and prepared his body yourself. He appreciates the gesture. As for his death, it was quite painless. The princess broke his neck before she ripped him open."

I gasped, and two tears spilled down my cheeks.

"I do not say these things to hurt you." Bartholomew quickly clarified.

"On the contrary, it is a relief to know he did not suffer." I ran my fingers over the smooth grain of the hairpin in my hand.

"There are more people I can ask about," I said. "The late king, my sister...are their voices among the shadows? Who's idea was it to give me the hairpin?"

Bartholomew lowered his eyes. "For your own good, Your Majesty, I think it best I not answer that question."

"I believe you just did," I said in a soft voice.

More whispers emerged from the shifting shadows.

"They are too ashamed to speak to you directly. But they understand what you must do, and they do not begrudge you for it." Bartholomew said.

"Thank you for the assurance," I said. "May I ask, how did you get into necromancy?"

"Ah," Bartholomew turned towards the shadows then, and stuffed his hands into the pockets of his long robes. "My daughter died. A long time ago. She was very young."

"I'm so sorry," I said. "How did she pass?"

"Illness," Bartholomew said. "I turned to necromancy. I became obsessed with my work. My wife tired of me living with one foot in the grave, and she left. She was right, of course."

Bartholomew stepped towards me and placed a hand on my shoulder. "There is a time for living, and a time for death, Your Majesty. Don't get confused about what side you're on, or you might miss out on what's right in front of you."

28
ALCHEMY

I wandered around Bartholomew's estate for a while after that, pondering what I had learned. Nature seemed to grow everywhere, from crumbling logs with mushrooms growing out of them, to climbing vines of ivy and wisteria, to wildflowers thriving in hidden nooks and crannies.

Eventually, I made my way back to the room I was sharing with Quincy. I pushed the door open just as he was sitting up in bed.

"How long was I out for?" Quincy asked, rubbing a hand across his face.

"A couple of hours," I said, going to sit beside him.

"Hm, how did things go with Bartholomew?"

I let out a deep sigh. "It went all right. Turns out he was expecting Aster and Senna. He also gave me this." I held up the hairpin, then tucked it into my travel bag.

"Dare I ask what you two spoke about?" Quincy questioned, tilting his head to one side.

"Not right now," I said, rubbing the back of my neck. "I'll tell you later. It's a lot to process."

"I understand." Quincy got out of bed and stretched. His large muscular frame formed a silhouette against the backdrop of the window.

I watched him for a moment, wondering if the shadows had ever whispered to him. It felt unfair to ask, so I decided against it. If Quincy wanted to tell me, he would.

We didn't see Bartholomew again for the rest of the night. He didn't join Quincy and me for dinner, either, although we were served a five course meal. It was a lovely gesture, but difficult to enjoy. The shadows didn't lie still, and they continued whispering in low, raspy voices.

Bartholomew did join us for breakfast the next morning. He chatted happily the entire time, sometimes to Quincy and me, and sometimes to the dead. It was disconcerting to see him switch back and forth with such ease. My eyes darted to Quincy's, and I saw he was as unsettled as I was.

At midday, as the three of us sat down for tea, the steward entered the room.

"Miss Aster and Miss Senna here to see you, sir." The steward said.

"Yes, of course. Let them in." Bartholomew said, standing from his seat.

The door opened, and the two women entered. Senna looked a little out of place, but Aster was more at ease.

"I was wondering when you two would arrive." Quincy rose from his seat and hugged them both.

"We were worried when you didn't stop in to see us," Senna explained. "You pass our house to get to Bartholomew's, and we're only a few hours off the main road."

"We were expecting you to stay one night with us, at least," Aster chastised.

"That's my fault," I said, hugging Senna and Aster in my turn. "We have so little time. I used magic to hurry our journey along."

"Well, we're here now," Aster said, taking a seat at the table. "Hello, Bartholomew."

"Hello, Aster, dear." Bartholomew inclined his head and lifted his teacup. "Hello to you as well, Senna."

"Hello," Senna squeaked out in a high voice. She hurried to her wife's side.

A frenzied voice rose from the shadows then. I was so startled by the tone of urgency that I almost dropped my teacup.

"All right, I'll ask her. Not that it's any of your business, mind." Bartholomew snapped. He turned to Aster. "Have you been remembering to polish your great-grandmother's chalice? Your mother is very keen to know."

Aster rolled her eyes, but one side of her lip quirked up in a smile. "The chalice is fine, Mother."

The whispering continued, the shadows swelling like a dark fog.

"Would you quiet down? I hardly think this is the time." Bartholomew said, puffing out his chest.

A look of frustration crossed over Aster's voice. "If she's asking about grandchildren again-"

"She is."

"Well, you can tell her to bugger off. We haven't decided yet." Aster put her nose in the air.

The whispering seemed to settle down then. The fog rolled back and light filtered into the room. From outside came the trilling of birdsong, along with a gentle wind through the trees.

I blinked a few times, disoriented by the sudden change.

"So, what's the plan?" Senna asked, pouring herself a cup of tea. There was still a touch of shrill apprehension in her voice.

I fished the spell out of my dress and handed it to Quincy. He passed it along to Aster and Senna.

"Hm," Aster frowned. "It's a bit advanced for me."

"Not for me," Senna said. "Ceridwen and I should be able to make this. I'm just not sure if a wand will be an effective weapon against a vampire."

"It's a lightning wand," I explained. "There are several steps to killing a vampire, with the last step being to set them on fire. Well, this is the last step. Lightning is heat. It will pass through her more quickly than a flame and destroy her almost instantly."

"That actually sounds brilliant, and efficient," Aster said, looking impressed.

"I've seen what lightning does when it passes through a person's body," Quincy said. "With any luck, if it burns her thoroughly enough, I won't have to...well, you know."

An image of Snow White lashed to a pyre crossed my mind.

Everyone at the table squirmed uncomfortably and shot me looks of pity. Everyone except Bartholomew. He hummed happily to himself and glanced over at the shadows. I wondered what he could see.

"Quincy and I went to the observatory this morning. It looks like a thunderstorm is headed directly for us. With any luck, now that you two are here, we should be able to complete the ritual tonight." I said.

"Are you sure we have all the supplies needed?" Senna asked.

"Quincy mentioned that yesterday," Bartholomew said. "I had my steward check the supply closet. All the tools you need are here and available for your use."

"That's a relief," Quincy said. "Thank you, Bartholomew."

"Of course, dear boy. Would you like my steward to show you the supply closet?" Bartholomew asked.

Senna moved to her feet. "I'd like to be the one to go, actually. If no one minds, that is. I'd like a chance to take stock of everything."

"It's no problem at all, young lady," Bartholomew said. He called his steward in, and Senna went with him, leaving the five of us alone.

"I know necromancy isn't the most palatable of magical crafts, but Senna seems really out of sorts," I commented.

Aster shrugged her shoulders. "She's never been close to someone who's passed. Her parents are both still living and her brother goes to the University. They're all close and see each other often."

"Well, that explains a lot," I said.

"Senna can not perceive the nature of the dead, so it makes her uncomfortable. As it would for anyone who does not understand the delicate balance between the two planes." Bartholomew said.

I recalled Bartholomew's words to me the day before.

"There is a time for living and a time for death," I murmured in a low voice.

"Precisely, Your Majesty." Bartholomew nodded.

I squeezed Quincy's hand, then stood up from the table. "I'll go check on Senna, see if she needs any help collecting what we need for tonight."

As I stood up and left the room, I heard the shadows once again start to whisper to each other.

"Are you sure this is going to work?" Quincy asked in a low voice.

I bit down on my bottom lip, my stomach twisting into a tight knot. "It has too."

Quincy cupped my face in his hands and kissed me on the forehead. "All right then, lover. On your lead."

I took a deep breath and glanced around the yard. Senna, Aster, and Bartholomew were looking at me expectantly. For some reason, they had all unofficially elected me as the leader of this campaign.

Turning my head up to the sky, I examined the dark, angry clouds rolling towards us. They crackled and snapped with lightning, occasionally emitting a burst of light.

The sun had long ago set, coating the Necromancer's backyard with an inky blackness. Rain drizzled down on us.

"We should begin," I said. "Quincy, Bartholomew, raise the lightning rod. Senna, Aster, get ready."

The storm was currently positioned above us. Every rumble of thunder made the ground beneath us come alive, bucking and rolling under our feet. The air was thick and moist. The damp air clung to our skin and raised the hackles on the back of our necks.

Quincy and Batholomew sprang into action. They began spinning the crankshafts on the lightning rod. The metal point began to rise into the sky, as high as the turrets on the Necromancer's house.

Senna and Aster stood beside me, tense, but firm in their convictions. We waited apprehensively by a metal dais with a copper bowl. The bowl was half full of water and contained a single piece of quartz crystal. A thin copper wire ran from the lightning rod to the metal dais, connecting the two.

Behind me was a small forge. There was a scrap of pure silver that was about two inches long, and a half inch thick resting in the fire. The forge wasn't meant to melt the silver, but to keep the metal soft enough to manipulate.

The sky rumbled, and a white flash among the clouds alerted me to what was coming.

"Stand clear!" I shouted. My voice sounded small as it echoed through the air.

Quincy grabbed Batholomew, and they sprinted away from the lightning rod.

The rumbling in the sky increased as clouds shifted and contorted. The wind picked up into a screaming gale that sent chills down my spine.

Then, finally, what we were all waiting for.

A flash of pure white lightning arced down from the sky. It spider-webbed against the darkness, almost in slow motion. We waited with bated breath until, at last, a white finger reached down and touched the tip of the lightning rod.

Everything happened very quickly then.

A sizzling hot bolt of energy shot down the turret, and traveled along the copper wire and into the dais. The water trembled, and the quartz moved around as though the bowl were being shaken. The crystal glowed, becoming so bright it was hard to look at.

Aster, Senna, and I shielded our eyes as a pure, white light filled the air. My heart raced in my chest. We all waited to see whether the crystal would crack, or if it could hold the lightening energy.

Finally, after what seemed like an eternity, the light dimmed. The three of us leaned over the bowl, eager to see if it worked.

The quartz crystal was glowing like a star.

"Aster, Senna, now!" I shouted.

Aster lifted a rod of ash, polished to a high shine, with a notch at the end. Senna held a pair of tongs in her hand that she used to gingerly lift the crystal.

"Careful now, careful," I muttered in a low voice.

Aster held the rod very still, a grim look on her face, while Senna wedged the crystal into the notch.

"It's in. Hurry, hurry." Senna urged.

I rushed over to the forge. Using another pair of tongs, I pulled the scrap of silver from the fire and laid it on the blacksmith's anvil.

"All right, here we go," Aster said. She carefully placed the ash rod on the scrap of metal. She made sure the silver covered the notch where the wood and crystal connected.

I stood next to Aster with a chasing hammer. The head was smaller than my fist and used specifically for wand making and jewelry. I began to softly tap the silver, molding it to the wand.

Quincy and Bartholomew moved closer to us, watching as the three of us worked.

Aster finished rotating the wand. I stopped hammering. The scrap of silver was beginning to cool and harden, cementing the wand and crystal together. The quartz still shone with all the brilliance of a star.

"There, it's done," Senna said, out of breath. "We can't cool the metal in water. The lightning magic wouldn't like that. But, it's finished."

"Yes, and the magic is holding well," Bartholomew said, clasping his hands together in front of him. "A fine bit of alchemy, that was."

I laid down the hammer and stepped back into Quincy's arms. He held me tightly, kissing me on top of the head.

"So, what do we do now?" Aster asked.

"There's nothing left for you to do," I said in a quiet voice. "The task is mine and Quincy's to finish."

"And now we have what we came for," Quincy said. "Our job here is done."

I took a deep breath and nodded. "Tomorrow, then, we make for Honeyvale."

It was late, so the five of us disbanded and went to bed. At least, Quincy and I went to bed. Below, we could just make out the sounds of Aster and Senna having drinks with Bartholomew.

Quincy soon fell into a deep sleep, but I tossed and turned next to him. Marcella haunted my dreams, as did Conrad and Iberius. They all seemed to be trying to tell me something, but their voices couldn't reach me.

I started awake more than once, comforted by Quincy's warm body and his arms around me.

Morning came sooner than I would have liked. I lay on my back, staring up at the ceiling, and watching the light creep slowly through the room. It seemed to be waging a slow battle against the shadows, and it was unclear which side would win.

Eventually, Quincy stirred beside me and sat up.

"You're awake." He noted, propping himself up on his elbow.

"I don't think I'll have a good night's sleep until our business in Honeyvale is complete," I said in a soft voice.

Quincy heaved a deep sigh. "I wish there was something I could say."

"I know." I threw back the covers and climbed out of bed. "Unfortunately, this isn't a scenario that can be made better with words. There is a grisly task before us. The best we can do is move forward and hope we make it through to the other side."

As we packed our meager possessions, I turned to Quincy and handed him a sealed bottle of water.

"What's this?" He asked, holding it up to the light.

"That's the water we used to make the lightning wand," I said. "Last night I couldn't sleep, so I went downstairs and collected it. I happened to bump into Bartholomew-"

Quincy snorted. "Nothing Bartholomew does is by happenstance."

"Well, anyway, I went downstairs and gathered the water. Bartholomew gave me this diamond vial to keep it in. I don't know if it's useful, or has any magical properties, but I wanted you to have it." I said.

"I shall treasure it, as I treasure you." Quincy drew me close and kissed me on the forehead. He drew his fingers through my hair and let out a deep sigh of contentment. Who knew how many moments like this we had left?

When we finished packing, we headed down to the stables. The stable master was already awake and nearly finished with saddling up Buttercup. Scout had already been seen to, and was patiently waiting to begin.

The three of us exchanged pleasantries, and then Quincy and I walked the horses down the lane and prepared to mount.

"WAIT!" a voice yelled, ringing out across the yard.

Startled, I turned back towards the house and saw Bartholomew racing out of the front door. His robe trailed behind him, revealing long, pale legs and slippers.

"I didn't want you to leave without something for breakfast," Bartholomew said. He thrust a package into my hands. It was a white cloth, tied together with a piece of twine.

"Thank you, Bartholomew," I said.

"Of course, my dear." He said with a slight bow.

"Where are Senna and Aster?" Quincy asked, craning his neck to see if his friends were coming.

"Sleeping, I'm afraid. They're both terribly worn out from last night."

Quincy snorted. "From the drinks, you mean, not the alchemy."

"Don't worry, I'll look after them," Bartholomew said in a cheery voice.

Without thinking, I moved forward and threw my arms around the necromancer's neck. We held each other tightly for a long moment, then broke apart.

"Be well, Your Majesty." Bartholomew gave me a sad smile, then helped me onto the horse. "Oh, Your Majesty?"

"Yes?" I asked, twisting in the saddle.

"You won't forget your gift, will you?" He asked.

I shook my head. "No, I won't."

"Goodbye, Bartholomew, and thank you for all your help," Quincy said, dipping his chin in farewell.

"Goodbye, so long, good luck, and do come visit again. Quincy always has the most interesting stories." Bartholomew said in a rambling voice.

We waved to each other and then started our journey back to Honeyvale. My tired and stressed mind kept revisiting Bartholomew's question, and wandering to the hairstick tucked away in my travel bag.

29
HONEY FESTIVAL

It took us twelve days to reach the Black Barrel in Honeyvale. I offered to use magic to speed our journey, but Quincy was vehemently against it. He wanted me to save my energy for the fight.

In the end, it turned out to be the right decision. The spell for the lightning wand had drained me more than I knew. Even though it was more alchemy than magic, a tremendous amount of energy had passed through me that night. I wondered if Aster and Senna were similarly affected.

My heart twisted as I realized I might never get the opportunity to ask them.

Thaddeus looked up as we entered the Black Barrel. A smile spread across his face.

"Welcome back! Welcome back! Well, not even a month gone, and already returning to my humble establishment? I'm flattered."

"Hello, Thaddeus." Quincy took a seat at the bar. "We'll take our usual room, if it's available."

"Yes, of course." Thaddeus bustled around behind the counter, then laid a key down in front of Quincy.

I also took a seat, dropping my travel bag on the floor beside us. "I'd like a drink before we go up. It's been a long journey."

"Right away, miss." Thaddeus placed two mugs in front of Quincy and me.

"So, Thaddeus, any news since we were here last?" Quincy asked, taking a sip of his mead.

"Well, now that you mention it." Thaddeus leaned over the counter and lowered his voice. "On the morning of your departure, it was discovered that several young men had vanished from their beds. We didn't even find their bodies, they were just gone. Since then, we've had a member of our community go missing every few days. There are no more survivors, no more blood-soaked sheets. They disappear without a trace."

My throat went dry, and I took another sip of mead. My eyes wandered to Quincy, who didn't seem at all phased.

"That's unfortunate," Quincy said, drumming his fingers against the counter. "I take it the monster you told us about is still here?"

"That I couldn't say." Thaddeus shrugged. "No one has seen her in some weeks. If it weren't for all the people that have gone missing, I'd say she packed up and left."

I frowned into my drink but didn't say anything.

Thaddeus crossed his arms and leaned against the counter, a serious look on his face. "I probably shouldn't be telling you folks this, but things are bad out here. Real bad. My advice? Stay long enough to enjoy the festival, then turn around and hightail it out of here, and don't look back."

Quincy and I exchanged a long look.

"Tell us about the festival," I said, turning back to Thaddeus.

"Oh, that'll be the Honey Festival. We have one every year, and there's something for everyone. People come from all over to hawk their wares; soaps, candles, mead, and just about anything you can think of. There's singing and dancing, traveling theaters, and drinking games."

I shifted in my seat, my curiosity piqued.

Quincy downed the rest of his drink, then got to his feet. "My thanks, Thaddeus. My wife and I will be going now."

Grabbing my bag, I followed Quincy up the stairs and into our room.

"So she's taking townsfolk from their beds," I said, once we were safely in our room with the door closed behind us. "What do you think she's doing with them? She can't turn them, not until the next full moon."

Quincy ran a hand through his long braids, looking stressed. "Aster has this theory. She thinks werewolves transform for five days. The full moon, two days before and two days after."

My throat went dry, and I licked my lips. "So, what you're saying is, on our last night in Honeyvale, Snow White was hunting for young men to transform into werewolves?"

"Ceridwen-"

"It was the last night of the month her werewolves would turn. She must have been getting them prepared for the next full moon. Don't you think?" My heart was racing in my chest. I felt sick and shaky, but I needed answers.

Quincy stopped and put his hands on the back of a chair. He leaned over, staring at the floor. "Yes, that is what I think."

My hand flew to my mouth, but a muffled sob escaped anyway.

"How long until the full moon?" Quincy asked.

"We still have another week," I said, sitting on the edge of the bed. "What's her plan, Quincy? What do you think Snow White is doing?"

Quincy ran a hand over his face and let out a sigh. "I think Snow White is being careful. She's not leaving bodies, evidence, or witnesses behind. She's being discreet. It could be she's afraid of attracting another hunter."

I chewed on my bottom lip for a moment. My heart slowed, and my hands stopped trembling. "Maybe it's not her. It could be a different creature. Is it possible she's moved on? Thaddeus said no one has seen her."

Quincy was slow to respond. He rubbed the back of his neck, staring out the window. "No, Ceridwen, I don't think that."

"Why?" I asked.

"Because," Quincy started, heaving a great sigh, "It sounds like she has given up on leaving people alive. I believe she is abducting people off the streets and hiding their corpses after."

The nausea and dizziness returned. I leaned forward, placing my head in my hands.

"Ceridwen," Quincy kneeled in front of me, gently touching my cheek.

"I'm all right." I gasped, sitting up.

Quincy licked his lips, looking nervous. "Hey, what do you say we go to that festival tomorrow, hm? We have an entire week until the next full moon, that's plenty of time. We'll take just one day to ourselves, one day for us, then get back to work."

"What about Snow White?" I asked.

Quincy wrinkled his nose. "Snow White will stay away from large crowds."

"What makes you say that?" I asked.

"Because she always has," Quincy stated in a simple voice. "That's what you said, isn't it? She's a recluse? She won't like the noise, or all the bodies pressed up against each other."

"Oh," I said, slowly. "I suppose you're right."

"Come on, what do you say?" Quincy asked, a smile pulling on the edges of his lips.

I hesitated. "It does sound...fun."

Thaddeus' description of the festival *had* piqued my interest, but could I really enjoy myself, knowing what was coming?

"The fact is, neither of us knows what's going to happen once we go up against Snow White," Quincy said in a soft voice. "So, let's take tomorrow for ourselves. What do you think?"

A smile spread across my face, and I reached out to touch Quincy's cheek.

"All right, let's do it. Let's take tomorrow for ourselves."

Quincy was gone when I woke the next morning. I rolled over, noticing his side of the bed was cool, indicating that he had probably been gone for a while. I sat up and rubbed the sleep from my eyes, wondering where Quincy would go without telling me.

That was when the door opened and Quincy tiptoed in. His face fell when he noticed me sitting up in bed.

"I wanted to surprise you." He said, laying a box down on the table. "I thought you should have something nice for today."

I smiled and slid out of bed. "Quincy, that is so thoughtful."

Going over to the table, I lifted the lid of the box and gasped. Inside was a deep scarlet dress made of silk. It had a box neckline, and the skirt was pleated. Tiny crystals were sewn into the bodice, and there was a sash belt with flowers on it.

"It's beautiful," I said. The fabric slid through my fingers like water.

"I know at the castle you must be used to having nice things-"

"Quincy, stop, please." Laughing, I placed a finger over his mouth, effectively silencing him. "It's beautiful, I love it."

I used the washroom, then changed into the dress Quincy had purchased. I swayed my hips, watching the fabric froth around my legs.

"If only the room had a full-length mirror," I said.

Quincy laughed, then kissed me on the forehead. "You'll just have to trust me when I say you're lovely. You'll be the most beautiful creature at the festival today."

I wrapped my arms around Quincy's elbow and smiled at him. "You flatter me. I'm glad we decided to do this, though."

"Me too," Quincy said, his voice soft. "Let's get started, shall we?"

Together, we descended the stairs and left the tavern. We were immediately greeted by the sights and sounds of a bustling festival. We wandered around for a bit, taking in the scenery and chatting with vendors.

"Oh, look, a traveling theater!" I exclaimed excitedly. "I haven't seen one of those since I was a little girl."

I pulled Quincy along behind me and placed some coins in a young girl's hand. We were let into an enclosure that was roped off. Towards the front was a wagon that had temporarily been transformed into a makeshift platform.

A jester made his way onto the stage and took a bow. Everyone began clapping, myself included. Quincy folded his arms across his chest, but there was a spark of amusement in his eye.

"Hear ye, all ye people." The jester started in a loud voice. "Once Cherida was a rich and prosperous land. We lived full, happy lives under the rule of our wise and benevolent ruler, King Iberius! Then, from out of the darkness, came two stars. You know well of who I speak, the Starbright sisters!"

A boo went through the crowd, and I felt Quincy stiffen beside me.

The jester clasped his hands together and gave a solemn nod. "Yes, their beauty blinded King Iberius to their amoral and corrupt ways. They enspelled the King, intent on seizing power and ruling Cherida. Thus begins our story of how the witch-sisters seduced the King, and took control of our country."

More actors appeared on stage, portraying an exaggerated romance between Marcella and Iberius.

"We should go," Quincy whispered in my ear.

"No." My lips were numb, and I could barely get my words out. "To leave now would only make us look suspicious."

"But, Ceridwen-"

"I'm fine, Quincy."

The next half hour was horrendous. I watched the people of Cherida laugh and boo my sister's name. They portrayed her as an evil witch, stripping away her humanity and all her good qualities.

Iberius was played as an intelligent and thoughtful king, who simply couldn't control himself around the Starbright sisters.

At last, the play was over, and the jester appeared back on stage.

"And so our tale of woe concludes." The jester said. "The Queen gave birth to a daughter of extraordinary beauty; hair black as midnight, lips red as blood, and skin white as snow. The babe was pure of heart, encompassing all of Iberius' good virtues. When the Queen saw this, she was so enraged she turned her head away and died. Thus, for a time, the King was free."

A smatter of applause went through the crowd, then the jester continued.

"For a time, all was well in the Kingdom, then the younger Starbright began to plot and scheme for her sister's throne. She finally managed to seduce the King-"

Here, I snorted. I hadn't meant to, but the story they concocted was too ridiculous.

"He then died under mysterious circumstances, only a few short years later."

I kept quiet this time, though I had to bite down on my tongue.

"The Queen Ceridwen is a vain and proud woman, reveling in her beauty and her powers of seduction. She hoards a magic mirror in her room, and every day she asks it who the most beautiful woman in all the land is."

My thoughts immediately went to the scrying mirror in my travel bag, and to my first meeting with Aster. Apparently, this rumor was more widespread than I had imagined.

"The Queen has terrorized Snow White, her stepdaughter, our princess. This poor young girl has been forced to dress in rags, stay indoors, and work as a servant."

An angry murmur spread through the crowd then. Quincy moved behind me and wrapped his arms around my shoulders. His body was tense, his muscles taut with anger and rage.

"But there is hope!" The jester continued. "The evil queen has fallen ill at her summer castle. With any luck, her reign of terror is coming to an end. Let us hope for the day when we may celebrate her demise, and cheer for the reign of our good and kind Queen Snow White!"

"I'm going to kill them, all of them." Quincy hissed in my ear. He made to move past me, pulling the ax from his belt.

"Quincy, no!" I said, grabbing the back of his shirt. "Let's just- Let's go, all right?"

Quincy hesitated, his eyes locked on the jester.

"Please, just get me out of here," I whispered in a small voice.

That seemed to do the trick. Quincy's eyes softened, and he looked down at me. After a long moment, he nodded.

"All right, let's go."

Quincy wasn't gentle as he shouldered his way through the crowd. We eventually made it back out onto the street, where he slowed down and took a deep breath.

"Right," He slung an arm over my shoulder and held me close. "There's lots to do here. We could always get something to eat or drink, buy you something pretty-"

"What's that?" I asked, pointing at a stall.

Quincy's eyes lit up when he saw what I was pointing at. "You've never had raw honeycomb before?"

I shook my head. "I thought you could only eat the honey."

Quincy became visibly excited. "Wait here, I'll be back."

Disappearing from my side, Quincy rushed to the vendor, where he purchased two slices of honeycomb. He returned and thrust a slice into my hand. The honeycomb was wrapped in large, green leaves and smelled divine.

"How do I eat it?" I asked, confused.

"Just take a bite," Quincy said. He demonstrated by sinking his teeth into the corner of his honeycomb and began chewing. "Mm, delicious."

I tentatively followed his example, my teeth breaking through the hexagonal cells and releasing the sweet honey within.

"Mmm..." I said, my eyes widening. "It is good!"

We continued our way through the festival while we finished our honeycomb. The beeswax was edible, though a bit waxy. When I finished mine, I licked my fingers clean.

Quincy laughed. "You really enjoyed that, didn't you?"

"I can't remember the last time I had something so good," I confessed.

Quincy chuckled and shook his head. "All those delicacies at the castle, and you're fawning over honeycomb."

I nudged him in the side with my elbow, and we both laughed.

Music washed over us as we walked, and we turned toward the source of the sound. There was a small band playing, one with a lute, and one with a crumhorn.

Another musician was beating her hand against a tabor, while a fourth danced with a tambourine.

Quite a few people were standing around in a semi-circle, clapping and throwing coins.

A couple eventually broke apart from the crowd. They grabbed each other's hands and began dancing. More couples joined in, laughing and smiling at each other.

A light appeared in Quincy's eyes. "Come on!" He shouted, reaching for my hand.

I froze in place, panic rooting my feet to the ground. "I can't."

Quincy quirked an eyebrow at me and tilted his head. "Why not?"

My face flushed hot, and I lowered my eyes. "I'm not very good at it."

Quincy's jaw dropped open. "I don't believe you."

"It's true!"

"But- But, Ceridwen," Quincy leaned in close to me and spoke in a low voice. "What about all that time you spent at the castle? Surely, you must have learned at some point."

I scowled. "If you must know, Marcella forced me to learn the basics, but I never enjoyed it."

"Forced you? So, that's the problem." A twinkle appeared in Quincy's eyes. "Let me teach you to enjoy dancing."

Reluctantly, I took Quincy's hand. He gave me a wicked grin and pulled me close to his chest. I wrapped my arms around his neck while he held me around the waist.

"Trust me." He whispered in my ear.

Just like that, we were off, moving fluently through the crowd of people, our feet dancing wildly.

It was better than I expected. There were no formal steps, no awkward conversations with a stiff partner, no judgmental eyes peering at me from a large crowd.

The moment seemed to last forever. Music pulsed through the air like magic. We became lost in a sea of happiness and laughter.

I was safe in Quincy's embrace. His scent of leather and tobacco was warm and familiar. His eyes were alight with an intoxicating mixture of love and mischief.

The music slowed, and so did we. I leaned into Quincy's embrace, soaking up his energy and fiery aura. Every detail of his face was etched in my mind's eye, and I knew this man wholly possessed my heart and soul in a way that made me ache.

If only this could go on forever.

Eventually, the band took a break and so did we. My cheeks were sore from smiling and laughing so much.

"Come on, I'll get us something to drink," Quincy said, moving us away from the crowd. He left my side and disappeared in the direction of a vendor selling honey and herb tea.

I wiped a few loose strands of hair out of my face. The tendrils were damp with sweat. I glanced around, spotting a seller from Theor.

My interest piqued, I moved towards them and examined their wares.

"Hello," a pretty woman said, smiling at me. Her raven hair was styled into tiny braids, just like Quincy's. Her dark skin had a jeweled undertone of dusky rose compared to Quincy's earthy copper. "See anything you like?"

"These silks," I said, leaning over her display table. "They're lovely."

"Ah, yes, our hair scarves. They're very popular in Theor. The silk has many benefits, both for the hair and the skin."

My eyes skimmed over the different colors. These scarves were just like the one Quincy wore when he tied back his braids. A deep, cobalt blue caught my eye then. It was the color of the sky right before the sun rises.

"How much is this?" I asked, running the tips of my fingers across the light fabric.

The woman quoted me a price. I fished a few coins out of my purse for her, and then I carefully folded the scarf and placed it in my pocket. I had just taken a few steps away from the vendor when Quincy appeared.

"Here, try this." Quincy thrust a cup into my hand.

I took a sip, and my eyes widened. "Mmm! What is it?"

Quincy put his arm around my shoulders, and we continued walking. "Honey, lavender, and lemon."

"Really?" I stared down at my cup. Those flavors didn't sound like they should go together, yet I couldn't deny the drink was delicious.

We enjoyed the festival for a while longer, but by then it was starting to get dark. Silently, we made our way back to the Black Barrel, each of us lost in our own thoughts.

"I bought something for you," I admitted in a shy voice, once we were back in our room.

Quincy pulled his shirt off over his head, revealing his broad shoulders and muscular chest. "For me?" He asked, excitement in his voice.

I pulled the hair scarf out of my pocket and handed it to him. "I hope you like it."

Quincy's face suddenly turned serious. He sat down on the edge of the bed, a hurt look in his eyes.

"I just thought- because you already have one, I thought you might like another." My words were coming out in a jumble. "Oh no, it's all wrong, isn't it? Quincy, I'm sorry. I just wanted to do something nice-"

Quincy moved from the bed suddenly and pressed his lips to mine. He cupped my face in his hands and deepened the kiss, pulling me closer. I was out of breath when we finally broke apart.

"I love it," Quincy said in a husky voice.

"You do?" I asked, confused. "It's just that, you looked so sad-"

"The hair scarf you've seen me wearing," Quincy interrupted. "It was a gift from my late wife."

I sucked in a breath. "Oh, Quincy, I'm so sorry."

"Don't be." Quincy shook his head. "I'll still wear her scarf sometimes, and think about her, and our son. But you've given me a reason to look forward, to the future. I haven't had that in a long time. Thank you."

"You're welcome, Quincy," I whispered.

He took me in his arms then, kissing me deeply until I was dizzy and breathless. Picking me up, Quincy laid me on the bed, and we quickly became entangled in each other's bodies.

When we finished, Quincy drifted off to sleep. He lay on top of me, his head on my stomach. I twirled his braids around my fingers and looked out the window.

Outside, the moon was waxing. It would be full in about a week. My stomach churned, and I wondered if Quincy and I would even be alive to see it.

A new thought struck me, then, and a jolt went through my body. Quincy murmured in his sleep and tightened his arms around me.

For a moment, I couldn't move. I was too stunned. When was the last time I had my moon blood? Shouldn't it have been here by now?

My breath became shaky. I stared at the ceiling, focusing on slowing my heart and relaxing my body. Eventually, the panic subsided, and I pushed my fears away.

Those thoughts would have to wait for another day. Tomorrow, we faced Snow White.

30
THE GIFT

The next morning was a quiet one. Quincy and I lay in bed, not speaking, just holding each other. We watched the sun through the window as it traveled across the sky.

Sometime after noon, we went to town and stocked up on supplies.

When we got back to our room, I put on a Carnelian belt and wound a necklace of nightshade around my throat. I wound my hair up into a tight bun and carefully slid the carnelian hairpin in, the one that Bartholomew had gifted me.

Quincy was checking on his crossbow. He had a sheath of silver-tipped quivers, along with a silver dagger. The vial of lightning water I gave him was tucked into his belt, as was the lightning wand.

"I think we should bring both horses," I said, looking at myself in the mirror. "We'll tie Buttercup to Scout. If anything happens to us, Scout can lead her to Senna and Aster's place."

Quincy nodded. "I think you're right. We might also need them for a quick escape."

"There's one other thing I need to say." I sat at the table next to Quincy. My fingers traveled across the table until I was able to caress his arm. "I love you. I love you so much, Quincy. Today will be hard, but I'll do everything in my power to protect you. I'll never forgive myself if I fail-"

"Ceridwen," Quincy leaned forward and took my hands in his, "You're not going in there alone. This burden does not fall squarely on your shoulders. I'll do everything I can to keep you safe, to get the job done. It's what you hired me for."

"I know you will." I gave him a watery smile, tears starting in my eyes.

"Come here." Quincy stood to his feet and pulled me with him. Wrapping his arms around me, he kissed me gently on the lips. "I love you, too. We're going to get through this together."

"Thank you," I said, looking up into his face.

"Come on," Quincy jerked his head towards the door. "We only have a few hours of daylight left. Let's get started."

Placing my hand in Quincy's, I let him lead me out the door and down to the stables.

He was right. I had hired him to do a job. Now, I had to trust that he could see it through.

I finished pouring salt around the miner's camp and looked up. Bartholomew's gift had proven useful, after all. It wasn't just any jar of salt he had given me, but one that never emptied, no matter how much was used.

Quincy was a few feet away from me, inspecting the line, and making sure there weren't any gaps.

"Everything looks good." He said, moving to my side. His hair was tied back with the cobalt scarf I had given him. Even as the sun was beginning to set, and our doom was nearing, I couldn't help but think about how handsome he looked. I stared into his face, committing every detail to memory.

After tonight, that might be all I have of him.

"Ceridwen." Quincy cupped my face in his hands, touching his forehead to mine. "I love you. I will always love you. Wherever I go, wherever I end up, no matter what happens tonight, I will carry you with me. Not even the devil himself could make me forget you."

"I love you, too, Quincy." Tears pricked the back of my eyes. "My heart will always belong to you."

We may not make it through the night alive, we may not make it through the night together, but nothing could take away our love. Whatever happened next, we would always have that.

The sun was the harbinger of our doom. Standing together, Quincy and I watched it dip below the horizon.

Just as the last rays of light were swallowed up by the darkness, the door to the mining lodge was flung open.

Seven men came loping out. Their movements were fluid and unnaturally swift. It was easy to tell the difference between the men who had already turned, and those who had only been bit.

Three of the werewolf men were large and unnaturally hairy, their muscles disproportionate to their bodies. Their teeth were sharpened into points, and their wild eyes glowed in the dark.

Those who were bitten, but had yet to transform, were also large and strong. However, their bodies were more human, and they lacked the wild aura that permeated their peers.

"You got this?" Quincy murmured into my ear.

I nodded, energy pulsing down my arms and into my palms. "On your signal."

Quincy hefted a crossbow into his arms. He took aim and fired.

The arrow arced through the air but didn't embed itself into a body. Instead, it landed in the ground. The men snarled. The group huddled closer together while continuing to race towards us.

Quincy fired another arrow. It grazed the arm of one of the wild men, who turned abruptly and moved closer to the pack, a murderous expression in his eyes.

Quincy lowered his crossbow. "I think that's as close as they're going to get."

I rubbed my hands together. "You did well."

"Let me just get off one more shot," Quincy muttered. He lifted the crossbow again, a gleam in his eyes.

The arrow flew through the air, landing near the back of the pack. The men yelped and picked up their pace, stumbling into the men in front of them.

At that same moment, the front of the pack slammed into the edges of the salt circle. Everything became a confusing tangle of limbs and legs as they fell over each other.

"Do it now, Ceridwen!" Quincy yelled above the noise.

I drew on the power of my carnelian belt, feeling the energy rush through me. Holding out my palms, fire roared across the clearing. It was a dry heat, like from a furnace, and the flames were orange and red, swirling with embers. Smoke plumbed into the sky.

Quincy and I waited with bated breath. At last, the smoke cleared. My breath caught in my throat as I took in the scene before me.

Seven burned corpses were before us. They were charred and ashen, barely resembling anything human. For a moment, I felt a pang of guilt. These creatures had been men once.

Quincy stepped over the salt line and held his hand out to me. "Come."

I took his hand in my own and followed. We advanced on the miner's lodgings, not speaking and moving quietly. My heart beat strangely in my chest.

We stopped in front of the door. Quincy put his crossbow down and pulled a wooden stake from his belt.

"All right," He whispered. "On the count of three. One, Two-"

BOOM.

Wood splinters flew through the air. The door exploded into tiny fragments, and a shadowy figure burst through.

For a moment all I saw was yellow, glowing eyes. They were wild and mad and untamed, filled with a murderous rage and brutal hunger.

Then the jaws parted. A lolling, red tongue tasted the air. Sharp fangs dripped with saliva, capable of tearing flesh and breaking through bone.

"Ceridwen!" Quincy bellowed. "It's the last werewolf!"

Hairy arms reached out, and just like that, Quincy was gone. The creature yanked my lover through the door and into the lodgings.

"Quincy!" I screamed. Throwing myself through the shattered entrance, I gave chase after them.

As I hurtled into the lodgings, I took in the man's appearance. He was grotesque and hairy, half human and half animal. His muscles bulged at odd angles. He also had a burn across his face and body. It took a moment to remember I had done that.

Quincy was pinned to the floor, underneath the creature.

The werewolf leaned forward, baring his teeth. His fangs were inches away from Quincy's throat.

"I haven't forgotten our last meeting, huntsman." The creature growled. "You owe me for the deaths of my brothers."

Quincy gave a menacing laugh. "You're welcome to try and collect."

Before I had a chance to do anything, Quincy brought up a silver dagger and buried it in the werewolf's side.

"AAAHHH!" The werewolf leaped back, his face contorting in pain.

Quincy came up swinging, his ax cutting through the air. As he aimed a blow at the werewolf's head, the creature grabbed the hilt of the weapon. They stumbled across the cabin, and then fell out a window. Glass shattered across the floor as the two men disappeared.

"No!" I yelled, rushing forward.

An unexpected blow to the chest caught me off guard. I gasped as the breath was driven from my body, and I found myself pressed against a wall.

"You came back." Snow White said, looking at me with wide, dark eyes. She was the picture of youth and innocence.

My heart twisted cruelly in my chest, and I let out a pained gasp.

"Snow White," I said, "This can't continue. These creatures...they were men once! Don't you understand? You've stolen them from their families! You've stolen their lives, their futures!"

Snow White gave an evil smile, and her veneer cracked. Behind the mask, I saw who she truly was, deranged, a murderer, bloodthirsty, someone who reveled in violence. "You were the one who raised me to rule."

"Not like this," I said in a firm voice.

"No?" Snow White raised one eyebrow. "Have you not stolen people's lives, their futures? Have you not broken up families? Do not think you can hide what you are from me. You're just as bloodthirsty as I am."

The breath went out of me, and bile rose in my throat. Was Snow White right? Could it be that we were the same?

Snow White cocked her head, the wheels turning behind her eyes. "I could turn you."

"What?" I gasped.

"I was telling the truth." Snow White said in a soft voice. "You are the only mother I've ever known. If I turned you, we could be together forever. Death will not haunt our footsteps. We would be immortal and strong. No one would dare defy us."

My breath hitched in my throat. Eternity with Snow White? My thoughts barreled out of control as the possibilities flashed before my eyes.

Never again would I have to run for my life. Never again would I worry about scheming royals and backstabbers. I wouldn't fear for Snow White's life. We could rule them all so easily. It wouldn't be difficult to bend the people to our will. Break them, even, if we so desired-

With a gasp, I brought myself back to the present. How close had that been to Marcella's dream?

"We won't have to worry about losing each other, not the way you lost your parents or your sister. Don't you see?" Snow White asked. "You don't have to be parted from any more of your family."

It was tempting, so tempting, to say yes.

I licked my lips, trying to come up with a coherent answer, when a stray thought arrived with all the gentleness of a summer breeze.

"There is a time for living, and a time for death, Your Majesty. Don't get confused about what side you're on, or you might miss out on what's right in front of you."

Bartholomew's quiet words surfaced in my mind, and my resolve crumbled. This was it. This was the gift Bartholomew was talking about the day he ran down the lane to bring Quincy and me breakfast.

The gift was living.

CRASH. BANG.

Quincy and the werewolf crashed through the side of the building. The lodgings exploded in a flurry of noise and fighting. As the werewolf sprawled across the ground, teeth snapping, Quincy got the upper hand in the fight. He loosed the ax from his belt and raised it high above his head.

Snow White saw what was about to happen, and rage flashed across her face. "Damn you!" She shrieked.

Quincy brought the blade of his ax down, cleanly cutting off the werewolf's head. He shifted the ax in his hand, turning his attention to Snow White and me. There was a murderous gleam in his eye.

Snow White turned to me with a hiss. "Make your choice. Now!"

"I don't want it." My voice was calm, certain. "I don't want to live forever, Snow White. I don't want to kill, or hunt people, or rule over them. That's not living, and I can't do it. I'm sorry."

Snow White bared her teeth at me. "How dare you! Do you know what I'm offering?"

"I said no-AH!" I shrieked as Snow White grabbed a fistful of my hair. She yanked my head back, exposing my throat. For one panic-stricken moment, I thought about Everald grabbing me in the same manner.

Snow White tilted her head back. Opening her jaw, she revealed her sharp fangs. "You'll thank me for this later," she said in a raspy voice.

"No!" Quincy yelled.

Snow White brought her teeth to my throat, then shrieked and released me.

"AAAHHH! Nightshade! You're wearing nightshade!" She yelled, cowering away.

"Leave her alone!" Quincy yelled. He raised his ax and ran in our direction.

"Go away! You're ruining everything!" Snow White screamed.

"I made a promise," Quincy growled. He lowered his ax. His other hand went to his belt, and he pulled out the lightning wand. He leveled it at Snow White, a determined look on his face. A burst of bright, hot light exploded from the crystal and filled the room with a dry, burning heat.

As the bolt of lightning shot across the room, Snow White proved faster. Moving at an inhuman speed, she darted out of the way. The bolt crashed in a corner of the room, causing a small explosion. The force knocked me onto the flat of my back, and even Quincy stumbled back a few steps.

Snow White hissed, baring her fangs at Quincy. He quickly raised the wand and sent another bolt in her direction. I shielded my eyes as fire and embers crashed against the far wall.

"Enough!" Snow White bellowed. She darted across the room, her movements a blur.

Grabbing Quincy's wrist, Snow White yanked his arm back and twisted. I flinched as a crack echoed through the air, and Quincy bellowed in pain. The lightning wand hit the ground and rolled across the floor. Snow White let out a growl, and her foot came down on the crystal. It cracked and shattered beneath her heel. Another flash of light filled the room, briefly blinding me.

I let out a cry and curled up on my side. For a moment, I wondered if I would ever see anything again. Struggling to my knees, I rubbed my palms against my eyes and pried my eyelids open.

"Did you think you could defeat me so easily?" Snow White raged. She held Quincy's broken arm in one hand. Her other hand came up and slammed into his chest.

Quincy flew across the cabin and hit the far wall, crumbling to the floor where he lay motionless.

"No, Quincy!" I yelled, attempting to run to his side.

Snow White grabbed me around the throat. She pulled me close, staring into my wide and frightened eyes.

"You smell like him." Snow White hissed. "You smell like that filthy huntsman."

"I love him," I said in a thick voice. "Please, Snow White, please, don't hurt him. Whatever you're feeling, take it out on me. Leave Quincy alone."

Snow White wrinkled her nose, like she found the thought distasteful. Then her gaze fell to my stomach. All at once, she froze. Her features became cold and still, like a marble statue. Her eyes flicked up to mine, and I saw a fiery rage there that scorched my soul.

"You're pregnant."

Her words were quiet, poised, and as deadly as a poisoned blade. Shock poured over me, like an icy rain.

Behind us, Quincy stumbled to his feet. There was a stunned look on his face, but beyond that, I couldn't tell what he was feeling.

Snow White spun on her heel, baring her teeth at Quincy.

"You did this! This is your fault!" She screamed.

Snow White's hand abruptly left off at my throat. I stumbled as she launched herself at Quincy.

"She is mine! You will not take her from me!" Snow White was yelling.

Appearing at Quincy's side, Snow White grabbed a fistful of his braids and yanked his head back. His throat was now exposed. She drew her lips back from her teeth and sank her fangs into the soft flesh of his neck.

"No!" I screamed so loud, and so long, that the breath went out of my body.

Snow White dropped Quincy to the ground. She made a choking sound, and her hands went to her throat.

Quincy collapsed, a pained expression on his face. There was also a look of triumph in his eyes, and I saw an empty vial roll across the floor.

The lightning water. Quincy had drank it, and poisoned his blood against Snow White.

Gasping, clawing at her throat, Snow White threw herself at me, baring her fangs.

I pulled out my hairpin, gripping it tightly in my hands and holding it like a stake.

Snow White grabbed onto my upper arms. Her gaze landed on my shoulder, and she lurched forward, trying to sink her teeth into my skin. Whether she was about to drain me dry, or still determined to turn me, I wasn't sure.

I still held the hairpin. Lifting my hand, I plunged the pointed end into Snow White's chest.

It was here that I understood the full potential of Bartholomew's gift. The carnelian cracked. A bolt of sunlight traveled down the coffin nail and straight into Snow White's heart. There was a brief flash of golden light beneath her skin. She gasped, a puff of smoke emanating from her mouth.

No more words were spoken between us. The strength went out from Snow White's legs, and I caught her in my arms. We sank to the floor together. I began to weep, cradling her head against my chest.

"I'm sorry. I'm sorry, I'm so sorry." Over and over, I repeated the words. Hot tears poured down my face, burning my skin as they traveled down my cheeks. I watched, sobbing quietly, as the light faded from Snow White's eyes.

31
GRIEF

I thought the grief of losing Snow White was going to kill me.

Quincy quickly put out a half dozen fires around the lodge while I sat in a corner, rocking back and forth and holding Snow White's body. When he finished, he managed to convince me to lay her down and follow him outside.

It was then that I noticed his arm was hanging at a funny angle, and blood was pumping from his neck.

"W-wait a moment," I mumbled through numb lips. Reaching into my belt, I pulled out a Howlite crystal and healed the bone in Quincy's arm. The puncture wounds on his neck I patched up with moss.

As soon as he was well enough, Quincy set about building a pyre. I watched in a daze, tears running down my face.

When he finished, Quincy disappeared into the cabin and re-emerged, carrying Snow White's small, lifeless body in his hands. She looked impossibly tiny in his strong arms.

As he placed her on the pyre, my knees gave way, but I somehow remained standing. Stumbling forward, I bent over Snow White's cold form and touched my forehead to hers. With a muffled gasp, I drew my fingers through her long, raven hair.

"She could be sleeping." I choked out.

Quincy stood next to the pyre, shifting uncomfortably. His dark eyes watched me with a mixture of pity and guilt. "Ceridwen, you need to look away. You don't want to see what happens next."

With an effort, I straightened, but couldn't bring myself to move back. Swiping a hand across my eyes, I blinked at Quincy and the ax he was holding.

"Oh, oh, Quincy, no. Please, not that." I begged.

Quincy dropped his eyes. "I take no pleasure from this, Ceridwen, but you know it has to be this way."

"Quincy, please," I begged, fighting the urge to climb onto the pyre and hold Snow White in my arms. My hands scrabbled across the wood until I found her icy hand. I clutched it tightly in my own. She was so small, but she had always been small for her age...

"Ceridwen," Quincy said, his voice a bit firmer. He came to my side and gently tugged at my skirts. "Turn away, my love."

"No!" I shrieked. I flung out my arms, grabbing Snow White by the shoulders. "I can't do it, don't make me! Let's just leave her here, Quincy. Surely, she can't hurt anyone now-"

Quincy wrapped his arms around my waist and lifted me in the air. I screamed and clawed and flailed against him until the strength drained from my body. Collapsing against his chest, I sobbed.

Through it all, Quincy said nothing. He held me tightly in his arms, stroking my hair with one hand.

Slowly, my crying subsided. Quincy put a hand under my chin and lifted my face, so our eyes met.

"Ceridwen." His voice was husky. "You still have something to live for."

Quincy took my hand and placed it over my belly.

"There is still some good in this world." He murmured in my ear. His breath ghosted across my skin.

I took a deep breath, inhaling Quincy's scent of tobacco and leather. My body relaxed the tiniest bit, and my mind cleared.

"All right," I said in a scratchy voice. I turned away from the pyre and faced the cabin.

"It will be over soon." Quincy put his hand on the back of my neck and gently kissed me on the forehead.

He disappeared from my sight then. I heard the *thump* of the ax and slapped both hands over my mouth. A scream welled up inside of me, but I tampered it down.

Following that, there was a rapid slicing sound that was mercifully quick. I stared at the cabin as numbness washed over me. After I few minutes, Quincy's voice floated over to me.

"I'm ready to begin, Ceridwen."

I turned back to Snow White. Quincy had wrapped a cloth around her neck, so I couldn't see where he had beheaded her. There was also a blanket tucked around her body.

"What did you do with her heart?" I asked in a hollow voice.

"I placed it under the pyre. It will burn first." Quincy explained. "Say your goodbyes."

I went to Snow White, pressing my forehead to hers. I ran my fingers through her hair as I cried, my tears falling on her face.

"Goodbye, my snow angel." I choked out. "Daughter of my heart, how I wish I could have done more. My child, my love, I'm so sorry I couldn't protect you."

Placing a tender kiss on Snow White's forehead, I whispered in her ear. "I will never forget you. All the days of my life, I will carry your memory with me."

I stepped back from the pyre, my hand going to my belly. It was a small comfort, knowing I would be bringing new life into the world. A new baby to love and hold and cherish, although I was too numb at the moment to really appreciate it.

Quincy moved to my side and slipped an arm around my waist. He kissed me tenderly on top of my head.

"I'm going to begin now." He said.

I nodded but didn't turn away. Instead, I watched as Quincy moved about the pyre, a torch in hand. He lit the kindling in various places, and soon Snow White was lost in a fiery blaze.

I don't know how long I stood there, watching. Long enough to see the pyre die down, leaving nothing but ashes behind. Long enough to see the sun rise, then set, and for the first stars appear, like diamond chips set in black velvet.

Quincy brought the horses into the clearing with us and set up a small camp. Going to his saddlebags, he pulled out a sleeping mat and unrolled it on the ground. Taking my hand, he led me to the makeshift bed where we lay down together. Eventually, I drifted off into a fitful slumber, his arms around me.

I woke the next morning, the previous day's events fresh in my mind.

With the sun low on the horizon, it was clear the day was just beginning. The sky was a pale, washed-out blue, and I suspected the last pink streaks of dawn had just faded. The air was crisp and cool, accented with the light trilling of birdsong.

The sound of soft footsteps had me reluctantly stir and move into a sitting position. I glanced around, finding Quincy poking at the pyre with the wooden handle of his ax. He seemed to be making sure there was nothing left but ashes.

As Quincy moved in a circular motion, his eyes landed on me.

"You're awake." He noted, then went back to his task.

"Yes," I said, swiping a hand across my eyes. "Did you get any sleep?"

"No," Quincy shook his head. "I wasn't tired."

I squeezed my eyes shut and let out a sigh. "I don't know how I was able to drift off after what we did yesterday."

When I opened my eyes, Quincy was crouched down in front of me. He cupped my chin in his hand, drawing his thumb over my cheek.

"You were exhausted." He said. "Be gentle with yourself."

"I'm trying." I gave Quincy a brittle smile and placed my hand over his.

A wave of gratitude washed over me. Whatever awful thing happened next, it soothed my heart to know this man, who I loved, would follow me anywhere and keep me safe.

"Are you hungry?" Quincy stood up and moved away from me. He grabbed his pack and rummaged through it. "I still have some cheese and apples from the tavern."

"Yes, please," I responded. My stomach rumbled with hunger.

Quincy came to sit beside me and handed me the food. I bit into an apple, staring sullenly into the distance. I should have been using this moment to plan ahead, to map out a future for Cherida, but Snow White's death had cast a pall over everything.

I would think about it later.

Carefully, Quincy reached out a hand and placed it on my stomach.

"Did you know?" He asked in a quiet voice.

I swallowed my bite of apple and shrugged. "I suspected the night of the festival, but I didn't know. Everything has been so chaotic these past few weeks. I haven't had time to think about it."

Quincy pulled me into his lap and nuzzled my neck.

"A baby." He said. "*Our* baby." His voice sounded gleeful.

I thawed out at Quincy's excitement. A spark of hope and joy started in my chest.

"Yes, we're going to have a baby," I said.

"I wonder if it will be a boy or a girl," Quincy mused.

I sank my teeth into my bottom lip, remembering Marcella's obsession with having a son. "Do you have a preference?"

Quincy shook his head. "I'm just excited to meet them. Whoever they are, whoever they want to be, I'm going to love them."

I smiled and ran my fingers through Quincy's braids. "Thank you for saying that."

"I can't wait to watch them grow up." Quincy went on. "I'll teach them how to whittle and how to build things. You can teach them about botany and magic."

Icy dread curled my stomach into a tight knot. My mouth went dry, and a tremble ran down my spine. I stood up and moved away from Quincy.

"Where are you going?" Quincy asked, noticing my sudden change in mood.

"We can't live in a fantasy, Quincy. We have to be realistic." I said.

Quincy blinked, uncomprehending. "All right, then, where do you suggest we start?"

I straightened my back in an attempt to steady myself. "Cherida, we must start with Cherida."

Quincy scowled and looked away. "Hang Cherida, why do we care? I just want you."

"I can't."

Quincy turned towards me, drawing his brow. "What do you mean?"

"I had an arrangement with Amara, Quincy. You know that. I can't abandon her." I said.

"So we go get her." Quincy stood to his feet and advanced on me. "We take her with us. We go somewhere, anywhere, but we do it together."

"It's not that easy, Quincy," I argued. "We can't leave Cherida without an heir. The country will go to war with itself."

"You don't know that," Quincy argued. "You're making an assumption. I'm sure there's someone high enough up in the ranks who can assume the throne."

"There isn't." I shook my head. "Snow White killed many important people. Not only that, but much of the court has been locked away in their summer castles. If they come out and see a vacancy in power, it will result in a power grab that could devastate the economy."

"I still don't understand why that's our problem." Quincy stood and folded his arms across his chest. "Why is it your responsibility to make sure a bunch of mad fools don't drive themselves to extinction?"

I looked at the ground, twisting my hands in my skirts. "Iberius trusted me on his deathbed. He bequeathed me with much of the country's army and land. He knew an uprising was possible, and he gave me the tools I needed to assume a position of power. It's the least I can do for him, especially after what Marcella and I did-"

"No, stop." Quincy shook his head. "Don't take responsibility for your sister's actions."

"I'm not," I said in a firm voice. "But I helped her summon that demon, that vampire. If it weren't for us, Iberius could have appointed another heir to the throne. He could have taken better precautions to prevent a war."

Quincy rocked back on his heels, folding his arms across his chest. "So, what do you suggest?"

I licked my lips, then moved towards Quincy.

"You could come with me." My voice was a hoarse whisper. "Come back with me to Cherida, to Aileen. I'll tell them you're head of the castle guard, that you're under my employment. They won't separate us. We can be together!"

"Oh, listen to yourself, Ceridwen!" Quincy bellowed. "You're asking me to watch someone else raise my child! To watch from afar as you marry another person!"

"I have responsibilities, Quincy!" I cried out. "You knew that before we slept together! You knew I was engaged, that I had to return to the castle!"

"But I thought you'd change your mind!" Quincy said. He moved towards me, cupping my face in his hands. "I thought that all changed when we fell in love. Don't you want something for yourself? Must your whole life be honor and duty?"

"Please, don't ask me that." I stepped back, away from Quincy. "You can't assume that because we fell in love that I'm going to change the whole trajectory of my life, that I'm going to turn my back on everyone who depends on me!"

"The country despises you," Quincy said in a gravely voice. "They hate and fear you. Whatever you have to offer them, they don't want it."

My heart throbbed like an open wound. I drew in a sharp breath. "Be that as it may, I will not turn back now. I am returning to Cherida. Are you coming with me or not?"

Quincy watched me for a long moment, then shook his head, staring at the ground.

"Not."

Pain tore at my chest, but I remained upright, my face impassive. "Fine," I said. "Goodbye, Quincy."

Without waiting for a response, I untethered Buttercup and began my long trek back towards the castle.

32
GOODBYE FOR NOW

I could have used magic to return more swiftly to the castle, but I found myself prolonging the journey.

Amara, at least, would be happy to see me. That is, until I told her about Snow White.

Snow White. How was I going to handle that?

Perhaps I could send Amara away, and claim my stepdaughter succumbed to the plague.

No, that would still risk civil war. Neither the court, nor the people, would accept me as heir apparent.

Amara could, possibly, continue impersonating Snow White. They had certainly fooled enough courtiers back in the day. They had even made a game of it. My mind wandered back to when I caught Amara dancing in the gardens. The crowd had been calling her Snow White and cheering for her.

I pushed the thought away. I was ashamed to think of how I acted then.

Anyway, it wouldn't be fair of me to ask Amara to give up her life for the crown. She wasn't born for that; it wasn't her responsibility.

Perhaps Amara would be amenable to sacrificing a few years. Then she could abdicate the throne in favor of someone else. It wouldn't be that difficult to convince the court that she'd rather be with her stepmother in Aileen. Of course, Amara would have to keep up the charade, but she was welcome with me anytime.

Then again, Amara might prefer to travel, to go somewhere else, to be someone new.

My thoughts went round and round in wild circles, keeping me up late at night. I would stare at the stars, wishing for some form of guidance. I often wondered what Marcella, or even Iberius, would think of the mess I'd gotten myself into.

Thinking about Quincy was too painful. Every time I envisioned his face, it was like a knife to the heart. Sometimes I would curl up into a little ball, my hands on my stomach, drawing a sense of calm from the part of Quincy that I carried with me.

A baby.

I had never actively thought about having children before. Not in a proactive way. I had never loved anyone enough that I wanted to try. Quincy was different. I knew, somehow, that this was a man who I was going to love for the rest of my life. Someone who, if our circumstances were different, I could have a real future with.

At last, the day dawned where my castle my silhouetted against the morning sky. I rode through town silently, casting an illusion over myself so I wouldn't be recognized. I was stressed and tired and weary down to the bone.

No one stopped me as I rode past the castle guards, through the gates, and into the stables. I handed Buttercup's reins over to a stable hand, who barely glanced at me.

I wandered through the castle, still not lifting my illusion. Funny, I had lived here for years, raised a child here, watched my sister get married here, but the homely familiarity I had been expecting was gone. Everything felt alien and foreign, as though my old life and I no longer fit together.

What had changed so much?

After some time, I tired of wandering the halls. I began to look for Amara in earnest. My search led me outdoors and into the extensive gardens on the castle grounds.

The garden paths were lined with neatly trimmed bushes, along with red and white roses that perfumed the air with a sweet and heady scent. Eventually, I caught sight of a cream-colored skirt disappearing around a corner. I quickened my pace when Amara's bell-like laughter came ringing through the air.

I paused, shock rippling through me. Amara had always been sweet and docile. But this? This sounded like a kind of wild joy I hadn't heard from her before.

Perhaps that was my fault.

I followed at a slower pace, peeking at Amara through foliage and around corners.

She was with Prince Liam. They walked close together, not quite touching. Amara's head was bowed, a blush coloring her cheeks, but she leaned in towards the King, looking up at him through her long, dark lashes.

Prince Liam was openly smitten with Amara. He kept tilting his head down, bending at the waist to catch a glimpse of her face. While Amara alternated her gaze between him and the ground, King Liam only had eyes for her.

I followed at a distance, watching as Liam gestured wildly with his hands. Whatever story he was telling, he was trying very hard to make her laugh.

He was soon rewarded with a peal of laughter as Amara rocked back on her heels.

She clutched her stomach with one hand, while the other drifted to land on Liam's chest. The pink in her cheeks deepened into a blush, and she snatched her fingers back, embarrassed. She looked away too quickly to notice him leaning into her touch.

I followed for a few more minutes, entranced by the scene before me.

Eventually, a courier made their way through the gardens, rushing to King Liam's side and whispering in his ear. A solemn look came over the King's face and he nodded. As the courier scuttled away, Liam murmured a brief explanation to Amara. He finished by kissing the back of her hand, then hurrying towards the castle.

Amara didn't move for a long moment. She watched the direction in which the king had left, a soft, dreamy expression on her face.

Dropping my illusion, I made my way around the corner and cleared my throat.

"Amara," I said.

Amara started, then turned in my direction. Her face lit up as her eyes landed on me.

"Ceridwen!" she squealed, rushing to my side. She paused a few steps away from me, noticing the expression on my face. She let out a soft gasp, clutching her hands to her chest.

I reacted quickly. Amara's knees buckled, and I jumped forward, wrapping both of my arms around her.

"Shhh," I soothed, holding her to my chest. I stroked one hand through her dark hair.

Amara made a strangled, gasping sound for another few breaths, then burst into tears.

I let her cry, knowing she likely wouldn't get a chance like this again. Who else but the two of us would grieve the loss of Snow White?

Eventually, Amara took a deep breath and straightened up. She took a step back and looked into my face.

"How did it happen?" She asked in a thick voice.

I sighed. "Unfortunately, making Snow White a golem wasn't an option. She was...something else, Amara. Not of the living world."

"I understand." Amara glanced at the ground. "I think we both suspected it was a fool's hope."

"Yes, it was." I let out a deep sigh.

"So, she is dead, then?" Amara asked in a trembling voice. "Did she suffer much?"

I shook my head. "Don't ask for details, Amara. I won't tell you anything you want to hear."

Amara made a pained noise, like I had stabbed her. "Snow White was my best friend. All my life, she was loyal and kind, and her love was unwavering. I shall miss her."

"Yes, so will I," I said.

"What happens now?" Amara asked, lifting her eyes to mine.

"I've been considering that my entire return journey," I confessed in a slow voice. "You and I have some decisions to make."

"Me?" Amara raised her brow, looking surprised.

"Yes," I nodded. "I am still engaged to the King, Amara, and Cherida needs a leader. I can resume my position at court, go to Aileen, and leave you in charge here. In a few years, you can abdicate the throne and come stay with me, or you can get married and continue to rule. If you find any of those options uncomfortable, we can fake your death. We'll tell everyone that Snow White succumbed to the plague. Rest assured, you will be generously rewarded for your loyalty. You can travel, settle down wherever you like, and live in the lap of luxury."

Amara grew pale when I mentioned my engagement to the king, though she kept her face still and betrayed no emotion.

"There is one more option," I said in a kind voice. "I saw the way you and the King looked at each other. Amara, do you love him?"

"I-I am loyal to the crown," Amara said in a trembling voice. "Tell me what you wish of me, Ceridwen, and I will do it."

I let out a soft chuckle and took Amara's hands in my own. "My only wish is for you to be happy. Now, tell me the truth. Do you think you could be content living out the rest of your days as Snow White? As King Liam's wife and queen?"

"Oh, I-" Tears sprang into Amara's eyes, and she nodded. "I love the King very much, Ceridwen. Loving him for the rest of my life? Why, that would be as easy as breathing. But how would we accomplish such a thing? Your engagement to King Liam has already been announced, and anyway, it is one of convenience. He seeks your council, and above all else, to heal his country. He-I mean, we-would not wish to sacrifice the health of our countries for personal gain."

I smiled at Amara and tutted her gently. "Amara, Snow White taught you everything there is to know about being royal. You two also worked together long ago, and successfully captured the hearts of the people of Cherida. I have no doubt you can do the same for the people of Aileen. You have some small gifts with magic, as well. Nobody will doubt that you are the daughter of a greenwitch."

Amara began to look hopeful, though there was still a trace of worry on her face. "Do you really think I have what it takes to lead?"

"You inspire love and loyalty in people," I said in a gentle voice. "You also have a kind heart. Leading already comes naturally to you."

Amara smiled then, her slight frame relaxing as though a heavy weight had lifted from her shoulders.

"That's kind of you to say, Ceridwen, but I still don't know how we could accomplish such a thing. Your engagement has already been announced. To break it would risk scandal." Amara pointed out. "It's a pretty dream, though."

"Well, I have no desire to cause scandal, not for you, at least," I said. "Truthfully, I no longer wish to live at court. My happiness lies elsewhere."

"You're leaving, then?" Amara looked distressed at the thought.

"I am leaving court." I clarified. "Although, I will probably stay in Cherida. It has been my home longer than Aileen. Unless Quincy wishes to go elsewhere-"

I paused, realizing I had said more than I meant to.

Amara's eyes sparkled with happiness. "So, you're in love too."

"Yes," I confessed. "Quincy and I are in love. We are also...expecting."

Amara's smile grew wider, and she gave me a quick hug. "I'm so happy for you both."

"Thank you." I paused, tapping a finger against my chin. "Let's say that, later today, a courier arrived with a message that I passed away from the plague at my summer castle. Do you think the King would make you an offer of marriage?"

"Yes, I believe so." Amara hesitated. "Will I see you again?"

"Of course, dearest," I said. "I'll send word once I'm settled."

The two of us gave each other another long, lingering hug. When we separated, there were tears in both of our eyes.

"Well, then I suppose this is goodbye." Amara's voice trembled as she spoke.

"It's goodbye for now," I said, cupping her chin in my hand. "Good luck to you, my love. I know you'll do great things."

"Thank you, Ceridwen." Amara said.

We had nothing more to say to each other, yet we could have stood there all day. Saying goodbye was painful, but I knew we each had bright futures ahead of us, and Cherida would survive and flourish under Amara and Liam.

Leaning in, I kissed her gently on the forehead, then turned and left the castle gardens for the last time.

33
FIRST STEPS

I went back to the stables and had Buttercup brought to me. I quickly ran a brush through her coat, whispering a few magical words in her ear that would refresh and energize her.

My illusion spell was recast, so no one would question my presence. After all, in a few hours, I would be dead.

Riding away from the castle, I felt lighter than I ever had while living there. Courtly intrigue suited Marcella just fine. She loved the finery, the gossip, and the power. It had taken a while, but I realized those were all things I could live without. A simple life in the country was far more agreeable to me.

Buttercup cantered down the road and out of the city. Once we were past the gates, I pulled on the reins and turned in the saddle to look at everything I was leaving behind.

It wasn't bittersweet, like I thought it would be. Instead, it felt like a weight had lifted from me. Quincy was right. For far too long, I had shouldered the burdens of others. It was time to find what made me happy.

I righted myself in the saddle and started down the road again. It was still early in the day, and I passed a few people who bowed and tipped their hats, calling good morning.

I smiled back and returned the greeting, smug in my anonymity.

Around noon, I spotted a figure on the road. He looked like a giant astride a large, black horse. Sunlight skimmed across umber skin, highlighting undertones of copper. Long, dark braids hung down past his shoulders and were tied back with a cobalt blue hair scarf. Strapped to his hip was an ax.

The breath went out of my body when I realized who it was.

It was Quincy.

I spurred Buttercup forward, urging her to a brisk trot. I adjusted my illusion so Quincy could recognize me.

Scout spotted me first and let out a loud *neigh*. He pranced forward a few steps, then broke into a gallop. Quincy's eyes lit up, and a wide smile spread across his face.

As we pulled up beside each other, Quincy dismounted and rushed to my side. I swung my leg over the saddle and jumped into his embrace. I nearly started sobbing when I felt his arms around me again.

"Ceridwen!" Quincy breathed into my hair. He held me tightly, lifting my feet off the ground.

"Oh, Quincy, I missed you!" I said, burying my face in the crook of his neck.

"I'm sorry, I'm so sorry." Quincy set me down and cupped my face in his hands. "You were right about everything. I shouldn't have expected so much from you. It wasn't fair."

"Quincy, wait, I-"

"No, Ceridwen," Quincy stated firmly. "Let me finish, please. I was being selfish. I thought I could have everything I wanted, without considering your responsibilities or what made you happy."

"You make me happy." I choked out in a watery voice. I put my hands on his chest and smiled up at him.

Quincy's face broke into a smile, but his eyes remained serious. "I'm happy to hear it, because I intend on sticking around for a long, long time."

My eyes widened as the full weight of his words became clear.

"Quincy, are you saying what I think you're saying-?"

"I love you, Ceridwen," Quincy said. "I told you once I would follow you anywhere just for the privilege of being by your side. Well, I'm a man of my word and I don't plan on breaking my promise, especially to you. Where you go, I will go. To Cherida, to Aileen; if you ask it of me, I will be by your side. Husband or no husband, near or far, I just want to be by your side. There, that's it, that's all I'm going to say."

A few tears trickled down my cheeks, and I couldn't help but give a small laugh.

"Oh, we really are a pair, aren't we?" I asked. "I love you, Quincy, but I won't ask you to follow me to Aileen."

"But, Ceridwen-"

"I won't ask," I interrupted, "Because I'm not going."

Quincy blinked at me, uncomprehending. "What?"

I shrugged. "As it turns out, Amara is managing the kingdom just fine on her own. She doesn't need me. Also, she's in love with the king, and he loves her."

"So you broke off the engagement?" Quincy asked, a note of surprise on his face.

"Er, not quite." I felt my cheeks flush with warmth. "I left a letter with a courier. He doesn't remember it, of course. In a few hours, he's going to have a vision of an urgent message arriving for the princess. He'll take the letter to Amara, which contains news of my death. Apparently, I succumbed to the plague at my summer castle. There will be no funeral, of course. The plague is too dangerous. They'll have to burn my body at once."

A muscle jumped in Quincy's jaw, and his dark eyes misted over. "You gave up everything for me."

"No," I shook my head. "This was never my dream. It was Marcella's. We have all paid dearly for her ambitions."

Snow White's face flashed before my eyes, followed by Iberius. Even Marcella's gaunt and drawn features while she lay on her deathbed surfaced.

I shook my head in an attempt to clear my mind. "I'm following my heart. For the first time in my life, I have a reason to. I've never loved anyone the way I love you."

Quincy put his arms around me, linking his hands together at the small of my back. The afternoon sun fell across his face. The gold in his eyes came alive, like sparks from a campfire. I reached a hand up, drawing my fingers lightly across his umber skin.

"So," Quincy said, "Command me, my queen. Where do you wish to go? Where shall I take you? What is your heart's desire?"

I laughed and shook my head. "I'm not a queen anymore, Quincy. From now on, I'm just Ceridwen."

Quincy raised an eyebrow, a mischievous twinkle in his eyes. "If I can't call you queen, may I at least call you wife?"

I raised my eyebrows, and my lips parted slightly in surprise. "What?"

Quincy reached a hand into his pocket, then pulled out a thin gold band.

"It's not very grand," Quincy muttered. "But Ceridwen, will you marry me? Would you consent to be the wife of a simple huntsman?"

Tears welled in my eyes, and I nodded. "Yes, Quincy, of course I'll marry you."

He smiled and slipped the ring on my finger. Then he lifted me in his arms and kissed me passionately.

As our lips parted, I looked down at Quincy, curious about one thing.

"Would you really follow me anywhere?" I asked.

"Of course," Quincy responded without hesitation.

"Well, what about a little cottage with room for chickens and an herb garden?" I asked. "Would you follow me there?"

A broad smile stretched across Quincy's face, and he nodded. "Yes, I think I can manage that."

Then he kissed me again.

I stood in Senna and Aster's backyard, dressed in a simple white gown. My rounded belly had been visible for a couple of months now.

Quincy was in an excellent mood. When he wasn't helping Aster set up for the wedding ceremony, he was hovering close to me, stealing kisses, touching my hair, or rubbing my baby bump.

Senna came out of her cottage. She was singing softly, her sweet voice like a chorus of bells. Bartholomew trailed behind her, holding the wedding cake.

"Look out, look out everyone!" Bartholomew said in a loud voice. "I'd hate for this cake to go to waste. Senna worked so hard on it."

Senna laughed and motioned for him to place it down on a nearby table. "Thank you for all your help today, Bartholomew."

I went to stand next to them, throwing my arms around his thin shoulders. "I'm so glad you could make it. Thank you for coming."

"Of course, my dear, I wouldn't miss this for the world." He patted me fondly on the cheek.

"Are we ready to get started?" Aster asked, standing underneath the flower arch.

Quincy turned and flashed me a smile. "Ready when you are, love."

"Oh, I've been ready," I said, going to his side. I slipped my hand in his and looked up at Quincy's perfect face. It seemed unreal that I would get to spend the rest of my life with this man. My heart was bursting with happiness.

Senna was my maid of honor. She came to stand beside me, her eyes bright and her cheeks flushed.

Bartholomew took a seat and watched eagerly.

Quincy and I turned to face each other, and the ceremony started.

It had taken longer to get married than I initially expected. After Quincy and I became engaged, we traveled the countryside so I could release all the golems I created.

I also watched over Amara carefully, ensuring that her succession went off without a hitch. Her coronation would take place in a few months' time, on her sixteenth birthday. It was public knowledge that she would announce her engagement to King Liam at this point. The people talked about her with an excitement and adoration that had never been extended to my sister and me.

I couldn't help but smirk when I heard people praise Amara. It amused me to imagine how horrified they would be if they ever found out her true parentage.

People also saw the passing of the Starbright sisters as a cause for celebration. My death was the subject of many gleeful conversations, with multiple individuals expressing their eagerness for the cleansing of the Starbrights' malevolence and impurity from their country.

Quincy didn't like hearing that. More than once I caught his hand straying towards his ax while he stared down some oblivious bystander, and I would have to act quickly to keep the peace.

Deep down, I wondered if the people were right to rejoice. I had committed horrible, evil treacheries in the name of protecting my family. My hands were stained with blood, and I would never be free of that. I couldn't explain why, but when Snow White died, the darkest parts of me had died with her. Killing Snow White had been a necessary evil, but I could also make it my last act of violence. I was finally free to embrace a more peaceful and loving side of myself.

"Please put your hands together," Aster said.

Quincy and I locked our fingers, smiling at each other.

"Senna?" Aster asked.

"Oh, I have it right here." Senna quickly handed her a piece of red silk.

Aster smiled at her wife, then turned back to Quincy and me. She wrapped the silk around our wrists.

"As this knot is tied, so are your lives bound. All the dreams of love and happiness you have both wished for are in this silk, infused into its very fibers. May this binding serve as a firm foundation for your marriage, providing strength in times of struggle and a constant source of light during difficult times," Aster said. She finished by knotting the fabric.

"May your love be a constant reminder of the sacred vows you have taken today. As you embark on this journey together, may the sun shine upon your path. May the bonds of your marriage remain strong and unbreakable. I now pronounce you a married couple in the spirit of love and unity." Aster finished.

"Can I kiss my wife now?" Quincy asked in an eager voice.

Aster laughed. "Yes, you may now kiss the bride."

Quincy pulled me close to him, pressing his lips gently against mine. It was a sweet kiss, full of promise.

"I love you, wife." He breathed.

"I love you, husband," I whispered back.

"Hurray!" Bartholomew stood to his feet and clapped loudly. Aster pulled Senna close and kissed her on the forehead.

"Oh, I always cry at weddings." Senna fanned her face, her eyes glassy.

"Let's have some cake," Bartholomew suggested. "Cake cheers everyone up!"

Senna laughed, then went to the table and began cutting slices for everyone. Aster disappeared into her house, then resurfaced with a pitcher.

"I got what you asked for, Quincy." She said, setting it down on the table. "It was rather difficult to find. I'm not sure why this is so important to you, but you better enjoy it."

"It's not for me," Quincy said.

Aster shot him a stern look that made him laugh.

"It's for all of us," Quincy corrected himself.

"What is it?" Bartholomew asked, peering into the pitcher.

"Here, I'll pour everyone a glass," Quincy said, standing up. After he served everyone, he came to sit next to me and handed me a cup.

I tentatively took a sip, and my eyes widened. "Quincy, is this the honey, lavender, and lemon drink they had at the Honey Festival?"

"It is." He sat back and examined me with a smile. "Surprised?"

"Oh, Quincy, you remembered." My eyes misted at how thoughtful and caring he was.

"Oh, don't start that!" Senna said with a laugh.

"Today is for celebrating!" Bartholomew exclaimed.

Aster smirked and sat down next to her wife. "Well, I'm happy to know I acquired that bottle for a good cause. It was a pain to track down."

"And it's delicious." Bartholomew smacked his lips together and looked pleased.

The five of us sat around talking and laughing for the rest of the day. Some moments were bittersweet. It pained me that my parents couldn't be here, that Snow White couldn't be my flower girl, that I didn't have Marcella to fuss over my hair and my dress.

Yet other moments were pure joy. I had friends I cared for deeply. Quincy and I were in love, and in a few months, we would welcome our child into the world.

As the evening rolled around, Quincy stood up and stretched. I admired his figure as he raised his muscular arms over his head and his shirt lifted, gifting me with a glimpse of his abs.

"Well, wife, I think it's about time you and I went home." He said, turning to me.

I blinked in surprise. "What?"

"Oh, I'm so excited." Senna gushed. "We're going to be neighbors!"

"Neighbors?" I glanced around the table, feeling confused. "What's going on?"

"Oh, show her already, Quincy," Aster said, batting his arm.

"All right, all right." Quincy laughed, adjusting his cobalt blue hair scarf. "Ceridwen, I have one more wedding present to show you."

I got to my feet then, puzzled over the sudden turn of events. "We're not staying here tonight?"

Aster laughed loudly at that. "I hope you weren't expecting to spend your honeymoon in our loft!"

"I-I'm not sure what I thought."

Bartholomew hurried to my side and kissed my temple. "Goodbye, my dear, though it won't be goodbye for long."

Senna slipped her arm around her wife's middle. "Don't be strangers."

"As if we could." Quincy teased.

"Oh, go on, you two," Aster laughed, swatting us away.

Quincy led us to where Buttercup and Scout were waiting for us. We quickly groomed and saddled them, then started on our journey.

"Where are we going?" I asked, for what felt like the hundredth time.

"You'll see," Quincy said. "It isn't far."

We took off at a brisk trot down the road, away from the town. After about fifteen minutes, we rode up beside a quaint cottage with a large front yard. I could tell by the wood that it was new. Off to the side was a chicken coop, although it was missing the chickens. Out front was space for a garden. In the back were several apple trees.

"Quincy," I gasped. "Did you build this?"

"I did." He answered. "Do you like it?"

"Oh, I love it." I gushed. "It's better than any castle."

"I believe you because I know how much you hated living at the castle." Quincy chuckled. "It just...well, it felt like the perfect place."

"For what?" I asked.

He laughed and drew me into his arms. "You, me, us, our family."

I sucked in a breath, tears starting in my eyes. "Yes, I believe you're right."

Quincy drew his thumb down my cheek. "I know we've both suffered. I thought this could be the start of a new chapter for us."

"I agree." I swiped a hand over my eyes and let out a watery laugh.

"Well then, wife," Quincy leaned down to kiss me on the nose, "let's go inside and get started."

Hand in hand, we moved towards the cottage, taking the first steps towards our new life together.

EPILOGUE

Epilogue

Many years went by. Quincy and I settled into our new home, next to Aster and Senna, with Bartholomew only a few days' ride away. We were close enough to the big city that outsiders were not viewed with suspicion, but far enough away that I didn't have to worry about my identity being discovered.

Amara married the King only a few months after her sixteenth birthday. Invitations were sent to Quincy and me, but we decided against going. It hurt my heart not to go, but Amara was still clinging to me, and her old life. She needed space to adjust and to step into her new role as queen. On her wedding day, I watched her carefully on my scrying mirror. She was as lovely as ever.

Three months after my own wedding, I gave birth to a baby girl. We named her Zanna. Two years later, we welcomed our son, Algar. Our third and last child came a year after that, in late spring. Another girl, Fern.

I sat on the porch, rocking Fern, when I heard the sounds of a royal carriage making its way down the road. A smile spread across my face. Amara always came at the beginning of summer, once a year. She had sent me a message on my scrying mirror that she would be arriving today, and I was excited to see her.

A luxurious carriage came down our small lane and stopped in front of our cottage. It had been freshly painted and trimmed in gold. It looked out of place next to my humble lodgings. Snow white horses tossed their manes and stomped their feet.

A footman jumped down and opened the door, revealing Amara on the other side. As she stepped down, I noticed she had a gently rounded belly, and her hand rested protectively over her stomach.

I stood up quickly, a smile spreading across my face. I tucked the baby into one arm and gave a short curtsy.

"My Queen," I said.

Amara looked almost startled when she met my eyes, as though she still couldn't quite accept that she was royalty, and I was common. She quickly smoothed her face of emotions and straightened her back.

"Good evening, Aunt. Should we go inside?" She asked in a polite voice.

"As you wish, Your Majesty." I held the door open and let her enter first.

I didn't worry what the footmen or driver would think about Amara calling me aunt. Addressing another by familial relations was seen as a sign of respect here in Cherida, like calling an elderly man 'grandfather'.

Quincy came out of the kitchen, dusting his hands. "Ho! I recognize that voice. Is that who I think it is?"

"Yes, Quincy, it's me." Amara giggled.

Quincy swooped in and lifted her in a bear hug. "Oh, it's good to see you again, Your Majesty! I trust you traveled well?"

"Quincy, be careful with her!" I urged in a sharp voice.

"I was," He said. "I'm always careful with our girl. Aren't I, Your Majesty?"

"I'm quite alright," Amara said, a delighted smile playing across her features.

"She's pregnant." I pointed out.

Quincy's eyes widened. He gently shifted Amara in his arms and set her down in a chair. I shook my head, an exasperated smile on my face, and took a seat on our settee.

"How far along are you?" Quincy asked, settling down next to me.

"Five months," Amara said. "You don't have to say those things, you know."

"Say what?" I questioned.

Amara fidgeted, looking uncomfortable. "You don't have to call me Your Majesty."

"I think you know we do," Quincy said in a gentle voice.

Amara looked at me for a long moment, biting down on her bottom lip. "It doesn't seem that long ago that you were royalty, and I was the commoner."

"Hm," I shifted Fern in my arms. "It seems a lifetime ago to me."

Amara's face broke into a smile. "You do seem very happy."

I looked into Fern's sleeping face and listened to my older two children playing in one of the bedrooms.

I nodded. "Yes, this is the happiest I've ever been. It's the first time I've had something that was...mine."

"I know the feeling." A slight blush blossomed across Amara's face.

"Tell us about life at the castle." Quincy encouraged.

Amara straightened up. "As you know, we've been staying in Aileen full time. We only come to Cherida for the summer months. Liam, I mean the King, made his younger brother steward of the realm."

"A wise decision. Our lands have been prosperous and our taxes low. Your husband could have done worse." I noted.

Amara let out a sigh of relief. "I'm happy to hear that."

"When are you expecting?" I asked.

Amara's face lit up. "Autumn. As you know, my son was born two years ago. The King and I were so happy. Although this time...Oh, I do hope it's a girl."

I tilted my head, carefully examining her belly. "I think it will be."

Amara rubbed her baby bump, then let out a deep sigh. "There is one matter that gives me cause for concern. We've told everyone you passed away of the plague in your summer castle yet...horrible, vile rumors persist. They're calling you evil. The evil stepmother."

"Yes, I've heard the rumors," I said.

"So have I," Quincy growled. His eyes darted to one of his axes hanging on the wall, out of reach of the children.

Amara looked uncomfortable. "I'm trying to put a stop to it. I can't seem to quell the rumors. It's quite distressing."

The anxiety was plain on Amara's face. I merely chuckled and shook my head.

"Amara, the rumors don't bother me. I won't lie and pretend I haven't done awful things. My sister was even more awful, unfortunately, and she forever branded us as the evil witches."

Amara looked sorrowful. "People will never know the things you've done, how you took care of me and Snow White. They'll never know what you sacrificed for the Kingdom."

"I know, and that's enough for me," I answered.

Zanna came into the living room then. She rushed towards Quincy, jumping into his lap.

"Hey, there's my Zanna girl!" Quincy lifted her in a bear hug, planting kisses on her cheeks.

Zanna laughed, then stilled when she saw Amara sitting in our living room.

"Pwin-thess?" Zanna asked, pointing one sticky finger.

Algar toddled into the room then, his chubby legs unsteady. "Bwa!" He announced proudly. Seeing Zanna on Quincy's lap, a comically determined look came over his face. He crawled up beside his sister and immediately tried to push her back onto the floor.

"Behave, you two. We have company." Quincy said in a stern voice.

Algar didn't care, but Zanna was entranced with Amara.

"Pwin-thess?" she asked again, turning to me.

I smiled at her. "Queen." I corrected.

Amara gave her a kind smile. "Hello, Zanna. It's nice to see you again."

Zanna sat back in Quincy's lap. "Pwetty. Pwetty kween."

The three of us sat and talked some more while Quincy and I wrangled the children.

"Oh," I looked up, suddenly embarrassed. "Would you like some tea, dearest? I should have offered earlier, but I'm ashamed to say it quite slipped my mind."

"Mine too," Quincy said, wincing as Algar grabbed a fistful of his braids and pulled.

With a sigh and a shake of her head, Amara stood from her seat. "I fear I have taken up too much of your time."

"Don't be silly, dearest, of course you haven't," I said.

"You're always welcome here," Quincy assured her.

Amara examined Quincy for a long moment, a bittersweet look in her eyes. "Thank you for taking care of her."

Quincy blinked, a hint of surprise on his face. "We take care of each other."

"I do hope...I wish you two...so many years of joy." Amara's eyes were misting. She sniffed and swiped at her cheeks.

I stood from my seat. "I'll see you out."

Amara followed after me, then stopped at the door.

"Ceridwen," Amara began, "there is something I need to tell you."

I paused. "Yes? What is it?"

Behind me, Quincy put Algar and Zanna on the floor and came to stand next to me. He slipped an arm around my waist, looking concerned.

Amara sucked in a deep breath and fidgeted with her skirts. "It's only that...I don't think I'll be able to come back here. My husband and the servants are beginning to ask questions. They want to know who this greenwitch is that I talk about so much. Liam is becoming suspicious due to my failure to make any introductions. Deep down, I think he knows I'm keeping a secret. He won't pry, not yet anyway. But I fear it's only a matter of time before he begins to press the issue."

My heart sank as Amara told me this. Fern moved in my arms, burrowing into my breast and making little baby noises. I clutched her to me, as I had once done with Snow White.

"Amara," I kept my voice gentle, "I suspected this day would come. We both did."

Amara sucked in a breath, looking hurt. "It's just that...well, I don't know what I'll do without the two of you."

"Have some faith in yourself. You'll be all right." Quincy soothed.

Amara turned towards the children, a faraway look in her eyes. "Our paths are moving in such different directions, pulling us away from each other."

I stepped closer and put my hand under Amara's chin. I raised her eyes to meet mine. "Worry not, my dear. Everything is as it should be. Do not cling to the past, especially when you have such a bright future ahead of you."

Amara's hands traveled down to her stomach, where she rubbed her rounded belly. The shadows finally left her eyes, and a smile came over her face.

"I'll never forget you, Ceridwen, or you, Quincy. Not ever." She whispered.

I leaned forward and grasped her in a tight hug. "Nor I, you."

Quincy wrapped both of us in his arms and kissed Amara on top of her head. For a long moment, the three of us stood there, holding each other.

When we finally broke apart, all three of us had tears in our eyes. Quincy opened the door, and our children spilled out into the yard. Zanna pranced around in the grass, her laughter ringing through the air. Algar toddled after on unsteady feet. He watched the horses with wide eyes.

"Big." He said, pointing one chubby finger.

I strode forward, Quincy at my side. He had one arm wrapped around my waist. Together, we watched Amara go to her carriage. A footman opened the door for her and bowed his head.

"Your Majesty." His voice was a dim echo on the wind.

The door closed, and Amara looked out the window. I held her gaze as the horses started down the road. Just before she left our sight, Quincy and I both lifted our arms and waved. For a moment, she was a blur on the horizon, then she was gone.

I let out a deep sigh and turned towards Zanna. She played with the flowers near our house. Algar clung to her skirts and babbled nonsensically.

They would never replace the loved ones we lost. There were still times I woke in the night, sobbing uncontrollably. Quincy would have to light a candle and rock me back to sleep, whispering soothing words in my ears.

Other times, Quincy would become silent and thoughtful. He would tie a forest green hairscarf in his hair and go for long walks where he was gone for most of the day. He would return misty-eyed and, after our children fell asleep, would hold them for hours.

No, the loved ones we lost could never be replaced, but out of the ashes, we had built something new and precious. We had learned that, despite the darkness we endured, life could be beautiful again.

Quincy tucked a strand of hair behind my ear. "Do you really believe that?"

I turned to face him, confused. "What?"

Quincy let out a sigh, his gaze falling to Fern. He traced a gentle finger over her chubby cheek.

"Do you believe everything is as it should be?" He asked.

I held our baby closer, then went into my husband's arms. I looked up into his dark eyes and smiled. "With all my heart."

NEWSLETTER SIGNUP

Sign up for Charlotte Eyle's Newsletter and receive a FREE ebook!

Everyone knew Queen Marcella was desperate for a baby, but what fueled that desperation? Black as Ashes is a short story prequel to Red as Blood and told from Marcella's point of view.

Get your free book at the link below:

https://dl.bookfunnel.com/56ims9xpcf

SNEAK PEAK

Turn the page for a sneak peek of Charlotte Eyle's next book, Castle Frankenstein

Germany 1870

Emeline Deschner is a fan of Mary Shelley's Frankenstein. Behind her favorite novel is speculation that the author based her work on local legends in Germany. Legends about the infamous alchemist, Johanne Dippel, who performed bizarre experiments on cadavers. When Emeline arrives at Castle Frankenstein, on vacation with her family, she uncovers a secret that changes everything she knows. Suddenly Emeline finds herself caught between a lonely, intelligent creature and an ancient society bent on destroying him. Despite the danger, Emeline can't help but feel drawn to Seth. She might even be falling in love with him. But what can Emeline do when following her heart means walking into peril? As the Ambrosia Brotherhood infiltrates Castle Frankenstein, Emeline must act quickly to save Seth and her family. Is she strong enough to prevail against her enemies, or will she be separated from Seth forever?

Read the first chapter now!

CASTLE FRANKENSTEIN

Chapter 1

Emeline Deschner couldn't get enough of her surroundings. Nudging her horse from a gentle walk into a trot, she watched one green hill roll into the next. Long grains of grass bent in the breeze, as though waving at their arriving guests.

"Em!" called an elderly woman, head hanging out of a carriage. "Do wait for us, my dear! We would never find you in this prairie!"

Emeline threw her head back and laughed. "Oh, Mother, you worry too much."

"She's right, you know." James, Emeline's older brother, rode up beside her. He was on the back of a spirited stallion. "Young girls are so fragile. You're as liable to break as a china doll!" He mocked.

"I am not!" Emeline retorted. Heat flooded her cheeks. Why did he insist on teasing her?

James smirked at the look on his sister's face. "Prove it then. Keep up with me!"

Digging his heels into the stallion's side, he took off in a blur.

Emeline gritted her teeth irritably, then did the same with her horse.

"Yah!" she shouted, flapping the reins. "No fair, James, you got a head start!"

He didn't respond, except to allow his laughter to come ringing back across the prairie.

Emeline wished her pudgy mare would go faster, but the sweet-tempered animal would only canter along the chosen path. After several minutes, they finally made it into the copse of woods where James had disappeared.

Slowing her horse to a walk, Emeline looked around with interest. The forest was dense and the air stagnant, but she didn't care. The trees offered shade from the beating sun and a handful of birds released merry chirps, their songs echoing through the air.

Humming a cheerful tune, she continued down the trial.

Crack.

The sudden breaking of a branch caused the mare to rear up on her hind legs.

Emeline was only half paying attention and had a loose grip on the reins. The move was so sudden she didn't have time to throw herself forward. Instead, she lost her balance and slid off the horse's back. She crashed to the ground.

"Oomph," Emeline grunted, rubbing her sore hip. At least the forest floor was covered in soft moss that cushioned her landing.

The horse danced around for a moment, then seemed to feel guilty over its skittish behavior and leaned down to nuzzle Emeline's cheek.

"Well, at least you had the sense not to trample me," Emeline said. Despite the pout on her lips, she reached up to rub the horse's long nose.

"Are you alone out here, girl?"

Emeline looked over her shoulder, observing a man in a filthy black duster coat. His long hair and beard were matted. A crescent-shaped scar sat near his right eye. He was short, with a pudgy belly.

Emeline shivered at the stranger's grimy appearance. She quickly stood to her feet. It took a minute to find her voice, but she answered with authority.

"No, my brother is nearby. My parents will also be along shortly. They are following in a carriage."

"Hm," the man grunted. "That is good. It is not wise to travel alone in this forest. Many strange things have happened here. Even with the sun out, one's safety is not guaranteed."

Emeline bristled. "Thank you, sir, but I'm quite able to look after myself."

Emeline paused to brush some leaves off of her dress, then squared her shoulders. She looked the stranger in the eye, unflinching.

"Are you now?" He breathed softly. His eyes wandered over to the mare. The hilt of Emeline's smallsword gleamed from the saddle.

"Humph," he smirked. "These days, most people use revolvers for protection. It's been a good long while since I've seen a sword carried in the open like that. Hardly a weapon, but good enough for a child, I suppose."

Emeline ground her teeth. She was on the verge of losing her temper when James came riding into view.

"I thought you would be halfway to the castle by now!" He hollered. "Aren't you always bragging about being the superior rider?"

As James' eyes connected with his sister and the stranger, his face contorted into an angry grimace. Leaping from his horse, he threw back his coat to reveal a revolver.

"Are you in need of assistance, sir?" James asked. His words were cordial but as bitterly cold as a winter morning.

The man took a step back and bowed his head. "Not at all, sir. The lady here took a tumble from her horse. I will leave her in your capable hands and be on my way."

With those parting words, he shrank back into the forest, disappearing from view.

James followed the stranger with his eyes, then moved towards Emeline.

"Come on, let me help you back onto your horse." He said.

"What an odd man," Emeline remarked, as her brother hoisted her into the saddle. "Suddenly I'm a lady now. Thank you, James. Oh, you should have heard the way he was talking to me!"

James snorted. "Odd? That was nearly disastrous. I'm glad you're all right, though. Just, let's not mention this to Mother and Father. Agreed?"

Emeline laughed. "You mean you don't want to be flayed alive by our parents? Fine, I will keep your, or should I say our, secret. But you must promise not to call me a little girl anymore. I've had enough of that to last a lifetime. Besides, at 21 you're only two years my senior."

James flashed a grin. "You have my word. Come on now. The castle is still some distance away, but I found a shortcut."

With the horses trotting side by side, Emeline and James set off down the trail. It was some time before they emerged from the trees. Through the slowly darkening sky, the castle was just visible.

The building was short and blocky. Icy stones seemed to emanate a cold, unwelcome chill that went straight to Emeline's bones. A white mist coated the ground, reaching wispy fingers into the air before dissipating with a sigh. Coal black storm clouds rolled against a sapphire blue sky. There was a faint *boom*, like that of a cannon, followed by a white flash of lightning.

"Well, what do you think?" James asked.

"I-I don't know," Emeline answered. "I feel like...it doesn't want to be disturbed."

James chuckled. "What's to disturb? It's just a castle."

He nudged his horse forward. "Come on, sister, where is your sense of adventure?"

Emeline didn't answer, but the hairs on the back of her neck prickled. Wheeling around in the saddle, Emeline peered into the forest but found nothing. Her mind wandered back to the stranger. Something told her she hadn't seen the last of him. With a sigh, Emeline gave herself a mental shake and followed her brother. She was on holiday and intended to enjoy every minute of her stay at Frankenstein's castle.

About the Author

Charlotte Eyle is an author who loves to explore fairy tales and breathe new life into them. When she isn't writing, she enjoys reading fantasy novels that allow her to fall into new worlds, playing Dungeons and Dragons with her family, and planning road trips where she explores unique locations along the West Coast. She draws inspiration from authors like Robin McKinley and J. R. R. Tolkien, who helped shape her love of reading and writing.

Stay in touch with Charlotte Eyle!
Website: https://authorcharlotteeyle.com/
Facebook: https://www.facebook.com/profile.php?id=61560789894036
Instagram: https://www.instagram.com/authorcharlotteeyle/
Tiktok: https://www.tiktok.com/@authorcharlotteeyle?lang=en
Youtube: https://www.youtube.com/@AuthorCharlotteEyle
Ko-Fi: https://ko-fi.com/authorcharlotteeyle

Made in the USA
Columbia, SC
21 August 2024

eeae85a5-9781-4471-8c57-320e961337a4R03